A STORY ABOUT A REAL MAN

BORIS POLEVOI

© 2009 Oxford City Press

CONTENTS

About the Author 7
Author's Note 9
Part One 17
Part Two 102
Part Three 203
Part Four 283
Postscript 334

ABOUT THE AUTHOR

By Hero of the Soviet Union ALEXEI MARESYEV

I met Boris Polevoi in the summer of 1943. Fierce fighting was raging in the Kursk Salient, and my regiment was committed to the battle. We flew several missions every day. One evening I returned from a mission tired, hungry, with my thoughts on what I would order at the canteen. As I climbed out of the cockpit I saw a stranger with a group of airmen, who were pointing in my direction.

"What a bore. Another correspondent," I thought, sighing and hurrying off to the canteen as fast as I could make it.

The stranger quickly overtook me and introduced himself saying: "I'm Boris Polevoi, *Pravda* war correspondent." I remember seeing the name in *Pravda* but for the life of me I could not recall what he wrote about. However, I took an instant liking to him. He was quick, impetuous and simple, and there was a smile in his eyes. I invited him to my dugout and we sat talking for a long time. Polevoi filled several notebooks, and still the questions came. Dawn was breaking when he was ready to go. Before leaving he said: "I'll give this a write-up, Alexei. Definitely. I can't say how exactly but I'll certainly write the story."

In the morning we were back in the thick of the battle. One mission followed another, and I soon forgot about the *Pravda* correspondent. To be more exact, I kept coming across his name in the newspapers. And I liked the people he wrote about. But these were meetings only on the pages of newspapers.

One day in 1947, I don't remember the exact date, I switched on the radio and heard the announcer ending a broadcast with the words: "You can hear the next instalment of Boris Polevoi's *A Story About a Real Man* at nine o'clock tomorrow." In my mind's eye I at once pictured the dark-haired newspaper man who had spent a night in my dugout. The next day I made a point of tuning in at nine o'clock in the morning. I could hardly believe my ears. Polevoi had written about me.

That same evening I called on him at his home and he told me that he had looked for me during the war but had been unable to find me. We travelled different roads to victory. He described his work in army archives and how he recapitulated the details of our talk with the aid of his hasty notes.

That evening saw the beginning of my close friendship with Boris Polevoi. Unfortunately we meet very rarely, only at conferences and meetings, and sometimes in our homes. But for me these are always memorable occasions, for Polevoi is a bottomless well of ideas and observations, and it's always a thrill just to listen to him.

But there was an occasion when we were together for quite a few days. It was in the United States where we were invited by American war veterans. It was Polevoi's second visit to the US. During his first visit a well-known journalist maintained that as an ex-airman he could not believe the story of Alexei Maresyev. He said it was all the work of Polevoi's imagination. On this visit Polevoi introduced me to the American as "material evidence". But I don't think even that made him change his mind.

Today Pelevoi is 60. He has been working in Soviet literature for more than forty years. He has written four novels and seventeen volumes of short stories and sketches. He does not think of rest, even in his sleep. It's the profession he has chosen. The profession of a journalist. I have not made a slip of the pen. He is a writer, but he's got the tenacity and vitality of a journalist. He's always travelling, always looking, always making notes.

Were I a man of letters I would most certainly have written *A Story About a Real Man*, of a courageous and mercurial war-time correspondent, of a distinguished writer and journalist, of a fine friend and a REAL MAN—of Boris Polevoi.

AUTHOR'S NOTE

I was born in Moscow on March 17, 1908 but I grew up in the town of Tver (which has been renamed Kalinin). That, I feel, gives me grounds for considering myself a native of Kalinin.

My father, a barrister-at-law, died of tuberculosis in 1916. I scarcely remember him, but judging from the fine library of classical Russian and foreign literature that he had put together and from what I heard from my mother, he must have been a progressive and widely-read man for his day. After his death, my mother, who was a doctor, went to work in a factory hospital and we moved to the houses belonging to the huge Morozov Textile Mill.

There I spent my childhood and youth.

We lived in the "houses for employees", but I had friends among the workers' children and went to school with them. My mother was often too busy at the hospital to give me any of her time, and so I spent most of the day with my friends in the workers' "bedrooms", as the hostels were called at that time, and on the outskirts of the settlements. In general, I did quite well at school, but I had no particular enthusiasm. My spare time was divided between the Tmaka, a grimy little factory stream, and the books from my father's library. Gorky was my favourite author. When my father and mother were students they worshipped him, and the family library contained almost all of his pre-revolutionary works.

The town's newspaper was called *Tverskaya Pravda*. A large worker-correspondents' organisation was set up at the factory in the 1920s and a branch editorial office was opened in the pump-house. We boys were awed by the people entering or coming out of that small brick building. They were worker-correspondents! They wrote for the newspaper. A fitter, who was the chairman of that organisation, became one of the most popular men at the factory.

It must have been in those far-off days that I was first drawn to journalism, which I thought was extremely exciting, very important and, as it seemed to me then, a little mysterious.

My first item was printed in *Tverskaya Pravda* when I was in the 6th form. As I remember it now, it consisted of seven lines and was about the visit S. D. Drozhzhin, the well-known peasant-poet, paid to our school. It was given an inconspicuous place on the back page and did not even carry a by-line. But I knew who wrote it and kept that issue of the newspaper until it virtually fell apart in my pocket. After that I began to write regularly for *Tverskaya Pravda*, and when they came to know me better I began to get assignments for features and sketches about the life of the town.

After finishing school I went to the Industrial College, where I studied chemistry and made quantitative and qualitative analyses. But at the bottom of my heart I was already yearning for the editorial offices with their smell of printer's ink, and during commercial classes I secretly wrote a sketch or a feature on a theme that had nothing to do with what the teacher was saying. In that way I gradually became associated with the glorious profession of a journalist, which to this day I regard as the most exciting and most fascinating of all literary specialities.

Work in newspapers taught me to observe life with the closest attention, to try and understand the things that were going on around me, and to write only when I had a good grasp of the subject.

My first book of feature articles was published in 1927. Friends from *Smena*, a Komsomol newspaper I was contributing to at the time, sent it to Maxim Gorky in Sorrento without my knowledge.

When I learned about it, I was horrified. I thought it was sacrilege to make a great writer read my immature and, as I was already quite aware, mediocre work. All the greater, therefore, was my surprise when I received a bulky packet bearing foreign stamps and my name and address written in a large and clear hand.

On six pages of foolscap Gorky reviewed my immature composition with the greatest attention and indulgence, advised that I should work hard to improve, and learn from the masters how to polish my style much as a "lathe operator polishes metal". That letter from the great writer was of tremendous value to me. I pondered over every word he wrote, striving to draw a correct and useful conclusion. Gorky helped me to realise that journalism and literature required unremitting work and as much, if not more, study than any other profession. I realised that a "by the way" attitude to journalism would lead to nowhere, that you had to put your heart and soul into it.

By that time I had graduated college and was working at the dyeing-and-finishing or, as it was popularly known, the "print" shop of the Proletarka Factory. After long reflection I left the factory and joined the staff of *Smena*.

I was with *Smena* and then with *Proletarskaya Pravda*, the Kalinin regional newspaper, right until the outbreak of the Great Patriotic War.

Parallel with my newspaper work, I wrote short stories but, remembering Gorky's advice, I published only a few.

In 1939 I had my first narrative, *Hot Shop*, published in the magazine *Oktyabr*. I have to admit that both the subject-line and the personalities were drawn from reality, so much so that old-timers at the Kalinin carriage-building works were quick to recognise their comrades. The whole thing ended by the prototype of the hero inviting me to his wedding. The bride was the prototype of my heroine. The guests at the wedding poked fun at me, saying that the hero and the heroine had to complete the work of the author by continuing his narrative and giving it a happy, albeit stereotype, ending.

Long experience as a newspaperman had helped me to write my first narrative. But I gained my most valuable experience as a writer during the Great Patriotic War, when I was a *Pravda* war correspondent.

It is no secret that the heroes of *A Story About a Real Man* and *We—Soviet People* are real, living men and women, most of whom appear under their own or slightly modified names. The idea of writing these books was born in the editorial offices of *Pravda*. It happened like this.

In February 1942 the newspaper carried a story headed *Exploit of Matvei Kuzmin*. That story, which I wrote hurriedly right after I returned from Kuzmin's funeral, describes an 80-year-old collective farmer who repeated the exploit of Ivan Susanin, legendary hero of the people's liberation struggle in Russia in the early 17th century. At the cost of his life he led enemy troops deep into an impassable forest from where none of them returned.

The story was raw and badly presented. As soon as I returned to Moscow from the front, I was summoned by the *Pravda* editor-in-chief, who told me that my write-up of that outstanding exploit had been too hasty and that it had been done in the style of a cub reporter.

"It could have been made into a beautiful story," he reproached me and, with his habit of generalising, added: "I have said it to the other war correspondents and I am saying it to you: make notes of everything out of the ordinary that you hear of or see performed. It is your civic duty. More, it is your duty as a member of the Party. To keep these exploits alive so that our people can learn now or later the full story of how their fellow-citizens fought fascism and triumphed you must write everything down."

I got myself a thick notebook in a stiff binding and began to write down all the conspicuous acts of heroism I came across at the front lines, noting down the civil address of the heroes themselves or of the witnesses.

Meanwhile, my work as a war correspondent kept me moving from one sector of the war to another, from the front to partisan territory behind the enemy lines, where intrepid task groups were harassing the enemy from bases in the forests, and then again to the front lines in Stalingrad, the Kursk Salient, Korsun-Shevchenkovsky, the Vistula, the Neisse, the Spree....

Altogether, I made notes of sixty-five such episodes. One of them, about an unusual meeting with Senior Guards Lieutenant Alexei Maresyev of the Air Force, developed into the book *A Story About a Real Man*. Of the others, I selected twenty-four, which I felt were the most dramatic, typical and revealing and used them for the stories in *We—Soviet People*.

To this day I have not lost the habit of making notes of what I see. In *The Return*, a short story, I endeavoured to draw a word-portrait of a noted Moscow steelmaker.

AUTHOR'S NOTE

The novel *Gold* is based on a true story of two modest bank employees—a girl and an old man—who carried a sack of gold across the firing lines during the war. The prototype of the heroine of the novel *Doctor Vera* is the surgeon of an army hospital who in 1942 remained behind in occupied territory near Kalinin and saved the lives of hundreds of wounded Soviet soldiers. *On a Wild Bank*, a novel about a huge building project in Siberia, is also based on real facts. I don't think this authenticity is extraordinary. Our socialist life, which is changing continually in its forward movement, daily, hourly lays bare before a writer unusually interesting, simple and yet remarkable subjects. Soviet people are attaining heights of labour and military valour and performing deeds in the name of their country that defy even the most fervid imagination. And what an endless variety of characters our Soviet reality unfolds to a writer!

Newspaper work constantly brings me into contact with the most interesting people of our day and permits me to observe their life and work. Journalism sharpens the eye and the ear. So far as I am concerned, facts brought out from life make up for any lack of artistic imagination.

I am not in the least embarrassed that my heroes continue the narration with the lives they lead outside the pages of my books. A writer experiences double joy as he observes these people living happy lives teeming with activity and creation.

There is great happiness in being a writer of the Land of Socialism!

B. POLEVOI

PART ONE

1

The stars were still glittering with a bright, cold light, but the faint glow of morning had already lit the eastern sky. The trees gradually emerged from the gloom. Suddenly, a strong, fresh breeze blew through their tops, filling the forest with loud, resonant sounds. The century-old pines called to each other in anxious, hissing whispers, and the dry powdery snow poured with a soft swish from their disturbed branches.

The wind dropped as suddenly as it had risen. The trees again sank into their frozen torpor. And then all the forest sounds that heralded the dawn broke out: the hungry snarling of the wolves in the glade near by, the cautious yelp of foxes, and the first, uncertain taps of the just awakened woodpecker, sounding so musical in the still forest that it seemed to be tapping a violin and not the trunk of a tree.

Again the wind blew through the heavy pine tops in noisy gusts. The last stars were gently extinguished in the now brighter sky; and the sky itself seemed to have shrunk and grown more dense. The forest, shaking off the last remnants of the gloom of night, stood out in all its verdant grandeur. From the rosy tint that struck the curly heads of the pines and the spires of the firs, one could tell that the sun had risen and that the day promised to be bright, crisp and frosty.

It was quite light by now. The wolves had retired into the thick of the forest to digest their nocturnal prey; and the foxes, too, had left the glade, leaving cunningly traced, winding tracks on the snow. The ancient forest rang with a steady, continuous sound. Only the fussing of the bird, the woodpecker's tapping, the merry chirping of the yellow tomtits darting from branch to branch, and the dry, greedy croak of jays introduced some variation into this mournful, anxious, long-drawn-out sound that rolled in soft waves through the forest.

A magpie, cleaning its sharp, black beak on the branch of an alder-tree, suddenly cocked its head, listened and squatted, ready to take flight. The branches creaked with a note of alarm. Somebody, big and strong, was pushing through the undergrowth. The bushes rustled, the tops of the young pines swayed restlessly, the crunching of the crisp snow was heard. The magpie screeched and darted away, its arrowlike tail sticking out.

From out of the snow-covered pines appeared a long brown muzzle, crowned by heavy, branching antlers. Frightened eyes scanned the enormous glade. Pink, velvety nostrils twitched convulsively, emitting gusts of hot, vaporous breath.

The old elk stood like a statue among the pines. Only its flocky skin quivered nervously on its back. Its ears, cocked in alarm, caught every sound, and its hearing was so acute that it heard a bark beetle boring into the wood of a pine-tree. But even these sensitive ears heard nothing in the forest except the twittering and chirping of the birds, the tapping of the woodpecker and the even rustle of the pine-tree tops.

Its hearing reassured the elk, but its sense of smell warned it of danger. The fresh odour of melting snow was mingled with pungent, offensive and sinister smells alien to this dense forest. The animal's sad, black eyes encountered dark figures lying on the crusty surface of the dazzling white snow. Without moving, it tightened every muscle, ready to dart into the thicket; but the figures on the snow lay motionless, close together, some on top of others. There were a great many of them, but not one moved or disturbed the virginal silence. Near them, out of the snow-drifts, towered strange monsters; it was from here that those pungent and sinister smells came.

The elk stood on the edge of the glade, gazing with frightened eyes, unable to grasp what had happened to this herd of motionless and seemingly harmless humans.

A sound from above startled the animal. The skin on its back quivered again and the muscles of its hind legs drew still tighter.

But the sound also proved to be harmless. It was like the low droning of cockchafers circling among the leaves of a budding birch-tree. Now and again a short, sharp, rasping sound, like the evening croak of a corncrake in the marsh, was added to their droning.

Then the cockchafers came in sight, dancing in the blue frosty sky with glittering wings. Again and again the corncrake croaked up on high. One of the cockchafers hurtled to the ground with outspread wings; the rest continued their dance in the azure sky. The elk relaxed its muscles, stepped into the glade and licked the crisp snow with a wary glance at the sky. Suddenly, another cockchafer separated from the dancing swarm, and leaving a bushy tail behind it, dived straight down into the glade. It grew in size, grew so rapidly that the elk barely had time to make one leap into the woods when something enormous and more frightful than the sudden burst of an autumn storm struck the tree tops and dashed to the ground with a crash that made the whole forest ring. The noise sounded like a groan, and its echo swept through the trees, overtaking the elk that was tearing into the depths of the forest.

The echo sank into the green depths of the pines. The powdery snow, disturbed by the falling aircraft, floated down from the tree tops, sparkling and glittering. The all-embracing and weighty silence reigned once again. Amidst this silence were distinctly heard a man's groan and the crunching of the snow beneath the paws of a bear, whom the unusual noises had driven from the depths of the forest into the glade.

The bear was huge, old and shaggy. Its unkempt fur stuck out in brown clumps on its sunken sides and hung in tufts from its lean haunches. Since the autumn, war had raged in these parts and had even penetrated this dense western forest, where formerly only the foresters and hunters came, and then not often. Already in the autumn the roar of battle in the vicinity had driven the bear from its lair just when it was preparing for its winter sleep, and now, angry from hunger, it roamed the forest, knowing no rest.

The bear halted at the edge of the glade, at the spot where the elk had just been. It sniffed the elk's fresh, savoury-smelling tracks, breathed heavily and greedily, twitched its lean sides and listened. The elk had gone, but near the place where it had been the bear heard sounds that seemed to be produced by a living and probably feeble being. The fur on the bear's withers bristled. It stretched out its muzzle. And again that plaintive sound, barely audible, came from the edge of the glade.

Slowly, stepping cautiously on its soft paws, under the weight of which the hard, dry snow crunched with a whine, the bear moved towards the motionless human figure lying half-buried in the snow.

2

Pilot Alexei Meresyev had been caught in a double pair of "pincers". It was the worst thing that could happen to a man in a dog fight. He had spent all his ammunition when four German aircraft surrounded him and tried to force him to proceed to their base without giving him a chance to dodge or change his course.

It came about in this way. A flight of fighter planes under the command of Lieutenant Meresyev went out to escort a flight of "Ils" that was to attack an enemy airfield. The daring operation was successful. The Stormoviks, "flying tanks", as the infantry called them, almost scraping the pine-tree tops, stole right up to the airfield, where a number of large transport Junkers were lined up. Suddenly diving out from behind the grey-blue pine forest, they zoomed over the field, their machine-guns and cannons pouring lead into the heavy transport planes, showering them with rocket shells. Meresyev, who was guarding the area of attack with his flight of four, distinctly saw the dark figures of men rushing about the field, saw the transport planes creeping heavily across the hard-packed snow, saw the Stormoviks return to the attack again and again and saw the crews of the Junkers, under a hail of fire, taxi their craft to the runway and take them into the air.

It was at this point that Alexei committed his fatal blunder. Instead of closely guarding the area of attack, he allowed himself to be "tempted by easy prey", as airmen call it. He put his craft into a dive, dropped like a stone upon a slow and heavy transport plane that had just torn itself off the ground, and found delight in stitching its motley-coloured, rectangular, corrugated duralumin body with several long bursts from his machine-gun. He was so confident that he did not trouble to see the enemy craft hurtle to the ground. On the other side of the field another Junkers rose into the air. Alexei went after it. He attacked—but was unsuccessful. His stream of tracer bullets trailed over the slowly rising enemy plane. He veered round sharply and attacked again, missed again, overtook his victim again, and this time sent it down away over the forest by furiously firing several long bursts into its broad, cigar-shaped body. After bringing down the Junkers and circling twice in triumph over the spot where a black column of smoke was rising out of the heaving, green sea of endless forest, he turned his plane back to the enemy airfield.

But he did not get there. He saw his three planes fighting nine "Messers", which had evidently been called up by the commander of the German airfield to beat off the attack of the Stormoviks. Gallantly hurling themselves at the Germans, who outnumbered them three to one, the airmen tried to keep the enemy away from the Stormoviks. They drew the enemy further and further away, as black grouse do, pretending to be wounded and enticing hunters away from their young.

Alexei was so ashamed that he had allowed himself to be tempted by easy prey that he could feel his cheeks burning under his helmet. He chose a target and, clenching his teeth, sped into the fray. The target he had chosen was a "Messer" which had separated itself somewhat from the rest and was evidently also looking for prey. Getting all the speed he possibly could out of his plane, Alexei hurled himself upon the enemy's flank. He attacked the German in accordance with all the rules of the art. The grey body of the enemy craft was distinctly visible in the weblike cross of his sight when he pressed his trigger, but the enemy craft slipped by unharmed. Alexei could not have missed. The target was near and was distinctly visible in the sight. "Ammunition!" Alexei guessed, and at once felt a cold shiver run down his spine. He pressed the trigger-button again to test the guns but failed to feel the vibration that every airman feels with his whole body when he discharges his guns. The magazines were empty; he had used up all his ammunition in chasing the "transports".

But the enemy did not know that! Alexei decided to plunge into the fight to improve at least the numerical proportion between the combatants. But he was mistaken. The fighter plane that he had unsuccessfully attacked was piloted by an experienced and observant airman. The German realised that his opponent's ammunition had run out and issued an order to his colleagues. Four "Messers" separated from the rest and surrounded Alexei, one on each flank, one above and one below. Dictating his course by bursts of tracer bullets that were distinctly visible in the clear, blue air, they caught him in a double pair of "pincers".

Several days before, Alexei heard that the famous German Richthofen air division had arrived in this area, Staraya Russa, from the West. This division was manned by the finest aces in the fascist Reich and was under the patronage of Goering himself. Alexei realised that he had fallen into the clutches of these air wolves and that, evidently, they wanted to compel him to fly to their airfield, force him to land and take him prisoner. Cases like that had happened. Alexei himself had seen a fighter flight under the command of his chum, Andrei Degtyarenko, Hero of the Soviet Union, bring a German observer to their airfield and force him to land.

The long, ashen-grey face of the German prisoner and his staggering footsteps rose before Alexei's eyes. "Taken prisoner? Never! That trick won't come off!" he determined.

But do what he would, he could not escape. The moment he tried to swerve from the course the Germans were dictating him, they barred his path with machine-gun fire. And again the vision of the German prisoner, his contorted face and trembling jaw, rose before Alexei's eyes. Degrading animal fear was stamped on that face.

Meresyev clenched his teeth tightly, opened the throttle of his engine as far as it would go and, assuming a vertical position, tried to dive under the German machine that was pressing him to the ground. He got out from under the enemy craft, but the German airman pressed his trigger in time. Alexei's engine lost its rhythm and every now and again missed a beat. The entire craft trembled as if stricken with mortal fever.

"I'm hit!" Alexei managed to plunge into the white turbidness of a cloud and throw his pursuers off his track. But what was to be done next? He felt the vibrations of the wounded craft through his whole body, as if it were not the death throes of his damaged engine but the fever of his own body that was shaking him.

Where was the engine damaged? How long could the plane keep in the air? Would the fuel tanks explode? Alexei did not think these questions so much as feel them. Feeling as if he were sitting on a charge of dynamite with the fuse already alight, he put his craft about and made for his own lines in order, if it came to that, to have his remains buried by his own people.

The climax was sudden. The engine stopped. The aircraft slid to the ground as if slipping down a steep mountain side. Beneath it heaved the forest, like the grey-green waves of a boundless ocean.... "Still, I won't be taken prisoner," was the thought that flashed through the airman's mind when the nearest trees, merged in a continuous strip, raced under the wings of his craft. When the forest pounced upon him like a wild animal he cut off the throttle with an instinctive movement. A grinding crash was heard and everything vanished in an instant, as if he and the machine had dived into a stretch of dark, warm, thick water.

The aircraft struck the tops of the pines as it came down. That broke the force of the fall. Breaking several trees, the machine fell to pieces, but an instant before that Alexei was thrown out of the cockpit, and dropping on to a broad-branched, century-old fir-tree, he slipped down its branches into a deep snow-drift which the wind had blown against the foot of the tree. That saved his life.

Alexei could not remember how long he lay there unconscious and motionless. Vague human shadows, the outlines of buildings and incredible machines flickered past him, and the whirlwind speed with which they flashed past gave him a dull, gnawing pain all over his body. Then, something big and warm of indefinite shape emerged from the chaos and breathed hot, stinking breath into his face. He tried to roll away from this object, but his body seemed to have stuck fast in the snow. Prompted by the unknown horror hovering about him, he made a sudden effort and at once felt the frosty air entering his lungs, the cold snow against his cheek and an acute pain, no longer over his whole body, but in his feet.

"I'm alive!" was the thought that raced through his mind. He tried to rise, but he heard the snow crunching under somebody's feet and a noisy, hoarse breathing near him. "Germans!" he thought at once, and suppressed an urge to open his eyes, jump to his feet and defend himself. "A prisoner! A prisoner, after all! What shall I do?"

He remembered that the day before his mechanic Yura, a Jack of all trades, had offered to fix the strap of his holster that had been torn off, but he had not taken up that offer. As a result he had to carry his pistol in the thigh pocket of his flying suit. To get at it now he had to turn over on his side, but he could not do that without attracting the enemy's attention; he was lying face downwards. He felt the sharp outline of the pistol against his thigh: but he lay motionless; perhaps the enemy would take him for dead and go away.

The German walked near him, sighed in a rather queer way, then went up to him again, crunching the snow. Alexei again felt the malodorous breath coming from his mouth. He knew now that there was only one German, and that gave him a chance of escape: if he watched him, jumped up suddenly, grabbed him by the throat before he could get at his gun.... But that would have to be done carefully and with the utmost precision.

Without changing his position, Alexei opened his eyes slowly, and through his lowered lashes saw not a German, but a brown, shaggy patch. He opened his eyes wider and at once shut them tight again: a big, lean, shaggy bear was squatting on its haunches in front of him.

3

Silent as only a wild animal can be, the bear squatted near the motionless human figure that barely protruded from the bluish snow glittering in the sun. Its filthy nostrils twitched slowly. From its half-open maw, in which old, yellow, but still powerful fangs were visible, a fine thread of thick saliva hung, swaying in the wind.

Robbed by the war of its winter sleep, it was hungry and angry. But bears do not eat carrion. After sniffing at the motionless body, which smelt strongly of petrol, the bear lazily walked round the glade where plenty of similar human bodies were lying frozen in the crisp snow; but a groan and a rustle brought it back again to Alexei's side.

And so it was now squatting beside Alexei. The pinch of hunger fought its aversion to carrion. Hunger was beginning to gain the upper hand. The beast sighed, got up, turned the body over with its paw and tore at the flying suit with its claws. The material held, however. The bear uttered a low growl. It cost Alexei a great effort at that moment to suppress a desire to open his eyes, roll aside, shout and push away the heavy body that had flung itself upon his chest. While his whole being was prompting him to put up a fierce and desperate defence, he compelled himself, slowly and imperceptibly, to slip his hand into his pocket, grope for the handle of his pistol, cock it carefully so that it did not click, and imperceptibly pull it out.

The beast tore at his flying suit with greater fury. The stout leather crackled, but still held. The bear roared in a frenzy, gripped the suit with its teeth and through the fur and wadding nipped the body. By a last effort of will Alexei suppressed a cry of pain, and just at the moment when the bear yanked him out of the snow-drift he raised the pistol and pressed the trigger.

The shot rang out in a sharp, reverberating crack.

The magpie fluttered its wings and flew swiftly away. The dry snow dribbled from the disturbed branches. The bear slowly released its prey. Alexei fell back into the snow, keeping his eyes fixed on the bear. The latter was squatting on its haunches; its black purulent eyes expressed bewilderment. A stream of thick, dull-red blood trickled between its fangs and dripped on to the snow. It uttered a hoarse, frightful roar, rose heavily on its hind legs and collapsed before Alexei could fire another shot. The bluish snow slowly turned scarlet and as it melted a light vapour rose near the bear's head. The beast was dead.

The tension under which Alexei had been labouring suddenly relaxed. Again he felt the sharp, burning pain in his feet. Falling back on the snow, he lost consciousness.

He came to when the sun was already high in the sky. Its rays, penetrating the thick pine tops, lit up the snow with glittering light. The snow in the shade was no longer a pale, but a deep blue.

"Did I dream about the bear?" was the first thought that entered Alexei's mind.

The brown, shaggy, unkempt carcass lay near by on the blue snow. The forest rang with sounds. The woodpecker resonantly tapped the bark; the swift, yellow-breasted tomtits chirped merrily as they skipped from branch to branch.

"I'm alive, alive, alive!" Alexei repeated to himself. And his whole being, his whole body, exulted as he became conscious of the mighty, magic, intoxicating sensation of being alive that overcomes a man every time he has passed through mortal danger.

Prompted by this mighty sensation he sprang to his feet, only to collapse upon the carcass of the bear with a groan. His head filled with a dull, rumbling noise, as if a couple of old, rough grindstones were turning and grinding and causing tremors in his brain. His eyes ached as if somebody were pressing them with his fingers. At one moment everything round him looked distinct and clear, flooded with the cold, yellow light of the sun's rays; at another moment everything vanished behind a grey, sparkling veil.

"Too bad. I must have got concussion when I fell. And something's wrong with my feet," thought Alexei.

Raising himself on his elbow he looked with surprise at the broad field beyond the edge of the forest and bordered on the horizon by the grey semi-circle of the distant forest.

Evidently, in the autumn, or more probably in the early winter, the fringe of this forest had been a defence line which a Soviet Army unit had held, not for long perhaps, but stubbornly, unto death. Blizzards had covered up the earth's wounds with a layer of snowy cotton wool;

but even beneath that layer the eye could still trace the line of trenches, the hillocks of wrecked machine-gun emplacements, the endless shell craters, large and small, stretching to the feet of the mutilated, beheaded or blasted trees at the forest edge. Dotted over this lacerated field were a number of tanks painted in the motley colours of pike's scales. They stood frozen to the snow, and all of them—particularly the one at the extreme end which must have been turned over on its side by a grenade, or a mine, so that the long barrel of its gun hung to the ground like an exposed tongue from the mouth—looked like the carcasses of strange monsters. And all over the field, on the parapets of the shallow trenches, near the tanks, and on the edge of the forest, lay the corpses of Soviet and German soldiers. There were so many that in some spots they lay piled up on top of each other; and they lay in the very same frozen postures in which death had struck them down in battle only a few months before, on the border-line of winter.

All this told Alexei of the fierce and stubborn fighting that had raged here, told him that his comrades-in-arms had fought here, forgetting everything except that they had to check the enemy and not let him pass. At a little distance, near the edge of the forest, at the foot of a thick pine which had been decapitated by a shell, and from whose tall, mutilated trunk yellow, transparent resin was now oozing, lay the bodies of German soldiers with smashed-in skulls and mutilated faces. In the middle, lying across one of the enemy bodies, was the prostrate body of a huge, round-faced, big-headed lad without a greatcoat, in just a tunic with a torn collar; and next to him lay a rifle with a broken bayonet and a splintered, blood-stained butt.

Further on, on the road leading to the forest, half-way out of a shell crater at the foot of a young, sand-covered fir-tree, lay the body of a dark-skinned Uzbek with an oval face that seemed to have been carved out of old ivory. Behind him, under the branches of the fir-tree, there was a neat stack of grenades; and the Uzbek himself held a grenade in his dead, upraised hand, as if, before throwing it, he had taken a glance at the sky and had remained petrified in that pose.

And still further on, along the forest road, near some motley-coloured tanks, on the edges of large shell craters, in the foxholes, near some old tree stumps, everywhere lay dead bodies, in padded jackets and trousers and in faded green tunics and forage-caps pulled over the ears; bent knees, upraised chins and waxen faces gnawed by foxes and pecked by magpies and ravens protruded from the snowdrifts.

Several ravens were circling slowly over the glade and this suddenly reminded Alexei of the mournful but magnificent picture of "The Battle of Igor" reproduced in his school history book from the canvas of a great Russian artist.

"I might have been lying here like them," he thought, and again the sense of being alive surged through his whole being. He shook himself. The rough grindstones were still turning slowly in his head, his feet burned and ached worse than before, but he sat down on the bear's carcass, now cold and silvery from the dry snow that powdered it, and began to ponder what to do, where to go, how to get to his own forward lines.

When he was thrown out of his aircraft he had lost his map case, but he could vividly picture the route he had to take. The German airfield, which the Stormovik had attacked, lay about sixty kilometres west of the forward lines. During the air battle his men had drawn the enemy about twenty kilometres east away from the airfield, and, after escaping from the double "pincers", he himself must have got a little farther to the east. Consequently, he must have fallen about thirty-five kilometres from the forward lines, far behind the forward German divisions, somewhere in the region of the enormous tract of forest land known as the Black Forest, over which he had flown more than once when escorting bombers and Stormoviks in short raids on near-by German bases. From the air this forest had always looked to him like a boundless green sea. In clear weather it heaved with the swaying tops of the pine-trees; but in bad weather, enveloped in a thin, grey mist, it looked like a smooth, dreary waste of water with small waves rolling on the surface.

The fact that he had fallen into the middle of this

huge forest had a good and bad side. The good side was that he was unlikely to meet any Germans here, for they usually kept to the roads and towns. The bad side was that his route, though not long, was very difficult; he would have to push through dense undergrowth, and was not likely to meet with human aid, to get shelter, a crust of bread, or a cup of something warm to drink. His feet.... Would they carry him? Would he be able to walk? ...

He rose slowly from the bear's carcass. Again he felt that acute pain starting from his feet and shooting over his whole body from the bottom up. A cry of agony escaped his lips and he sat down again. He tried to remove his fur boots, but they would not budge; with every tug he uttered a groan. Clenching his teeth and shutting his eyes tight he wrenched one of the boots off with both his hands—and at once lost consciousness. When he came to he carefully unwound the foot cloth. The foot had swelled and it looked like one whole, livid bruise. It burned and ached in every joint. He rested his foot on the snow and the pain subsided somewhat. With a similar desperate wrench, as if he were pulling one of his own teeth, he removed the other boot.

Both his feet were useless. Evidently, when he was thrown out of the cockpit of his aircraft, something must have caught his feet and shattered the bones of the instep and toes. Under ordinary circumstances, of course, he would not have dreamed of attempting to stand up on feet in such a frightful condition. But he was alone in the depths of a virgin forest, in the enemy's rear, where to meet a human being meant not relief, but death. So he resolved to push on, eastward, through the forest, making no attempt to seek convenient roads or human habitation; to push on at all costs.

He resolutely got up from the bear's carcass, gasped, ground his teeth and took the first step. He stood for an instant, tore the other foot from the snow and took another step. Noises filled his head, and the glade swayed and floated away.

Alexei felt himself growing weaker from exertion and pain. Biting his lips, he continued to push on and reached a forest road that ran past a wrecked tank, past the dead

Uzbek holding the grenade, and into the depths of the forest, eastward. It was not so bad hobbling on the soft snow, but as soon as his foot touched the wind-hardened, ice-covered, humped surface of the road, the pain became so excruciating that he dared not take another step and halted. He stood, his feet awkwardly apart, his body swaying as if blown about by the wind. Suddenly a grey mist rose before his eyes. The road, the pine-trees, the greyish pine tops and the blue, oblong patch of sky between them vanished.... He was in his airfield, by a fighter, his fighter, and his mechanic, lanky Yura, his teeth and eyes, as always, glistening on his unshaven and ever smutty face, was beckoning him to the cockpit, as much as to say: "She's ready, off you go!..." Alexei took a step towards the plane, but the ground swayed, his feet burned as if he had stepped upon a red-hot metal plate. He tried to skip across this fiery path of ground on to the wing of his plane, but collided with the cold side of the fuselage. He was surprised to find that the side of the fuselage was not smooth and polished but rough, as if lined with pine bark.... But there was no fighter; he was standing on the road, stroking the trunk of a tree.

"Hallucinations? I am going out of my mind from the concussion!" thought Alexei. "It will be torture, going by this road. Should I turn off? But that will make the going slower...." He sat down on the snow and with the same short, resolute wrenches pulled off his fur boots, tore open the uppers with his teeth and finger-nails to make them easier for his fractured feet, took off his large, fluffy angora woollen scarf, tore it into strips, which he wound round his feet, and put his boots on again.

It was easier to walk now. But it is not quite correct to say walk: not walk, but move forward, move forward carefully, stepping on his heels and raising his feet high, as one walks across a bog. After every few steps his head swam from pain and exertion. He was obliged to halt, shut his eyes, lean against the trunk of a tree, or sit down on a snow hummock to rest, conscious of the acute throbbing of the blood in his veins.

And so he pushed on for several hours. But when he turned to look back, he could still see at the end of the forest cutting the sunlit turn of the road where the dead

Uzbek lay like a small dark patch on the snow. Alexei was extremely disappointed. Disappointed, but not frightened. It made him want to push on faster. He got up from the hummock, tightly clenched his teeth and moved on, choosing close targets, concentrating his mind upon them—from pine-tree to pine-tree, from stump to stump, from hummock to hummock. And as he moved on he left a winding, irregular track on the virgin snow on the deserted forest road, like that left by a wounded animal.

4

And so he moved on until the evening. When the sun, setting somewhere behind him, threw its cold, red glare upon the tree tops and the grey shadows began to thicken in the forest, he came to a hollow overgrown with juniper, and there a scene opened before his eyes that made him feel as if a cold wet towel was being passed down his spine, and his hair stood on end under his helmet.

Evidently, while the fighting was proceeding in the glade, a medical company had been posted in this hollow. The wounded had been brought here and laid on beds of pine-needles. And here they were, still lying in the shelter of the bushes, some half-buried and others completely buried under the snow. It was clear from the first glance that they had not died from their wounds. Somebody had cut their throats with skilful strokes of a knife, and they all lay in the same posture, with their heads thrown back as if trying to see what was going on behind them. And here too was the explanation of this frightful scene. Under a pine-tree, next to the snow-covered body of a Soviet Army man, sat a nurse, waist-deep in the snow, holding the soldier's head in her lap, a small, frail-looking girl wearing a fur cap, the ear-flaps of which were tied under her chin with tape. Between her shoulder-blades protruded the highly polished handle of a dagger. Near by lay the bodies of a fascist, in the black uniform of the SS, and of a Soviet Army man with a blood-stained bandage on his head. The two were clutching each other by the throat in a last mortal grip. Alexei guessed at once that the one in black had murdered the wounded, and the Soviet Army man, who had been still alive, had rushed upon the murderer at the very moment that he was stabbing the nurse and had clutched the enemy by his throat with all the remaining strength in his fingers.

And so the blizzard had buried them all—the frail girl in the fur cap sheltering the wounded man with her body, and these two, the murderer and the avenger, holding each other by the throat, lying at her feet, which were encased in old army top-boots with broad leggings.

Alexei stood there transfixed for several moments, then hobbled towards the nurse and pulled the dagger out of her back. It proved to be an SS dirk, fashioned like an ancient German sword, with a silver SS emblem on the mahogany hilt. On the rusty blade the inscription: *"Alles für Deutschland"* could still be discerned. Alexei removed the leather scabbard of the dirk from the German's body; he would need the weapon on his journey. Then he dug the hard, frozen ground sheet out from under the snow, tenderly covered the nurse's body with it and laid a few pine branches upon it. . . .

By that time, dusk set in. The strips of light between the trees died out. Dense and frosty darkness enveloped the hollow. It was quiet here, but the evening wind swept through the tree tops and the forest sang, at one moment a soothing lullaby, at another a melody of anxiety and alarm. The fine dry snow, no longer visible to the eye, but swishing softly and pricking the face, was blown into the hollow.

Born in Kamyshin, in the Volga steppe, a town-dweller, inexperienced in woodcraft, Alexei had not taken the trouble to prepare for the night, or to light a fire. Overtaken by the intense darkness and conscious of excruciating pain in his fractured and weary feet, he had not the strength to collect firewood; he crawled into the thick undergrowth of a young pine, sat down under the tree, hunched his shoulders, rested his head upon his knees which he clasped in his arms and, warming himself with his own breath, sat quite still, enjoying the quiet and repose.

He kept his pistol cocked, but it is doubtful whether he would have been able to use it on that first night in the forest. He slept like a log and heard neither the steady rustling of the pines, nor the hooting of an owl somewhere near the road, nor the distant howling of wolves—none of the noises of the forest that filled the dense, impenetrable darkness which closely enveloped him.

He woke with a start, as if somebody had shaken him, as soon as the first streaks of dawn appeared and the trees loomed in vague silhouettes in the frosty gloom. On waking he remembered what had happened to him, and where he was, and the carelessness with which he had spent the night in the forest frightened him. The intense cold penetrated his fur-lined flying suit and pierced him to the marrow. He shivered as if with ague. But the worst were his feet; the pain was more acute than ever, even now when he was at rest. The very thought of having to stand up terrified him. But he rose resolutely, with a wrench, in the same way as he had torn the boots from his feet the day before. Time was precious.

To all the torments that had afflicted Alexei was added that of hunger. The day before, when he had covered the nurse's body with the ground sheet, he had seen a canvas Red Cross satchel lying by her side. Some small animal had already busied itself with it and crumbs were scattered on the snow near some holes the animal had gnawed. Alexei had paid scarcely any attention to this the day before, but now he picked the satchel up and found in it several field dressings, a large tin of meat, a packet of letters and a small mirror, at the back of which was the photograph of a thin-faced, aged woman. Evidently the satchel had also contained some bread, but the birds or animals had made short work of that. Alexei put the tin and the bandages into the pockets of his flying suit, saying to himself: "Thank you, dear," adjusted the ground sheet which the wind had blown off the young woman's feet, and made his way slowly towards the east, which was already ablaze with orange-coloured flame behind the network of tree branches.

He now possessed a kilogram tin of meat, and he resolved to eat once a day, at noon.

5

To divert his mind from the pain every step cost him, Alexei began to think over and calculate his route. If he did ten or twelve kilometres every day he would reach his destination in three days, in four at most. "That's all right! Now, what does ten or twelve kilometres mean? A kilometre is two thousand paces; consequently, ten kilometres are twenty thousand paces, but that's a lot, considering that I will have to rest after every five hundred or six hundred paces...."

The day before, in order to ease the going, Alexei had set himself certain visible targets; a pine-tree, a tree stump, or a pitfall in the road, and strove towards each one as a halting place. Now he reduced all these to figures—into a given number of paces. He decided to make each stretch a thousand paces, that is, half a kilometre, and to rest by the clock—not more than five minutes. He calculated that, with difficulty, he could do ten kilometres from sunrise to sunset.

But how hard the first thousand paces were! He tried counting them in order to take his mind off the pain, but after counting up to five hundred he lost count and after that could think of nothing except the burning, throbbing pain. Yet, he covered those thousand paces. Lacking the strength to sit down, he dropped face downwards into the snow and greedily licked it, pressed his forehead and burning temples to it and felt indescribable pleasure at the icy touch.

He shuddered and looked at his watch. The second hand was ticking off the last seconds of the allotted five minutes. He watched the moving hand with fear, as if expecting something terrible at the end of the round; but as soon as it reached the figure sixty, he sprang to his feet with a groan and pushed on farther.

By midday, when the semi-darkness of the forest sparkled with the fine threads of sun-rays that pierced the dense pine branches, and when the pungent smell of resin and melting snow pervaded the forest, he had covered only four of these stretches. At the end of the last one he dropped down into the snow, not having the strength to crawl to the trunk of a big birch-tree that was lying almost within arm's reach. There he sat for a long time, his head dropped on his chest, thinking of nothing, seeing and hearing nothing, not even feeling the pangs of hunger.

He took a deep breath, threw a few pinches of snow into his mouth, and overcoming the torpor that fettered his body, he drew the rusty tin of conserves from his pocket and opened it with the German dirk. He put a piece of frozen, tasteless fat into his mouth and wanted to swallow it, but the fat melted. Instantly, he was overcome by such ravenous hunger that he could barely tear himself away from the tin, and began to eat snow, only to have something to swallow.

Before proceeding farther he cut himself a pair of walking-sticks from a juniper-tree. He leaned on these sticks, but with every step he found it more and more difficult to walk.

6

...The third day of Alexei's painful walk through the dense forest, in which he found not a single human trail, was marked by an unexpected event. He awoke with the first rays of the sun, shivering from the cold and inward fever. In a pocket of his flying suit he found a cigarette lighter which his mechanic had made from an empty rifle cartridge and had given him as a souvenir. He had entirely forgotten about it, or that he could and should have lit a fire. Breaking some dry, mossy branches from the fir-tree under which he had slept, he covered them with pine-needles and set fire to them. Brisk, yellow flames shot out from the grey smoke. The dry, resinous wood burned quickly and merrily. The flames reached the pine-needles and, fanned by the wind, flared up, hissing and groaning.

The fire hissed and crackled, radiating dry, beneficent heat. A cosy feeling overcame Alexei. He pulled down the zipper of his flying suit and drew from his tunic pocket some tattered letters, all written in the same hand. In one of the letters he found, wrapped in a piece of cellophane, a photograph of a slim girl in a flowered frock, sitting on the grass with her legs drawn in. He gazed at the photograph for some time and then wrapped it up again in the piece of cellophane, put it back into the envelope, held it in his hand thoughtfully for a moment, and returned it to his pocket.

"Never mind, everything will be all right," he said, whether to the girl or to himself it is hard to say. And thoughtfully he repeated: "*Never mind....*"

Now, with an accustomed movement, he whipped off his fur boots, unwound the strips of woollen scarf and examined his feet. They were more swollen, the toes spread in all directions; the feet looked like inflated rubber bladders and were even of a darker colour than they had been the day before.

Alexei sighed, cast a farewell glance at the dying fire and again laboured on, his sticks crunching the ice-hard snow. He proceeded, biting his lips and sometimes almost losing consciousness. Suddenly, amidst the usual sounds of the forest to which his ears had already grown so accustomed that they almost failed to catch them, he heard the distant throbbing of automobile engines. At first he thought this was a hallucination due to his weariness, but the sounds grew louder, now running at low gear and now subsiding. Evidently they were Germans, and they were going in his direction. Alexei at once felt a coldness in his stomach.

Fear lent him strength. Forgetting his weariness and the pain in his feet, he turned off the road and made for a fir thicket. He crawled into its depths and dropped on to the snow. It was difficult, of course, to see him from the road, but he could see the road distinctly, lit up by the midday sun that was already high above the spiked fence of fir-tree tops.

The sounds drew nearer. Alexei remembered that his lone trail was distinctly visible on the road that he had abandoned, but it was too late to attempt to go farther away, the engine of the leading vehicle was heard quite close now. Alexei pressed deeper into the snow. Through the branches he saw a flat, wedge-shaped, whitewashed armoured car. Swaying, its chains clanging, it drew near to where Alexei's trail turned off the road. Alexei held his breath. The armoured car rolled on. It was followed by a general-purpose car. Somebody in a high-peaked cap, his nose buried deep in his brown fur collar, was sitting beside the driver, and behind him were several machine-gunners in field-grey greatcoats and steel helmets, sitting on high benches and swaying with the motion of the car. A larger general-purpose car brought up the rear, its motor roaring and its treads clanging. In it, sitting in rows, were about fifteen Germans.

Alexei pressed closer to the snow. The vehicles came so close that the fumes of the exhaust gas beat in his face. He felt the hair at the nape of his neck rise and his muscles contracted into tight balls. But the vehicles swept by, the smell of the fumes was dissipated, and soon the sound of the engines was barely heard.

When all had become quiet, Alexei got out on to the road, on which the tracks left by the cars were distinctly visible, and pursued his way eastward, following these very tracks. He pushed on in the same measured stretches, took the same spells of rest and ate as before, after covering half of the day's route. But now he proceeded like a forest animal, with the utmost caution. His vigilant ears caught the slightest rustle, his eyes roamed from side to side as if he were aware that a big and dangerous beast was lurking in the vicinity.

An airman, accustomed to fighting in the air, this was the first time he had seen the enemy on the ground. Now he was wandering in their tracks, and he laughed vengefully. They were not having a good time here; they found no cosiness, no hospitality in the land they had occupied! Even in this virgin forest, where for three days he had not seen a single sign of a human being, their officer was obliged to travel under such a heavy escort!

"Never mind, everything will be all right!" said Alexei to cheer himself up, and he pushed on, step by step, trying to forget that the pain in his feet was growing more and more acute and that he himself was perceptibly losing strength. His stomach could no longer be deceived by the piece of young fir bark which he kept on chewing and swallowing, nor by the bitter birch buds, nor by the tender and sticky young linden bark that stretched in the mouth like chewing-gum.

By the time dusk fell he had barely covered five laps. At night he lit a big fire, piling large quantities of pine branches and dry brushwood around a huge, half-decayed birch-tree trunk lying on the ground. While this tree trunk smouldered with a dull glow, radiating pleasant warmth, he slept stretched out on the ground, conscious of the life-giving warmth, instinctively turning over in his sleep, and waking in order to add brushwood to revive the flames that were lazily lapping the sides of the log.

A blizzard sprang up in the middle of the night. The pine-trees overhead swayed, rustled, creaked and groaned in alarm. Clouds of prickly snow swept across the ground. The rustling gloom swirled around the sizzling, sparkling fire. But the snow-storm did not disturb Alexei; he was immersed in deep, sound slumber, protected by the warmth of the fire.

The fire protected him from the beasts of the forest. As for the Germans, there was no need to worry about them on a night like this. They would not dare to go deep into the forest during a snow-storm. For all that, while his weary body rested in the smoky warmth, his ear, already trained to the caution of the denizens of the forest, caught every sound. Just before dawn, when the blizzard had abated and a dense white mist hung over the now silent earth, Alexei thought that above the rustle of the swaying pine-trees and the soft swish of the falling snow he heard the distant sounds of battle, explosions, bursts from machine-guns, and rifle fire.

"Can the front line be so near? So soon?"

7

But when, in the morning, the wind dispersed the fog, and the forest, which had grown silvery in the night, glistened bright and frosty in the sun and, as if rejoicing at this sudden transformation, the feathered fraternity chirped and twittered and sang in anticipation of the coming spring, Alexei, however much he strained his ears, could catch no sound of battle, neither rifle fire nor even the rumble of artillery.

The snow-flakes, sparkling like crystals in the sun, dribbled from the trees in white, smoky streams. Here and there heavy drops of moisture fell on the snow with a light patter. The spring! This was the first time it had announced its coming so emphatically and resolutely.

Alexei decided to eat the miserable remnants of the tinned meat—a few shreds of meat coated with savoury fat—in the morning, for he felt that if he did not do so he would not have the strength to rise. He cleaned the tin out thoroughly with his forefinger, cutting his hand here and there on its jagged edges, but it seemed to him that there were still some scraps of fat left. He filled the tin with snow, scraped away the grey ashes from the dying fire and placed the tin on the glowing embers. Later he sipped the hot water with the slightly meaty flavour with the utmost relish. When he finished he slipped the tin into his pocket, meaning to use it for making tea. To drink hot tea! This was a pleasant discovery, and it cheered him somewhat when he proceeded on his way again.

But here a great disappointment awaited him. The blizzard had completely obliterated the road, barring it with sloping, conical snow-drifts. Alexei's eyes smarted from the monotonous, bluish glare. His feet sank into the fluffy, as yet unsettled snow and he could pull them out only with great difficulty. His sticks were of little service to him, for they, too, sank deep into the snow.

By midday, when the shadows under the trees grew black and the sun looked over the tree tops into the forest cutting, Alexei had covered only about fifteen hundred paces, and he was so weary that every new step cost him a tremendous effort of will. He felt giddy. The ground slipped from under his feet. Every now and again he fell, lay motionless for an instant on top of a snow-drift, pressing his forehead to the crisp snow, and then got up and walked another few paces. He felt an irresistible inclination to sleep, to lie down and forget everything, not moving a single muscle. Come what may. He halted, stood benumbed, swaying from side to side, and then, biting his lips until they hurt, he pulled himself together and walked a few paces, barely able to drag his feet along.

At last he felt that he could go on no longer, that no power on earth could shift him from the spot, that if he sat down now he would never get up again. He cast a longing glance around him. By the roadside stood a young, curly pine tree. Mustering his last ounce of strength, Alexei stepped towards it and flung himself upon it. His chin rested on the fork of the branches. This took some of the weight off his fractured feet and he felt a little relief. He leaned against the springy branches and enjoyed the repose. Wishing to make himself more comfortable, he stretched one leg and then the other, still keeping his chin on the fork of the tree, and his feet, completely relieved of the weight of his body, were easily lifted out of the snow-drift. A brilliant idea struck him.

"Why, of course! It would be easy to cut down this small tree, lop off the branches, leaving the fork, throw the staff forward, rest my chin on the fork and transfer the weight of my body to it, and then throw my feet forward, just as I am doing now. It will be slow going. Yes, slow, of course, but I won't get so tired, and I will be able to push on without having to wait until the snow-drifts harden."

He dropped to his knees, cut the young tree down with his dirk, lopped off the branches, wound his pocket handkerchief and bandages round the crutch and set off at once. He threw the staff forward, rested his hands and chin upon the fork, put one foot forward and then the other, threw the staff forward again and took another two steps forward. And so he kept on, counting the paces and fixing a new rate of progress for himself.

No doubt an onlooker would have thought it strange to see a man wandering through the dense forest in this queer fashion, moving over deep snow-drifts at a snail's pace, pushing on from sunrise to sunset and covering no more than five kilometres. But the only witnesses of this strange proceeding were the magpies; and having convinced themselves of the utter harmlessness of this strange three-legged, clumsy animal, they did not fly away at his approach, but merely hopped reluctantly out of his way, cocked their heads and gazed mockingly at him with their black, inquisitive, beady eyes.

8

And so he hobbled along the snow-covered road for two days, throwing out his staff, resting upon it and drawing his feet up. By this time his feet were quite numb and felt nothing, but his body was convulsed with pain at every step. He no longer felt the pangs of hunger. The spasms and cutting pains in his stomach had become a dull, constant ache, as if the empty stomach had hardened and turned, pressing against his insides.

Alexei's food consisted of young pine bark which he stripped off the trees with his dirk in his rest intervals, the buds of birch- and lime-trees, and also the soft, green moss which he dug up from under the snow and stewed in boiling water during his nightly bivouacs. A joy to him was the "tea" he brewed from lacquered bilberry leaves which he gathered on thawed patches of ground. The hot liquid sent a warm glow through his whole body and even created the illusion of satiety. Sipping the hot brew that smelt of smoke and leaves, he felt soothed, and his journey did not seem so endless and terrible.

On his sixth bivouac he again lay under the green tent of a spreading fir-tree and lit his fire round an old, resinous tree stump, which, he calculated, would smoulder and give off heat the whole night. It was still light. Overhead an invisible squirrel was busy in the top branches of the fir-tree, shelling fir-cones and throwing the empty and mutilated cones to the ground. Alexei, whose mind was now constantly concentrated on food, wondered what it was that the squirrel found in the cones. He picked up a cone, stripped off one of the scales and beneath it found a winged seed about the size of a millet grain. In appearance it looked like a tiny cedar nut. He put the seed in his mouth, crushed it between his teeth and felt the pleasant flavour of cedar oil.

He collected a few fir-cones that were lying around, put them on the fire, added a handful of brushwood, and when the cones opened from the heat he shook the seeds into his hand, crushed them between his palms, blew the winged husks away and threw the tiny nuts into his mouth.

The forest hummed with faint sounds. The resinous tree stump smouldered, giving off a mild, fragrant smoke that reminded Alexei of incense. The small flames flickered, now burning brightly, now dying down, causing the trunks of the golden pines and silvery birches to stand out in a circle of light and then to recede into the murmuring gloom.

Alexei threw some more brushwood on the fire and shelled some more cones. The smell of cedar oil recalled to his mind a long-forgotten scene of his childhood.... A small room crowded with familiar objects. The table under the lamp hanging from the ceiling. His mother, in holiday attire, just returned from vespers, solemnly taking a paper bag from the chest and emptying cedar nuts from it into a bowl. The whole family—Mother, Grandmother, his two brothers and himself, the youngest of all—sitting round the table and the solemn shelling of cedar nuts—the holiday luxury—beginning. Nobody uttered a word. Grandmother pried the kernels out with a hairpin, Mother did the same with a pin. She skilfully cracked the shells with her teeth, extracted the kernels and collected them on the table; and when she had quite a heap, she swept them into the palm of her hand and put the lot into the open mouth of one of the children; and the fortunate one felt her hand against his lips; it was rough and toil-worn, but this being a holiday, it smelt of scented soap.

Kamyshin ... childhood! It was cosy living in that tiny house on the outskirts of the town!... But here, amidst the noises of the forest, your face is burning hot while the piercing cold strikes you in the back. An owl is hooting in the darkness, the yapping of a fox is heard. Huddled at a fire and gazing thoughtfully at the dying, flickering embers, sat a hungry, wounded and mortally weary man, alone in this vast, dense forest; and before him, in the darkness, lay an unknown road, full of unexpected dangers and trials.

"Never mind, everything will be all right!" the man suddenly exclaimed, and by the light of the last red flicker of the fire one could have seen his cracked lips stretch in a smile at some remote thought.

9

On the seventh day Alexei learned where the noise of a distant battle had come from on that night of the snowstorm.

Utterly worn out, halting every moment to take a rest, he was dragging himself along the thawing forest road. The spring was no longer smiling from a distance, it had arrived in this virgin forest with its warm, gusty winds, with its bright sun-rays that broke through the branches and swept the snow from hummock and hillock, with the mournful croak of the ravens in the evenings, the slow and staid rooks on the now brownish hump of the road, the wet snow, now porous like honeycomb, glistening puddles in the hollows from the melting snow, and that powerful, intoxicating smell which makes every living thing giddy with joy.

Alexei had loved this time of the year since his childhood, and even now, as he dragged his aching feet encased in the sodden and bedraggled fur boots through the puddles, hungry, fainting from pain and weariness, cursing the puddles, the slushy snow and early mud, he greedily inhaled the moist, intoxicating fragrance. He no longer picked his way among the puddles, he stumbled, fell, got up, leaned heavily on his staff, swaying and mustering his strength, then threw the staff forward as far as he could and slowly continued on his way eastward.

Suddenly, at a point where the forest road abruptly turned to the left, he halted and stood transfixed. At a spot where the road was exceptionally narrow and hedged in on both sides by closely growing young pines, he saw the German motor vehicles that had passed him a few days before. Their road was barred by two huge pines. Next to these trees, with its radiator lodged between them, stood the wedge-shaped armoured car, no longer a patchy white, but a rusty red, and it stood low on the rims of its wheels, for its tyres had been burnt away. Its turret was lying on the snow under a tree like a monstrous mushroom. Near the armoured car lay three corpses—its crew—in short, black, greasy tunics and cloth helmets.

The two general-purpose cars, also rusty-red and charred, stood behind the armoured car in the melting snow that was blackened by fumes, ashes and charred wood. All around, by the roadside, under the bushes and in the ditches, lay the bodies of German soldiers. It was evident that they had fled in horror, that death had struck at them from behind every tree, behind every bush, screened by the snowy mantle spread by the blizzard, and that they had died not really knowing what had happened. The body of the officer, minus his trousers, was tied to a tree. To his green tunic with the dark collar was pinned a scrap of paper on which was written: "You got what you came for", and beneath this inscription, in another hand, was written with an indelible pencil the word—"cur".

Alexei searched this scene of battle, looking for something to eat. All he found was a stale, mouldy rusk, trampled into the snow and pecked by birds. He at once put it to his mouth and greedily inhaled the sourish flavour of rye bread. He wanted to put the whole rusk into his mouth and chew, chew and chew the fragrant, pulpy bread, but he suppressed the desire and broke the rusk into three pieces, pushed two of them deep into his thigh pocket and then began to pick the third into crumbs and to suck each crumb as though it were a sweet, to draw out the pleasure as long as possible.

Once again he went over the scene of battle, and here an idea struck him: "There must be partisans somewhere round about here! They must have trampled the slushy snow in the bushes and around the trees!" Perhaps they had already seen him wandering among the corpses, and somewhere from the top of a fir-tree, or behind a bush, a partisan scout was watching him? He cupped his hands round his mouth and shouted with all his might:

"O-ho! Partisans! Partisans!"

He was surprised that his voice sounded so faint and feeble. Even the echo that came reverberating from the depth of the forest, re-echoing against the tree trunks, seemed louder.

"Partisans! Pa-artisans! O-ho!" he called over and over again, sitting in the black, greasy snow amidst the silent enemy corpses.

He strained his ears for a reply. His voice was hoarse and cracked, he now realised that having done their job and collected their trophies, the partisans had gone long ago—indeed, what was the use of their staying in this deserted wilderness?—but he kept on calling, hoping for a miracle, hoping that the bearded men that he had heard so much about would suddenly emerge from the bushes, pick him up and take him to a place where he could rest for a day, even for an hour without having to bother about anything or striving to get anywhere.

Only the forest answered with its reverberating, vibrating echo. But suddenly, above the deep and melodious humming of the pines he heard—or thought he heard, considering the tenseness with which he listened—dull and rapid thuds, now quite distinct, and now faint and confused. He started up as though a distant friendly call had reached him in this wilderness. He could not believe his ears, and sat for a long time listening intently with outstretched neck.

No! He was not mistaken! A moist wind blew from the east and carried to him the distant sounds of artillery fire; and this fire was not slow and sporadic like the sounds he had heard during the past months when the combatants, having entrenched and fortified themselves on firm defence lines, listlessly exchanged shots to harass each other. This firing was rapid and intense, sounding as if somebody were unloading cobble-stones, or drumming his fists on the bottom of an upturned oak barrel.

Of course! It was a fierce artillery duel. Judging by the sounds, the front line must be about ten kilometres away and something serious was happening there, somebody was launching an attack, and somebody was putting up a desperate defence. Tears of joy rolled down Alexei's cheeks.

He kept his eyes turned to the east. True, at the spot he was, the road turned abruptly in the opposite direction and a snowy carpet lay in front of him; but it was from the east that he heard the inviting sounds; it was in that direction that the dark tracks of the partisans were leading; it was somewhere in the forest over there that these brave men of the forest lived.

And Alexei mumbled: "Never mind, it's all right, comrades, everything will be all right." He vigorously threw his staff forward, rested his chin on it and putting all the weight of his body upon it he placed one foot and then the other on the snow and turned from the road, moving forward with difficulty but resolutely.

10

That day he did not even make a hundred and fifty paces over the snow. Dusk compelled him to halt. Again he picked out an old tree stump, piled dry brushwood around it, unwrapped his cartridge cigarette lighter, jerked the little steel wheel, jerked it again—and turned cold; the lighter had run dry. He shook it, blew into it in the endeavour to quicken the last remnants of gas, but in vain. Night fell. The sparks that flew from the flint like flashes of lightning parted for an instant the gloom around his face. He kept jerking the wheel until the flint was completely worn out, but he failed to get any fire.

He had to grope his way to a clump of young pine-trees, huddle up, rest his chin on his knees, clasp his knees with his hands and sit silently listening to the rustling of the forest. He might have dropped into despair that night, but in the slumbering forest the sound of artillery fire was even more distinct and it seemed to him that he was even able to distinguish the sharp reports of the shots from the longer booms of the exploding shells.

He woke up in the morning with an unaccountable sensation of alarm and grief. At once he asked himself: "What was it? A bad dream?" He remembered: the cigarette lighter. But warmed by the kindly rays of the sun, with everything around—the slushy snow, the trunks of the trees, and even the pine-needles—shining and glistening—he took a less serious view of this misfortune. But something worse happened. Unclasping his numbed hands, he found that he could not get up. After several attempts to rise he broke his forked staff and collapsed to the ground like a sack. He rolled over on his back to rest his swollen limbs and gazed through the pine branches at the infinite blue sky, across which white, fluffy clouds, with curly golden edges, were hurrying. His body gradually came to, but something had happened to his legs. They could not bear him even for a moment.

Holding on to the pine-tree, he made another attempt to rise and at last succeeded, but as soon as he tried to bring his legs up to the tree he collapsed from weakness, and from a frightful, new itching pain in the feet.

Was this the end? Was he to perish here, under the pines, where, perhaps, nobody would find and bury his bones, picked clean by the beasts of the forest? Overpowering weakness pressed him to the ground. But in the distance the guns rumbled. Fighting was going on over there, and his own people were there. Would he be unable to muster enough strength to cover these last eight or ten kilometres?

The rumble of the guns put new courage into him, called him persistently, and he responded to the call. He got up on his hands and knees and ambled on like an animal, at first instinctively, hypnotised by the sounds of the distant battle, and later consciously and deliberately, realising that it was easier to go through the forest this way than with the aid of the staff. Not having to bear any burden, his feet hurt less, and he could move faster on his hands and knees. And again he felt a lump rising in his throat from sheer joy. As though encouraging somebody else who had lost heart and doubted the possibility of progressing in this incredible fashion, he said aloud:

"Never mind, my boy, everything will be all right now!"

After completing one of his laps, Alexei warmed his frozen hands by holding them under his arm-pits, then crept up to a young fir-tree, cut out two square pieces of bark and, breaking his finger-nails in the process, tore several long strips of bast from the trunk. He then took the strips of woollen scarf from his fur boots and wound them round his hands; over his knuckles he placed the pieces of bark, fastened them with the bast strips and then tied the whole with the bandage of one of the dressings. On the right hand he thus obtained a broad and very convenient mitten. But he was not so successful with the left hand, which he had to tie up with the aid of his teeth. But for all that, his hands were now "shoed", and Alexei proceeded on his way, feeling the going easier. At the next stop he tied pieces of bark to his knees too.

By midday, when it was getting appreciably warm, he had made a considerable number of "paces" on his hands. Whether it was due to the fact that he was drawing nearer to the place from where the sounds of artillery fire came or to some acoustical illusion, but those sounds were louder. It was now so warm that Alexei opened the zipper of his flying suit.

As he was crawling across a moss-covered bog in which green clumps were appearing from the melting snow, fate had another gift in store for him: on the greyish, soft, damp moss he noticed the fine stems of a plant bearing rare, pointed, polished leaves, between which, right on the surface of the clumps, lay scarlet, slightly crushed, but still luscious cranberries. Alexei bent his head down to the clump and with his lips began to pick berry after berry from the warm, velvety moss that smelt of the dankness of the bog.

The pleasant sweetish-sour taste of the cranberries, this first real food he had eaten for the past few days, gave Alexei cramps in the stomach. But he had not the strength of mind to wait until these cramps passed. He wriggled from clump to clump and, like a bear, picked the sweet and sour berries with his tongue and lips. In this way he cleared up several clumps, feeling neither the spring water in his sodden boots, nor the burning pain in his feet, nor weariness—he felt nothing but the sweetish-tart taste in his mouth and a pleasant heaviness in the stomach.

He vomited, but still he could not restrain himself and set about picking the berries again. He removed the self-made "footwear" from his hands and filled the old meat tin with berries; he also filled his helmet, tied it by the tape to his belt and crawled on further, overcoming with difficulty the languor that was spreading over his whole body.

That night, after creeping under the shelter of an old fir-tree, he ate the berries and chewed bark and fir-cone seeds. Then he turned in, but his sleep was that of the anxious watcher. Several times he thought that somebody was noiselessly creeping up to him in the darkness. He opened his eyes and strained his ears so hard that they began to buzz, took out his pistol and sat stock-still, starting at the sound of a falling cone, the crunch of the night-hardened snow and the low ripple of the tiny springs that ran from under the snow.

Only before dawn did he fall asleep. He woke up when it was quite light and around the tree under which he had been sleeping he saw the winding imprints of a fox's paws, and between them the long traces left by its dragging tail.

"So that's what disturbed my sleep!" From the tracks it was evident that the fox had prowled around, had squatted and had prowled again. A disturbing thought flashed through Alexei's mind. Hunters say that this cunning animal senses the approaching death of a human being and begins to follow him. Had this premonition drawn this craven beast to him?

"Nonsense! How utterly absurd! Everything will be all right," he said to cheer himself up, and going down on his hands and knees he crawled and crawled, trying to get away from this sinister place as fast as he could.

That day he had another stroke of luck. In a fragrant juniper bush, the dull-grey berries of which he was plucking with his lips, he saw a strange heap of fallen leaves. He touched the heap with his hand, but it held firm. He began to pull the leaves away and suddenly something pricked his finger. He guessed at once that it was a hedgehog. It was a big, old hedgehog that had crept into the thicket to hibernate; and to keep warm it had rolled itself up in fallen autumn leaves. Alexei was overcome with frenzied joy. Throughout his painful journey he had dreamed of killing an animal or a bird. How many times had he drawn his pistol and had taken aim at a magpie, a jay, or a rabbit, and each time had with difficulty fought down the desire to shoot; for he had only three bullets left—two for the enemy, and the third for himself if need be. He had forced himself to put the pistol away; he could not afford to take risks.

And here a piece of meat actually fell into his hands! Not pausing to remember that the hedgehog was according to common belief an unclean animal he rapidly removed the remaining leaves. The animal slept on, rolled up, looking like a funny big bean with bristles. Alexei killed the animal with his dirk, unrolled it, clumsily tore off its armour and the yellow skin from its underside, cut the carcass up into pieces and began voraciously to tear with his teeth the warm, grey, sinewy flesh that tightly adhered to the bones. The animal was consumed to the very last. Alexei crunched all the small bones and swallowed them, and only then did he become aware of the repugnant dog taste of the meat. But what was that smell compared with a full stomach that sent a feeling of satiety, warmth and languor through the whole body?

He examined and sucked every bone again, and lay down in the snow enjoying the warmth and repose. He might have fallen asleep had he not been roused by the cautious yap of a fox that came from the bushes. Alexei pricked up his ears, and suddenly, above the distant rumble of artillery, which he had heard all the time coming from the east, he distinguished the rattle of machine-gun fire.

Throwing off all weariness, forgetting the fox and the need of rest, he crawled forward again into the depths of the forest.

11

Beyond the bog across which he had crawled, there was a glade through which ran a double barred fence of weather-beaten poles fastened with strips of bast and willow to stakes driven into the ground.

Between the poles there peeped, here and there, from under the snow, the track of an abandoned, untrodden road. There must be a human habitation near by! Alexei's heart jumped. It was hardly likely that the Germans had got to this remote place; but even if they had, there would also be his own people somewhere around, and they, of course, would shelter a wounded man and help him in every way they could.

Sensing an early end to his wanderings, Alexei pushed on with all his might, taking no rest. He crawled, gasping for breath, falling face down into the snow, losing consciousness from the strain; he crawled hurriedly to reach the top of a hillock from which, he was convinced, he would be able to see the village that was to be a haven of refuge. Straining every nerve to reach the habitation he failed to notice that except for this fence and the track of the road that was rising more and more distinctly out of the snow, there was nothing to indicate that human beings were in the vicinity.

At last he reached the top of the hillock. Panting and gasping for breath, Alexei raised his eyes—and at once dropped them again, so ghastly was the scene that lay before him.

There could be no doubt that only recently this had been a small forest village. Its contours could be easily distinguished by the two uneven rows of chimneys that towered above the snow-covered remains of gutted houses. All he could see were a few gardens, wattle fences, and a rowan tree that had grown outside a window. Now they jutted out of the snow, dead and charred by fire. It was a bare, snow-covered field on which the chimneys stuck out, like tree stumps in a forest clearing, and in the middle, looking altogether incongruous, reared the crane of a well, from which was suspended an old, ironbound wooden bucket that swung slowly in the wind on its rusty chain. At the entrance to the village, near a garden surrounded by a green fence, there was a pretty arch, under which a gate creaked as it swung slowly on its rusty hinges.

Not a soul, not a sound, not a wisp of smoke. A desert. Not a sign of a living human being anywhere. A hare, which Alexei had scared out of the bush, scampered away and made straight for the village, kicking up its hind legs in the funniest fashion. It stopped at the wicket-gate, sat up, raised its forepaws and cocked an ear; but seeing this large, strange creature continuing to crawl in its tracks, it scuttled off again along the line of charred and deserted gardens.

Alexei continued mechanically to push forward. Big tears rolled down his unshaven cheeks and dropped into the snow. He halted at the wicket-gate where the hare had been a moment before. On the gate were the remains of a board with the letters "Kind...." It was not difficult to guess that the neat premises of a kindergarten had stood behind this green fence. There were even a few low benches which the village carpenter had made and, in his love for the children, had planed and scraped smooth with glass. Alexei pushed open the gate, crawled to a bench and wanted to sit on it, but his body had grown so accustomed to a horizontal position that he could not straighten up. When, at last, he did sit down, his whole spine ached. In order to rest he lay down on the snow and half curled up, as a tired animal does.

His heart was heavy and sad.

Around the bench the snow was melting, exposing the black earth from which warm moisture was rising, visibly curling and quivering in the air. Alexei scooped up a handful of the warm, thawing earth; it oozed between his fingers like grease and smelt of dankness and dung, of the cowshed and the home.

People had lived here, had, at some time or other, long, long ago, won this patch of ground from the Black Forest, had furrowed it with a plough, had raked it with a wooden harrow, had manured and tended it. It had been a hard life of constant struggle against the forest and the beasts of the forest, of constant worry about making ends meet until the next harvest. Under Soviet rule a collective farm was formed and they began to dream of a better life; farming machines came in, and with them a sufficiency. The village carpenters built a kindergarten, and, in the evenings, watching the rosy-cheeked children romping in this very garden, the men of the village must have thought that it was time they set about building a club and a reading-room where, cosy and warm, they could spend a winter evening while the blizzard raged outside; they must have dreamed of having electricity here, in the depths of the forest. Now it was nothing but a wilderness, a forest with its eternal, undisturbed silence.

The more Alexei pondered over this the more active his mind became. The vision of Kamyshin, that small, dusty Volga town in the flat, arid steppe, rose before his eyes. In the summer and autumn the sharp wind of the steppe blew through the town carrying clouds of dust and sand, which pricked the face and hands, blew into the houses, seeped through the closed windows, blinded the eyes and gritted in the teeth. These clouds of sand from the steppe were called "Kamyshin rain", and for many generations the people of Kamyshin had dreamed of stopping this sand and of breathing their fill of pure, fresh air. But this dream came true only in a socialist country. The people conferred together and launched a campaign against the wind and sand. Every Saturday the entire population came out with picks and shovels and axes and, in time, a park arose in the former vacant city square and young, slender poplar-trees lined the narrow streets. The people carefully watered and pruned these trees as if they were flowers growing on their own windowsills. Alexei remembered how, in the spring, all the inhabitants, young and old, rejoiced when the thin, bare branches sprouted and garbed themselves in green.... Suddenly, he pictured to himself the Germans in the streets of his native Kamyshin. They were cutting down the trees, which the people had tended so carefully, to use them for firewood. His native town was enveloped in smoke, and on the spot where his home had been, where he had grown up and where his mother had lived, reared a bare, sooty, monstrous chimney, like this one here.

His heart was torn with pain and anguish.

"They must not be allowed to go any farther! We must fight them while there is breath left in our bodies, like that Russian soldier had done who lay on top of the enemy bodies in that forest glade."

The sun was already touching the grey tops of the trees.

Alexei crawled down what had once been the village street. The smell of corpses came from the heaps of ashes. The village seemed more deserted than the forest. Suddenly, a strange sound brought him to the alert. Near a heap of ashes at the very end of the street he saw a dog. It was a shaggy, flap-eared house dog, just an ordinary Bobik or Zhuchka. Growling softly, it was worrying a piece of flabby meat that it held between its paws. On catching sight of Alexei, this dog, which is supposed to be the most genial of animals, the object of the constant scolding of housewives and the favourite of urchins, suddenly snarled and bared its teeth. Its eyes burned so fiercely that Alexei felt a shiver run down his spine. He threw off his "mitten" and reached for his pistol. For several moments the man, and the dog that had become a wild beast, stood glaring at each other, and then some recollection must have dawned on the animal, for it lowered its muzzle, wagged its tail guiltily, snatched up the piece of meat and ran behind the ash heap with its tail between its legs.

Away! Away from here, as quickly, as possible! Taking advantage of the last streaks of light, not choosing any road, but going straight across the snow, Alexei crawled into the forest, almost instinctively moving in the direction from which the sounds of artillery fire were now distinctly heard. They drew him like a magnet, and the nearer he approached them the greater was their power of attraction.

12

And so Alexei crawled on for another two or three days. He had lost count of time; everything had merged into one continuous chain of automatic effort. At times sleep, or, perhaps, oblivion, overcame him. He fell asleep as he crawled, but the force that drew him on to the east was so strong that even in this state of oblivion he continued to crawl slowly until he collided with a tree or bush, or until his hand slipped and he fell face downward in the melting snow. All his will, all his vague thoughts were concentrated on one spot like focussed light: crawl on, keep moving, moving onwards, at all costs.

On his way he inspected every bush in the hope of finding another hedgehog. His food consisted of berries he found under the snow, and moss. Once he came upon a huge ant-hill that towered up in the forest like a haystack, washed and combed by the rain. The ants were still asleep and their habitation seemed dead. Alexei plunged his hand into this soft stack and withdrew it covered with ants tenaciously clinging to the skin. He began to eat these insects with great relish, feeling in his dry, cracked mouth the spicy, tart taste of formic acid. He plunged his hand into the hill again and again until the whole population was roused by this unexpected invasion.

The tiny insects fiercely defended themselves; they stung Alexei's hand, lips and tongue, they got under his flying suit and stung his body. But the burning sensation was pleasant if anything, the bite of the formic acid acted as a tonic. He felt thirsty. Among the clumps he saw a small puddle of brownish forest water and stretched out to drink, but at once recoiled—out of the dark water, against the background of the blue sky reflected in it, a strange horrible face had peered at him. It was the face, of a skeleton covered with a dark skin and overgrown with untidy, already curling bristle. Large, round, wildly shining eyes stared out of the deep sockets, and unkempt hair hung down on the forehead in bedraggled strands.

"Is that me?" Alexei asked himself, and fearing to look again he did not drink the water but put some snow into his mouth instead and crawled on eastward, drawn by that same powerful magnet.

That night he chose for his bivouac a large bomb crater surrounded by a breastwork of yellow sand that had been thrown up by an explosion. He found the bottom of the crater quiet and cosy. The wind did not blow into it, it merely rustled the sand that dribbled in from the breastwork. From it the stars seemed unusually large and appeared to be suspended low over his head. A shaggy branch of a pine-tree that swayed to and fro beneath the stars looked like a hand holding a rag and wiping and polishing those shining lights. Before dawn it grew cold. A raw mist hung over the forest. The wind changed. Now it blew from the north, converting this mist into ice. When the dull, belated light at last broke through the branches, the dense mist descended and gradually dissolved, and the ground all round was found to be covered with a slippery, icy crust. The branch overhead no longer looked like a hand holding a rag, but like a wonderful crystal chandelier with small, suspended prisms tinkling gently in the wind.

Alexei woke up feeling weaker than ever. He did not even chew the pine bark of which he kept a stock in the bosom of his flying suit. He tore himself off the ground with difficulty, as if his body had been glued to it during the night. Without brushing the ice from his clothes, beard and moustache, he attempted to clamber up the side of the crater, but his hands slipped on the sand that had frozen during the night. Again and again he tried to get out, but each time he slipped back to the bottom. His efforts grew more and more feeble. At last he realised to his horror that he would be unable to get out without assistance. This thought impelled him to make one more effort to climb up the slippery side, but he succeeded in raising himself only a little when he slipped down again, exhausted and helpless.

"This is the end! Nothing matters now!"

He curled up at the bottom of the crater, conscious of a frightful sense of repose that unmagnetised and paralysed his will, creeping over his whole body. Listlessly he drew the tattered letters from his tunic pocket, but he had no strength to read them. He took out from its cellophane wrapper the photograph of the girl in the print frock sitting on the grass in a meadow. With a sad smile, he asked her:

"Is it really good-bye?"—and suddenly he gave a start and remained transfixed with the photograph in his hand. It seemed to him that he had heard a familiar sound up in the cold, frosty air, high up above the forest.

He at once cast off his lethargy. There was nothing particular about that sound. It was so faint that even the sensitive ear of a forest animal would have been unable to distinguish it from the monotonous rustle of the ice-covered tree tops. But by a peculiar whistling note in it Alexei guessed unerringly that it came from an "Il-16", the type of plane that he flew.

The drone of the engine drew nearer, grew in volume and changed now to a whistle and now to a groan as the craft veered in the air, and, at last, high up in the grey sky, Alexei saw a tiny, slowly-moving cross, disappearing into and emerging from the grey, misty clouds. He could already see the red stars on its wings, and right over his head it looped the loop, glistening in the sun as it did so, banked and flew away. Soon the drone of its engine ceased, drowned by the gentle rattle of the ice-covered branches swaying in the wind, but for a long time after Alexei thought that he still heard that subtle, whistling sound.

He pictured himself in the cockpit. In an instant, even before a man could smoke a cigarette, he could be back in his own forest airfield. Who was in that plane? Perhaps it was Andrei Degtyarenko, out on a morning patrol. He used to climb high on those flights in the secret hope of encountering an enemy.... Degtyarenko.... The plane.... The boys....

Impelled by a fresh burst of energy, Alexei glanced at the icy side of the crater. "I'll never get out that way," he said to himself. "But I can't lie here and wait for death!" He drew his dirk from its scabbard and began with listless, feeble strokes to hack footholds in the icy side, scraping the frozen sand away with his finger-nails. He scraped until his finger-nails broke and his fingers bled, but he kept hacking away with his dirk with unrelaxing energy. Then, clinging to the dents with his hands and knees, he slowly climbed up the side and at last reached the breastwork. Another effort to lie across the breastwork and roll over and he would be saved, but his feet slipped and down he went, striking his face painfully against the ice. He was severely hurt, but the drone of the aircraft engine still rang in his ears. He climbed up the side again, and again slipped to the bottom. Then, after critically examining the dents he had made he began to deepen them, making the edges of the top ones sharper; and when he had finished he started to climb again, cautiously exerting his failing strength.

With enormous difficulty he threw himself across the sandy breastwork and helplessly rolled down to the ground. Then he crawled in the direction in which the aircraft had flown, and from which the sun had risen over the forest, dispelling the snow-devouring mist and causing the ice crust to sparkle like crystal.

13

But he found it extremely hard to crawl. His arms trembled and gave way, unable to bear the weight of his body. Several times his face hit the melting snow. It seemed as though the earth had enormously increased its force of gravity, it was impossible to resist it. Alexei wanted very much to lie down and rest for at least half an hour, but the determination to press on amounted to a frenzy today; and so he crawled and crawled, fell, got up, crawled again, conscious of neither pain nor hunger, seeing nothing, hearing nothing except the sound of artillery and machine-gun fire.

When his arms ceased to support him, he tried to crawl on his elbows, but this proved to be very awkward, so he lay down and, using his elbows as levers, tried to roll. He found he could do that. Rolling over and over was easier than crawling and did not call for much exertion. But it made him giddy, and every now and again he lost consciousness. He had to stop often, sit up and wait until the earth, the forest and the sky had stopped whirling round.

The trees began to thin out and here and there were open spaces where the trees had been felled. The trails of winter roads appeared. Alexei was no longer thinking of whether he would reach his own people, but he was determined to go on rolling as long as he had the strength to move. When he lost consciousness from the frightful strain to which all his enfeebled muscles were subjected, his arms and his whole body continued automatically to make these complicated movements, and he kept rolling on in the snow—towards the sound of gun fire—eastward.

Alexei did not remember how he spent that night, or whether he made much progress next morning. Everything was submerged in the gloom of semi-oblivion. He only had a vague recollection of the obstacles he encountered in his path: the golden trunk of a felled pine-tree that exuded amber-coloured resin, a stack of logs, and sawdust and shavings that were lying about everywhere, a tree stump clearly showing the yearly rings at the cross-cut.

An unusual sound called him out of his state of semi-oblivion, restored him to consciousness and caused him to sit up and look round. He found himself in a big forest clearing that was flooded with sunlight and strewn with felled and as yet undressed trees and logs. Standing apart were neat stacks of firewood. The midday sun was high in the sky, the strong smell of resin, heated conifers and of snow dampness pervaded the air, and high above the as yet unthawed earth a lark was singing, pouring all its soul into its simple melody.

Filled with a sensation of indefinable danger, Alexei cast his eyes round the clearing. It was fresh, it did not look as if it were abandoned. The trees had been felled only recently, for the branches on the undressed trees were still fresh and green, the honeylike resin still oozed from the cuts and a fresh smell emanated from the chips and raw bark that lay around everywhere. Hence, the clearing lived. Perhaps the Germans were preparing logs here for their dugouts and emplacements? In that case he had better clear out as quickly as possible, for the lumbermen might turn up at any moment. But his body felt petrified, fettered by dull, heavy pain, and he had not the strength to move.

Should he crawl on? The instinct that he had cultivated during these days of life in the forest put him on the alert. He did not see but felt that somebody was closely and relentlessly watching him. Who was it? Quiet reigned in the forest, the lark was singing in the sky above the clearing, the hollow pecking of a woodpecker was heard and the tomtits darting among the drooping branches of the felled trees angrily twittered to each other. But in spite of all, Alexei felt with every fibre of his body that he was being watched.

A branch cracked. He looked round and among the grey clumps of young pine-trees whose curly tops were swaying in the wind he saw several branches that seemed to be acting independently, they did not sway in unison with the rest. And it seemed to him that he heard low, agitated whispers coming from there: the whispers of human beings. Again, as when he had encountered the dog, he felt a cold shiver run down his spine.

He quickly drew his pistol from the bosom of his flying suit. The pistol had already grown rusty and he had to use both hands to cock it. The click seemed to startle somebody hidden among the pines. Several of the tree tops swayed heavily, as if somebody had pushed against them, but soon everything was quiet again.

"What is it, a man or an animal?" Alexei asked himself, and it seemed to him that he heard somebody in the clump of trees, also asking: "Is it a man?" Was it his imagination, or did he really hear somebody in the clump speak Russian? Why, yes, Russian! And because it was Russian he was suddenly overcome with such mad joy that, not stopping to think whether it was a friend or foe, he emitted a triumphant yell, sprang to his feet, rushed towards the spot the voice had come from and at once collapsed as if he had been felled, dropping his pistol in the snow....

14

Collapsing after an unsuccessful attempt to get up, Alexei lost consciousness, but the sense of imminent danger immediately brought him round. No doubt there were people hiding in the pines, watching and whispering to each other.

He rose up on his arms, picked his pistol up from the snow, keeping it out of sight, close to the ground, and began to watch. Danger had completely drawn him out of his state of oblivion. His mind was working with precision. Who were these people? Perhaps lumbermen whom the Germans had forced to come here to prepare firewood? Perhaps they were Russians who, like himself, were surrounded, and were now trying to get through the German lines to their own people? Or, perhaps, peasants living in the vicinity? After all, he did hear somebody exclaim distinctly: "A man!"

The pistol trembled in his hand that was numb from crawling; but he was prepared to fight and make good use of his remaining three bullets....

Just at that moment an excited childish voice called from the clump of trees:

"Hey! Who are you? Doitch? Fershteh?"

These strange words put Alexei on the alert, but it was undoubtedly a Russian who called, and undoubtedly a child.

"What are you doing here?" another childish voice inquired.

"And who are you?" retorted Alexei and stopped, amazed at the faintness and feebleness of his voice.

This question must have caused a sensation among the trees, for whoever were there held a long whispered consultation, accompanied, evidently, with excited gesticulations, for the branches swayed wildly.

"Stop kidding, you can't fool us! I can tell a German miles off. Are you Doitch?"

"Who are you?"

"What do you want to know for? Nicht fershteh...."

"I am Russian."

"You are fibbing. Bust my eyes if you ain't. You are a fascist!"

"I am Russian, Russian! An airman. The Germans shot me down."

Alexei cast all caution to the winds now. He was convinced that his own people were behind those trees, Russian, Soviet people. They did not believe him. Thas was natural. War teaches one to be cautious. And now, for the first time since he started out on his journey, he felt absolutely done in, he felt that he could not move either hand or foot, neither move nor defend himself. Tears rolled down the dark hollows of his cheeks.

"Look, he's crying!" came a voice from behind the trees. "Hey, you! Why are you crying?"

"I am a Russian, a Russian like you, an airman."

"From what airfield?"

"But who are you?"

"What do you want to know for? Answer!"

"From the Mochalov airfield. Why don't you help me? Come out! What the hell...."

There was another, more animated, whispered consultation behind the trees. Alexei distinctly heard the words:

"Do you hear? He says he's from the Mochalov airfield.... Perhaps he's telling the truth.... And he's crying...." Then came a shout: "Hey, you, airman! Chuck your gun! Drop it, I tell you, or we won't come out! We'll run away!"

Alexei threw his pistol away. The branches parted, and two boys, alert, like a couple of inquisitive tomtits ready to dart off in an instant, cautiously, hand in hand, approached Alexei. The older one, a thin, blue-eyed lad with flaxen hair, held an axe. The younger one, a red-haired, freckle-faced little fellow, his eyes shining with irrepressible curiosity, followed a step behind the first and whispered:

"He's crying. He is really crying. And skinny! Look how skinny he is!"

The older boy, still holding the axe, approached Alexei, kicked the pistol farther away with his huge felt boot—it was probably his father's—and said:

"You are an airman, you say. Have you got any papers? Let's look!"

"Who is here, our people or Germans?" Alexei asked in a whisper, smiling in spite of himself.

"How do I know, living here in the forest? Nobody reports to me," answered the older boy diplomatically.

Alexei had no alternative but to put his hand in his tunic pocket and take out his identity card. The sight of the red officer's card with the star on the cover had a magical effect upon the youngsters. It was as if their childhood, which they had lost during the German occupation, was suddenly returned to them by the appearance of one of their own beloved Soviet airmen.

"Yes, yes, our people are here. They've been here for three days."

"Why are you so skinny?"

"...Our men gave them such a licking! Didn't they give it to them, though! There was a terrible big fight here! And an awful lot of them were killed. Awful!"

"...And didn't they run! It was funny to see 'em. One of them harnessed a horse to a washtub and rode off in it. Two of them, wounded they were, held on to a horse's tail and another rode on its back, like a baron. You should have seen them!... How did they shoot you down?"

After chattering for a while, the youngsters got busy. They said that they lived about five kilometres away. Alexei was so weak that he could not even turn over to lie more comfortably on his back. The sleigh, which the lads had brought to get brushwood at the "German lumber camp", as they called the clearing, was too small to take Alexei; and besides, he would have been too heavy for them to haul over the untrodden snow. The older boy, whose name was Seryonka, told his brother Fedka to run to the village as fast as he could for help, while he remained to guard Alexei from the Germans, as he explained, but actually because, in his heart, he did not trust him. "You can never tell," he thought to himself. "These fascists are a sly lot—they can pretend to be dying and even get Soviet Army papers...." Gradually his fears were dispelled and he began to talk freely.

Alexei lay dozing on a soft bed of pine-needles, with half-closed eyes, listening absent-mindedly to the boy's chatter. Only a few disjointed words reached his mind through the haze of restful languor that had at once spread over his whole body; and although he did not grasp what these words meant, the sounds of his native language gave him the utmost pleasure. Only later did he hear the story of the disaster that befell the inhabitants of the village of Plavni.

The Germans had arrived in this forest and lake region as far back as October, when the birches were glowing with yellow leaves and the aspen-trees seemed to be ablaze with a sinister red fire. There had been no fighting in the immediate vicinity of Plavni. About thirty kilometres to the west of the village, the German columns, headed by a powerful tank vanguard, after wiping out a Soviet Army unit that had made a stand at a hastily built defence line, moved round Plavni, which was hidden near a lake away from the road, and rolled on eastward. They were in a hurry to reach Bologoye, the big railway junction, capture it, and thus disconnect the Western and North-Western fronts. Here, at the far approaches to this town, all through the summer and autumn, the inhabitants of Kalinin Region, townspeople, peasants, women, the aged and children, people of all ages and all professions, had toiled night and day, in the rain, in the heat, suffering from mosquitoes, the dampness from the marsh and bad drinking water, digging and building defence lines. The fortifications ran from south to north for hundreds of kilometres, through forest and marsh, round the shores of lakes, and along the banks of small rivers and streams.

Great were the sufferings of the builders, but their labour was not in vain. The Germans broke through some of the defence lines in their stride, but were checked at the last one. The fighting changed to positional warfare. The Germans failed to break through to Bologoye; they had to shift the weight of their attack further south, and on this sector to pass to the defensive.

The peasants of Plavni, who supplemented the usually meagre crops they raised on their sandy, clayey soil with successful fishing in the forest lakes, were already rejoicing that the war had passed them by. In obedience to the orders of the Germans, they renamed the chairman of their collective farm village elder, but continued to carry on as a collective farm, in the hope that the fascists would not for ever trample on Soviet soil and that they would be able to live quietly in their remote haven until the storm blew over. But the Germans in field-grey uniforms were followed by others in black uniforms with skull and crossbones on their forage-caps. The inhabitants of Plavni were ordered, on pain of severe penalties, to provide within twenty-four hours fifteen volunteers for permanent work in Germany. The volunteers were to muster in the building at the end of the village that served as the collective-farm office and fish shed, and to have with them a change of underclothing, a spoon, knife and fork and a ten days' supply of provisions. But nobody turned up at the appointed hour. It must be said that, taught by experience, the black-clad Germans, evidently, had not had much hope that anyone would turn up. To teach the village a lesson, they seized the chairman of the collective farm, that is, the village elder, Veronika Grigorievna, the elderly patron of the kindergarten, two collective-farm team-leaders, and ten other peasants they chanced to lay their hands on, and shot them. They gave orders that the bodies should not be buried and said that they would treat the whole village in the same way if the volunteers failed to turn up at the appointed place next day.

Again nobody turned up. Next morning, when the Hitlerites from the SS *Sonderkommando* went through the village, they found every house deserted. Not a soul was in the place, neither young nor old. Abandoning their homes, their land, all the belongings they had accumulated by years of toil, and almost all their cattle, the people had vanished, under cover of the night fogs that are prevalent in those parts, without leaving a trace. The entire village, down to the last man, went off to an old clearing, deep in the forest, eighteen kilometres away. After making dugouts for their habitation, the men went to join the partisans, while the women and children remained to rough it until the spring. The *Sonderkommando* burnt the recalcitrant village to the ground, as they did most of the villages in this district, which they called a dead zone.

"My father was the chairman of the collective farm, village elder, they called him," said Seryonka, and his words reached Alexei's mind as if they came from the other side of a wall. "They killed him. And they killed my big brother. He was a cripple. He had only one arm. He had his arm crushed on the threshing-floor and had to have it cut off. Sixteen they killed.... I saw it myself. The Germans made us all come and look. My father yelled and swore at them. 'You'll suffer for this, you scoundrels! You'll weep tears of blood for this!' he told them."

Alexei felt a strange sensation sweeping through him as he listened to this fair-haired boy with the large, sad, tired eyes. He seemed to be floating in a dense mist. Unconquerable weariness bound his whole body, which had been subjected to such superhuman strain. He was unable to move a finger, and he simply could not believe that he had been on the move only two hours before.

"So you live in the forest?" he asked the boy in an almost inaudible voice, releasing himself with difficulty from the fetters of sleep.

"Yes, of course! There are three of us now. Fedka, Mother and I. I had a sister, Nyuska her name was. She died in the winter. She got all swelled up and died. And my little brother, he died too. So there are three of us.... The Germans aren't coming back, are they? What do you think? Grandfather, my mother's father, that is, he's our chairman now; he says they won't; he says: 'The dead don't come back from the graveyard.' But Mother, she's frightened. She wants to run away. They may come back again, she says.... Look! There's Grandad and Fedka."

At the edge of the clearing stood red-haired Fedka, pointing to Alexei; and with him was a tall, round-shouldered old man in a ragged, light-brown homespun coat tied at the waist with cord and wearing a high, German officer's peaked cap.

This was Grandad Mikhail, as the boys called him. He had the benevolent face of St. Nicholas as depicted in the simple village icons, the clear, bright eyes of a child and a soft, thin, floating beard which was quite silvery. He wrapped Alexei in an old sheepskin coat, which was all in multi-coloured patches, and as he lifted and rolled his light emaciated body, he kept on saying with naive surprise:

"Poor, poor lad! Why, you're wasted away to nothing! Heavens, you're nothing but a skeleton! The things this war is doing to people! It's hard!"

As carefully as if he were handling a new-born babe he laid Alexei on the sleigh, tied him down with a rope, thought for a moment, took off his coat, rolled it up and put it under Alexei's head. Then, going in front of the sleigh, he harnessed himself to a small horse collar made of sackcloth, and handing a trace to each of the boys, he said: "God be with us!" And the three of them hauled the sleigh over the thawing snow, which clung to the runners, creaked, and gave way under the feet.

15

During the next two or three days Alexei felt as though he were enveloped in a dense, hot mist, through which he could obtain only a hazy picture of what was going on. Reality mingled with delirious fantasy, and it was only a considerable time later that he was able to piece together the actual events in their proper order.

The fugitives lived in the depths of the virgin forest. Their dugouts, roofed with pine branches, were still covered with snow and were hardly discernible. The smoke that rose from them seemed to come straight from the ground. The day Alexei arrived was windless and raw, and the smoke clung to the moss and wound among the trees, so that it seemed to Alexei that the place was surrounded by a dying forest fire.

All the inhabitants—mainly women and children and a few old men—on learning that Mikhail was bringing a Soviet airman who had got here nobody knew how, and who, Fedka had told them, looked like "a real skeleton", poured out to meet them. When the "troika" was seen through the trees, the women ran towards it, and chasing away the children who had come flocking too, surrounded the sleigh and accompanied it to the dugouts, weeping and wailing. They were all in rags, and all seemed equally aged. The smoke and soot from the fire-places in the dugouts had darkened their faces, and only by their sparkling eyes and their teeth, which glistened white against their dark skin, was it possible to tell the young women from the old.

"Women! Oh, you women! What have you collected around here for? This isn't a show!" Grandad Mikhail exclaimed angrily, tugging harder at his collar. "Get out of the way, for heaven's sake! Good Lord, they're like a lot of sheep! Daft!"

And from the crowd of women Alexei heard voices saying:

"Oh, how thin he is! He really looks like a skeleton. He isn't moving. Is he alive?"

"He's unconscious. What is the matter with him? Oh, how thin he is, how thin!"

And then the ejaculations of amazement ceased. The unknown but frightful experiences the airman must have gone through deeply impressed these women, and while the sleigh was being hauled along the edge of the forest, drawing nearer to the underground village, a dispute arose among them as to which of them was to take Alexei into her dugout.

"My place is dry. Sand, all sand, and there is plenty of air.... And I have a stove," argued a little, round-faced woman with merry eyes, the whites of which glistened like those of a young Negro.

"A stove! But how many of you are living there? The smell alone is enough to send you to kingdom come! Put him into my place, Mikhail. I have three sons in the Soviet Army, and I have a little flour left. I'll bake him some flat cakes!"

"No, no! Put him into my place. I've got plenty of room. There's only two of us, and we have a lot of space. Bring your flat cakes to me, it makes no difference to him where he eats them. Ksyusha and I will take care of him, you can be sure of that. I have some frozen bream and some mushrooms.... I'll cook him some fish, and mushroom soup...."

"What good will fish do to him when he's got one foot in the grave? Put him in my place, Grandad, we have a cow, and we'll be able to give him milk!"

But Mikhail pulled the sleigh to his own dugout, which was situated in the middle of the underground village.

...Alexei remembered that he lay on a bunk in a small, dingy cave dug in the earth, with a smoky spluttering rush-light stuck in the wall and shooting off sparks. By its light he could see a table made from the planks of a German mine crate and resting on a stump nocked into the ground, several sawn logs around the table to serve as stools, a slim figure in the black kerchief and old woman's clothes bending over the table—this was Varvara, Grandad Mikhail's youngest daughter-in-law—and Mikhail's head with its thin, grey locks.

Alexei was lying on a striped straw mattress, still covered with the patched sheepskin coat, which gave off a pleasant, sourish, homelike smell.... And although his body ached as if he had been stoned, and his feet burned as though hot bricks had been put to them, it was pleasant to lie motionless like this, knowing that he was safe, that he did not have to move, or think, or be constantly on the alert.

The smoke from the fire in the hearth in the corner of the dugout rose to the ceiling in grey, living, intertwining layers, and it seemed to Alexei that not only this smoke, but the table, the silvery head of Grandad Mikhail, who was always busy over something, and Varvara's slim body, were also floating, swaying and dissolving. He shut his eyes. He opened them when he was roused by a gust of cold air from the door that was lined with sacking. A woman was standing at the table. She had placed a bag on the table and held her hands on it as if pondering whether she should take it back again. She sighed and said to Varvara:

"This is some farina I have had since before the war. I have been saving it for my Kostyunka, but he doesn't need anything now. Take it and cook some of it for your lodger. It's for babies, just what he needs now."

She turned and went out, affecting everybody in the dugout with her sorrow. Somebody else brought some frozen bream, another brought flat cakes baked on hearth-stones, filling the dugout with the sourish, warm smell of fresh-baked bread.

Seryonka and Fedka came. Removing his forage-cap with peasant-like gravity Seryonka said: "Good morning", and placed on the table two lumps of sugar with crumbs of tobacco and bran on them.

"Mother sent it. Sugar is good for you, eat it," he said, and turning to Mikhail he added in a business-like tone: "We've been to the old place again. We found an iron pot, two spades, almost undamaged, and an axe head. They may come in handy."

Meanwhile, Fedka, standing behind his brother, looked with greedy eyes at the sugar on the table and sucked noisily, as his mouth watered.

Later, when he had pondered over all this, Alexei fully appreciated the value of these gifts that were brought to him in the village, about a third of the inhabitants of which had died of starvation that winter, where there was not a family that did not mourn the loss of one or even two of its members.

"Oh, women, women, you are priceless! D'you hear what I say, Alexei? I say the Russian woman is priceless. You only have to touch her heart and she will give her last away, will sacrifice her head if need be. That's what our women are like. Am I not right?" Grandad Mikhail would say as he accepted these gifts for Alexei, and then he would turn again to the job he always had in hand— mending a harness, a horse collar, or a pair of worn-out felt boots. "And in work too, our women are not behind us men. To tell the truth, they can give us a point or two! It's their tongues that I don't like! They'll be the death of me, those women will be the death of me, I tell you! When my Anisya died, I thought to myself: 'Thank the Lord, I'll have a bit of quiet now!' But there, you see, God punished me for it. All our men who were not taken into the army, all joined the partisans to fight the Germans, and I, for my sin, became a commander over women, like a billygoat in a sheep run.... It's hard, I tell you!"

Alexei saw many things in this forest habitation that greatly astonished him. The Germans had robbed the inhabitants of Plavni of their homes, their belongings, their farm implements, cattle, domestic utensils and clothing, of everything that had been acquired by the toil of generations, and at present the people were living in the forest in great distress, in constant danger that the Germans would discover them. They starved and suffered from the cold—but the collective farm did not fall to pieces; on the contrary, the great disaster of the war had welded the people closer together. They even made the dugouts collectively and moved into them, not haphazardly, but according to the teams they had worked in on the farm. When his son-in-law was killed, Grandad Mikhail took over the duties of collective-farm chairman, and in the forest he sacredly adhered to all the collective-farm customs. And now, under his direction, the cave village, deep in the virgin forest, was preparing for the spring in brigades and teams.

Though starving, the peasant women brought to the common dugout all the grain they had managed to save when they had fled from their village—all, to the last seed. The greatest care was taken of the calves born from the cows that had been saved from the Germans. These people starved, but they did not slaughter the collectively-owned cattle. At the risk of their lives, the boys of the village went to the old, gutted village and, rummaging among the ash heaps, found plough-shares, turned blue by the heat. These they brought to the underground village and put wooden handles on those best fit for use. Out of sacking the women made yokes to harness the cows for the spring ploughing. The women's teams had taken turns to catch fish in the lake and had thus provided food for the whole village in the winter.

Although Grandad Mikhail grumbled and growled at "his women" and put his hands to his ears when they indulged in long and angry quarrels in his dugout about some matter connected with the collective farm, the import of which was unintelligible to Alexei, and although, when driven out of patience, he bawled at them in his high, falsetto voice, he appreciated their worth and, taking advantage of the compliance of his silent listener, he praised the "female tribe" to the skies.

"But look what's happened, my dear Alexei," he said. "A woman will always cling to a thing with both her hands. Am I not right? Why does she do that? Because she is stingy? Not a bit! She does it because this thing is dear to her. It is she who feeds the children; whatever you may say, it is she who runs the home. Now listen to what happened here. You can see how we are living; we count every crumb. Yes, we are starving. Well, this was in January. A band of partisans suddenly turned up. No, not our men. Our men are fighting somewhere near Olenin, so we heard. These men were strangers to us, from the railway. They burst in on us and said: 'We are dying from hunger.' Well, what do you think? Next day these women filled those men's knapsacks with food, and yet their own children were swollen from starvation, too weak to walk. Well? Am I right? I should say so! If I were a big commander, when we have kicked out the Germans, I would muster all our best troops and line them up in front of a woman and order them to march past and salute this Russian woman. That's what I would do! ..."

The old man's chatter had the effect of a lullaby on Alexei and he often had a short nap while the old man talked. Sometimes, however, he felt an urge to take the letters and the girl's photograph from his pocket and show them to him, but he did not have the strength to move. But when Grandad Mikhail began to praise his women, Alexei thought he could feel the warmth of those letters through the cloth of his tunic.

At the table, also always busy with something, sat Grandad Mikhail's silent daughter-in-law. At first Alexei had taken her for an old woman, Grandad's wife, but later he saw that she could be no more than twenty or twenty-two, that she was light-footed, graceful and pretty, and he noticed that whenever she glanced at him in her frightened, anxious way, she always heaved a trembling sigh, as if she were swallowing a lump. Sometimes at night, when the rushlight had burnt out and in the smoky gloom of the dugout the cricket—which Grandad Mikhail had found in the gutted village and had brought home in his sleeve with some scorched utensil to make it feel homelike—began to chirp, Alexei thought he heard somebody on the other bunk crying softly and trying to deaden the sounds by biting the pillow.

16

On the morning of the third day that Alexei had been staying with Grandad Mikhail, the old man said to him in an emphatic tone:

"You are lousy, Alexei, that's what! Lice are worse than dung beetles. And it's hard for you to scratch yourself. I'll tell you what I'll do, I'll give you a bath. What do you say to that? A steam bath. That will be fine! I'll wash you down and steam your bones a bit. It will do you good after what you've gone through. What do you say? Am I right?"

And he set about arranging the bath. He made the fire on the hearth in the corner so hot that the hearthstones cracked loudly. Outside the dugout another big fire was lit, and, as Alexei was told, a large stone was heated. Varya filled an old wooden tub with water. Golden straw was laid out on the floor. After that Grandad Mikhail, stripped to the waist, remaining only in his underwear, quickly dissolved some alkali in a small wooden bucket and stripped a piece of bast matting to make a bath sponge. When the dugout grew so hot that cold drops of water began to fall heavily from the ceiling, the old man hurried out and soon returned with the red-hot stone on a piece of sheet iron. He dropped the stone into the tub. A great cloud of steam shot up to the ceiling, spread out under it and then broke up into a curly fleece. Nothing could be seen through the mist, but Alexei felt that he was being undressed by the deft hands of the old man.

Varya assisted her father-in-law. Owing to the heat she threw off her padded coat and kerchief. Her heavy plaits, the existence of which could scarcely have been suspected under her tattered kerchief, fell loose down her back, and suddenly, slim, large-eyed and light-footed, she was transformed from a pious old woman into a young girl. This transformation was so unexpected that

Alexei, who had paid no attention to her up till now, became ashamed of his nakedness.

"Never mind, Alexei, lad, never mind," Grandad Mikhail said reassuringly. "It can't be helped. We've got to do this job with you. I've heard that in Finland men and women take their bath together. What? It's not true? Perhaps they told me a lie. But Varya, here, she is something like a hospital nurse now, tending a wounded soldier, so there is nothing to be ashamed of. Hold him, Varya, while I take his shirt off. Goodness, it's quite rotten! It's falling to pieces!"

Alexei saw a look of horror in the young woman's large, dark eyes. Through the swaying curtain of steam he saw his own body, for the first time since the catastrophe. On the golden straw lay a human, skin-covered skeleton with prominent knee-caps, angular pelvis, an absolutely hollow abdomen, and sharply outlined ribs.

The old man stirred the alkali water in the bucket, dipped the bast sponge into the grey, oily liquid and raised it over Alexei's body. Through the hot steam he caught sight of the emaciated form lying on the straw and his arm remained in the air holding the sponge.

"Good Lord!" he exclaimed. "You are in a shocking state, Alexei! You are in a bad way, I say. What? You managed to get away from the Germans, but will you escape...."

And suddenly he turned angrily upon Varya who was supporting Alexei's back.

"What are you staring at a naked man for, you hussy? What are you biting your lips for? You women, you're all alike! And you, Alexei, don't think about anything, don't worry! We won't let that fellow with the scythe get at you. That we won't! We'll nurse you back to health, put you to rights. Take my word for it!"

Carefully and deftly, as if he were handling an infant, he washed Alexei down with the alkali water, rolled him on his sides, pouring water over him, and rubbed with such vigour that his hands positively squeaked as they slipped over the protruding ribs.

Varya helped him in silence.

But the old man had had no reason for scolding her. She was not looking at the frightful, gaunt body that was lying helplessly in her arms. She tried to keep her eyes away from it, but when, through the steam, they involuntarily lighted upon Alexei's leg, or arm, a gleam of horror flashed in them. She began to imagine that this airman was not a stranger who had come into their home, goodness knows how, but her own Misha; that it was not this unexpected guest, but her husband, with whom she had lived only one spring, a broad-shouldered fellow with big, bright freckles on his face, with eyebrows so fair that he seemed to have none, with enormous, powerful hands, that the fascist monsters had reduced to this state. That it was her Misha's seemingly lifeless body that she was holding in her arms. And horror overcame her, her head swam, and only by biting her lips could she keep herself from falling into a swoon.

...Later, Alexei lay on the thin, striped mattress, in a long, heavily-patched but clean and soft shirt that belonged to Grandad Mikhail, conscious of a feeling of freshness and vigour in his whole body. After the bath, when the steam had evaporated through the hole in the ceiling over the hearth, Varya gave him some hot, smoky bilberry tea. He sipped it with tiny pieces of the two lumps of sugar which the boys had brought him and which Varya had broken up and handed to him on a strip of white birch bark. Then he fell asleep—the first sound, dreamless sleep since the catastrophe overcame him.

He was awakened by loud conversation. It was almost dark in the dugout, the rushlight barely smouldered. Amidst this smoky gloom he heard the cracked, high-pitched voice of Grandad Mikhail:

"Just like a woman! Where are your brains? The man's not had so much as a millet seed in his mouth for eleven days, and you go and boil them hard!... Why, these hard-boiled eggs will kill him!" Then his voice assumed a pleading tone: "It's not eggs he needs now. D'you know what'd be good for him, Vasilisa? Some nice chicken broth! That's what! It would put new life into him. Now, if you were to bring us your Partisanka ... eh?"

But the grating voice of a frightened old woman interrupted him:

"I won't! I won't and won't! It's no use asking, you old devil! Don't dare say any more about it! Give my Partisanka?... Chicken broth!... Look how much they've brought already. Enough for a wedding! What will you think of next?"

"Vasilisa, you ought to be ashamed of yourself for talking in that woman's way!" came the old man's cracked voice again. "You yourself have two sons at the front, and yet you talk in this silly way! This man, you might say, has crippled himself for us, has shed his blood...."

"I don't want his blood! My sons are shedding their blood for me! It's no use asking. I said I won't ... and I won't!"

The dark silhouette of an aged figure glided to the door and as it opened a beam of spring light burst into the dugout, so dazzling that Alexei shut his eyes tight and groaned. The old man hastened to his side:

"Weren't you asleep, Alexei? Did you hear this talk? Did you? But don't condemn her, Alexei, don't condemn her for her words. Words are the shell; the kernel in it is sound. Do you think she begrudges the chicken? Not a bit, Alyosha! The Germans wiped out her whole family and it was a big family, there were ten of them. Her oldest son is a colonel. The Germans found this out, and the whole of the colonel's family, all except Vasilisa, were taken to the ditch at the same time. And they burned their home. You can imagine what it means for a woman at her age to be left without kith and kin! All that she has left is one chicken. It's a cunning bird, let me tell you, Alyosha. In the very first week the Germans cleaned up all the chickens and ducks. They are very fond of poultry, those Germans are. All you could hear was: 'Chicken, Ma, chicken!' But this one escaped! It's not an ordinary chicken, I tell you! It would do for a circus! When a fascist came into the yard, she would get into the loft and remain there quite still as if she wasn't there at all. But if any of our people came into the yard, she was not a bit disturbed. How she knew the difference, goodness only knows! And so it was the only chicken left in the whole village. And for her cunning we named her Partisanka."

Meresyev dozed with open eyes; he had grown accustomed to that in the forest. His silence must have disquieted Grandad Mikhail. Busying himself around the dugout and doing something at the table, he resumed the subject he had been talking about:

"Don't condemn the woman, Alexei! Try to understand her, my friend. She was like an old birch-tree in a big forest, protected from the wind on every side. But now she is like an old, rotten stump in a clearing, and her only consolation is that chicken. Why don't you say something? Are you asleep? Well, sleep, sleep."

Alexei was asleep and not asleep. He lay under the sheepskin coat that was pervaded with the sourish smell of bread, the smell of an old peasant habitation; he heard the soothing chirp of the cricket and was reluctant to move even a finger. He felt as though his body was boneless and had been filled with warm cotton wool, through which the blood pulsated and throbbed. His fractured, swollen feet burned, ached with an intense, gnawing pain, but he had not the strength to turn over or even move.

In that state of semi-oblivion Alexei was conscious of the life around him in snatches, as if it were not real life, but the flickering of a series of fantastic, disconnected scenes on a cinema screen.

Spring was here. The fugitive village was passing through its most difficult days. The inhabitants were eating the last of the provisions they had managed to conceal in the ground, and which they had surreptitiously unearthed at night in the gutted village and had brought into the forest. The ground was thawing. The hastily built dugouts "wept tears"; water dripped from the walls and ceiling. The men who were waging partisan warfare in the Olenin Forest, to the west of the underground village, used to visit the place singly and at night; but now they were cut off by the front line. Nothing was heard of them. This worsened the already hard lot of the women. And now spring was here, the snow was melting and they had to think of planting the crops and digging the vegetable gardens.

The women went about care-worn and irritable. Every now and again noisy quarrels and mutual recrimination would break out in Grandad's dugout, during which the women would enumerate all their old and new grievances, real and imaginary. Sometimes sheer pandemonium reigned; but it was enough for the wily old man to cast into this turmoil of angry women's voices some practical suggestion concerning their collective-farm affairs, such as: "Isn't it time somebody went to the old village to see whether the ground has thawed?" or: "There's a nice breeze blowing now. Perhaps we ought to air the seed. It has grown moist from the damp earth in the underground barn," for the quarrelling to die down at once.

One day Grandad came into the dugout looking pleased and yet troubled. He brought with him a green blade of grass. He laid it gently in his calloused palm and showed it to Alexei.

"Look at this," he said, "I've just come from the fields. The ground is thawing, and, thank God, the winter crop is showing. There's been plenty of snow. Even if we don't get the spring crop in, the winter crop will provide us with bread. I'll go and call the women. It will gladden their hearts, poor things!"

Outside the dugout the women chattered like a frock of magpies; the blade of green grass brought from the fields gave them fresh hope. In the evening Grandad Mikhail came in rubbing his hands and said:

"What do you think my long-haired cabinet of ministers have decided, Alexei? Not a bad thing, I tell you. One team is to plough the patch in the hollow, where the going is heavy. They will harness the cows. Not that you can do much with them. We've only got six left out of the whole herd. The second team will take the higher field, that's drier. They'll dig with spades and mattocks. We dig our vegetable plots that way, don't we? The third team will go up on the hill. It's sandy soil there; we'll prepare it for potatoes. That's easy work. We'll put the youngsters on that job, and the weaker women. And before long we'll get help from the government. But even if we don't, we shall manage. We'll do it ourselves, and we won't let any of the land go waste, I can assure you of that. Thanks to our men for kicking the fascists out of here; we'll be able to live now. We are a tough race and can stand anything, no matter how difficult!"

Grandad could not fall asleep for a long time. He twisted and turned on his straw bed, coughed, scratched himself and groaned: "O Lord! O my God!" got up several times, went to the water bucket, rattled the dipper, and drank in big, greedy gulps, like a winded horse. At last he could stand it no longer. He got up, lit the rushlight, touched Alexei, who was lying with open eyes in a state of semi-consciousness, and said:

"Are you asleep, Alexei? I am lying here and thinking. Lying here and thinking, I say. In the old village, over there, there's an oak standing in the square. About thirty years ago, during the first big war, when Nicholas was on the throne, this oak was struck by lightning, which burnt the top off. But it was a sturdy tree, powerful roots and plenty of sap. The sap had nowhere to go upwards, so it produced a side shoot, and you should see what a fine, new, curly head it's got.... It's the same with our Plavni.... If only the sun shines and the earth is fertile; what with our own, Soviet government, we, brother Alexei, will put everything to rights again in about five years. We are stickers, make no mistake about that! If only the war ends soon! We'll smash them up, and then set to work, all of us together. What do you think?"

That night Alexei's condition worsened.

Grandad's bath acted like a stimulant upon Alexei and roused him out of his stupor. He became more conscious than ever of his utter exhaustion and weariness, and of the pain in his feet. He rolled feverishly on his mattress, moaned, ground his teeth, called for somebody, railed at somebody, demanded things.

Varya sat up with him all night, her legs drawn up, her chin resting on her knees, and her large, round, mournful eyes staring straight in front of her. Every now and again she put a cold wet rag to Alexei's head or breast, or adjusted the sheepskin which he kept throwing off, and all the time she was thinking of her husband who was far away, blown hither and thither by the wind of war.

At the first streak of dawn the old man woke up, glanced at Alexei, now quiet and dozing, and whispering something to Varya, made ready for a journey. He pushed his felt-booted feet into galoshes which he himself had made from an automobile tyre, tightly belted his coat with a bast girdle and took up a juniper stick which had been polished by his hand and which always accompanied him on his long journeys.

He went out without saying a word to Alexei.

17

Meresyev was in such a state that he did not notice the departure of his host. He was unconscious the whole of the next day, and came to only on the third day, when the sun was already high in the sky and a bright and solid beam of sunlight, piercing the grey, stratified smoke of the hearth, stretched through the whole dugout from the skylight to Alexei's feet, intensifying the gloom rather than dispersing it.

There was nobody in the dugout. Varya's low, husky voice was heard through the door. Evidently busy over something, she was singing an old song that was popular in this forest region. It was a song about a lonely ash-tree that was longing to go over to an oak that also stood lonely some distance away.

Alexei had heard this song more than once before; it was sung by the girls who had come in merry groups from the surrounding villages to level and clear the airfield. He liked the slow and mournful melody. Before, however, he had not paid attention to the words, and in the bustle of army life they had slipped through his mind without leaving any impression. But now they emerged from the lips of this young, large-eyed woman full of such tender sentiment, and they expressed so much real and not merely poetical, feminine longing, that Alexei at once felt the full depth of the melody and realised how much Varya the ash-tree longed for her oak.

> ...But the ash-tree is not fated
> By the lonely oak to stay.
> 'Tis clear she must, poor orphan,
> Alone for ages sway...

sang Varya, and in her voice was felt the bitterness of real tears. When she stopped singing, Alexei could picture her sitting outside under the trees flooded with spring sunlight and her large, round, longing eyes full of tears. He felt a tickling in his own throat and an irresistible desire to see, not read, but see those old letters—the contents of which he knew by heart—that lay in his tunic pocket, to look at the photograph of the slim girl sitting in the meadow. He made an attempt to reach his tunic, but his arm dropped helplessly upon the mattress. Again everything floated in that grey gloom spotted with rainbow-coloured rings. Later, in that gloom, which rustled with curious stabbing sounds, he heard two voices—Varya's and another, the voice of an old woman that was also familiar to him. They spoke in whispers.

"He doesn't eat?"

"No, he can't. Yesterday he chewed a piece of flat cake—the tiniest bit—and it made him vomit. That's no food for him! He takes a little milk, so we give him some."

"Look, I've brought some broth.... Perhaps the poor boy would like a little broth."

"Aunty Vasilisa!" exclaimed Varya. "Have you really...."

"Yes, it's chicken broth. What are you surprised at? Nothing extraordinary about it. Wake him up, perhaps he'll take a little."

And before Alexei—who had heard this conversation—could open his eyes, Varya shook him vigorously, unceremoniously, and cried out with joy:

"Alexei Petrovich! Alexei Petrovich! Wake up! Grandma Vasilisa has brought you some chicken broth! Wake up, I say!"

The rushlight stuck in the wall near the door spluttered and burned up brighter. In the flickering, smoky light Alexei saw a little, bent old woman with a hooked nose and wrinkled, shrewish face. She was busying herself at the table unwrapping something large; first she removed a piece of sackcloth, then an old woman's coat, then a sheet of paper, and finally exposed a small iron pot which filled the dugout with such a delicious odour of fat chicken broth that Alexei felt spasms in his empty stomach.

Grandma Vasilisa's wrinkled face preserved its stern and shrewish expression.

"There, I've brought you this," she said. "Please, don't refuse it. Eat it and get well. Perhaps, please God, it will do you good."

And Alexei remembered the sad story about this old woman's family, and the story about the chicken that bore the name of Partisanka, and everything—the old woman, Varya, and the steaming iron pot on the table emitting that delicious smell—floated in a welter of tears through which he saw the stern eyes of the old woman gazing at him with infinite pity.

"Thank you, Granny," was all that he could say as the old woman made for the door.

And when she had reached the door he heard her say:

"Don't mention it. What is there to thank me for? My sons are in the war too. Perhaps somebody will give them broth. Eat it. May it do you good. Get well."

"Granny! Granny!" Alexei tried to get up, but Varya restrained him and gently pushed him back on the mattress.

"Lie down, lie down! Here, take some of this broth." She offered him the aluminium lid of a German army billycan, from which rose a deliciously fragrant vapour, and turned her head away, evidently to hide the tears that came unbidden to her eyes. "Take some," she repeated.

"Where is Grandad Mikhail?"

"He's out. He's gone on business. To find out where the District Committee is. He won't be back for a long time. But take this broth. Take it."

Right under his nose Alexei saw a large, chipped, wooden spoon, black with age, and filled with amber-coloured broth.

The first spoonfuls roused in him a wolfish appetite; so ravenous was he that he felt painful spasms in the stomach; but he permitted himself to take only ten spoonfuls and a few shreds of the tender white chicken meat. Although his stomach imperatively demanded more and more, he resolutely pushed the food away, knowing that in his present state an extra spoonful might prove to be poison for him.

Grandma's broth worked miracles. Alexei fell asleep, not into a swoon, but into a real, sound, health-giving sleep. He woke up, ate a little more and fell asleep again, and could not be roused either by the smoke from the hearth, the talking of the women, or by the touch of

Varya's hand—for fearing that he was dead, she would bend over him every now and again to feel whether his heart was beating.

He was alive; he breathed regularly and deeply. He slept for the rest of the day, all night, and went on sleeping as if no power on earth could wake him.

Early next morning a distant, monotonous droning could be heard indistinctly above the sounds that filled the forest. Alexei gave a start, raised his head from his pillow and listened with strained attention.

Wild, irrepressible joy filled his whole being. He lay motionless, his eyes flashing with agitation. He could hear the loud cracking of the stones cooling on the hearth, the feeble chirping of the cricket, tired after its night's performance, the calm and regular beat of the swaying old pine-trees that grew over the dugout, and even the patter of the heavy drops of spring moisture outside the door. But above all these sounds the steady droning could easily be distinguished. Alexei guessed that the sound came from the engine of a "U-2" aircraft. The sound now grew in volume, now subsided, but it never died out entirely. Alexei held his breath. It was evident that the aircraft was somewhere in the vicinity, that it was circling over the forest, either scouting or looking for a place to land.

"Varya, Varya!" Alexei called, trying to raise himself on his elbow.

But Varya was not in the dugout. Excited women's voices and hurrying footsteps were heard outside. Something was happening there.

The door of the dugout opened for an instant and Fedka's freckled face appeared.

"Aunty Varya! Aunty Varya!" the boy cried out, and then added in an excited voice: "The plane! It's circling over us!" and vanished before Alexei could say a word.

With an effort Alexei sat up. The thumping of his heart, the blood throbbing in his temples and the pain in his injured feet sent tremors through his whole body. He counted the circles the aircraft up there was making: one, two, three, and, overcome by excitement, fell back on the mattress and again plunged swiftly and irresistibly into that sound, health-giving sleep.

He was roused by a young, resonant, booming bass voice. He would have picked that voice out from any chorus. The only man in the Fighter Wing with a voice like that was Squadron Commander Andrei Degtyarenko.

Alexei opened his eyes, but he thought he was still asleep and that it was in a dream that he saw the broad, high-cheeked, rough-hewn, good-natured face of his friend, with the livid scar on his forehead, light-coloured eyes and equally light and colourless "pig's eyelashes", as Andrei's enemies called them. A pair of light-blue eyes peered inquiringly, through the smoky semi-darkness.

"Now, Grandpa, show me your trophy," boomed Degtyarenko with a marked Ukrainian accent.

The vision did not melt away. It really was Degtyarenko, although it seemed absolutely incredible that his friend should be here, in the underground village in the depths of the forest. He was standing there, tall, broad-shouldered, with his tunic collar unbuttoned as usual. He was holding his helmet with the wires of his radiophone dangling from it, and also some packets and parcels. The rushlight was burning behind him, and his golden, close-cropped, bristling hair shone like a halo.

From behind Degtyarenko peeped the pale, weary face of Grandad Mikhail, his eyes bulging with excitement; and next to him stood a hospital nurse: it was snub-nosed, impudent Lenochka, peering through the gloom with live curiosity. She held a canvas Red Cross satchel under her arm and pressed some strange-looking flowers to her breast.

Everybody stood silent. Degtyarenko looked around in perplexity, evidently blinded by the gloom. Once or twice his eyes passed indifferently over Alexei's face; nor could Alexei accustom himself to the idea that his friend should suddenly appear in this place, and he trembled lest all this should turn out to be a feverish dream.

"Good Lord, can't you see him? Here he is," whispered Varya, pulling the sheepskin from Meresyev.

Again Degtyarenko cast a bewildered look at Alexei's face.

"Andrei!" called Meresyev feebly, trying to raise himself on his elbows.

Andrei looked at him in amazement and scarcely concealed fright.

"Andrei! Don't you recognise me?" whispered Meresyev, feeling that he was beginning to tremble all over.

Andrei looked for another instant at the living skeleton covered with dark, seemingly charred skin, trying to discern the merry features of his friend, and only in his eyes, enormous and almost round, did he catch the frank and determined Meresyev expression that was familiar to him. His helmet dropped to the floor, the packets and parcels came undone, and apples, oranges and biscuits were scattered on the floor.

"Lyoshka! Is that you?" His voice was husky with emotion and his long, colourless eyelashes dropped. "Lyoshka! Lyoshka!" he cried again. He picked the feeble body from the bed as lightly as though it were that of an infant, pressed it to his breast and kept on repeating: "Lyoshka! Lyoshka!"

He held Alexei out in his arms for an instant and gazed at him, as if trying to convince himself that it was really his friend, and again pressed him to his breast.

"Yes, it's you! Lyoshka! You son of the devil!"

Varya and the nurse tried to tear the weak body out of his powerful, bearlike grasp. "For God's sake, let go of him, there's hardly any life in him!" Varya whispered angrily.

"It's bad for him to get excited. Put him down!" the nurse said, speaking rapidly.

But Andrei, convinced at last that this dark, shrunken, imponderable body was really that of Alexei Meresyev, his comrade-in-arms, his friend, whom the whole wing had given up for dead, put Alexei on the bed, clutched his own head, uttered a wild cry of triumph, clutched Alexei by the shoulders, peered into his dark eyes that were shining with joy out of their deep sockets and shouted:

"Alive! Holy Mother! Alive, the devil take you! Where have you been all these days? What happened to you?"

But the nurse, the chubby little creature with the snub nose, whom everybody in the wing, ignoring her rank of lieutenant, called Lenochka, or "sister of medical science", as she, to her own undoing, had introduced herself to her superior, always singing and laughing Lenochka, who was in love with all the lieutenants at the same time, firmly pushed the excited airman away from the bed and said sternly:

"Comrade Captain, leave the patient alone!"

Throwing on to the table the bunch of flowers, for which the day before someone had flown to the regional centre, and which were now absolutely superfluous, she unfastened the canvas Red Cross satchel and, in a business-like manner, proceeded to examine the sick man. She deftly tapped his legs with her stubby fingers and asked him:

"Does it hurt? Here? And here?"

Alexei had a good look at his legs for the first time. The feet were terribly swollen and almost black. The slightest touch caused a pain to shoot through his whole body like an electric shock. The look of the tips of the toes worried Lenochka most. They had turned quite black and were insensitive to all feeling.

Grandad Mikhail and Degtyarenko sat down at the table. Surreptitiously taking a pull at the airman's flask to celebrate the occasion, they engaged in an animated conversation. In his cracked, high-pitched voice, Grandad Mikhail began evidently not for the first time to tell how Alexei was found.

"Well, our youngsters found him in the clearing. The Germans had felled logs for their dugouts, and the boys' mother, my daughter, that is, sent them there for chips. That's how they found him. 'Aha! What's that funny thing over there?' At first they thought it was a wounded bear rolling over and over and took to their heels at once. But curiosity got the better of them and they went back. 'What kind of a bear is it? Why is it rolling? There's something funny about this!' They went back and saw this thing rolling over and over groaning."

"What do you mean 'rolling'?" inquired Degtyarenko doubtfully, offering Grandad his cigarette case. "Do you smoke?"

Grandad took a cigarette from the case, drew a folded piece of newspaper from his pocket, tore off a strip, emptied the tobacco from the cigarette into it, rolled it and, after lighting up, inhaled with deep relish.

"Smoke? Of course I smoke," he said after another draw. "Oh yes! Only, I've not seen any tobacco since the Germans came. I smoke moss, and also dry spurge leaves, yes!... As for how he rolled, ask him. I didn't see that. The boys say that he rolled from his back to his belly and from his belly to his back. You see, he had no strength to crawl on his hands and knees. That's the kind of fellow he is!"

Every now and again Degtyarenko jumped up to look at his friend, whom the women were rolling in the grey army blankets which the nurse had brought with her.

"Sit still, my boy, sit still. It's not a man's business to put diapers on!" said Grandad. "Listen to what I'm telling you. And don't forget to tell it to one of your higher-ups. That man did a big thing. You see what he is like now. All of us, the whole collective farm, have been nursing him for a week, and yet he can't move. But he had the strength in him to crawl through our forest and marshes. There aren't many that could do a thing like that. Even the holy saints in their vigils didn't do anything like it. What's standing on a pillar? Am I right? I should say so! But listen, my boy, listen!..."

The old man bent over towards Degtyarenko's ear, tickling him with his soft, fluffy beard, and said in almost a whisper:

"I hope, though, he isn't going to die. What do you think? He got away from the Germans, but can you get away from that fellow with the scythe? Nothing but skin and bones—how he managed to crawl I can't imagine! He must have wanted to get to his own people pretty bad, eh? All the time he was unconscious he kept saying: 'airfield', 'airfield', and other words, and he also mentioned Olga. Is there a girl at your place with that name? Perhaps it's his wife. Are you listening to me? Did you hear what I said? Hey, airman!"

But Degtyarenko was not listening. He was trying to picture this man, his comrade, who had seemed quite an ordinary lad, crawling with frozen and fractured legs, over the melting snow, through forest and marsh, crawling, rolling, to get away from the enemy and to reach his own people. His own experience as a fighter-pilot had inured him to danger. When he rushed into the fray he never thought of death and even felt a joyous thrill. But for a man to do a thing like that, all alone in the forest. . . .

"When did you find him?"

"When?" The old man moved his lips and took another cigarette from the open case. "Now, when was it? Why, of course! It was just a week ago."

Degtyarenko ran over the dates in his mind and calculated that Alexei Meresyev had crawled eighteen days. For a wounded man to crawl all that time, and without food—it seemed incredible.

"Well, Grandpa, thank you very much!" the airman tightly embraced the old man and pressed him to his breast. "Thank you, brother!"

"Don't mention it. There's nothing to thank me for. 'Thank you,' he says! What am I? A stranger, a foreigner, or what?" And then he angrily shouted at his daughter-in-law who was standing in bitter reflection with her cheek resting on her hand. . . . "Pick those provisions off the floor! Fancy throwing such precious stuff about! . . . 'Thanks', he says!"

Meanwhile, Lenochka had finished preparing Meresyev for his journey.

"It's all right, it's all right, Comrade Senior Lieutenant," she twittered, her words dropping fast like peas from a bag. "Now, in Moscow, they'll put you on your feet in a trice. Moscow is a big city, isn't it, now? They heal worse cases than yours!"

From her exaggerated animation and the way she kept on repeating that Meresyev would be put on his feet in a trice, Degtyarenko guessed that her examination had shown that the case was serious and that his friend was in a bad way. "Chattering like a magpie", he growled to himself, scowling at the "sister of medical science". Suddenly he remembered that nobody in the wing took this girl seriously, and that everybody said in jest that all she could cure anybody of was love—and that consoled Degtyarenko somewhat.

Wrapped in the blankets, from which the head alone was visible, Alexei reminded Degtyarenko of the mummy of a Pharaoh he had seen in the illustrations of his school textbook on ancient history. He passed his big hand down his friend's cheeks, which were covered with hard, thick, reddish stubble.

"It's all right, Alexei! You'll be back on your feet again! We've received orders to send you to Moscow, to a fine hospital. All professors! As for the nurses"—he clicked his tongue and winked at Lenochka—"they make the dead walk! You and I will make ourselves heard in the air yet...." And here Degtyarenko caught himself speaking with the same affected, lifeless joviality that Lenochka was assuming. Suddenly he felt moisture under his hands as he stroked his friend's cheeks. "Where is the stretcher?" he demanded angrily. "Let's take him out! What's the use of dilly-dallying?"

Assisted by the old man, they gently placed Alexei, rolled up in the blankets, on the stretcher. Varya collected his belongings and tied them up in a bundle.

"Grandad!" said Alexei, stopping Varya as she was pushing the SS dirk into the bundle. Prompted by his thrifty habits, Grandad Mikhail had often examined the dirk with curiosity, had cleaned it, sharpened it, and had tried it on his thumb. "Take this as a souvenir."

"Thank you, Alexei! Thank you! It's a fine piece of steel. And look! It's got something written on it not in our language," he added, showing the dirk to Degtyarenko. The latter read the inscription on the blade and translated it: *Alles für Deutschland*—"Everything for Germany".

"Everything for Germany," echoed Alexei, remembering how he had acquired the dirk.

"Now then, old man, pick him up, pick him up!" cried Degtyarenko, grasping the handles at one end of the stretcher.

The stretcher swayed and, with difficulty, passed through the narrow doorway of the dugout, knocking the earth down from the walls.

All those who had crowded into the dugout rushed out to see the foundling off. Varya alone remained. She unhurriedly trimmed the rushlight, went up to the striped mattress that still bore the imprint of the human body that had lain on it, and stroked it with her hand. Her eyes fell upon the bunch of flowers that had been forgotten in the hurry. Several sprigs of hot-house lilac, pale and wilted, like the inhabitants of this fugitive village who had spent the winter in cold, damp dugouts. The young woman picked up the flowers, inhaled the tender smell of spring, so faint that it was barely perceptible amidst the fumes and soot, flung herself on a bunk and burst into bitter tears.

18

The whole of the available population of the village of Plavni came out to say farewell to their unexpected guest. The aircraft had landed behind the forest on a small, elongated lake, the ice of which, though melting at the edges, was still strong and firm. There were no roads to this lake. There was a track to it, which Grandad Mikhail, Degtyarenko and Lenochka had trodden in the soft, yielding snow an hour before. Along this track a crowd of people were making for the lake, headed by the boys of the village, with staid Seryonka, and Fedka, bubbling over with enthusiasm, right in front. By right, as an old friend who had found the airman in the forest, Seryonka was walking solemnly in front of the stretcher, laboriously pulling his feet, encased in the huge felt boots left him by his father, out of the snow and sternly scolding the other white-toothed, grimy-faced, fantastically ragged boys. Degtyarenko and Grandad, keeping in step, carried the stretcher, while Lenochka walked on the untramped snow by the side, now adjusting Alexei's blankets, and now wrapping her scarf round his head. Behind trailed the women, girls and the old folks, chattering as they went.

At first the bright light reflected by the snow dazzled Alexei. The fine spring day struck his eyes so forcibly that he had to close them and he nearly swooned. Slightly raising his eyelids he let his eyes get used to the light and then gazed around him. A picture of the underground village unfolded before him.

The old forest stood like a wall whichever way you looked. The tops of the trees almost met overhead and cast the ground below in semi-gloom. It was a mixed forest. The trunks of the still bare birch-trees, the tops of which looked like smoke frozen in the air, stood side by side with the golden trunks of pine-trees, and among them, here and there, showed the dark, peaked tops of fir-trees.

Beneath the trees, which hid them from enemy eyes from the ground and from the air, at a spot where the snow had long been trampled by hundreds of feet, were the dugouts. Infants' diapers were drying on the branches of century-old fir-trees, pots and pitchers were being aired on the stumps of pine-trees, and under an old fir-tree, from the trunk of which beards of grey moss were dangling, between its sinewy roots where, according to all the rules, a beast of prey should be lying, lay a greasy rag doll with a flat, genial face traced with indelible pencil.

The crowd, preceded by the stretcher, moved slowly down the trampled, moss-carpeted "street".

In the open air Alexei at first felt an upsurge of instinctive, animal joy, but this gave way to feeling of sweet, silent sadness.

Lenochka wiped the tears from his face with a tiny pocket handkerchief and, interpreting these tears in her own way, told the stretcher-bearers to go slower.

"No, no! Faster! Go faster!" said Meresyev, hurrying them on.

It seemed to him that they were going too slowly. He began to fear that he would not be able to get away, that the aircraft from Moscow would fly away without waiting for him and he would never reach the clinic. He moaned softly from the pain caused him by the hurried pace of the stretcher-bearers, but he kept on repeating: "Faster please, faster!" He hurried them on in spite of the fact that he heard Grandad Mikhail panting for breath and saw him slipping and stumbling. Two women took the old man's place at the stretcher; he continued to plod along by the side of the stretcher opposite to Lenochka. Wiping his perspiring bald head, flushed face and wrinkled neck with his officer's cap he mumbled contentedly:

"Whipping us up, eh? In a hurry!... Quite right, Alexei, you are absolutely right, hurry them up! When a man's in a hurry it shows there's life in him, and it's beating strong. Aren't I right, dearly beloved foundling?... Write us from the hospital. Remember the address: Kalinin Region, Bologoye District, the future village of Plavni, what? Future, I say. Don't be afraid, it will reach us. Don't forget. The address is right!"

When the stretcher was lifted into the aircraft and the pungent smell of aircraft fuel struck Alexei's nostrils he felt another upsurge of joy. The celluloid hood was drawn over his head. He did not see the people who had come to see him off waving their hands; he did not see the little old woman with the hooked nose, looking in her grey kerchief like an angry raven, struggling against fear and the wind raised by the propeller, push towards Degtyarenko, who was already in the cockpit, and hand him a packet with the rest of the chicken; he did not see Grandad Mikhail fussing round the aircraft, scolding the women and driving away the children; and how, when the wind had torn his cap from his head and sent it bowling over the ice, he stood bareheaded with his glistening bald patch and thin silvery locks, looking like St. Nicholas in the simple village icons. He stood, waving his hand to the departing aircraft, the only man among the motley crowd of women.

Hopping off the icy surface of the lake, Degtyarenko flew the plane over the heads of the crowd and cautiously, with the runners almost touching the ice, he flew along the lake under cover of its high, steep shore, and vanished behind a wooded island. This time, the daredevil of the wing who had received more than one dressing-down from his superior for recklessness in the air, flew cautiously; he did not fly, he crept, hugging the ground, following the courses of small rivers and taking cover under the shores of the lakes. Alexei saw nothing and heard nothing. The familiar smell of petrol and lubrication, and the joyous sensation of flying, caused him to lose consciousness. He came to only at the airfield when the stretcher was being lowered from the aircraft to transfer him to an emergency Red Cross craft that had already arrived from Moscow.

19

He arrived at his own airfield at the busiest time of the day, when it was working to its utmost capacity, as it did every day during that hectic spring.

The roar of engines did not cease for a moment. The place in the air of one squadron that landed for refuelling was taken by another, and that by a third. Everybody, from the airmen to the petrol-tank drivers and storekeepers, worked until they dropped. The Chief of Staff had lost his voice and could now speak only in hoarse whispers.

But notwithstanding the intense activity and the general tension, everybody had been eagerly looking forward to Meresyev's arrival.

"Hasn't he come yet?" the pilots had shouted to the mechanics above the roar of their engines even before they had taxied to their caponiers.

"Anything heard of him?" the "petrol magnates" had inquired as they taxied their petrol carriers to the tanks buried in the ground.

And everybody had strained his ears to hear whether the sounds of the familiar wing Red Cross plane were coming from over the woods.

When Alexei came to and found himself lying on a springy, swaying stretcher, he saw a close ring of familiar faces around him. He opened his eyes. Exclamations of joy went up from the crowd. Right next to the stretcher he saw the youthful, immobile face and restrained smile of the Wing Commander. Next to it he saw the red and perspiring face of the Chief of Staff, and the round, full, pale face of the Commander of the M.C.B.—Maintenance Crew Battalion—whom Alexei detested for his formalism and stinginess. How many familiar faces! The front stretcher-bearer was Yura, who stumbled every time he turned his head to look at Alexei. Next to him hurried a little red-haired girl, the sergeant at the meteorological station. Before, Alexei had imagined that she disliked him for some reason; she had tried to keep out of his sight and had stealthily watched him with a strange look in her eyes. He called her in jest the "meteorological sergeant". Near her Kukushkin came tripping, a little fellow with an unpleasant, jaundiced face, who was disliked in the squadron because of his unsociable habits. He too was smiling and trying to keep in step with Yura's enormous paces. Meresyev remembered that just before his flight he had, in a large company, twitted Kukushkin for failing to pay him a debt and was convinced that this vindictive fellow would never forgive him. But now he was running beside the stretcher, carefully supporting it and elbowing aside the bystanders to prevent them from pushing.

Alexei never suspected that he had so many friends. That's what people are like when they truly reveal themselves! He now felt sorry for the "meteorological sergeant" who seemed afraid of him for some reason: he felt ashamed of himself in the presence of the M.C.B. Commander, about whose stinginess he had circulated so many jokes and anecdotes in the division, and he felt that he wanted to apologise to Kukushkin and to tell the boys that he was not such an unpleasant and unsociable felow after all. Alexei felt that after all the torments he had gone through he had at last come home to his own family, where everybody sincerely rejoiced at his return.

He was carefully carried across the field to the silvery Red Cross plane standing masked on the edge of a bare birch wood. The mechanics were already starting its engine.

"Comrade Major," said Meresyev suddenly, addressing himself to the Wing Commander and trying to speak as loudly and confidently as possible.

The Commander, with the customary quiet, enigmatic smile, bent over Alexei.

"Comrade Major ... permit me not to fly to Moscow, but to remain here, with you...."

The Commander pulled off his helmet which prevented him from hearing.

"I don't want to go to Moscow. I want to remain here, at the medical battalion...."

The major took off his fur glove, groped for Alexei's hand under the blanket and, pressing it, said:

"You funny chap! You need real, serious treatment."

Alexei shook his head. He felt so good and restful here. Neither the experiences he had gone through nor the pain in his feet seemed terrible to him now.

"What's he saying?" inquired the Chief of Staff in his hoarse voice.

"He wants to remain here with us," answered the Commander, smiling.

And at that moment his smile was not enigmatic as it usually was, but friendly and sad.

"Fool! Romantics! An example for *Pionerskaya Pravda*," said the Chief of Staff. "They do him the honour of sending a plane from Moscow for him by order of the Army Commander himself, but he.... What do you think of him?..."

Meresyev wanted to answer and say that he was not romantic, that he was simply convinced that here, in a tent at the medical base, where he had once spent a few days with a sprained ankle after a crash landing in a damaged plane, that here, in familiar surroundings, he would recover much more quickly than among the unknown conveniences of a Moscow clinic. He had already thought of the words with which to give the Chief of Staff a stinging reply, but before he could utter them the siren emitted its mournful wail.

Every face at once assumed a grave and business-like air. The major issued several curt orders and the men began to bustle like ants; some ran to the planes standing under cover on the edge of the woods, some to the command post, distinguished by a small mound on the edge of the field, and some to the machines that were hidden in the woods. Alexei saw a distinct trail of smoke in the sky and the grey, slowly dissolving trail of a multiple-tailed rocket. He understood what it was: the "alert". His heart began to thump, his nostrils quivered, and he felt a cold thrill run down his spine, as he always felt in moments of danger. Lenochka, the mechanic Yura and the "meteorological sergeant", who had no particular job to do amidst the feverish bustle of the airfield when the alarm was sounded, snatched up the stretcher and ran, all three of them, to the nearest point on the edge of the wood, trying to keep in step and, of course, failing to do so in their excitement.

Alexei groaned. They dropped into a walking pace. In the distance the automatic anti-aircraft guns were already chattering convulsively. One after another flights of aircraft crept out on to the runway and hopped off. Above the familiar sound of their engines Alexei soon heard coming from the woods an irregular, undulating drone which caused his muscles to contract automatically like tightened springs; and this man, bound to the stretcher, imagined that he was in the cockpit of a fighter speeding to meet the enemy.

The stretcher would not go into the narrow slit. Yura and the girls wanted to carry him down in their arms, but Alexei protested, demanding that the stretcher be put down on the edge of the wood under a big, stout birch-tree. Lying there he witnessed the events that took place with a swiftness that occurs in a heavy dream. Airmen have rare opportunities to watch an air battle from the ground. Meresyev, who had fought in the Air Force since the first day of the war, had never witnessed an air battle from the ground. And now, accustomed as he had been to lightning speeds in air fighting, he was amazed how slow and harmless an air battle seemed from the ground, how listless the movements of the old, blunt-nosed fighter planes and how harmless the rattle of their machine-guns sounded above, reminding him of something domestic—like the whir of a sewing-machine, or the ripping of calico when it is torn.

Twelve German bombers, in V formation, bypassed the airfield and vanished in the bright rays of the sun, now high in the sky. From behind the clouds, the edges of which were so dazzling from the sun that it hurt the eyes to look at them, came the low droning of the engines like the buzzing of cockchafers. The anti-aircraft guns in the woods barked and snarled more furiously than ever. The smoke from their bursting shells floated in the sky like fluffy dandelion seeds. But nothing was seen except a rare flash of the wings of a fighter plane.

More and more often the buzzing of the cockchafers was interrupted by the sound of tearing calico: r-r-r-ip, r-r-r-ip, r-r-r-ip! Amidst the dazzling sun-rays a battle was raging, but from below it was so unlike that which the participants in an air fight see, and seemed so insignificant and uninteresting that Alexei watched it without the slightest thrill.

Even when from above came a piercing screech increasing in volume and a stick of bombs rapidly growing in size came hurtling down like black drops shaken from a brush, Alexei was not afraid and slightly raised his head to see where they would fall.

At this moment the conduct of the "meteorological sergeant" amazed Alexei. When the screaming of the bombs reached the highest pitch, the girl, who was standing waisthigh in the slit and, as always, stealthily glancing at him, suddenly jumped out, made a dash for the stretcher, dropped to the ground and covered Alexei with her body, trembling with fear and agitation.

For an instant he saw, close to his own eyes, a tanned, quite childish face, full lips and a peeling snub nose. The roar of an explosion was heard from somewhere in the forest, immediately followed much nearer by a second, a third, a fourth. The fifth was so terrific that the earth trembled and swayed. The crown of the tree under which Alexei was lying, severed by a splinter, came hurtling to the ground with a noise. Again he saw the pale, terror-stricken face of the girl and felt her cool cheek against his; and in the interval between the crashes of two sticks of bombs, this terrified girl whispered:

"Darling! Darling! ..."

Another stick of bombs shook the earth with a terrific roar and it looked as though whole trees shot up out of the ground into the sky over the airfield, their crowns burst apart, and then clumps of frozen earth fell to the ground with a thunderous rumble, leaving in the air a trail of brownish, acrid smoke that smelt like garlic.

When the smoke dispersed, it was already quiet all round. The sounds of the air battle were barely audible from behind the forest. The girl had already jumped to her feet, her cheeks were no longer sallow but flushed. Blushing furiously and seeming ready to cry, she said apologetically, keeping her eyes away from Alexei:

"I didn't hurt you, did I? What a fool, Lord, what a fool I am! I'm very sorry!"

"No use apologising now," growled Yura, ashamed that it had not been he, but the girl from the meteorological station, who had dashed to protect his friend.

Grumbling, he shook the sand from his overalls, scratched the back of his head and looked wonderingly at the jagged stump of the beheaded birch-tree, from the trunk of which the transparent sap was oozing in profusion. This sap of the wounded tree, glistening in the sun, trickled down the mossy bark and dripped to the ground, clear and transparent, like tears.

"Look! The tree is crying!" said Lenochka, who even in the midst of danger did not lose her air of impudent curiosity.

"So would you cry!" answered Yura gloomily. "Well, the show's over. Let's go! I hope the ambulance plane isn't damaged."

"Spring is here!" said Meresyev, gazing at the mutilated tree trunk, at the glistening, transparent sap dripping to the ground, and at the snub-nosed "meteorological sergeant" in the greatcoat much too large for her, whose name he did not even know.

As the three of them, Yura in front and the two girls behind, were carrying him to the plane, winding their way between the still smoking bomb craters into which the water from the thawing snow was trickling, Alexei cast curious side glances at the small, strong hand that emerged from the coarse cuff of the greatcoat and firmly grasped the handle of the stretcher. What was the matter with her? Or did he, in his fright, imagine he heard those words?

On that day which was portentous for him, Alexei Meresyev was the witness of another event. The silvery Red Cross plane and the flight mechanic walking around it, shaking his head and looking to see whether it had been damaged by a splinter or a blast, were already in sight when, one after another, the fighter planes returned and began to land. They shot over the forest, glided down without the usual circle, landed, and taxied to their caponiers on the edge of the wood.

Soon all was quiet in the sky. The airfield was cleared and the whir of engines in the woods was silenced. But men were still standing at the command post and scanning the sky, shading their eyes from the sun with their hands.

"Number nine has not returned! Kukushkin has got stranded somewhere," said Yura.

Alexei recalled Kukushkin's little, jaundiced face which always bore a discontented expression, and remembered how carefully he had supported his stretcher that morning. Could he have been.... That thought, so ordinary for an airman on hectic days, made him shudder now that he was excluded from the life of the airfield.

At that moment they heard the drone of an engine.

Yura jumped up with a cry of joy:

"There he is!"

There was animation among the men at the command post. Something had happened. "Number nine" did not land, but flew in a wide circle round the airfield, and as it flew over Alexei's head he saw that part of its wing had been shot away, and what was far worse, only one "leg" was visible under the fuselage. Two red rockets shot into the air, one after the other. Kukushkin flew overhead once again. His plane looked like a bird circling over its ruined nest, not knowing where to perch. He started on a third circle.

"He'll bail out in a minute. His fuel has run out. He's flying on the last drops!" whispered Yura, his eyes glued to his watch.

In cases like this, when a landing was impossible, airmen were permitted to gain altitude and to bail out. Probably "number nine" had already received an order to that effect, but it obstinately kept circling round.

Yura kept glancing at the plane and then at his watch. When it seemed to him that the engine had slowed down he squatted on his haunches and turned his head away. "Is he thinking of saving the plane?" Everybody present thought to himself: "Jump! Jump, man!"

A fighter plane with a figure "1" on its tail darted into the air and with the first swerve skilfully came alongside the wounded "number nine". By the cool, skilful way in which the plane was handled, Alexei guessed that it was being piloted by the Wing Commander himself. Evidently deciding that Kukushkin's radio set was out of order, or that the pilot had lost his head, he had hastened to his assistance. Signalling with his wings: "Do as I do," he veered to the side and then climbed up. He ordered Kukushkin to veer and bail out. But at that moment Kukushkin reduced his gas and prepared to land. His plane with the broken wing dashed right over Alexei's head and rapidly neared the ground. It abruptly heeled over to port, landed on its sound "leg", taxied a little way on one wheel, reduced speed, heeled over to starboard and, catching the ground with its sound wing, spun round, raising clouds of snow.

When the clouds of snow subsided something dark was seen lying near the crippled plane. Men came running towards this dark object, and, sounding its siren, an ambulance car dashed towards it.

"He saved his plane! So that's the kind of man Kukushkin is! When did he learn to do that?" thought Meresyev, lying on the stretcher and envying his comrade.

He felt an urge to run with all his might to the spot where lay this little, universally disliked fellow who had proved to be such a brave and skilful pilot. But he was bound to the stretcher and fettered by excruciating pain, which overwhelmed him again as soon as the nervous tension relaxed.

All these events took no more than an hour, but they had been so numerous and swift that Alexei had not been able at once to analyse them in his mind. Only when his stretcher had been fixed into the special sockets in the Red Cross plane and when he again happened to catch the fixed stare of the "meteorological sergeant" did he really appreciate the significance of the words that had escaped the girl's pale lips during the bombing. He was ashamed to think that he did not even know the name of this splendid self-sacrificing girl.

"Comrade Sergeant," he called softly, looking at her with grateful eyes.

It is doubtful whether she heard him amidst the roar of the engine, but she stepped forward and held out a small packet, saying:

"Comrade Senior Lieutenant, these are letters for you. I saved them because I knew that you were alive and that you would come back. I knew it, I felt it."

She placed the small batch of letters on his chest. Among them he saw several from his mother, folded in triangles, the addresses written in an irregular, aged hand, and several in the familiar envelopes like those he always kept in his tunic pocket. His face beamed when he saw those envelopes and he made a movement to free his hand from the blanket.

"Are these from a girl?" inquired the "meteorological sergeant" sadly, blushing again, while tears came to her eyes and glued her long, bronze eyelashes together.

Meresyev realised that he had not imagined those words during the explosions, and realising this, dared not tell the truth.

"From my married sister. She has a different surname now," he answered, feeling disgusted with himself.

Voices were heard above the roar of the engine. The side door opened and a surgeon, a stranger wearing a white smock over his greatcoat, boarded the plane.

"One of the patients is here already? Good!" he said, looking at Meresyev. "Bring the other one in. We'll be off in a minute. And what are you doing here, Madame?" he inquired, gazing through his vapour-dimmed spectacles at the "meteorological sergeant" who was trying to hide behind Yura. "Please go, we'll be off in a minute. Hey! Put the stretcher in!"

"Write, for God's sake write, I will wait!" Alexei heard the girl whisper.

Assisted by Yura, the surgeon hauled into the plane a stretcher on which somebody was moaning softly. As it was being fixed into its sockets, the sheet with which it was covered slipped down and Meresyev saw Kukushkin's face, contorted with pain. The surgeon rubbed his hands, looked round the cabin, and patting Meresyev on the stomach, said:

"Fine, excellent! A fellow-passenger to keep you company, young man. What? And now, all those not flying leave the plane, please! So that Lorelei with the sergeant's stripes has gone, eh? Good! Let's start! . . ."

Yura seemed reluctant to go. The surgeon finally pushed him out. The door was closed, the plane shuddered, started, hopped and then quietly and smoothly soared into its native element accompanied by the regular beat of the engines. The surgeon, holding on to the wall, went up to Meresyev.

"How are you?" he inquired. "Let me feel your pulse." He looked inquisitively at Meresyev, shook his head and muttered: "M'yes. A strong character!" And then to Meresyev he said: "Your friends tell things about your adventures that are simply incredible, something like a Jack London story."

He dropped into his seat, made himself more comfortable, at once grew limp and dozed off. It was evident that this pale-faced man, no longer young, was dead tired.

"Something like a Jack London story," thought Meresyev and remote recollections of his boyhood came to his mind, the story of a man with frozen legs crawling through the desert followed by a sick and hungry wolf. Lulled by the steady drone of the engines, everything began to float, to lose its outline, to dissolve in the grey gloom, and the last strange thought that passed through Alexei's mind as he fell asleep was that there was no war, no bombing, no continuous, torturous, gnawing pain in the feet, no aircraft speeding towards Moscow, that all this was something from a wonderful book that he had read in his boyhood in the remote town of Kamyshin.

PART TWO

1

Andrei Degtyarenko and Lenochka did not exaggerate when they described to their friends the magnificence of the hospital in the capital into which Meresyev and Lieutenant Konstantin Kukushkin were placed. Before the war, this had been the clinic of an institute at which a celebrated Soviet scientist had conducted research to devise new methods of rapidly restoring people to health after sickness or injury. The institute possessed firmly-established traditions and enjoyed world-wide fame.

When the war broke out, the scientist converted the clinic into a hospital for wounded army officers. The hospital continued to provide its patients with every form of treatment known to progressive science at that time. The battles that raged outside of Moscow caused such an influx of wounded that the number of beds had to be increased fourfold compared with the number the clinic had been designed for. All the auxiliary premises—the visitors' rooms, the reading and recreation rooms, the staff's rooms and the dining-rooms—were converted into wards. The scientist even gave up his own study next to his laboratory and transferred himself, with his books, to a tiny room that had served for the nurse on duty. Even then it was often found necessary to place beds in the corridors.

From behind the glistening white walls, which looked as though they had been deliberately designed for the solemn silence of the temple of medicine, were heard the groaning, moaning and snoring of the sick who were asleep, and the raving of those in delirium. The place was thoroughly impregnated with the oppressive stuffy odours of war—of blood-stained bandages, inflamed wounds, the decaying flesh of living human beings—which no amount of airing could eliminate. Folding camp-beds stood side by side with the comfortable beds made according to the scientist's own design. There was a shortage of utensils. In addition to the clinic's beautiful porcelain crockery, dented aluminium bowls were used. The blast from a bomb which had exploded in the vicinity had shattered the glass of the huge Italian windows, and these had to be boarded up with plywood. There was even a shortage of water; every now and again the gas shut off, and instruments had to be sterilised over antiquated spirit-stoves. But the stream of wounded continued. They were brought in increasing numbers—in aircraft, automobiles and trains. And their number grew in proportion to the increase in the might of our offensive.

In spite of all this the entire hospital staff—from its chief, the Merited Scientist and member of the Supreme Soviet, to the ward maids, cloakroom attendants and porters—all these tired, sometimes half-starving people, who never knew a full night's rest, continued fanatically to adhere to the established rules of their institute. The ward maids, who sometimes took two and three spells of duty in succession without a rest, took advantage of every spare moment to clean and wash and scrub. The nurses, thin, aged, staggering from weariness, continued, as before, to appear on duty in white, starched robes, and were as scrupulous as ever in carrying out the instructions of the doctors. The house surgeons, as usual, were severe in their strictures on finding even a spot on any of the patients' bed linen, and they rubbed the walls, balustrades and door handles with their pocket handkerchiefs to see whether they were perfectly clean. And twice a day, at fixed hours, the chief himself, a tall, florid-faced old man, a regular martinet, with greying hair standing up from a wide forehead, a black moustache and grey-streaked imperial beard, made the rounds of the wards, just as he did before the war, accompanied by a suite of house surgeons and assistants in starched smocks, perused the case cards of the new patients and gave advice in severe cases.

During those restless days he had an enormous amount of work to do outside of the hospital too, but he always found time to attend to the institute of his creation at the expense of rest and sleep. When scolding a member of the staff for some delinquency—and he did this boisterously, passionately, always at the scene of the "crime"—he invariably insisted that the clinic must continue to function as a model institution even in alert, blacked-out, war-time Moscow, that this was their retort to those Hitlers and Goerings; he refused to listen to any excuses on the grounds of war-time difficulties and said that slackers and idlers could get to hell out of here, and that precisely now, when things were difficult, there must be especially strict order in the place. He himself continued to make his rounds with such punctuality that the ward maids, as before, set the ward clocks by his appearance. Even air raids did not disturb the punctuality of this man. It was this that stimulated the staff to perform miracles and maintain pre-war order in the clinic under incredible difficulties.

During one of his morning rounds the chief, we will call him Vasily Vasilyevich, came upon two beds standing side by side on the staircase landing on the second floor.

"What's this exhibition?" he barked and shot such a fierce glance from under his shaggy eyebrows at the house surgeon that the latter, a tall, round-shouldered person, no longer young, of impressive appearance, stood to attention like a schoolboy and said:

"Arrived only last night.... Airmen. This one has a fractured thigh and right arm. Condition normal. But that one"—he pointed to a gaunt figure of indefinite age lying motionless with eyes closed—"is a severe case. Compound fracture of the insteps, gangrene in both feet, but chiefly, extreme exhaustion. I don't believe it, of course, but the medical officer, who accompanied them here, reports that the patient with fractured feet had crawled for eighteen days behind the German lines. This, of course, is an exaggeration...."

Not listening to the house surgeon, Vasily Vasilyevich lifted the blanket. Alexei Meresyev was lying with his arms crossed on his chest. From these dark-skinned arms, which stood out distinctly against the background of the fresh white shirt and sheets, one could study the bone structure of man. The professor gently replaced the blanket and, interrupting the house surgeon, growled:

"Why are they lying here?"

"There is no more room in the corridor. You yourself...."

"You yourself! You yourself! What about forty-two?"

"That's the colonels' ward."

"Colonels'!" the professor burst out. "What fool invented that?"

"But we were told: 'Leave a reserve for Heroes of the Soviet Union.'"

"Heroes! Heroes! In this war all are heroes! But why are you trying to teach me? Who is in charge here? Put these men into forty-two at once. Inventing all sorts of nonsense like 'colonels' ward'!"

He went off, accompanied by his now subdued retinue, but soon turned back, bent over Meresyev's bed, and placing his puffy hand, the skin of which was peeling from the effects of all sorts of disinfectants, upon the airman's shoulder, he asked him:

"Is it true that you crawled behind the German lines for over two weeks?"

"Have I got gangrene?" inquired Meresyev, in his turn, in a sinking voice.

The professor cast an angry glance at his retinue that had halted at the door, looked straight into the airman's large black eyes that expressed grief and anxiety, and bluntly said:

"It would be a sin to deceive a man like you. Yes, it's gangrene. But keep your chin up. There are no incurable diseases, just as there are no hopeless situations. Did you get that? That's right!"

And he stalked off, tall and brisk, and soon, through the glass door of the corridor, the distant rumble of his growling voice was heard.

"A funny old boy," said Meresyev, following the departing figure with his heavy eyes.

"He's crazy. Did you hear him? Playing up to us. We know these simple ones," answered Kukushkin from his bed with a crooked smile. "So we have the honour of being put into the 'colonels' ward'."

"Gangrene," said Meresyev softly, and repeated sadly, "gangrene."

2

The so-called colonels' ward was situated at the end of the corridor on the second floor. Its windows faced south and east, so that the sun shone in it all day, its beams slowly crawling from one bed to another. It was a small ward. Judging by the dark patches on the parquet floor, there had formerly been only two beds here, two bedside cupboards, and a round table in the middle. Now there were four beds in the room. On one lay a wounded man swathed in bandages, looking like a bundled-up new-born infant. He lay on his back and through slits in his bandages stared at the ceiling with vacant, motionless eyes. On another bed, next to Alexei's, lay a man with a wrinkled, pock-marked, soldierly face and thin, fair moustaches, obliging, talkative and vivacious.

People in hospital soon make friends. By the evening Alexei already knew that the pock-marked man was a Siberian, chairman of a collective farm, a hunter, and in the army a sniper, and a skilful sniper at that. Beginning with the famous battles near Yelna, when he with his Siberian Division, in which his two sons and son-in-law also served, entered the fighting, he had "ticked off", as he expressed it, seventy fascists. He was a Hero of the Soviet Union, and when he told Alexei his name, Alexei looked curiously at this homely figure. That name was widely known in the army at the time, and the principal newspapers had even written editorials about him. Everybody in the hospital—the nurses, the house surgeon and Vasily Vasilyevich himself—respectfully addressed him as Stepan Ivanovich.

The fourth inmate of the ward, all in bandages, had said nothing about himself the whole day; in fact, he had not uttered a word. But Stepan Ivanovich, who knew everything in the world, quietly told Meresyev his story. His name was Grigory Gvozdev. He was a lieutenant in the Tanks, and he too was a Hero of the Soviet Union. He had graduated from the Tank School and had been in the war from the very start. He had fought his first engagement on the frontier, somewhere near the fortress of Brest-Litovsk. In the famous tank battle near Byelostok his tank was put out of action, but he at once got into another, the commander of which had been killed, and with the remnants of the tank division covered the troops retreating towards Minsk. In the battle on the Bug he was wounded and lost his second tank. Again he got into another tank the commander of which had been killed and took over command of the company. Later, finding himself in the enemy's rear, he formed a roaming tank group of three machines, and for about a month stayed far behind the German lines, harassing enemy transports and troops. He replenished his stocks of fuel, ammunition and spare parts on the fields of recent battles. In the green hollows by the side of high roads, in the forests and marshes, there were any number of wrecked machines of every type.

He was a native of a place near Dorogobuzh. When he learned from the communiqués of the Soviet Information Bureau, which the tankmen regularly received on the WT set of the commander's machine, that the fighting line was nearing his native place, he was unable to restrain himself, and after blowing up his three tanks, he, with his eight surviving men, made his way through the forest to rejoin our forces.

Just before the war broke out Gvozdev had been home on leave in a little village on the bank of a small river that winds through wide meadows. His mother, the village school-teacher, had fallen seriously ill, and his father, an old agronomist and a member of the Regional Soviet of Working People's Deputies, had wired him to come home.

Gvozdev recalled the low log cabin near the school, his mother, a little, emaciated woman lying helpless on an old couch, his father, in an old-fashioned shantung jacket, standing by his mother's couch coughing and pinching his short, grey beard with anxiety, and his three little, dark-haired sisters who closely resembled their mother. He also recalled the village doctor, slim, blue-eyed Zhenya who rode with him on the cart right to the railway station to see him off, and to whom he had promised to write every day. Prowling like a wild beast through the trampled fields and gutted, deserted villages of Byelorussia, avoiding towns and highways, he, with aching heart, tried to guess what he would see in his native home, wondered whether his folks had succeeded in getting away, and what had become of them if they had not.

What he actually saw when he reached his native village exceeded his worst expectations. He found neither his house, nor his kin, nor Zhenya, nor the village itself. From a half-daft old woman who, shuffling her feet as if stepdancing, and mumbling to herself, was cooking something at a stove among a heap of charred ruins, he learned that when the Germans were approaching, the school-teacher was so ill that the agronomist and his daughters dared not take her away, nor go away and leave her. The Germans found out that a member of the Regional Soviet of Working People's Deputies and his family had remained in the village. They seized the whole family, hanged them that very night on a birch-tree outside the house, and burnt the house down. The old woman also told him that Zhenya had gone to the superior officer to plead for the Gvozdev family, but the officer tormented her for a long time to compel her to yield herself to him. What actually happened the old woman did not know, but next day the girl was carried out dead from the house in which the officer had taken up his quarters, and for two days her body lay on the riverbank. Later, the Germans burnt the whole village down because somebody had set fire to their fuel tanks that were standing in the collective-farm stable. That had occurred only five days before.

The old woman led Gvozdev to the charred remains of his home and showed him the birch-tree. In his boyhood his swing had hung from a stout branch of that tree. It was withered now, and five rope ends hung from the charred branch, swaying in the wind. Shuffling her feet and mumbling a prayer to herself, the old woman led Gvozdev to the river and showed him the spot where had lain the body of the girl he had promised to write to every day and had never found the time to do so. He stood amid the rustling sedge for a while and then returned to the forest where his men were waiting for him. He did not say a word or shed a tear.

At the end of June, during General Konev's offensive, Grigory Gvozdev and his men succeeded in breaking through the German lines. In August he was given a new tank, the T-34, and before the winter became famous in the battalion as the "man who knew no limit". Stories were told and written about him that seemed incredible, but were true, nevertheless. One night, sent out to reconnoitre, he dashed at top speed through the German lines, safely crossed their minefield and, firing his guns and sowing panic among the enemy, he broke through to a village that was half surrounded by the Soviet Army and rejoined his own lines on the other side, causing no little confusion in the enemy's ranks. On another occasion, operating with a mobile group behind the German lines, he dashed out from ambush and charged a German transport column, crushing the horses and waggons under his treads.

In the winter, at the head of a small tank group, he attacked the garrison of a fortified village near Rzhev, where a small enemy operative staff had its headquarters. On the outskirts of the village, as his tanks were crossing the defence zone, his own tank was hit by a bottle of inflammable liquid. Sooty, suffocating flames enveloped the tank, but the crew remained in action. The tank raced through the village like a huge torch, firing all its guns, twisting and turning, and chased and crushed the fleeing German soldiers. Gvozdev and his crew, which he had picked from the men who had been in the enemy rear with him, were aware that they were likely to be blown up any moment by the explosion of the fuel tank or ammunition; they were suffocating from the smoke, burnt themselves against the red-hot armour, their clothing was already smouldering, but they fought on. A heavy shell that burst under the treads overturned the tank and, either by the force of the blast or by the clouds of sand and snow that it raised, blew the flames out. Gvozdev was taken out of the tank, suffering from frightful burns. He had been in the turret next to the dead body of the gunner, whose place he had taken.

For two months the tankman had been lying between life and death without hope of recovery, taking no interest in anything, and sometimes not uttering a word for days.

The world of severely wounded men is usually limited by the four walls of their hospital ward. Somewhere beyond those walls war is raging, events of major and minor importance are taking place, passion is at its height, and every day leaves a fresh mark on the soul of every man. But the life of the outer world is not permitted to enter the "severely wounded" ward, and only remote, subdued echoes of the storm raging beyond the hospital walls reach it. The life of the ward is confined to its own, minor interests. A sleepy, dusty fly appearing on the sun-warmed window-pane is an event. The new, high-heeled shoes worn today by nurse Klavdia Mikhailovna, in charge of the ward, who intends to go to the theatre that evening straight from the hospital, is news. The stewed prunes served for the third course at dinner instead of the apricot jelly that everybody is fed up with, is a subject for conversation.

But what always fills the tormentingly long hospital days of the "severely wounded" man, the thing on which all his thoughts are concentrated, is his wound, which has torn him out of the ranks of the fighters, out of the strenuous life of war, and has flung him on to this soft and comfortable bed which he began to hate from the moment he was put in it. He falls asleep thinking of this wound, swelling or fracture, he sees it in his sleep, and the moment he wakes he wants to know whether the swelling has gone down, whether the inflammation is gone, whether his temperature is lower or higher. And just as the alert ear is inclined at night to magnify every rustle, so, here, this constant concentration of mind on one's infirmity intensifies the painfulness of the wound and compels even the staunchest and strongest-willed men who, in battle, had calmly looked death in the face, fearfully to catch the intonation of the professor's voice and with quaking heart to guess from the expression on his face the course his illness is taking.

Kukushkin was continuously grousing and grumbling. He thought that his splints had not been put on right, that they were too tight and that, as a consequence, the bones would not set properly and would have to be broken again. Grisha Gvozdev, submerged in despondent semi-consciousness, said nothing. It was easy to see, however, with what eager impatience he looked at his inflamed body and tattered skin when Klavdia Mikhailovna threw handfuls of vaseline into his wounds when changing his bandages, and how intently he listened to the consultations of the surgeons. Stepan Ivanovich was the only man in the ward who could move about, bent almost double, it is true, and clutching at the bed rails, constantly cursing that "fool of a bomb" that had knocked him out, and that "damned sciatica" brought on by the concussion.

Meresyev tried hard to conceal his feelings and pretended that he was not interested in what the surgeons were saying to each other. But every time his feet were unbandaged for electrical treatment and he saw that the sinister inflammation was creeping, slowly but steadily, along the insteps, his eyes opened wide with horror.

He became restless and gloomy. A clumsy jest from a fellow-patient, a crease on the bed sheet, or a broom slipping from the hands of the aged ward maid, sent him into a rage, which he suppressed with difficulty. True, the strict, gradually increasing ration of excellent hospital food quickly restored his strength, and the sight of his gaunt body when the bandages were being changed, or when he took electrical treatment, no longer called forth the terrified glances of the girl medical students. But the stronger his body grew, the worse his feet became. The inflammation now completely covered the insteps and was rising up the ankles. The toes were completely insensitive; the surgeon pricked them with needles, forcing them deep into the flesh, but Alexei felt no pain. They succeeded in checking the swelling by a new method which bore the strange name of "blockade", but the pain in his feet increased. It became absolutely unbearable. In the day-time Alexei lay quietly with his face buried in his pillow. At night, Klavdia Mikhailovna gave him morphia.

More and more often the surgeons, during their consultations, mentioned the frightful word "amputate". Vasily Vasilyevich would sometimes stop at Meresyev's bed and inquire:

"Well, and how is the crawler today? Perhaps we'll amputate, eh? One snip—and they're off!"

Alexei turned cold and shivered. Clenching his teeth to prevent himself from shouting, he merely shook his head, and the professor growled:

"Well, bear it, bear it—it's your affair. We'll see what this does." And he prescribed some new treatment.

The door closed behind him, his footsteps died down in the corridor, but Meresyev lay in his bed with eyes closed. "My feet, my feet, my feet...." Was he to be without feet, to be a cripple on wooden stumps like old Arkasha, the ferryman in his native Kamyshin? To unfasten and leave his feet on the river-bank when he went bathing and crawl into the water like a monkey, as that old man did?

These bitter reflections were aggravated by still another circumstance. On the very first day he arrived at the hospital he read the letters he had received from Kamyshin. The small, triangle-folded letters from his mother were, as always, brief, half consisting of greetings from relatives and assurances that they were all well, thank God, and that he, Alyosha, need not worry about her, and half of pleadings that he should take care of himself, not to catch cold, not to get his feet wet, not to rush into danger and to beware of the German's cunning, about which she had heard enough from her neighbours. The contents of all these letters were the same, except that in one she informed him that she had asked a neighbour to pray for him in church, not that she was religious herself, but in case there was somebody up above after all; in another she wrote that she was worried about his elder brothers who were fighting somewhere in the South and had not written for a long time; and in the last one she wrote that she had dreamed that during the spring flood on the Volga all her sons had returned to her; that they had come back from a successful fishing expedition together with their father—who was dead—and that she had baked for them their favourite pie—vyaziga pie*— and that the neighbours had interpreted the dream as meaning that one of her sons would certainly come home from the front. She therefore begged Alexei to ask his superior whether he would not let him go home, at least for a day.

The blue envelopes, addressed in a large, round, schoolgirl's hand, contained letters from a girl who had been a

---

* Pie stuffed with the spinal cord of a sturgeon.—*Tr.*

fellow-pupil at the factory apprenticeship school. Her name was Olga. She was now a technician at the Kamyshin saw-mill, where he himself had worked as a metal turner. This girl was something more than a boyhood friend, and her letters were out of the ordinary. It was not surprising that he read each one several times, picked them up again and again and perused the simplest lines in the endeavour to find in them some other, joyous, hidden meaning, although it was not quite clear even to himself what he sought in them.

She wrote that she was up to her ears in work, that she did not even go home at night but slept at the office so as not to lose time going and coming, that Alexei would probably not recognise the saw-mill now, and that he would be amazed, would simply go crazy with joy, if he knew what they were making now. Incidentally, she wrote that on the rare days off, not more than once a month, she went to see his mother, that the old lady was very worried about not hearing from her elder sons, that she was having a hard time, and lately had been in failing health. The girl begged Alexei to write to his mother more often and at greater length, and not to disturb her with bad news about himself as, probably, he was now her only joy.

Reading and rereading Olga's letters, Alexei saw through his mother's little ruse in telling him about the dream. He realised that his mother was longing for him, resting her hopes in him, and he also realised what a frightful shock it would be to her, and to Olga, if he wrote them about his legs. He pondered a long time over what to do, and had not the courage to write and tell the truth. He decided to withhold that for a time and to write them both that he was well, that he had been transferred to a quiet sector; to explain the change of address and make it sound plausible, he wrote that he was on a special assignment with a unit in the rear and would stay there for a long time.

And now, when the word "amputate" was mentioned more and more often by the surgeons in their consultations near his bed, a feeling of horror overcame him. How could he return home to Kamyshin a cripple? How was he to show Olga his wooden stumps? What a terrible blow that would be to his mother, who had lost her other sons at the front and was waiting for him, her last son, to return! Such were the thoughts that ran through his mind as he lay amidst the sad, oppressive silence of the ward, listening to the angry twang of the mattress springs under Kukushkin's restless body, to the sighs of the silent tankman, and to Stepan Ivanovich, bent almost double, standing at the window, where he spent most of the day, drumming his fingers on the window-pane.

"Amputate? No! Anything but that! Far better to die.... What a cold, frightful word: 'amputate'—sounds like a dagger thrust. Amputate? Never! That must not be!" thought Alexei. He dreamed of this frightful word in the shape of a great steel spider, tearing at his flesh with sharp, crooked claws.

3

For a week the inmates of number forty-two lived four in the ward. But one day Klavdia Mikhailovna, looking worried, came in accompanied by two orderlies, and told them that they would have to squeeze up a little. Stepan Ivanovich's bed was shifted right up to the window, to his great delight. Kukushkin's bed was shifted into the corner next to Stepan Ivanovich's, and in its place was put a nice, low bed with a soft spring mattress.

Kukushkin flew into a fit of rage at this. His face turned pale, he banged his fist on his bedside cupboard and in a high, squeaky voice abused the nurse, the hospital and even Vasily Vasilyevich, threatened to complain to somebody or other, and let himself go to such an extent that he nearly threw a mug at poor Klavdia Mikhailovna, and would have done so had not Alexei, his gypsy eyes flashing fiercely, pulled him up with a stern ejaculation.

Just at that moment the fifth patient was brought in.

He must have been of great weight, for the stretcher creaked and bent heavily in rhythm with the footsteps of the stretcher-bearers. A round, clean-shaven head rolled helplessly from side to side on the pillow. The broad, bloated, waxen face seemed lifeless. The full, pale lips bore a fixed expression of suffering.

It looked as though the new patient was unconscious; but as soon as the stretcher was placed on the floor he opened his eyes, rose up on his elbow, looked round the ward with curiosity, winked at Stepan Ivanovich for some reason, as much as to say: "How's life, not so bad?" and gave a deep cough. Evidently his heavy body was severely battered and he was in great pain. At the first glance Meresyev did not, for some reason, like the look of this big bloated figure, and it was with unfriendly eyes that he watched the two orderlies, two ward maids and the nurse jointly lift him from the stretcher and place him on the bed. They awkwardly jerked his stiff, log-like legs, and Alexei saw the face of the new patient suddenly grow pallid and break out in beads of perspiration, and he saw the wince of pain that crossed his lips. But the patient uttered not a sound; he merely ground his teeth.

As soon as he found himself on the bed, he smoothed the end of the top sheet over his blanket, piled the books and notebooks he had brought with him in neat stacks on top of his bedside cupboard, carefully laid out his tooth-paste and brush, eau-de-Cologne, shaving tackle and soap-box on the lower shelf, ran a critical eye over his handiwork, and then, as if feeling at home at once, said in a deep, rolling voice:

"Well, let's get acquainted. Regimental Commissar Semyon Vorobyov. Quiet. Non-smoker. Please, take me into your company."

He looked round at his wardmates with calm interest, and Meresyev managed to catch the sharp, critical glance of his keen, narrow, golden eyes.

"I will not be among you long. I don't know about the others, but I haven't much time to lie around here. My troopers are waiting for me. When the ice goes and the road's dry—I'm off! 'We're the Red Army Cavalry....' What?" he chattered, filling the ward with his cheerful, rolling bass voice.

"None of us is here for long. As soon as the ice breaks—we'll all be off—feet first, into ward number fifty," snapped Kukushkin, and abruptly turned to the wall.

There was no ward number fifty in the hospital. That was the name the patients had given to the mortuary. It is doubtful whether the Commissar had already heard this, but he at once caught the sinister meaning of the jest. He did not take offence, however; he merely looked at Kukushkin in surprise and inquired:

"And how old are you, my friend? Ah, greybeard, greybeard! You seem to have aged rather early!"

4

The appearance in ward number forty-two of the new patient, the Commissar, as they called him among themselves, changed the entire life of the ward. By the second day of his presence in it, this heavy and seriously wounded man had made friends with them all and, as Stepan Ivanovich put it later, had managed "to find a key to fit each one's heart".

With Stepan Ivanovich he talked to his heart's content about horses and hunting, of which both were very fond, and on which both were experts. With Meresyev, who was fond of philosophising about war, he argued vigorously about present-day methods of employing aircraft, tanks and cavalry, and tried to prove, not without some heat, that while, of course, aircraft and tanks were very useful, the horse was not obsolete and would yet demonstrate its usefulness, and that if the cavalry were well remounted, and supported by tanks and artillery, and if a large number of bold and intelligent young officers were trained to assist the old veteran commanders, our cavalry would yet surprise the world. He even found subjects for conversation with the silent tankman. It turned out that the division in which he had served as Commissar had fought at Yartsevo and later had taken part in General Konev's counter-attack at Dukhovshchina, where the tankman and his group had broken through the German lines. And the Commissar enthusiastically enumerated the villages they both knew, related how hot they had made it for the Germans, and where. The tankman kept silent, as usual, but he did not turn his head away when spoken to as he had done hitherto. His face could not be seen because of the bandages, but he nodded his head in agreement. Kukushkin's anger was converted into good humour the moment the Commissar invited him to play a game of chess. The chess-board was placed on Kukushkin's bed and the Commissar played "blindfold", lying on his bed with his eyes shut. He beat the grumbling, grousing lieutenant hands down, and thereby rose immensely in the latter's estimation.

The effect of the Commissar's appearance in the ward was like the fresh, moist air of the early Moscow spring that blew into the ward in the morning when the maid opened the windows, and when the oppressive silence of the sick-room was broken by the invasion of the many noises of the street. It cost the Commissar no effort to rouse this animation. He was simply full of life, boisterous, bubbling life, and forgot, or forced himself to forget, the torments caused by pain.

When he woke in the morning he sat up in bed and did his "jerks"—stretched both arms above his head, bent his body first to one side and then to the other, and rhythmically bent and turned his head. When water was taken round for washing, he insisted on having his as cold as possible, splashed and snorted over the bowl for a long time and then rubbed himself down with his towel with such vigour that his swollen body turned red; and watching him, the other patients longed to do the same. When the newspapers were brought in he eagerly snatched them from the nurse's hand and hurriedly read the communiqué of the Soviet Information Bureau, and after that calmly and slowly read the reports of the war correspondents from the different fronts. He had a way of his own in reading, which might be called "active reading". At one moment he would repeat in a whisper a passage in a report that pleased him and mutter "that's right", and mark the passage; or suddenly he would exclaim: "He's lying, the son of a bitch! I bet my head to a beer bottle he was not near the place. The rascal! And yet he writes!" One day he got so angry over something a highly imaginative war correspondent had written that he at once wrote a postcard to the newspaper stating in irate terms that such things don't and can't happen in war, and requesting that some restraint be put on this "unmitigated liar". At other times a report would set him thinking; he would lean back against his pillow with open eyes, lost in reflection, or else would tell some interesting story about his cavalry unit, every man of which, if he was to be believed, was a hero, "a downright brave lad". And then he would start reading again. And strange as it may seem, these remarks of his, these lyrical digressions, did not divert the attention of his listeners, but, on the contrary, helped them better to understand what he read.

For two hours a day, between dinner and the medical treatments, he studied German, learnt words by heart, constructed sentences and sometimes, suddenly struck by the sounds of the foreign words, he would say:

"Do you know what 'chicken' is in German, boys? *'Küchelchen'*. That sounds nice. You know, it gives you the impression of something tiny, fluffy and tender. And do you know what 'little bell' is? *'Glöckling'*. There's a tinkle in that word, isn't there?"

One day Stepan Ivanovich, unable to restrain himself, inquired:

"What do you want to learn German for, Comrade Commissar? You're only tiring yourself uselessly. It would be better if you saved your strength...."

The Commissar looked at the old soldier slyly and said:

"Ekh, you greybeard! Is this a life for a Russian? In what language will I talk to the German girls in Berlin when we get there? In Russian?"

Sitting on the edge of the Commissar's bed, Stepan Ivanovich wanted, quite reasonably, to answer that for the time being the fighting line was running not far from Moscow and that it was still a long way to the German girls, but there was such a ring of cheerful confidence in the Commissar's voice that the old soldier coughed and answered seriously:

"No, not in Russian, of course. But still, Comrade Commissar, you ought to take care of yourself after what you have gone through."

"The pampered horse is the first to come a cropper. Haven't you heard that before? It's bad advice you're giving me, greybeard."

None of the patients in the ward had a beard, but for some reason the Commissar called them all "greybeards", and there was nothing offensive about the way he said it; on the contrary, it had a ring of kindly humour and the patients felt soothed by it.

Alexei watched the Commissar for days on end, trying to fathom the source of his inexhaustible cheerfulness. There could be no doubt that he was enduring frightful suffering. As soon as he fell asleep and lost control of himself he began to moan, throw himself about and grind his teeth, while his face was contorted with pain. Evidently, he was aware of this and tried not to sleep in the day-time, he always found something to do. But when awake he was always calm and even-tempered, as if he suffered no pain at all. He talked leisurely with the surgeons, cracked jokes when the latter tapped and examined the injured parts of his body, and only by the way his hand crumpled his bed sheet and by the beads of perspiration that broke out on the bridge of his nose was it possible to guess how difficult it was for him to restrain himself. The airman could not understand how this man could suppress such frightful pain and muster such energy, cheerfulness and vivacity. Alexei was all the more keen on solving this riddle, for in spite of the increasing doses of drug that he was getting he could no longer sleep at night, and sometimes lay with open eyes until morning, biting his blanket to suppress his groans.

More and more often and persistently during the surgeon's inspection he heard the sinister word "amputate". Feeling that the frightful day was approaching, Alexei decided that without feet life would not be worth living.

5

And that day came. On one of his visits, Vasily Vasilyevich stood for a long time tapping Alexei's livid and totally insensitive feet and then, abruptly straightening his back and looking straight into Alexei's eyes, he said: "They must come off!" And before the airman, turning deathly pale, could utter a word, the professor repeated sternly: "They must come off! Not another word, do you hear? Otherwise you are done for! Do you understand me?"

He stalked out of the ward without even glancing at his retinue. An oppressive silence filled the ward. Meresyev lay with petrified face and wide-open eyes. Hovering before him, as if in a mist, were the livid, unsightly stumps of the old ferryman, and again he saw the latter crawling on the sand into the river like a monkey.

"Alexei," the Commissar called him softly.

"What?" answered Alexei in a distant, absent voice.

"You've got to, my boy."

In that instant it seemed to Alexei that it was not the ferryman but he himself who was crawling on stumps, and that his girl, his Olya, was standing on the sandy riverside in a bright-coloured frock blown about by the wind, light, radiant and beautiful, gazing at him intently and biting her lips. That's how it will be! And he broke into a fit of convulsive, silent weeping, burying his face in his pillow. Everybody in the ward was deeply affected. Stepan Ivanovich, grunting and groaning, got out of his bed, put on his robe and, shuffling his slippered feet and holding on to the bed rails, hobbled towards Alexei's bed, but the Commissar held up a warning finger, as much as to say: "Don't interfere. Let him have a good cry."

And indeed, Alexei felt better after that. Soon he calmed down and even felt that relief a man always feels when he has, at last, settled a question that had been tormenting him for a long time. He uttered not a word until the evening, when the orderlies came to take him to the operating theatre. Nor did he utter a word in that dazzling white room. Even when he was told that the state of his heart would not permit his being put to sleep and that the operation would have to be performed under a local anaesthesia, he only nodded. During the operation he uttered neither a groan nor a cry. Several times Vasily Vasilyevich, who performed the simple operation himself and, as usual, growled angrily at the nurses and assistants, looked anxiously at the assistant who was watching Alexei's pulse.

When the bones were sawn the pain was frightful; but Alexei was now accustomed to bear pain, and he did not even understand what these people in white robes and with faces masked with white gauze were doing at his feet. When he was being carried back to the ward, however, he lost consciousness.

The first thing he saw when he came to was the sympathetic face of Klavdia Mikhailovna. Strangely enough, he remembered nothing, and he even wondered why the face of this good-looking, kind-hearted, fair-haired woman looked anxious and inquiring. Seeing that he had opened his eyes, her face beamed and she softly pressed his hand under the blanket.

"You've been simply splendid," she said, and at once took his wrist to feel his pulse.

"What's she talking about?" Alexei wondered. Then he felt a pain higher up the leg than before, and it was not the former burning, tearing, throbbing pain, but a dull ache, as if cords had been tied tightly below his knees. Suddenly he realised from the folds of the blanket that his body was shorter than it had been before, and in a flash he remembered: the dazzling white room, Vasily Vasilyevich's fierce growling, the dull thuds in the enamelled pail. "Already?" he wondered rather listlessly, and said to the nurse with a forced smile:

"It looks as though I have grown shorter."

It was a wry smile, more like a grimace. Klavdia Mikhailovna gently smoothed his hair and said:

"Never mind, dear, you'll feel easier now."

"Yes. Less weight to carry."

"Don't! Don't say that, dear! But you really have been splendid. Some shout, and some even have to be strapped down. But you did not make a sound. Oh, this horrible war!"

At this the angry voice of the Commissar was heard in the evening twilight:

"Stop your wailing, now! Give him these letters, nurse. Some fellows are lucky. Makes me envious. Fancy getting so many letters all at once!"

The Commissar handed Meresyev a batch of letters. They were from Alexei's wing; they bore different dates, but for some reason had been delivered at the same time. And now, lying with his feet amputated, Alexei read these friendly messages which told him of a life, far away, full of arduous labour, hardships and dangers, which drew him like a magnet, but which was now lost to him for ever. He eagerly read the big news and the minor events they wrote to him about from his wing: that a political officer at Corps Headquarters had let it drop that the wing had been recommended for the Order of the Red Banner; that Ivanchuk had received two awards at once; that Yashin had gone out hunting and had killed a fox, which for some reason proved to be without a tail, and that Styopa Rostov had a gumboil, and this had spoiled his love affair with Lenochka—all this was to him of equal interest. For an instant his mind carried him to the airfield hidden in the forest which the airmen cursed because of the treacherous ground, and which seemed to him now to be the best spot on earth.

He was so absorbed with the contents of the letters that he did not notice the different dates, nor did he catch the Commissar winking to the nurse and pointing in his direction as he whispered to her: "My medicine is better than all your barbitals and veronals." Alexei never learned that, foreseeing this contingency, the Commissar had withheld some letters from him in order to mitigate the terrible blow by letting him read the friendly greetings and news from his beloved airfield. The Commissar was an old soldier. He knew the value of these hurriedly and carelessly written scraps of paper, which, at the front, are sometimes more precious than medicine or bread.

The letter from Andrei Degtyarenko, simple and rugged, like himself, contained a small note written in a tiny, curly hand and bristling with exclamation marks. It read:

"Comrade Senior Lieutenant! It is too bad of you that you do not keep your promise!!! In the wing they often mention you; I'm not telling a lie, all they do is talk about you. A little while ago the Wing Commander said in the dining-room: 'Now Alexei Meresyev, he is a man!!!' You know yourself that he talks in that way only about the very best. *Come back soon, everybody is expecting you!!!* Big Lyolya from the dining-room asks me to say that she won't argue any more and will give you three helpings of the second course at dinner, even if she loses her job for it. It's too bad, though, that you don't keep your promise!!! You have written to the others, but you have not written to me. I feel very hurt about it, and that is why I am not sending you a separate letter. But please write to me—in a separate letter—and tell me how you are, and all about yourself! . . ."

At the end of this amusing note there was the signature:

"The meteorological sergeant." Meresyev smiled, but his eye again caught the words: "come back soon, everybody is expecting you", which were underlined. He sat up in his bed and with the air of one who is searching in his pockets and finds that he has lost an important document, he groped convulsively in the place where his feet had been. His hand touched empty space.

Only in that instant did Alexei fully realise the gravity of his loss. He would never return to the wing, to the Air Force, to the front. He would never again go up in a plane and hurl himself into an air battle, *never!* He was now disabled, deprived of his beloved occupation, pinned to one spot, a burden at home, unwanted in life. And this would go on until the end of his days.

6

After the operation the worst that can happen to a man in such circumstances happened to Alexei Meresyev —he withdrew into himself. He did not complain, he did not weep, he was never irritable. He just kept silent.

For whole days he lay motionless on his back, his eyes concentrated on the winding crack in the ceiling. When his wardmates spoke to him he answered "yes" or "no", often inappropriately, and fell silent again, staring at a dark crack in the plaster as if it were a hieroglyph, the deciphering of which meant salvation for him. He obediently carried out all the doctor's orders, took everything he prescribed for him, ate his dinner listlessly, without zest, and stretched out on his back again.

"Hey, greybeard!" the Commissar called. "What are you thinking about?"

Alexei turned his head in the Commissar's direction and looked at him with a blank stare as if he did not see him.

"What are you thinking about, I'm asking you?"

"Nothing."

One day Vasily Vasilyevich came into the ward and asked him in his customary bluff manner:

"Well, crawler, are you alive? How's things? You are a hero, a hero, I say. You didn't even murmur. Now I can believe that you crawled on all fours for eighteen days, getting away from the Germans. I have operated on more people in my time than the number of potatoes you've eaten, but I've never operated on a fellow like you." The professor rubbed his hands; they were red and peeling and the finger-nails were corroded. "What are you scowling for? I praise him, but he scowls! I am a lieutenant-general in the Medical Corps. I order you to smile!"

Stretching his lips with difficulty into a vacant, rubber smile, Meresyev thought: "If I knew it would end like this, I wouldn't have taken the trouble to crawl. I had three bullets left in my pistol."

In one of the newspapers the Commissar read a war correspondent's description of an interesting battle. Six of our fighter planes engaged twenty-two German planes, brought down eight and lost only one. The Commissar read this story with such zest that one would have thought that it was not airmen he did not know, but his own cavalrymen, that had distinguished themselves. Even Kukushkin showed enthusiasm in the argument that ensued, when each tried to picture how it had all happened. But Alexei lay and thought: "Lucky fellows, they are flying and fighting, but I will never go up again."

The communiqués of the Soviet Information Bureau became more and more laconic. All the signs went to show that somewhere in the rear of the Soviet Army a mighty force was being mustered for another blow. The Commissar and Stepan Ivanovich gravely discussed where that blow would be struck and what effect it would have upon the Germans. Only recently Alexei had led conversations like that; now he tried not to listen to them. He too sensed the approach of big developments of gigantic and, perhaps, decisive battles. But the thought that his comrades, probably even Kukushkin who was rapidly recovering, would take part in those battles, while he was doomed to vegetate in the rear, that nothing could be done about it, was so bitter to him that when the Commissar read the newspaper, or when a conversation about the war commenced, Alexei covered his head with his blanket and rubbed his cheeks on his pillow in order not to see and not to hear. And for some reason the familiar line from Maxim Gorky's *Song of the Falcon* kept running through his mind: "Those who are born to creep cannot fly."

Klavdia Mikhailovna brought in a few sprigs of pussy-willow—how they got into stern, wartime, barricaded Moscow heaven knows—and placed a sprig in a glass at each bedside. The reddish sprigs and white, fluffy bolls smelt so fresh that it seemed as though spring itself had come into ward forty-two. Everybody that day felt joy and animation. Even the silent tankman mumbled a few words through his bandages.

Alexei lay and reflected: In Kamyshin, turbid streams are running down the muddy sidewalks into the glistening, cobble-stoned road, there is a smell of warmed earth, fresh dampness and horse dung. It was on a day like this that he and Olya had stood on the steep bank of the Volga and the ice had floated smoothly past them on the limitless expanse of the river amidst a solemn silence, broken only by the silver, bell-like strains of the larks. And it had seemed as though it was not the ice that was floating with the stream, but he and Olya, who were noiselessly floating to meet a stormy, choppy river. They had stood there without saying a word, dreaming dreams of such future happiness that in that spot overlooking the wide expanse of the Volga, in the freely blowing breezes of the spring, they had struggled for breath. Those dreams would never come true, now. She will turn away from him. And even if she does not, can he accept this sacrifice, can he permit her, so bright and fair and graceful, to walk by his side while he hobbled along on stumps?... And he begged the nurse to remove the naive harbinger of spring from his bedside.

The sprig of willow was removed, but he could not so easily rid himself of his bitter reflections: What will Olya say when she learns that he has lost his feet? Will she leave him, obliterate him from her life? His whole being protested against this. No! She is not like that! She will not throw him up, will not turn away from him! But that would be even worse. He pictured to himself her marrying him from an impulse of her noble heart, marrying him, a cripple, and for his sake giving up her dream of a higher technical education, harnessing herself to office drudgery to keep herself, a crippled husband and, perhaps, who knows, even children.

Had he the right to accept such a sacrifice? They were not bound to each other yet, they were engaged, but not yet husband and wife. He loved her, loved her dearly, and therefore decided that he had no such right, that he himself must sever their ties, at once, at one stroke, in order to save her not only from a burdensome future, but also from the torments of a present dilemma.

But then a letter arrived bearing the Kamyshin postmark, and it upset all these decisions. It was a letter from Olya, and every line breathed anxiety. As if labouring under a foreboding of disaster, she wrote that she would remain with him for ever, no matter what happened to him, that she lived only for him, that her thoughts were with him every spare moment, and that these thoughts helped her to bear the hardships of war-time, the sleepless nights at the saw-mill, the digging of trenches and tank ditches on free days and nights, and, why conceal it, her existence of semi-starvation. "That last small photograph you had taken, sitting on a tree stump with a dog and smiling, is always with me. I have put it in Mother's locket and wear it round my neck. When I feel depressed I open the locket and look at you... I believe that as long as we love each other, we need fear nothing." She also wrote that his mother had been very anxious about him lately, and again urged him to write to the old lady more often, but not to disquiet her with bad news.

These letters from home had always been a happy event, an event that had warmed his heart amidst the hardships of life at the front; but now, for the first time, they gave him no joy. They made his heart heavier and he committed the blunder that caused him so much torment later: he dared not write home to say that his feet had been amputated.

The only one he wrote to in detail about his misfortune and about his joyless reflections, was the girl at the meteorological station. They were scarcely acquainted, and it was therefore easier to tell her about these things. Not knowing her name, he addressed his letters to her as follows: "F.P.O. so-and-so, Meteorological Station, for the 'meteorological sergeant'." He knew what value was attached to letters at the front and hoped that his would reach even this strange address sooner or later. Even if they did not, it would not matter, he simply wanted to give expression to his feelings.

Alexei Meresyev spent his monotonous days at the hospital in bitter reflection. And although his iron constitution had borne the skilfully performed amputation easily and the wounds healed quickly, he grew perceptibly weaker, and in spite of all the measures taken to counteract this, everybody saw that he was pining away and wasting more and more every day.

7

Meanwhile, spring was surging outside.
It forced itself into ward forty-two, into this room that reeked of iodoform. It came through the window, bringing the cool, humid breath of melting snow, the excited twittering of the sparrows, the merry, ringing whoop of the street-cars as they turned the corner, the resounding footsteps on the now snow-free asphalt and, in the evening—the low, monotonous strains of an accordion. It peeped through the side window out of which could be seen a sunlit branch of a poplar-tree on which longish buds covered with a yellowish gum were swelling. It came into the ward in the form of the golden freckles on the kind, pale face of Klavdia Mikhailovna, defying every type of face powder, and causing the nurse no little annoyance. It persistently drew attention to itself by the merry drumming of heavy drops of moisture on the tin-covered outside windowsills.

As always, the spring softened hearts and awakened dreams.

"Ah, it would be nice to be in some forest clearing with a gun now, wouldn't it, Stepan Ivanovich?" mused the Commissar longingly. "To lie in wait for game, in a shack, at dawn ... can anything be nicer? You know—the rosy dawn, crisp and a little frosty, and you are sitting there. Suddenly—gl-gl-gl, and the flutter of wings—few-few-few.... And it perches over your head—tail spread out like a fan—and then comes a second, and a third...."

Stepan Ivanovich heaved a deep sigh and made a sucking noise as if his mouth were watering, but the Commissar went on indulging in his dream:

"And then you light a fire, spread out your cape, make some nice, fragrant tea with a smoky taste, and just a nip of vodka to warm every muscle of your body, eh? After your honest labours...."

"Oh, don't talk about it, Comrade Commissar!" answered Stepan Ivanovich. "Do you know the kind of hunting we get in our parts at this time of the year? For pike! You wouldn't believe it, but it's true. Haven't you heard about it? It's good fun, and, of course, you can make a bit of money, too. As soon as the ice breaks on the lake and the rivers overflow, they all swarm to the banks, on to the grass and moss which the spring waters have covered. They get into the grass and cast their spawn. You walk along the bank and you see what looks like sunken logs, but it's pike! You bang away with your gun. Sometimes you get so many that you can't stuff them all into your bag, I give you my word!..."

And an interchange of hunters' reminiscences would begin. Imperceptibly the conversation would veer round to the war and they wondered what was doing just now in the division, or in the company, whether the dugouts made in the winter were "weeping", or whether the fortifications were "creeping", and how the Germans were getting on, considering that in the West they were accustomed to asphalt roads.

After dinner they fed the sparrows. This was a form of amusement that Stepan Ivanovich had invented. He was unable to sit idle and was always doing something with his thin, restless hands. One day he suggested that the crumbs left over from dinner be scattered on the outside windowsill for the birds. This became a custom, and it was not only leftover crumbs they threw out of the window; they deliberately left slices of bread and crumbled them, so that a whole flock of sparrows was "put on the ration list", as Stepan Ivanovich expressed it. It gave all the inmates of the ward immense pleasure to watch the small, noisy creatures pecking away at a large crust, chirping and quarrelling, and, after cleaning up the windowsill, perching and preening themselves on the bough of the poplar, and then, with a whir of their wings, flying off to attend to their particular affairs.

Feeding the sparrows became a favourite pastime. The patients began to recognise some of the birds and even gave them names. A favourite among them was a stub-tailed, impudent, brisk little fellow that had probably lost its tail as a result of its pugnacious habits. Stepan Ivanovich named it "Submachine-Gunner".

It is an interesting fact that it was precisely this amusement with these noisy little creatures that drew the tankman out of his moroseness. When he first saw Stepan Ivanovich, bent almost double and supporting himself on his crutches, trying to get on to the radiator to reach the open ventilating pane, he watched him listlessly and with little interest. But next day, when the sparrows came flying to the window, he, wincing with pain, even sat up in bed to get a better view of the fussy little creatures. The day after that he saved a good piece of pie from his dinner, evidently believing that this hospital titbit would be particularly welcome to the vociferous cadgers. One day "Submachine-Gunner" failed to turn up and Kukushkin surmised that a cat had gobbled it up, an that it served it right. The morose tankman flared up and called Kukushkin a "grouser", and when, on the following day, the stub-tailed sparrow did turn up and again chirped and fought on the windowsill, cocking its head and flashing its impudent, beady eyes triumphantly, the tankman burst out laughing; it was his first laugh for many months.

After a little time Gvozdev brightened up completely. To everybody's surprise he turned out to be a cheerful, talkative chap, easy to get on with. This was the Commissar's doing, of course, for he was a past master at finding a key to fit every heart, as Stepan Ivanovich put it. And this is the way he did it.

The happiest hour in ward forty-two was when Klavdia Mikhailovna appeared at the door with a mysterious look on her face and her hands behind her back and, scanning each inmate with beaming eyes, inquired:

"Well, who's going to dance today?"

That meant that the mail had arrived. Before handing the lucky recipients their letters, Klavdia Mikhailovna made them jerk in their beds, if only a little, in imitation of a dance. Most often it was the Commissar who was obliged to do this, for sometimes he received as many as ten letters at a time. He received letters from his division, from the rear, from his fellow-officers, from privates, from fellow-officers' wives, writing for old time's sake, or requesting him to "pull up" husbands who had got out of hand, from the widows of fellow-officers who had been killed in action, asking for advice or assistance in arranging their affairs, and even from a Young Pioneer in Kazakhstan, the daughter of a regimental commander who had been killed in action, a girl whose name he could never remember. He read all these letters with the greatest interest and scrupulously answered them all; and he also wrote to the competent authority requesting assistance for the wife of Commander So-and-so, to the husband who had "got out of hand", giving him a good wigging, to a house manager, threatening to come himself and "screw his head off" if he did not put a stove into the apartment occupied by the family of Commander So-and-so who was at the front, and to the girl in Kazakhstan with the difficult name he could not remember, chiding her for getting bad marks for grammar in the second quarter.

Stepan Ivanovich too conducted a lively correspondence with the front and the rear. He received letters from his sons, who were also successful snipers, and letters from his daughter, a team-leader in her collective farm, containing innumerable greetings from all relatives and acquaintances and informing him that although the collective farm had sent more people on new construction jobs, such and such plans had been overfulfilled by so many per cent. These letters Stepan Ivanovich gladly read aloud the moment he received them, and the whole ward, all the ward maids, nurses and even the house surgeon, a dry, jaundiced fellow, were kept regulary informed about his family affairs.

Even unsociable Kukushkin, who seemed to be at loggerheads with the whole world, received letters from his mother, who lived somewhere in Barnaul. He would snatch the letter out of the nurse's hand, wait until everybody in the ward was asleep and then read it, whispering the words to himself. During those moments his harsh features softened and his face assumed a mild and solemn expression that was totally alien to his nature. He dearly loved his mother, an old village doctor, but for some reason he was ashamed of this sentiment and did his best to conceal it.

The tankman was the only one who did not share those joyous moments when a lively interchange of news was going on in the ward. He became gloomier than ever, turned to the wall and pulled his blanket over his head. He had nobody to write to him. The larger the number of letters the ward received, the more acutely he felt his loneliness. But one day Klavdia Mikhailovna appeared at the door with her face beaming even more than usual. Trying to keep her eyes away from the Commissar she said hurriedly:

"Well, who's going to dance today?"

She looked towards the tankman's bed and her kindly face lit up with a broad smile. Everybody felt that something extraordinary had happened. The ward was tense with expectation.

"Lieutenant Gvozdev, it's your turn to dance. Now then, step it out."

Meresyev saw Gvozdev give a start and turn round sharply, and he saw his eyes flash through the slits in his bandages. Gvozdev at once restrained himself, however, and said in a trembling voice which he tried to lend a tone of indifference:

"It's a mistake. There must be another Gvozdev in the next ward." But his eyes looked eagerly, hungrily towards three letters which the nurse held up high, like a flag.

"No! There's no mistake," said the nurse. "Look! 'Lieutenant G. M. Gvozdev', and even the number of the ward: forty-two. Well?"

A bandaged hand darted from under the blanket. It trembled while the lieutenant put a letter to his mouth and convulsively tore the envelope open with his teeth. His eyes flashed with excitement. A strange thing! Three girl friends, medical students of the same year, at the same university, in different handwriting and in different words, wrote approximately the same thing. On learning that Lieutenant Gvozdev, the hero tankman, was lying wounded in Moscow, they had decided to enter into correspondence with him. They wrote that, if the lieutenant was not offended by their importunity, would he not write and tell them how he was getting on? And one of them, who signed herself Anyuta, wrote, asking whether she could be of assistance to him in any way, did he need any good books, and if he did need anything, he was not to hesitate and ask her for it.

All day long the lieutenant turned those letters over and over, read the addresses and scrutinised the handwriting. He was, of course, aware that correspondence of this kind was carried on and had himself once conducted such with an unknown correspondent, a kindly note from whom he had found in the thumb of a pair of woollen mittens he had received as a holiday gift. But this correspondence ceased of its own accord when his correspondent sent him a jesting note with a photograph of herself, a middle-aged woman, with four children. But this was something different. The only thing that perplexed and surprised him was that the arrival of these letters was unexpected, and they had all come together. And another thing he could not understand was: how did these medical students get to know about his activities in the war? The whole ward wondered about this, and most of all the Commissar. But Meresyev caught the significant glances he exchanged with Stepan Ivanovich and the nurse, and guessed that he was at the bottom of it.

Be that as it may, next morning Gvozdev asked the Commissar for some writing paper and without waiting for permission unbandaged his right hand and wrote till the evening, crossing out lines, crumpling the letter and starting a new one, until, at last, he composed replies to his unknown correspondents.

Two of the girls soon stopped writing, but kind-hearted Anyuta continued to write for the three of them. Gvozdev was a man of communicative disposition and now the whole ward knew what was going on at the third-year course of the medical department of the university, what a thrilling subject biology was and how dull organic chemistry, what nice voice the professor had and how well he presented his subject, what a bore lecturer So-and-so was, how much firewood the students had loaded on to the freight street-cars at the last voluntary-aid Sunday, how hard it is to combine study with work at the base hospital, and about the "airs" a certain stupid student, not a nice girl at all, gave herself.

Gvozdev not only began to talk. He seemed to blossom out and was soon well on the road towards recovery.

Kukushkin had his splints removed. Stepan Ivanovich was learning to walk without crutches and could already move about fairly upright. He now spent whole days at the window, watching what was going on in the "wide world". Only the Commissar and Meresyev grew steadily worse as the days passed by. This was particularly the case with the Commissar. He could no longer do his morning jerks. His body assumed a sinister, yellowish, almost transparent bloatedness. He bent his arms with difficulty and he could no longer hold a pencil or a spoon.

In the morning the ward maid washed him and fed him, and one could see that it was not the severe pain but this helplessness that was depressing and tormenting him most. But he did not become despondent. His bass boomed just as cheerfully as before, he read the newspapers with his former zest and even continued to study German; but he was no longer able to hold his books when reading, so Stepan Ivanovich made him a book-rest out of wire and fixed it over his bed, and he would sit at his bedside to turn the pages over for him. In the morning, before the newspapers came, the Commissar would eagerly ask the nurse what the last communiqué was, what news had been given over the radio, what the weather was like, and what was heard in Moscow. He obtained Vasily Vasilyevich's permission to have a radio set extension fixed at his bedside.

It seemed as though the feebler his body grew the stronger became his spirit. He continued to read the numerous letters he received with unflagging interest and to answer them, dictating to Kukushkin and to Gvozdev in turn. One day Meresyev was dozing after taking some treatment, but was aroused by the Commissar's thundering bass voice.

On the wire book-rest over his bed lay a copy of the divisional newspaper which, in spite of the stamped order: "Not to be taken away", somebody sent him regularly.

"Have they gone crazy out there, or what, while on the defensive?" he roared. "Kravtsov a bureaucrat? The best veterinary surgeon in the army a bureaucrat? Grisha, take this down at once."

And he dictated to Gvozdev an irate letter to a member of the Army Military Council requesting that restraint be put on the newspapermen who had undeservedly thrown discredit upon a good and zealous officer. He continued to scold "those pen-pushers" even after he had given the nurse the letter to post, and it was strange to hear those words of passion from a man who could not even turn his head on his pillow.

That evening something more remarkable happened. In that quiet hour when the lights were not yet on and the shadows were beginning to darken in the corners of the room, Stepan Ivanovich was sitting at the window, thoughtfully gazing at the embankment. Some women in canvas aprons were cutting ice on the river. They hacked long strips of ice with crow-bars from the edge of a dark, square ice hole, broke the strips into oblong blocks with one or two strokes of their bars, and then, with the aid of boat-hooks, dragged these blocks up the wooden boards out of the water. The blocks lay in rows—greenish and transparent below and yellow and crumbling on top. A long train of sleighs, tied one behind the other, trailed along the river-bank to where the ice was being cut. An old man wearing an ear-flapped cap, wadded trousers and a coat of the same kind girdled with a belt from which hung an axe, led the horses to where the ice was lying, and the women loaded the ice blocks on the sleighs.

Stepan Ivanovich's experienced eye told him that the work was being done by a collective-farm team but was badly organised. There were too many people on the job and they only got into each other's way. A plan of operations arose in his practical mind. He mentally divided the team into groups of three—enough to drag the ice blocks out of the water without difficulty. He then assigned each group to a definite section and fixed the pay not at a round sum for the whole team, but for each group separately, according to the number of blocks they hauled. He saw an active, round-faced, rosy-cheeked young woman in the team and he mentally suggested to her that she should initiate socialist emulation among the groups.... He was so absorbed in his reflections that he did not see one of the horses go so near to the edge of the ice hole that its hind legs slipped, and it fell into the water. The weight of the sleigh kept the horse on the surface, but the swiftness of the current was pulling it under the ice. The old man with the axe fussed helplessly, now dragging at the rail of the sleigh and now tugging at the horse's bridle.

Stepan Ivanovich gasped and shouted at the top of his voice: "The horse is drowning!"

The Commissar, with an incredible effort, his face going ashen-grey from pain, rose up on his elbow and, leaning his chest on the windowsill, looked out and whispered: "The blockhead! Doesn't he understand? The traces!... Cut the traces! The horse will get out by itself. Oh! He'll kill the beast!"

Clumsily, Stepan Ivanovich clambered on to the windowsill. The horse was drowning. The turbid water was already splashing over it, but it was making desperate efforts to get out and dug its iron-shod forehoofs into the edge of the ice.

"Cut the traces!" shouted the Commissar, as if the old man on the river could hear him.

Stepan Ivanovich made a megaphone with his hands and through the ventilating pane shouted the Commissar's advice across the street:

"Hey! Old man! Cut the traces! You've got an axe in your belt—cut the traces, hack them!"

The old man heard this, what seemed to him, heaven-sent advice. He snatched the axe from his belt and cut the traces with a couple of strokes. Released from harness, the horse at once clambered on to the ice, stood away from the edge of the ice hole and, panting, shook itself like a dog.

"What's the meaning of this?" a voice demanded at this moment.

Vasily Vasilyevich, with his smock unbuttoned and without the white skull-cap he usually wore, was standing at the door. He flew into a towering rage, stamped his foot and would hear no explanations. He said the ward had gone mad, that he would send them all to the devil out of here, and went out panting and upbraiding everybody without having ascertained what had really happened. A few moments later Klavdia Mikhailovna came into the ward with tear-stained face and looking very much upset. She had just received a severe dressing-down from Vasily Vasilyevich, but she caught sight of the ashen-grey, lifeless face of the Commissar who was lying motionless with eyes shut, and rushed to him.

In the evening the Commissar felt very ill. They gave him an injection of camphor, and then they gave him oxygen, but he remained unconscious for a long time. The moment he came to, however, he tried to smile at Klavdia Mikhailovna, who was standing over him with the oxygen bag.

"Don't worry, nurse, I'll come back even from hell to bring you the stuff the devils use to get rid of freckles."

It was terrible to watch this big, powerful man growing feebler every day in the fierce struggle he was waging against his infirmity.

8

Meresyev too grew weaker with every passing day. In the next letter he wrote her, he even told the "meteorological sergeant", the only person to whom he now confided his grief, that he would probably not leave the hospital alive and that that would be for the best, for an airman without feet was like a bird without wings, which could still live and pick its food, but fly—never! He did not want to be a wingless bird and was prepared for the worst, if only it came soon. It was cruel to write like that, for in the course of their correspondence the girl had confessed that for a long time now she had not been indifferent to "Comrade Senior Lieutenant" and that if it had not been for his terrible blow she would never have disclosed her secret.

"She wants to get married. Men are at a premium now. What does she care about a fellow having feet or not as long as the pension is good," commented Kukushkin, as surly as ever.

But Alexei remembered the pale face pressing against his in that hour when death howled over their heads, and he knew that it was not as Kukushkin said. He knew too that it made the girl's heart ache to read his mournful confessions. Not even knowing the name of the "meteorological sergeant", he continued to confide his joyless reflections to her.

The Commissar was able to find a key to fit every heart, but so far he had not been able to find one to fit Meresyev's. On the day after he underwent his operation, Ostrovsky's *How the Steel Was Tempered* appeared in the ward. The book was read aloud. Alexei realised that this reading was meant for him, but the story brought him little comfort. Pavel Korchagin had been one of his boyhood heroes. "But Korchagin was not an airman," Alexei reflected now. "Did he know what 'yearning for the air' means? Ostrovsky did not write his books in bed at a time when all the men and many women of the country were fighting, when even snotty-nosed boys, standing on crates because they were not tall enough to reach the lathes, were turning shells."

To put it short, on this occasion the book was not a success. So the Commissar tried a flanking movement. Casually, he began to tell the story of another man whose legs were paralysed, and who held a big public post in spite of that. Stepan Ivanovich, who was interested in everything that happened in the world, gasped with astonishment, and remembered that where he came from there was a doctor who only had one arm, but was for all that the best doctor in the district, rode a horse, loved to go hunting and handled a gun so expertly that he could hit a squirrel in the eye. Here the Commissar recalled the late Academician Williams, whom he had known personally. That man was half paralysed, could use only one arm, and yet he directed the work of the Agricultural Institute and conducted research on a vast scale.

Meresyev listened and smiled: it is possible to think, to talk, to write, issue orders, heal people and even go hunting without legs, but he was an airman, a born airman, an airman since boyhood, from the day on which— when guarding the melon field where among the limp leaves on the cracked earth lay enormous striped melons that were famous all over Volga region—he heard, and then saw, a small silvery dragon-fly, its double wings glistening in the sun, gliding slowly over the dusty steppe somewhere in the direction of Stalingrad.

From that moment the dream of becoming an airman had never left him. His mind was filled with it during the lessons at school, and later, when he operated a lathe in a factory. At night, when everybody was asleep, he and the famous airman Lyapidevsky found and rescued the Chelyuskin expedition, and with Vodopyanov he landed heavy aircraft on the pack ice at the North Pole, and with Chkalov opened the unexplored air route to the United States across the Pole.

The Young Communist League sent him to the Far East and there he helped to build the city of youth in the taiga—Komsomolsk-on-the-Amur—but he carried his dream of flying even to that distant place. Among the builders of the city, he found young men and women like himself, who also dreamed of flying, and it was hard to believe that with their own hands they actually built an air club for themselves in that city, which in those days existed only in blueprints. In the evenings, when mist enveloped the huge construction project, the builders would withdraw into their barracks, close the windows and light smoky fires of damp twigs outside the doors to drive away the swarms of mosquitoes and gnats which filled the air with a sinister, high-pitched buzzing. At that hour, when all the other builders were resting after the day's labours, the members of the air club, led by Alexei, their bodies smeared with kerosene which was supposed to keep the mosquitoes and gnats away, went into the taiga with axes, picks, saws, spades and T.N.T. There they felled trees, blew up tree stumps and levelled the ground to win space from the taiga for an airfield. And they won this space, tearing several kilometres out of the virgin forest with their own hands.

It was from that airfield that Alexei soared into the air for the first time in a training craft, at last realising the dream of his boyhood.

Later, he studied at an army aviation school and became an instructor himself. He was at this school when the war broke out. In spite of the opposition of the school authorities he gave up his job and joined the army. His whole object in life, all his interests, joys, plans for the future, and all his successes were bound up with aviation.

And yet they talked to him about Williams.

"But Williams was not an airman," said Alexei, and turned to the wall.

But the Commissar persevered in his efforts to "unlock" him. One day, when he was in his usual stupor, Alexei heard the Commissar say:

"Lyosha! Read this. It's about you."

Stepan Ivanovich was already carrying the magazine to Meresyev. It contained a short article marked with a pencil. Alexei ran his eye down the page looking for his own name, but did not find it. It was an article about Russian airmen of the First World War. Gazing at him from the page of the magazine was the unknown face of a young officer with a short moustache twisted to fine points, and wearing a forage-cap with a white cockade on one side of his head so that it touched his ear.

"Read it, read it, it was written for you," the Commissar urged.

Meresyev read the article. It was about a Russian army airman, Lieutenant Valerian Karpovich, who was hit in the foot by a German dumdum bullet while flying over the enemy's lines. In spite of his shattered foot, he managed to take his "Farman" across the lines and land at his base. The foot was amputated, but the young officer wanted to stay in the army. He invented an artificial foot and had it made from his own designs. He trained perseveringly for a long time and, as a result, returned to the army towards the end of the war. He was appointed inspector at an army aviation school and, as was stated in the article, "sometimes risked a flight in his aircraft". He was awarded the officer's St. George Cross and successfully served in the Air Force until he was killed in a crash.

Meresyev read the article once, twice and a third time. The lean, young lieutenant with the tired but determined face gazed at him with a rather strained but, on the whole, gallant smile. Meanwhile, the entire ward tensely watched Alexei. He ran his fingers through his hair;

keeping his eyes glued to the magazine he groped for a pencil on his bedside cupboard and with deliberate strokes traced a square around the article.

"Have you read it?" inquired the Commissar with a sly look in his eyes. Alexei remained silent, his eyes still scanning the lines of the article. "Well, what do you say?"

"But he only lost a foot."

"But you are a Soviet airman."

"He flew a 'Farman'. It wasn't much of a plane. A whatnot, rather. It was simple to fly. No technique or speed was needed."

"But you are a Soviet airman!" the Commissar persisted.

"A Soviet airman," Alexei repeated mechanically, still staring at the article. Then his face lit up with some sort of an inner light and he looked at each of his fellow-patients in turn with eyes filled with joy and wonder.

That night Alexei put the magazine under his pillow and remembered that in childhood, when he climbed into the bunk he shared with his brothers, he used to hide in much the same way an ugly little Teddy bear his mother had made for him out of an old plush jacket. He laughed loudly at this recollection.

He did not sleep a wink that night. The ward was wrapped in heavy slumber. Gvozdev tossed about on his bed, causing the mattress springs to twang. Stepan Ivanovich snored with a whistle as if his insides were bursting to get out. Now and again the Commissar turned over, uttering a low groan through clenched teeth. But Alexei heard nothing. Every once in a while he pulled the magazine out from under his pillow and by the light of the night-lamp gazed at the smiling face of the lieutenant. "You had a hard job, but you pulled it off," he mused. "Mine is ten times harder, but I'll pull it off too, you'll see!"

In the middle of the night, the Commissar suddenly lay quite still. Alexei raised himself on his elbow and saw him lying pale and calm, seeming not to breathe. He seized the bell and rang furiously. Klavdia Mikhailovna ran into the ward, bare-headed, with sleepy eyes and her plait hanging down her back. A few moments later the house surgeon was called. He felt the Commissar's pulse, gave him a camphor injection and put the nozzle of the oxygen bag to his mouth. The surgeon and the nurse busied themselves around the patient for about an hour, seemingly without avail. At last the Commissar opened his eyes, smiled feebly, almost imperceptibly, at Klavdia Mikhailovna and said softly:

"I'm sorry I gave you all this trouble for nothing. I didn't reach hell, and haven't brought you the stuff for your freckles. So you will have to put up with them, my dear. It can't be helped."

The jest made everybody breathe with relief. A stout oak that man was, and perhaps he would withstand even such a storm as this. The house surgeon left the ward, the squeaking of his shoes slowly dying in the corridor, the ward maids also went away, and only Klavdia Mikhailovna remained. She sat sideways on the edge of the Commissar's bed. The patients fell asleep again, except for Meresyev, who lay with eyes shut, thinking of artificial feet that could be attached to the pedals of his aircraft, even if it were with straps. He remembered the instructor at the air club speak about a Civil War airman who had short legs and had small blocks of wood attached to the pedals of his machine in order to be able to reach them.

"I'll be as good as you, my lad," he kept on assuring Karpovich. And the words "I will fly, I will fly" rang joyously in his mind, driving away sleep. He lay quiet with his eyes shut. Looking at him, one might have thought that he was deep in slumber and smiling in his sleep.

And lying there, he heard a conversation which he later recalled on more than one occasion during difficult moments.

"Oh, but why do you behave like that? I think it is terrible to laugh and joke when you are in such pain. My heart freezes when I think of the suffering you are going through. Why don't you want to go into a separate ward?"

It sounded as though it was not the kind and pretty but seemingly passionless nurse Klavdia Mikhailovna who was speaking, but a woman, ardent and protesting, and her voice expressed grief and, perhaps, something else besides. Meresyev opened his eyes. In the light of the night-lamp that was shaded with a kerchief, he saw the Commissar's pale, swollen face against the background of his pillow, his kind, flashing eyes, and the soft, feminine profile of the nurse. The light falling against the back of her head made her soft, fair hair shine like a halo, and Meresyev, although conscious that this was not the right thing to do, could not tear his eyes away from her.

"Now, now, little nurse, you mustn't cry! Shall we give you some bromide?" said the Commissar, as if speaking to a little girl.

"There! You are joking again! What an awful man you are! It is monstrous, really monstrous to laugh when one ought to cry, to soothe others when one's own body is being rent with pain. My dear, dear good man, don't dare, do you hear, don't dare behave like that any more!"

She lowered her head and wept silently. With sad, kindly eyes the Commissar gazed at her thin, white-robed, shuddering shoulders.

"It's too late, too late my dear," he said, "I have always been scandalously late in my own private affairs. I was always too busy with other things. And now, I think, I am too late altogether."

The Commissar sighed. The nurse raised her head and looked at him with eyes filled with tears and eager expectation. He smiled, sighed again and, in his customary kindly and slightly jocular tone, continued:

"Listen to this story, my clever little girl. I have just remembered it. It happened a long time ago, during the Civil War, in Turkestan. Yes. A cavalry squadron went in such hot pursuit of the *Basmachi* that before long it found itself in a desert, so wild that the horses dropped dead, one after another. They were Russian horses and not used to the sandy desert. So from cavalry we were converted into infantry. The Squadron Commander decided to abandon all baggage and, carrying nothing but weapons, make for the nearest big city. It was a hundred and sixty kilometres away, and we had to march across bare sand. Can you picture it, little girl? We marched one day, two days, three days. The sun was scorching hot. We had no water. Our mouths were so parched that the skin cracked. The air was full of sand, sand crunched under our feet, gritted in our teeth, pricked our eyes, blew down our throats. It was horrible, I tell you! If a man stumbled and fell, he would lie face downwards in the sand, unable to get up. We had a Commissar, a chap called Yakov Pavlovich Volodin. A flabby intellectual by the look of him—he was an historian. But he was a staunch Bolshevik. One would think that he would have been the first to drop, but he kept on, and encouraged the others. 'Not far to go now. We'll be there soon,' he would keep on repeating; and if anybody lay down he would level his pistol at him and say: 'Get up, or I'll shoot!'

"On the fourth day, when we were only about fifteen kilometres from the city, the men were completely played out. We staggered along as if we were drunk, and the trail we left zigzagged like that of a wounded animal. Suddenly the Commissar started a song. He had an awful, thin voice and the song he started was silly, the marching song they used to sing in the old army, but we all chimed in and sang it. I gave the order: 'Fall into line!' and had the men march in step. You wouldn't believe it, but the going became easier.

"After this song we sang another, and then a third. Can you picture it, little girl? We sang with dry, cracked mouths, and in such a scorching heat! We sang all the songs we knew and at last arrived, without leaving a single man in the desert.... What do you think of that?"

"What about the Commissar?"

"What about him? He's alive and well. He's a professor of archaeology. Digs up prehistoric settlements. True, that march cost him his voice. Speaks in a hoarse whisper. But what does he want a voice for?... Well, no more stories tonight. Go along, little girl, I give you my word as a cavalryman not to die any more tonight."

At last Meresyev fell fast asleep and dreamt about a strange desert, about cracked, bleeding mouths emitting the strains of songs, and about the Commissar Volodin who, in the dream, for some reason resembled Commissar Vorobyov.

He woke up late, when the sunbeams were already playing in the middle of the ward, which indicated that it was noon, and he woke with a joyous feeling in his heart. A dream? What dream? His eye caught the magazine which he had tightly gripped in his hand while asleep; from the crumpled page Lieutenant Karpovich was still smiling that strained, gallant smile. Meresyev carefully smoothed out the magazine and winked at the lieutenant.

The Commissar, already washed and combed, was watching him with a smile.

"What are you winking at him for?" he asked, feeling pleased.

"I'm going to fly," answered Alexei.

"How? He had only one foot missing, but you've lost both."

"But I am Soviet, Russian!" responded Alexei.

He uttered those words in a tone that suggested they were a guarantee that he would score a point over Lieutenant Karpovich and fly.

At lunch he ate everything the ward maid brought him, looked in surprise at his empty plate and asked for more. He was nervously excited, sang, tried to whistle, and argued with himself aloud. When the professor came on his round, Alexei took advantage of the special favour he showed him to badger him with questions about what he must do to hasten his recovery. The professor answered that he must eat more and sleep more. After that, at dinner, Alexei demanded two helpings of the second course and forced himself to eat four cutlets. He could not fall asleep after dinner although he lay for an hour and a half with his eyes closed.

Happiness is inclined to make one egotistical. When Alexei bombarded the professor with questions, he failed to notice what had attracted the attention of the whole ward. Vasily Vasilyevich appeared in the ward as usual, punctually at the moment when the sunbeam, after slowly crossing the whole floor of the ward, touched the spot where a piece of parqueting was missing. The professor was attentive as usual, but everybody noticed a sort of abstracted look about him they had never seen before. He did not rail and scold as he usually did, and the veins at the corners of his inflamed eyes continuously throbbed. On the evening round he looked shrunken and perceptibly aged. In a low voice, he reproved the ward maid for leaving a duster on the door handle, looked at the Commissar's temperature chart, prescribed something for him and walked out silently, followed by his also silent and disturbed-looking retinue. At the threshold he stumbled and would have fallen had not somebody caught him by the elbow. It seemed entirely out of place for this tall, heavy, hoarse-voiced, boisterous martinet to be so quiet and polite. The inmates of ward forty-two followed him out with wondering eyes. They had all learned to love this big, kind-hearted man, and the change in him disquieted them.

Next morning they learned the reason. Vasily Vasilyevich's only son, whose name was likewise Vasily Vasilyevich, who was also a medical man and a promising scientist, his father's pride and joy, was killed on the Western Front. At the usual hour the entire hospital waited with bated breath to see whether the professor would arrive for his customary round of the wards. In ward forty-two everybody closely watched the slow, almost imperceptible movement of the sunbeam across the floor. At last it touched the spot where the piece of parqueting was missing and they all glanced at each other as if saying he will not come. But at that very moment the familiar heavy tread and the footsteps of the numerous retinue were heard in the corridor. The professor even looked a little better. True, his eyes were inflamed and the eyelids and nose were swollen, as happens when one has a severe cold, and his puffy, peeling hands trembled noticeably when he picked the Commissar's temperature chart up from the table; but he was as energetic and business-like as ever. His boisterousness and raillery had vanished, however.

As if by common agreement, the wounded and sick vied with each other that day to please him in every way they could. Everybody assured him that they felt better, even the severest cases made no complaint and averred that they were on the road to recovery. And everybody zealously praised the arrangements in the hospital and testified to the positively miraculous effect of the various treatments provided. It was a friendly family united by a great and common grief.

Going round the wards, Vasily Vasilyevich wondered why he was meeting with such extraordinary success that morning.

But did he wonder? Perhaps he saw through this naive, silent conspiracy; and if he did see through it, perhaps it enabled him more easily to bear the severe, unhealable wound he had sustained.

9

The branch of the poplar-tree outside the window facing east had already thrown out small, pale-yellow, sticky leaves, beneath which hung red, fluffy catkins resembling fat caterpillars. In the morning, the leaves glistened in the sun and looked as if they were made of oil-paper. They gave off a pungent, acrid smell of briny freshness which penetrated the open ventilating pane and overpowered the hospital smell that pervaded the ward.

The impudence of the sparrows, which had grown plump as a result of Stepan Ivanovich's generosity, now knew no bounds. In celebration of the spring, "Submachine-Gunner" had got himself a new tail and was more fussy and pugnacious than ever. In the morning, the birds held such noisy meetings on the outside windowsill that the ward maid, who cleaned up the ward, lost patience with them, grumblingly climbed up on the windowsill and, poking her arm through the ventilating pane, shooed them off with her duster.

The ice on the Moskva River had gone. After a brief, boisterous period, the river calmed down, returned to its banks and obediently placed its mighty back at the disposal of ships, barges and river-trams, which during those stern days served to supplement the sadly depleted automobile service of the metropolis. Despite Kukushkin's gloomy forecast, nobody in ward forty-two was "washed away" by the spring flood. Everybody, except the Commissar, was making good progress, and most of the conversation in the ward now was about being discharged from the hospital.

The first to leave the ward was Stepan Ivanovich. On the day before his discharge, he wandered about the hospital with mixed feelings of anxiety, joy and excitement. He could not keep still for a moment. After chatting with some patients in the corridor, he would return to the ward, sit down at the window, begin to fashion something out of bread, but at once jump up and leave the ward again. Only in the evening, when dusk had already fallen, did he climb up on the windowsill and sit there in deep reflection, grunting and sighing. This was the hour when the patients took their various treatments, and there were only two other patients in the ward: the Commissar, who was silently watching Stepan Ivanovich, and Meresyev, who was trying hard to fall asleep.

Quiet reigned. Suddenly the Commissar turned his head towards Stepan Ivanovich—whose profile was clearly outlined in the light of the last rays of the setting sun—and said in a barely audible voice:

"It is twilight in the country now, and quiet, oh, so quiet. The smell of the thawing earth, damp manure, and the wood smoke. The cow's in the barn, stamping her straw bedding; she is restless, it's time for her to calve. Springtime.... I wonder whether the women managed to spread the manure on the fields. And what about the seed, and the harness? Do you think everything is all right?"

It seemed to Meresyev that Stepan Ivanovich looked at the smiling Commissar not so much with surprise as with fright when he said:

"You must be a wizard, Comrade Regimental Commissar, to guess other people's thoughts like this.... Yes, women are very practical, of course, that's true, but the devil knows how they are managing without us.... That's a fact."

Silence reigned again. A ship on the river sounded its siren and the echo went rolling merrily over the water and resounded between its granite banks.

"Do you think the war will be over soon?" asked Stepan Ivanovich, speaking in a whisper for some reason. "Will it be over before the hay-making?"

The Commissar answered: "What are you worrying about? The men of your age have not been called up.

You are a volunteer. You have done your share of fighting. If you apply, you will get your discharge, and then you will be able to take command over the women. Practical men are needed in the rear too, aren't they? What do you say, greybeard?"

As he said this the Commissar looked so kindly at the old soldier that the latter jumped down from the windowsill, animated and excited.

"Get my discharge, you say!" he exclaimed. "That's what I'm thinking too. I was just saying to myself: suppose I put in an application to the commission? After all I've been through three wars: the imperialist war, the Civil War, and a bit of this one. Perhaps that's enough, eh? What would you advise me to do, Comrade Regimental Commissar?"

"Say in your application that you want your discharge because you want to join the women in the rear. Say that there are others to protect you from the Germans," shouted Meresyev from his bed, unable to restrain himself.

Stepan Ivanovich looked guiltily at him. The Commissar puckered his eyebrows angrily and said:

"I don't know what to advise you, Stepan Ivanovich. Ask your heart. It's a Russian heart you've got. It will give you the advice you need."

Next day, Stepan Ivanovich received his discharge from the hospital. He came into the ward in his military uniform to say good-bye. Of short stature, in his old, faded tunic that had become white in the wash, tightly belted and so well drawn in at the back that there was not a single fold in front, he looked at least fifteen years younger than he was. On his breast he wore the gold Hero of the Soviet Union star, polished to a dazzling brightness, the Order of Lenin and the "For Valour" medal. He had his hospital gown thrown over his shoulders like a cape. And the whole of him, from the tips of his old, army top-boots to the tips of his moustaches jauntily turned up in "awls", smacked of the dashing Russian soldier as depicted in the Christmas cards of the period of the First World War.

The soldier stepped up to each of his wardmates to say good-bye, addressing him by his military title and clicking his heels so smartly that it was a pleasure to look at him.

"Came to say farewell, Comrade Regimental Commissar," he rapped out with exceptional warmth when he reached the end bed.

"Good-bye, Styopa. A safe journey," answered the Commissar, and overcoming the pain it caused him he turned towards the soldier.

The soldier went down on his knees and took the Commissar's big head in his hands, and, in accordance with the old Russian custom, they kissed three times.

"Get well, Semyon Vasilyevich. May God give you health and long life. You've got a heart of gold. You've been more than a father to us. I'll remember you as long as I live," murmured the soldier with deep emotion.

"Go now, go, Stepan Ivanovich! He must not get excited," said Klavdia Mikhailovna, tugging the soldier's sleeve.

"And thank you, nurse, for your kindness and care," said Stepan Ivanovich, addressing the nurse in the most solemn tone and making her a deep, reverential bow. "You are our Soviet angel, that's what you are!"

Quite confused now, not knowing what else to say, he backed to the door.

"What address shall we write to you to, Siberia?" inquired the Commissar with a smile.

"Why ask, Comrade Regimental Commissar? You know where to write to a soldier on active service," answered Stepan Ivanovich with embarrassment, and, making another deep bow, to everyone this time, vanished behind the door.

A hush ensued and the ward seemed empty. Later they began to talk about their regiments, about their comrades, and about the big operations that awaited them at the front. They were all recovering now, and so these were no longer dreams, but practical realities. Kukushkin was already able to walk about the corridor, where he found fault with the nurses, teased the other convalescent patients, and had managed to quarrel with many of them. The tankman also got out of bed now and often stood for a long time in front of the mirror in the corridor examining his face, neck and shoulders, which were now unbandaged and healing up. The more lively his correspondence with Anyuta became, and the more closely he became acquainted with her university affairs, the more critically did he scrutinise his scorched and disfigured face. In the twilight, or in the dimly-lit ward, it did not look so bad, it looked good, in fact: fine features, a high forehead and a short, slightly hooked nose, short black moustache that he had grown in the hospital, and fresh, stubborn, youthful lips. But in a bright light it could be seen that his face was covered with scars around which the skin was drawn tight. Whenever he got excited, or came back flushed from his bath treatment, these scars made him look hideous, and examining himself in the mirror at such a moment, he was ready to weep. In an endeavour to console him, Meresyev said:

"What are you moping for? You are not going to be a screen actor, are you? If that girl of yours is genuine, it won't make any difference to her. If it does, it shows that she is a fool. In that case, tell her to go to hell. A good riddance. You'll find one of the real sort."

"All women are alike," interjected Kukushkin.

"What about your mother?" asked the Commissar. Kukushkin was the only man in the ward whom he addressed in the formal way.

It is difficult to describe the effect this calm question produced on the lieutenant. He sprang up in his bed, his eyes flashing fiercely and his face turning whiter than a sheet.

"There you are! So you see that there are some good women in the world," said the Commissar in a conciliatory tone. "Why do you think Grisha won't be lucky? That's what happens in life: the seeker always finds."

In short, the entire ward became reanimated. The Commissar was the only one whose condition steadily grew worse. He was kept alive with morphine and camphor, and sometimes, as a result of this, he would toss restlessly about in his bed for whole days in a semi-drugged condition. After Stepan Ivanovich's departure he seemed to sink more rapidly. Meresyev requested that his bed be shifted closer to the Commissar's so as to be able to help him if need be. He felt drawn more and more to this man.

Alexei was aware that without feet life would be much harder and more complicated for him than for other people, and he was instinctively drawn to a man who knew how to live a real life and who, in spite of his infirmity, attracted people like a magnet. The Commissar now emerged more and more rarely from his state of semi-oblivion, but when he was quite conscious he was the same as ever.

One day, late in the evening, when the bustle in the hospital had died down and the silence that reigned was disturbed only by the low, barely audible snores, groans and delirious muttering that came from the wards, the familiar loud, heavy footsteps were heard in the corridor. Through the glass panes of the door, Meresyev could look down the whole length of the dimly-lit corridor, at the far end of which a nurse sat at a table, endlessly knitting a jumper. At the end of the corridor, the tall figure of Vasily Vasilyevich appeared, walking slowly with his hands behind his back. The nurse jumped up but he waved her aside with a gesture of annoyance. His smock was unbuttoned, he was bare-headed, and strands of his thick, grey hair hung over his brow.

"Vasya's coming," Meresyev whispered to the Commissar, to whom he was explaining his latest design for a special type of artificial foot.

Vasily Vasilyevich halted as if he had met some obstacle, supported himself against the wall, muttered something, then pushed himself away from the wall and entered ward forty-two. He stopped in the middle of the room, rubbing his forehead, as if trying to remember something. He smelt of spirits of wine.

"Sit down for a minute, Vasily Vasilyevich, and let's have an evening chat," said the Commissar.

The professor walked over to the bed, dragging his feet, sat down on the edge so heavily that the springs groaned, and rubbed his temples. On previous occasions, when making his rounds, he had stopped at the Commissar's bed to talk briefly about the course of the war. It was evident that he singled out the Commissar from among his other patients, so there was nothing strange about his late evening visit. But Meresyev had a feeling that these two men had something to talk about not meant for another's ears, so he shut his eyes and pretended to be asleep.

"It's the twenty-ninth of April today, his birthday. He is—no, he would have been... thirty-six," the professor said in a low voice.

With great difficulty the Commissar pulled his large, swollen hand out from under his blanket and laid it on Vasily Vasilyevich's. An incredible thing happened: the professor broke into tears. It was painful to see this big, strong man weeping. Alexei involuntarily hunched his shoulders and covered his head with his blanket.

"Before leaving for the front, he came to see me," continued the professor. "He told me that he had joined the People's Volunteers and asked me to appoint someone to take over his work. He worked with me here. I was so amazed that I yelled at him. I simply could not understand why a Candidate in medicine and a talented scientist should take up a rifle. But he said—I remember every word—he said: 'There are times, Dad, when a Candidate in medicine must take up a rifle.' That is what he said and asked me again: 'Who is taking over from me?' All I had to do was to make one phone call—and nothing, nothing would have happened, nothing, do you understand? He was in charge of a department in a military hospital. I'm right, aren't I?"

Vasily Vasilyevich stopped, breathing heavily with a hoarse rattle. Then he went on:

"Don't do that, dear boy. Take your hand away. I know how painful it is for you to move. Yes, I sat up all night, thinking what to do. You understand, I knew of another man—you know who I mean—who had a son, an officer, and he was killed in the very first day of the war. Do you know what that father did? He sent his second son to the war, sent him as a fighter-pilot, the most dangerous speciality in the war.... I remembered that man then and felt ashamed of my thoughts, and so I did not telephone...."

"Are you sorry now?"

"No. Do you call it being sorry? I go about asking myself: Am I the murderer of my only son? He could have been here now with me, and both of us would have been doing very useful work for our country. He had real talent—vigorous, daring, brilliant. He might have become the pride of the Soviet medical profession—if only I had telephoned then!"

"Are you sorry you did not telephone?"

"What do you mean? Ah, yes.... I don't know. I don't know."

"Suppose this were to happen now, would you act differently?"

Silence ensued. The regular breathing of the patients was heard. The bed creaked rhythmically—evidently the professor, in deep reflection, was rocking his body to and fro—and the valves clicked in the central heating pipes.

"Well?" asked the Commissar in a tone that rang deep with sympathy and understanding.

"I don't know.... I haven't a ready answer to your question. I don't know. But I think that if everything were to repeat itself, I would do what I did all over again. I am no better and no worse than other fathers.... What a frightful thing war is...."

"And believe me, it is no easier for other fathers to bear the dreadful news than it is for you. No easier."

Vasily Vasilyevich sat silent for a long time. What was he thinking, what thoughts were passing behind that high, wrinkled forehead during those slowly passing moments?

"Yes, you are right," he said at last. "It was no easier for him, and yet he sent his second son.... Thank you, dear chap, thank you. Oh, well, there's nothing to be done about it."

He got up from the bed, gently replaced the Commissar's hand under the blanket, tucked the blanket round him and silently walked out of the room.

Late that night the Commissar had a severe relapse. Unconscious, he tossed about in his bed, grinding his teeth, moaning loudly. Then he would fall silent and stretch out full length, and everybody thought the end had come. His condition was so bad that Vasily Vasilyevich—who, after his son was killed, had moved from his big, empty apartment to his small office in the hospital where he slept on an oilcloth-covered couch—ordered a screen to be put round his bed, which, as everybody knew, was an indication that the patient was likely to be taken to "ward number fifty".

With the aid of camphor and oxygen, they got his pulse going again, and the night surgeon and Vasily Vasilyevich went away to get what sleep they could for the remaining part of the night. Klavdia Mikhailovna, with tear-stained and anxious face, remained at the patient's bedside behind the screen. Meresyev could not fall asleep. He lay thinking with horror: "Is this really the end?" The Commissar was evidently still in great pain. He was delirious and kept repeating a word which sounded to Meresyev like "give". "Give, give me...."

Klavdia Mikhailovna, thinking that the patient wanted a drink, came from behind the screen and with a trembling hand poured some water into a glass.

But the patient did not want to drink. The glass tinkled against his set teeth and the water splashed on to the pillow; but he still kept repeating, now in an imperative and now in a pleading tone, the word that sounded like "give". Suddenly Meresyev realised that the word was not "give" but "live", and that with every remaining fibre of his being this big man was fighting to keep off death.

A little later, the Commissar calmed down and opened his eyes.

"Thank God!" murmured Klavdia Mikhailovna with relief and began to fold the screen.

"Don't! Leave it!" protested the Commissar. "Don't take it away, nurse dear. It's cosier this way. And don't cry; there is too much rawness on earth as it is.... Why are you crying, my Soviet angel?... What a pity we meet angels, even such as you, only on the threshold... of that place."

10

Alexei was experiencing something he had never felt before.

From the moment he began to believe that it was possible, by training, to learn to fly a plane without feet, and that he could become an airman again, he was overcome by a passionate desire for life and activity.

He now had an object in life: to fly a fighter plane; and he set out to pursue that object with the same fanatical stubbornness as he had displayed when he crawled to the partisans. Accustomed from early youth to look ahead, he first of all precisely defined for himself what he must do in order to achieve his object, without wasting precious time. And so he decided, first, that he must recover quickly, recover the health and strength he had lost when he had starved, and, therefore, that he must eat more and sleep more. Second, he must recover the fighting qualities of an airman and therefore develop himself physically by such gymnastic exercises as a bedridden man is capable of doing. Third, and this was the most important and difficult part, he must train what was left of his legs so as to preserve their strength and agility, and later, when he received his artificial limbs, to learn to fly a plane with them.

Even to walk is not an easy matter for a footless man. Meresyev, however, was determined to pilot an aircraft, and a fighter plane at that. To do that, particularly in an air battle, when everything is calculated to a fraction of a second and movements must synchronise to a degree equal to that of an unconditioned reflex, the feet must be able to perform operations as precise, skilful and above all as rapid as those performed by the hands. He must train himself to such a degree that the pieces of wood and leather attached to the stumps of his legs should perform these operations like living members of the body.

A man familiar with the technique of flying would regard this as impossible, but Alexei was now convinced that it was possible, and that being the case, he would achieve it without fail. And so he set about carrying out his plan. He began to take all the treatments and medicines prescribed for him with a punctiliousness that surprised himself. He ate a great deal and always asked for a second helping even if he had no particular appetite. Whatever the circumstances, he forced himself to take the prescribed number of hours of sleep and even trained himself to take an after-dinner nap, which was abhorrent to his active and vivacious nature.

It was not difficult for him to force himself to eat, sleep and take his medicine. Gymnastics were a different matter. The ordinary exercises which he had regularly taken in the past were unsuitable for a footless, bedridden man. He therefore invented a new set of exercises: for hours on end he bent his body forward, backward and sideways, from right to left and back again, with his hands on his hips, and he turned his head this way and that with such vigour and zeal that his spine creaked. His wardmates good-naturedly chaffed him over these exercises, and Kukushkin ironically congratulated him and called him the Znamensky brothers, Ladoumegue, or by the names of other famous sprinters. Kukushkin detested these gymnastics and regarded them as just another hospital fad. As soon as Alexei began his exercises, he would hasten to the corridor, grumbling and grousing.

When the bandages were removed from his legs and he was able to move more freely in his bed, Alexei added another exercise. He would insert the stumps of his legs between the rails at the foot of the bedstead, put his hands on his hips and slowly bend his body forward as far as it would go and then bend backward. Every day he reduced the speed of the bends and increased the number of "bows". Then he devised a series of exercises for his legs. He would lie on his back and bend each leg in turn, drawing the knee towards his chest, and then throw the leg out again. When he performed this exercise the first time, he realised what enormous, and perhaps insuperable, difficulties awaited him. Stretching his legs, of which the feet had been amputated to the shins, caused him acute pain. The motions were hesitant and irregular. They were as difficult to calculate as to pilot an aircraft with a damaged wing or tail. Mentally comparing himself to an aircraft, Alexei realised that the ideally calculated structure of the human body was, in his case, disturbed and that although his body was still strong and sound, it would never again acquire the harmony of action of its different parts that it had been trained to since childhood.

The leg exercises caused Meresyev acute pain, but every day he did them a minute longer than he had the previous day. There were dreadful moments during which unbidden tears welled up in his eyes, and he bit his lips until they bled to suppress an involuntary groan. But he forced himself to perform these exercises, at first once and later twice a day. After every spell, he fell helplessly back on his pillow, wondering whether he would be able to repeat them. But when the hour arrived he set to work again. In the evening, he felt the muscles of his thighs and calves and noted with satisfaction that they were no longer the flabby flesh and fat that he had felt under his hand at the beginning of the exercises, but the firm muscle that he had possessed in the past.

His legs occupied all Meresyev's thoughts. Sometimes, when lost in thought, he felt a pain in the feet and shifted the position of his legs, and only then did he remember that he had no feet. For a long time, due to some nervous anomaly, the amputated feet still lived with the body; suddenly they would begin to irritate, ache in damp weather, and there would even be an agonising pain in them. His mind was so taken up with his feet that sometimes in his sleep he saw himself quick in his movements. He dreamed that the "alert" was sounded and that he ran to his plane, leapt on to the wing, climbed into the cockpit and tried the pedals with his feet while Yura removed the cover from the engine. At another time, he and Olya would be running barefoot, hand in hand in the flower-bedecked steppe, enjoying the pleasant feel of the warm and moist ground. How good that was! But how disappointing to wake up and find that he had no feet!

After dreams like that, Alexei sometimes became dejected. He began to think that he was tormenting his body in vain, that he would never fly again, just as he would never run barefoot in the steppe with that lovely girl in Kamyshin who became dearer and more desirable to him the longer time kept them apart.

His relations with Olya gave Alexei no joy. Almost every week Klavdia Mikhailovna made him "dance", that is, jerk his body in bed and clap his hands to entitle him to receive a letter addressed in the familiar round, neat, schoolgirl's hand. These letters became more and more lengthy and endearing, as if the girl's young love that had been interrupted by the war was maturing more and more. He read those lines with longing and anxiety, knowing that he had no right to reciprocate.

Schoolmates, who had attended the apprenticeship school at the sawmill together, they had been filled with romantic sentiments which they had called love just to imitate grownups. Later, they had parted for six or seven years. First the girl went away to study at the technical school. When she returned to the sawmill as a mechanic, Alexei had already left the town and was studying at the aviation school. They met again just before the outbreak of the war. Neither had sought that meeting, and they had probably even forgotten each other—so much water had flowed under the bridge since their parting. One evening Alexei was in the street accompanying his mother somewhere and a girl passed them. He paid no attention to the girl except that he noticed that she had well-shaped legs.

"Why didn't you greet the girl? It was Olya!" his mother reproved him, mentioning the girl's surname.

Alexei looked back. The girl too had turned round to look back. Their eyes met and Alexei felt his heart skip. Leaving his mother, he ran towards the girl, who had halted under a bare poplar-tree.

"You?" he exclaimed in surprise, looking at her as if she were a rare and beautiful creature from overseas who had in some strange way appeared in this quiet, muddy street on this spring evening.

"Alyosha?" exclaimed the girl in the same surprised and incredulous tone.

They saw each other for the first time after a separation of six or seven years. Alexei saw before him a girl of miniature proportions, a graceful and supple figure with a pretty, round, boyish face and a few golden freckles on the bridge of her nose. She looked at him with large, grey, sparkling eyes, slightly raising her softly traced eyebrows that were somewhat bushy at the ends. There was little about this fresh, graceful girl of the sturdy, round-faced, rosy-cheeked, rather rough child, walking proudly in her father's greasy jacket with the sleeves rolled up, that she had been at the time they had last met at the apprenticeship school.

Forgetting about his mother, Alexei stood admiring the girl, and it seemed to him that he had never forgotten her during these years and had been dreaming of this meeting.

"So that's what you are like now!" he said at last.

"Like what?" she inquired in a ringing, throaty voice that was also quite unlike the one he had heard when they were at school together.

A gust of wind blew round the corner and whistled through the bare branches of the poplar-tree. The girl's frock fluttered against her well-shaped legs. With a ripple of laughter she stooped and held her frock down with a simple, graceful movement.

"Like that!" answered Alexei, no longer concealing his admiration.

"Well, like what?" the girl asked again, laughing.

The mother looked at the two young people for a moment, smiled sadly and went on her way. But they kept standing there admiring each other, chatting vivaciously, interrupting each other and interspersing their conversation with exclamations, such as "D'you remember?..." "D'you know?..." "Where is?..." "What's happened to?..."

They stood chatting like that for a long time until Olya pointed to the windows of the near-by houses at which, over geranium pots and sprigs of fir, inquisitive faces could be seen.

"If you have time let's go to the riverside," suggested Olya. Holding hands, a thing they had not done even as children, and forgetting everything, they went to a tall hill that ran steeply down to the river and from which a magnificent view could be had of the broad expanse of the Volga and of the solemn procession of ice floes on its flood waters.

From that time onwards the mother rarely saw her beloved son at home. Not usually fastidious about clothes, he now ironed his trousers every day, polished the buttons of his uniform with chalk, put on his white-topped peak cap with the Air Force badge, shaved his bristly chin every day, and in the evening, after twisting and turning in front of a mirror for a time, went to meet Olya at the gates of the sawmill. In the day-time too he would vanish every now and again, was absent-minded and gave inappropriate answers to questions put to him. Her maternal instinct told his mother what was happening to him, and understanding, she forgave him, consoling herself with the adage: the old grow older, the young must grow.

Not once did young people speak of their love. Every time he returned home from a ramble on the high bank of the slowly flowing Volga that glittered in the evening sun, or through the melon patches outside the town where on the ground, thick and black like tar, already lay the vines with dark green web-foot-shaped leaves, he counted the remaining days of his rapidly waning leave and resolved to open his heart to Olya. But evening came again. He met her at the mill gates and accompanied her to the small, two-storey, wooden house where she rented a tiny room, as clean and bright as the cabin in an aircraft. There he waited patiently while she changed behind the open door of her wardrobe, and tried to keep his eyes away from her bare elbows, shoulders and legs that peeped from behind the door. Then she went to wash and returned fresh, rosy-cheeked and with wet hair, always in the same white silk blouse that she wore on week-days.

And they went to the cinema, to the circus, or to the park. It made no difference to Alexei where they went. He did not look at the screen, at the arena, or at the people strolling in the park; he had eyes only for her, and looking at her he thought: "Now tonight I must, absolutely must propose to her on the road home!" But the road ended and his courage failed him.

One Sunday morning, they went for a walk through the meadows on the other side of the Volga. He called for her dressed in his best white duck trousers and a shirt with an open collar which, his mother said, wonderfully suited his dark, broad face. Olya was ready when he arrived. She handed him a parcel wrapped in a table napkin and they went to the river. The old ferryman—a disabled veteran of the First World War, a favourite with the small boys in the vicinity, who had taught Alexei, when a boy, to catch gudgeon near the sandbanks—hobbling on his wooden stumps, pushed the heavy boat off and began to row with short strokes. Cutting the current at an angle, the boat crossed the river in short jerks to the low, bright green bank on the other side. The girl sat in the stern in deep reverie with her hand over the gunwale, allowing the water to run through her fingers.

"Uncle Arkasha, don't you remember us?" asked Alexei.

The ferryman looked at the young faces with indifference and said: "I don't."

"Why, I am Alyoshka Meresyev. You taught me how to catch gudgeon near the sandbanks with a fork!"

"Perhaps I did. There were lots of nippers like you playing about here. I can't remember them all."

The boat passed a pier at which was moored a broad-bowed cutter bearing the proud name *Aurora* on its peeling bows, and cut into the sandy beach with a crunch.

"This is my place now. I don't work for the municipality any more, I'm on my own. You know what I mean—private enterprise," explained Uncle Arkasha, getting into the water to push the boat up the bank. But his wooden stumps sank into the sand, the boat was heavy and he could not shift it. "You'll have to jump," he said phlegmatically.

"How much for the ride?" asked Alexei.

"I leave it to you. You ought to pay a little extra, you look so happy. But I don't remember you, that I don't."

Jumping from the boat they wet their feet, and Olya suggested that they take their shoes off. They did so, and the touch of their bare feet on the moist, warm river sand made them feel so happy and free that they wanted to run, leap and caper on the grass like children.

"Catch me!" cried Olya, darting off across the shallows towards the low, emerald-green meadow, her strong, tanned legs flashing as she ran.

Alexei ran after her, seeing in front of him only the motley patch formed by her light, brightly-coloured frock. As he ran the wild flowers and plumes of horse sorrel painfully whipped his bare feet and he felt the soft, moist, sun-warmed earth yielding under his soles. It seemed to him to be a matter of vital importance to catch Olya, that a great deal in their future lives depended upon it, and that here, on this flowery meadow, amidst the intoxicating fragrance, it would be easy to tell her

11—1872

all that he had up till now lacked the courage to say. But each time he caught up with her and stretched out his hand the girl turned abruptly, evaded his grasp with the litheness of a cat, and ran off in a different direction with a merry, rippling laugh.

She was determined not to be caught, and he did not catch her. She herself turned from the meadow to the riverside and threw herself down on the hot golden sand, her face flushed, her mouth open, with heaving bosom greedily inhaling the air and laughing. Later he took her photograph on the flowery meadow, amidst the white, starry daisies. Then they bathed, and later he obediently went behind a bush and turned the other way while she dressed and wrung her bathing-suit.

When she called him he found her sitting on the sand, her sunburned legs drawn in, dressed in her thin, light frock with a Turkish towel wound round her head. Spreading the clean white napkin on the grass and placing pebbles on the corners to keep it down, she laid out the contents of the parcel. They lunched on salad, cold fish that had been carefully wrapped in oil-paper, and also home-made biscuits. She had not even forgotten the salt, nor even the mustard, which she brought in small cold cream jars. There was something charming and touching in the grave and skilful way this slip of a girl acted the hostess. Alexei said to himself: "No more dilly-dallying. This settles it. I'm going to propose to her this evening. I will prove to her, convince her that she must become my wife."

They sunned themselves on the sand, bathed once more, and after arranging to meet again in Olya's room in the evening, they walked slowly to the ferry, tired and happy. For some reason, neither the cutter nor the ferry-boat was there. They called Uncle Arkasha long and loud until they were hoarse. The sun was already setting in the steppe. Beams of bright pink sunlight, gliding over the crest of the hill on the other side of the river, gilded the roofs of the houses and the now motionless, dusty tops of the trees in the town. The windows shone blood-red. The summer evening was hot and quiet. But something must have happened in town. The streets, which were usually deserted at this hour, were teeming; two lorries filled with people rode past; a small group was marching in military formation.

"Uncle Arkasha must have got drunk," surmised Alexei. "Suppose we have to spend the night here?"

"I'm not afraid of anything when I'm with you," answered Olya, looking at him with her large, sparkling eyes.

He put his arms round her and kissed her, kissed her for the first and only time. The clicking of rowlocks was heard from the river; the ferry-boat loaded with people was approaching from the other side. Now they looked at the boat with disgust, but they obediently went to meet it as if urged by a foreboding of what it was bringing them.

The people jumped out of the boat in silence. All were in their best dresses, but their faces were troubled and gloomy. Men with grave faces and seemingly in a hurry, and women with eyes red from weeping, passed the young couple without uttering a word. Not knowing what had happened, the two jumped into the boat. Without looking at their happy faces Uncle Arkasha said:

"War... it was on the air this morning."

"War? With whom?" asked Alexei, almost jumping off his seat.

"With those damned fascists, who else?" growled Uncle Arkasha, angrily tugging at his oars. "The men have already gone to the District Military Commissariat. Mobilisation."

Alexei went straight to the Military Commissariat without going home, and at night he was already on the 12:40 train, on his way to the aircraft unit to which he was appointed, scarcely having had time to run home for his suitcase, and not even having said good-bye to Olya.

* They corresponded rarely, not because their sentiments towards each other had cooled, or because they were forgetting each other. No. He looked forward impatiently for those letters written in the round, schoolgirl's hand, kept them in his pocket and, when alone, read them over and over again. It was these letters that he pressed to his heart and gazed at during the terrible time

he had crawled in the forest. But the relations between these two young people had been broken off so abruptly, and at such an indefinite stage, that in the letters they wrote they communicated with each other as good, old friends, fearing to add to this that bigger thing that had, after all, remained unspoken.

And now, finding himself in hospital, he noticed with perplexity, which increased with each letter he received, that Olya herself had suddenly gone out to meet him, as it were, that now in her letters she wrote quite frankly of her longing, regretted that Uncle Arkasha had come for them just at that particular moment that evening, assured him that whatever happened to him there was one upon whom he could always rely, and begged him to remember when wandering far from home that there was a corner which he could regard as his own, to which he could return when the war was over. It seemed as though it was a new, a different Olya who was writing. Whenever he looked at her photograph, he always thought that if a breeze were to blow she would fly away in her flowered frock, like the parachute seeds of ripe dandelion. But those letters were written by a woman— a good, loving woman who was longing and waiting for her beloved. This gladdened and saddened him; gladdened him in spite of himself, saddened him because he thought he had no right to such love. Why, he had not had the courage to write that he was no longer the vigorous, sunburned youth that she had known, but a cripple like Uncle Arkasha. Not having dared to write the truth for fear it would kill his invalid mother, he was now obliged to deceive Olya and became more and more entangled in this deception with every letter he wrote.

That is why the letters he received from Kamyshin roused such contradictory feelings in him—joy and sorrow, hope and anxiety—they cheered and tormented him at one and the same time. Having told a falsehood once, he was obliged to go on inventing others, but he was a bad hand at such inventions, and that is why his answers to Olya were curt and dry.

He found it easier to write to the "meteorological sergeant". Hers was a simple but devoted soul. In a moment of despair after his operation, when he felt the need of expressing his grief to somebody, he wrote her a long and gloomy letter. Shortly afterwards, he received an answer written on a page torn from an exercise book, in a twiddly hand, the sentences liberally interspersed with exclamation marks that looked like caraway-seeds sprinkled on a bun, and the whole ornamented with tear blots. The girl wrote that if it were not for military discipline she would throw up everything at once and go to him to nurse him and share his sorrow. She implored him to write more often. There was so much naive, half-childish sentiment in this confused letter that it made Alexei sad, and he cursed himself for having told the girl when she handed him Olya's letters that Olya was his married sister. A girl like that ought never to be deceived. And so he frankly wrote and told her that he had a sweetheart in Kamyshin, and that he had not dared to tell her, or his own mother, the truth about his misfortune.

The answer from the "meteorological sergeant" came with what was, in those days, an incredible speed. The girl wrote that she was sending the letter with a major, a war correspondent who had visited their wing. He had courted her, but, of course, she had ignored him, although he was a nice, jolly fellow. From the tone of the letter it was evident that she was disappointed and offended, had tried to restrain her feelings but without avail. Chiding him for not having told her the truth that time, she asked him to regard her as his friend. This letter ended with a postscript written not in ink, but in pencil, assuring the "Comrade Senior Lieutenant" that she was his devoted friend and telling him that if "that one in Kamyshin" were unfaithful to him (she knew how the women in the rear were behaving), or if she ceased to love him, or was repelled by his being disabled, then let him not forget the "meteorological sergeant", only he must always write her nothing but the truth. The person who brought the letter also brought a neatly-packed parcel containing several embroidered handkerchiefs made from parachute silk and bearing Alexei's initials, a tobacco-pouch with a plane depicted on it, a comb, a bottle of "Magnolia" eau-de-Cologne, and a piece of toilet soap.

Alexei was aware how precious all these things were to the girls serving in the army in those hard times. He knew that a piece of soap or a bottle of eau-de-Cologne received as a holiday gift was treasured by them as though it were a sacred amulet which reminded them of civil life before the war.

He knew the value of these gifts and was therefore glad and ashamed when he laid them out on top of his bedside cupboard.

Now that he, with his characteristic energy, was training his crippled legs and dreaming of the possibility of flying and fighting again, he was torn by mixed feelings. The fact that he was obliged to prevaricate and tell half-truths in his letters to Olya, his love for whom grew stronger every day, and to be frank with a girl whom he scarcely knew, weighed heavily upon his conscience.

But he solemnly pledged himself to speak to Olya about love again only when his dream came true, when he had recovered his fighting fitness and had returned to the ranks. And this still further stimulated the fanatical zeal with which he drove himself towards his goal.

11

The Commissar died on the first of May.

Nobody knew how it happened. In the morning, after he was washed and combed, he questioned the woman barber who was shaving him about the weather and about what Moscow looked like on this holiday. He was glad to hear that the barricades were being removed from the streets, lamented the fact that there would be no demonstration on this glorious spring day, and teased Klavdia Mikhailovna, who on the occasion of the holiday had made an heroic attempt to conceal her freckles with face powder. He seemed better, and everybody began to hope that he had turned the corner and was now, perhaps, on the road to recovery.

For some time, since he was no longer able to read the newspapers, he had a wireless set with ear-phones at his bedside. Gvozdev, who knew about wireless sets, did something to it, and now the talking and singing could be heard all over the ward. At nine o'clock, the announcer, whose voice was known and listened to all over the world in those days, began to read the Order of the Day of the People's Commissar of Defence. Everybody remained absolutely silent, with necks craned towards the two black discs hanging on the wall, afraid to miss a single word. Even after the words: "Under the invincible banner of Great Lenin—forward to victory!"... had been pronounced, intense silence reigned in the ward.

"Now, please, explain this to me, Comrade Regimental Commissar..." Kukushkin began, and suddenly he cried out in horror—"Comrade Commissar!"

Everybody looked round. The Commissar was lying straight, stiff and stern on his bed, staring with motionless eyes at a point in the ceiling; his face, haggard and pale, bore a calm, solemn and majestic expression.

"He's dead!" cried Kukushkin, dropping on his knees at the bedside. "Dead!"

The dismayed ward maids ran in and out, the nurse rushed about, the house surgeon flew in, still fastening his smock. Ill-tempered, unsociable Lieutenant Konstantin Kukushkin was lying across the body of the dead man, paying no attention to anybody, his face buried in the blanket like a child's, his shoulders heaving and body trembling in a paroxysm of sobbing and weeping....

That evening a new patient was brought into now half-empty ward forty-two. He was Major Pavel Ivanovich Struchkov, of a fighter unit of the Moscow Defence Division. The fascists had decided to carry out a big air raid on Moscow on the holiday, but their bombers, flying in several echelons, were intercepted and after a fierce battle were routed somewhere in the region of Podsolnechnaya. Only one Junkers succeeded in breaking through. It made its way towards Moscow at a high altitude. Evidently, its crew was determined to carry out the assignment at any price in order to mar the holiday celebrations. In the heat of the battle Struchkov saw that the bomber was escaping and at once went in pursuit. He was flying a splendid Soviet machine, one of the type with which the fighter units were being equipped at that time. He overtook the German plane high up in the air, about six kilometres above the ground, already over the suburbs of Moscow. He skilfully manoeuvred into the enemy's rear, got him clearly into his sight and pressed the button of his guns. He pressed it, but to his surprise he failed to hear the familiar rattle. The button didn't work.

The German plane was a little ahead of him. He hung on to it, keeping in the dead zone, protected from the twin machine-guns in its stern by the keel of its tail. In the clear light of that bright May morning, Moscow loomed on the horizon like a heap of grey piles enveloped in mist. Struchkov resolved on a desperate stroke. He unfastened his straps, threw back the hood of his cockpit and tightened his muscles as if preparing to spring. He steered his plane in perfect line with that of the bomber and for a moment the two planes flew one behind the other as if tied by an invisible thread. Through the transparent hood of the Junkers, Struchkov distinctly saw the eyes of the German turret gunner watching every manoeuvre he made, waiting for at least a bit of his wing to appear outside the dead zone. He saw the German pull his helmet off in excitement, and even saw his hair, fair and long, hanging over his forehead in strands. The two black snouts of the heavy machine-guns were turned in Struchkov's direction and moved like living things, waiting for their opportunity. For an instant Struchkov felt like an unarmed man upon whom a robber had trained his gun, and he did what plucky, unarmed men do in such a situation—he hurled himself upon the enemy, but not with his fists, as he would have done on the ground; he jerked his plane forward and aimed the glistening circle of his propeller at the enemy's tail.

He did not hear the crash. In the next instant, thrown upward by the terrific impact, he felt that he was somersaulting in the air. The ground flashed over his head, stopped and then rushed towards him, bright green and shining. He released his parachute, but before he lost consciousness and hung suspended from the ropes, he saw out of the corner of his eye the cigar-shaped hull of the Junkers, minus its tail, hurtling past him and revolving like a maple leaf torn off by the autumn wind. Swinging helplessly from the parachute ropes, Struchkov heavily struck the roof of a house and fell unconscious into the festive street of a Moscow suburb, the inhabitants of which had watched his magnificent ramming operation from the ground. They picked him up and carried him to the nearest house. The adjacent streets at once became so crowded that the doctor who had been called could scarcely make his way to the house. As a result of the impact with the roof, Struchkov's knee-caps were damaged.

The news of Major Struchkov's heroic feat was immediately broadcast in a special issue of the "Latest News". The Chairman of the Moscow Soviet himself arrived to take him to the best hospital in the metropolis. And when Struchkov was brought into the ward he was followed by orderlies carrying flowers, fruit and boxes of chocolate— all gifts from the grateful inhabitants of Moscow.

He proved to be a cheerful and sociable fellow. No sooner had he crossed the threshold of the ward than he asked the patients what the "grub" was like, if the rules were strict, and whether there were any pretty nurses in the place. And while his knees were being bandaged he told Klavdia Mikhailovna an amusing story about the eternal subject of the army canteen, and paid her a rather bold compliment on her good looks. When the nurse left the ward he winked in her direction and said:

"Nice girl that! Strict? I suppose she puts the fear of God into you, eh? But we'll not take to our heels. Haven't you been taught tactics? Women are no more impregnable than fortresses, and there isn't one that cannot be taken," and with that he broke into a loud chuckle.

He behaved like an old-timer, as if he had been in the hospital a whole year. He at once began to address everybody by their first names and when he wanted to blow his nose he unceremoniously picked up one of Meresyev's parachute-silk handkerchiefs that the "meteorological sergeant" had so painstakingly embroidered.

"From your lady love?" he asked with a wink at Alexei and hid the handkerchief under his pillow. You've got plenty, and if you haven't, your girl will be only too glad to make you another one."

Notwithstanding the rosy flush that broke through the tan of his cheeks, he looked no longer young. Deep wrinkles radiated from the corners of his eyes to his temples like crow's feet, and everything about him spoke of the old soldier who is accustomed to regard the place where his kit-bag is, and where his soap-box and toothbrush are on the shelf over the wash-stand, as his home. He brought a great deal of boisterous cheerfulness into the ward and did it in such a way that nobody took offence and he made everybody feel that they had known him for years. Everybody took a liking to the new-comer, except that Meresyev was rather repelled by his obvious weakness for the opposite sex, which, incidentally, he made no attempt to conceal, and on which he dilated on the slightest pretext.

Next day the Commissar's funeral took place.

Meresyev, Kukushkin and Gvozdev sat on the sill of the window facing the courtyard and saw the team of artillery horses haul in the heavy gun-carriage, saw the brass band line up, their instruments glistening in the sun, and saw a military unit march in. Klavdia Mikhailovna came into the ward and ordered the patients to leave the window. She was, as usual, quiet and energetic, but Meresyev noticed that her voice trembled as she spoke. She had come to take the new patient's temperature, but at that moment the band struck up a funeral march. The nurse turned pale, the thermometer dropped from her hands and tiny, shining balls of mercury rolled about the parquet floor. Klavdia Mikhailovna ran out of the ward hiding her face in her hands.

"What's the matter with her? Was he her sweetheart?" asked Struchkov, nodding in the direction of the window from which the strains of mournful music came.

Nobody answered him.

Leaning out of the window, they all gazed at the open red coffin on the gun-carriage as it emerged from the gates into the street. Amidst a mass of wreaths and flowers lay the body of the Commissar. Behind the gun-carriage men were carrying his decorations pinned on cushions—one, two, five, eight. Generals marched behind with bowed heads. Among them was Vasily Vasilyevich, also in a general's greatcoat, but, for some reason, bareheaded. And then, at a little distance from the rest, in front of the slowly marching soldiers, came Klavdia Mikhailovna, bare-headed, in her white smock, stumbling, and evidently not seeing what was in front of her. At the gates, somebody had thrown a coat over her shoulders, but as she walked the coat slipped and fell to the ground, and the men marching behind her opened ranks to avoid trampling upon it.

"Who is it, boys?" asked the major.

He too, wanted to raise himself to the window, but his legs were bound in splints.

The procession passed out of sight. The mournful strains of the solemn music now came from somewhere down the river, subdued and distant, softly echoed by the walls of the houses. The lame woman janitor had already come out to close the iron gates, but the inmates of ward forty-two still stood at the window, seeing the Commissar off on his last journey.

"Can't you tell me who it is? You all seem to have been turned into blocks of wood!" exclaimed the major impatiently, still trying to raise himself to the window.

At last Kukushkin answered in a dry, cracked voice:

"It's the funeral of a real man ... a Bolshevik."

The expression: "a real man", sank into Meresyev's mind. A better description could not have been imagined. And Alexei was filled with a desire to become a real man, like the one who had just been taken on his last journey.

12

With the death of the Commissar, the whole life of ward forty-two changed.

There was no one to dispel with a kindly word the gloomy silence that sometimes envelops a hospital ward, when everybody becomes suddenly absorbed in his melancholy reflections and everybody's heart is heavy. There was nobody to draw Gvozdev out of his dejection with a merry quip, nobody to give Meresyev advice, nobody to curb Kukushkin's grousing with a witty but inoffensive remark. The magnet that drew all these different characters together and welded them into one, was gone.

But this was not needed so much now. Medical treatment and time had done their work. All the patients were rapidly recovering, and the nearer they drew to the time of their discharge the less they spoke about their infirmities. They dreamed of what awaited them outside the hospital, of how their particular units would greet them when they returned, and what activities lay ahead. All of them longed for the army life they had grown accustomed to, and their hands itched, as it were, in their eager desire to be out of the hospital in time to take part in the new offensive, which could be felt in the air like an impending storm and could be guessed from the calm that had suddenly descended upon the fronts.

There was nothing unusual in a soldier returning to active service from the hospital, but for Meresyev it became a problem: would skill and training compensate for the absence of feet; would he be able to get into the cockpit of a fighter plane again? He strove towards his goal with ever-increasing zeal and determination. Having gradually increased the time, he now exercised his legs and did training exercises—general gymnastics—for two hours every morning and evening. But even this seemed not enough to him. He began to do his exercises in the afternoon. Looking at him sideways with a merry, mocking twinkle in his eyes, Struchkov would announce, like a showman:

"And now, citizens, you will see the riddle of nature, the great shaman, Alexei Meresyev, who has no equal in the forests of Siberia, show you his bundle of tricks."

There was, indeed, something in the exercises, that he performed with such fanatical fervour, that made Alexei resemble a shaman. It was so hard to watch the endless bending of the body backward and forward and from side to side and the exercises for the neck and arms which he performed so resolutely and with the regularity of a swinging pendulum, that while he was thus engaged his wardmates who were able to walk left the room to roam about the corridor; and bed-ridden Struchkov pulled his blanket over his head and tried to fall asleep. Nobody in the ward believed, of course, that it was possible for a man with no feet to fly, but their wardmate's perseverance won their respect and, perhaps, their reverence, which they concealed with quips and jests.

The fractures in Struchkov's knee-caps proved to be more serious than was at first supposed. They healed slowly, his legs were still in splints, and although there was no doubt that he would recover, the major never ceased to curse his "damned joints" that were causing him so much trouble. His grumbling and growling grew into a steady rage; he would go into a frenzy over some trifle and curse and swear at everybody and everything. At such moments it seemed he would strike anybody who attempted to reason with him. By common consent his wardmates left him alone during such fits, let him "use up his ammunition", as they put it, and waited until his natural cheerfulness gained the upper hand over his war-shattered nerves.

Struchkov himself attributed his growing impatience to the fact that he was unable to go and have a smoke in the toilet and also to the fact that he was unable to go into the corridor to see the red-haired nurse from the operating-room with whom, so he alleged, he had already exchanged winks when he was having his legs rebandaged. There may have been some truth in this, but Meresyev noticed that these fits of irritation broke out after the major had seen aircraft flying over the hospital, or when the radio and the newspapers reported a new interesting air battle, or the achievement of some airman he knew. This also made Meresyev irritably impatient, but he gave no sign of it, and comparing himself with Struchkov he was conscious of a feeling of triumph. It seemed to him that he was coming at least a little bit nearer to the model he had chosen of the "real man".

Major Struchkov remained true to himself: he ate a great deal, laughed heartily and was fond of talking about women, appearing to be a woman-lover and a woman-hater at the same time. For some reason he was particularly severe in his criticism of the women in the rear.

Meresyev detested the talk that Struchkov indulged in. When listening to him he always had before his eyes a vision of Olya, or of that funny little girl at the meteorological station, who, as was related in the wing, had chased a too enterprising sergeant-major from the Maintenance Crew Battalion out of her sentry-box with the butt of her rifle and nearly shot him in her excitement; Alexei had an idea that it was these women that Struchkov was maligning. One day, after listening to one of

Major Struchkov's stories, which he ended with the remark "they are all alike", and that you can get on to any of them "in two ticks", Meresyev was unable to restrain himself and asked, clenching his teeth so tight that his cheek-bones paled:

"Any of them?"

"Yes, any of them," replied the major coolly.

At this moment Klavdia Mikhailovna entered the ward and was surprised to see the tense expression on the faces of the patients.

"What's the matter?" she asked, adjusting a strand of hair under her kerchief with an unconscious gesture.

"We're discussing life, nurse. We're like a lot of old codgers, now. Nothing to do but talk," the major answered with a beaming smile.

"What about her?" demanded Meresyev in an angry voice when the nurse left.

"Do you think she's made of different stuff?"

"Leave Klavdia Mikhailovna alone," Gvozdev said sternly. "We had an old chap here who called her a Soviet angel."

"Who wants to bet?"

"Bet?" cried Meresyev, his dark eyes flashing fiercely. "What are you staking?"

"Let's say a pistol bullet, as officers used to do: if you win, I'll be your target, and if I win you'll be my target," Struchkov said, laughing and trying to turn the whole thing into a joke.

"Bet? On that? You seem to forget that you're a Soviet officer. If you're right you may spit in my face." Alexei narrowed his eyes. "But watch out that I don't spit in yours."

"You don't have to bet if you don't want to. I'll prove it to you fellows just for the hell of it that we have no cause to quarrel over her."

From that day onward, Struchkov zealously paid his attentions to Klavdia Mikhailovna: he amused her with comic stories, in the telling of which he was a past master; in violation of the unwritten rule that an airman should be reserved in telling a stranger about his war adventures, he related to her many of his truly great and interesting experiences; with heavy sighs he even hinted at his unfortunate family affairs and complained of his bitter loneliness, although everybody in the ward knew that he was unmarried and had no particular family troubles.

It is true Klavdia Mikhailovna showed him a little more favour than the rest; she would sit on the edge of his bed and listen to the tales of his adventures, and he, unconsciously, as it were, would take her hand, and she would not withdraw it. Anger grew in Meresyev's heart, the entire ward was mad at Struchkov, for he behaved as if he wanted to prove to his wardmates that Klavdia Mikhailovna was no different from any other woman. He was gravely warned to stop this dirty game, and the ward was preparing resolutely to interfere in the matter when the affair suddenly took a totally different turn.

One evening, during her spell of duty, Klavdia Mikhailovna came into the ward not to attend to any of the patients, but just for a chat—it was for this that the patients liked her particularly. The major began one of his stories and the nurse sat down by his bed. Nobody noticed how it happened, but suddenly she jumped up. Everybody looked round. With an angry frown and flushed cheeks, the nurse glared at Struchkov—who looked ashamed and even frightened—and said:

"Comrade Major, if you were not a patient and I a nurse, I'd slap your face!"

"Oh, Klavdia Mikhailovna, I give you my word I didn't mean to.... And besides, what is there in it?..."

"Oh! What is there in it?" She looked at him now not with anger, but with contempt. "Very well. There's nothing more to be said. Do you hear? And now I ask you, in front of your comrades, never to speak to me again except when you need medical attention. Good night, comrades!"

And she left the ward with a step unusually heavy for her, evidently trying hard to appear calm.

For a moment silence reigned in the ward. Then Alexei's vicious, triumphant laugh was heard, and everybody pounced upon the major:

"So you got what was coming to you!"

Gloatingly, Meresyev asked with mock politeness:

"Do you want me to spit in your face now or later?"

Struchkov looked abashed, but he would not confess defeat. He said, not very confidently, it is true:

"M'yes. The attack was repulsed. Never mind, we'll try again."

He lay quiet until midnight, whistling softly, and sometimes ejaculating, as if in answer to his thoughts: "M'yes!"

Shortly after this incident Konstantin Kukushkin was discharged from the hospital. He showed no emotion on leaving, and when bidding his wardmates farewell he merely remarked that he was fed up with hospital life. He carelessly said good-bye to all, but begged Meresyev and the nurse, if any letters came from his mother, to take care of them and send them on to him to his wing.

"Write and tell us how you get on, and how the comrades welcomed you," were Meresyev's parting words.

"Why should I write to you? What do you care about me? I won't write, it would only be wasting paper, you wouldn't answer, anyhow!"

"Just as you please!"

Evidently, Kukushkin did not hear that last remark; he walked out of the ward without turning round again. And also without a parting backward glance he walked out of the hospital gates, proceeded along the embankment and turned the corner, although he knew perfectly well that, according to custom, all his former wardmates were at the window watching him.

Nevertheless, he did write to Alexei, and rather soon. It was a letter written in a dry, matter-of-fact tone. All he wrote about himself was that the wing appeared to be glad to see him back, but he forthwith added that the wing had suffered heavy casualties in recent battles and, of course, they would be glad to have back anyone with any experience. He gave a list of the killed and wounded, wrote that Meresyev was still remembered in the wing, and that the Wing Commander, who had been promoted to the rank of lieutenant-colonel, on hearing of Meresyev's gymnastic feats and of his determination to return to the Air Force, had said: "Meresyev will come back. He's the kind that sticks to a resolve," and that in reply to this the Chief of Staff had said that one could not do the impossible, to which the Wing Commander had retorted that nothing was impossible for men like Meresyev. To Alexei's surprise there were even a few lines about the "meteorological sergeant". Kukushkin wrote that this sergeant had bombarded him with questions so heavily that he had been obliged to order: "About turn! March!" Kukushkin concluded his letter by stating that on the very first day of his return to the wing he made two flights, that his legs were completely healed, and that within the next few days the wing would get new planes—"La-5's", which were to arrive soon, and about which Andrei Degtyarenko, who had tried them out, had said that in comparison with them the German craft of all types were mere suitcases filled with junk.

13

Summer set in early. It peeped into ward forty-two from that same poplar-tree branch, the leaves of which had become hard and bright. They rustled impetuously as if whispering to each other. Towards evening they lost their brightness owing to the dust from the street. The red catkins had long ago changed into bright green brushes, which had now burst and a light fluff was blown from them. At noon, the hottest part of the day, this warm poplar fluff was blown about Moscow, flew into the open windows of the hospital and lay in pink piles at the doors and in the corners into which the warm breezes had carried it.

One cool, bright, golden summer morning, Klavdia Mikhailovna, looking very solemn, came into the ward accompanied by an elderly man wearing steel-rimmed spectacles tied with string and a new, stiffly starched white smock, which, however, could not conceal the fact that he was an old craftsman. He carried something wrapped in a white cloth. He placed the bundle on the floor at Meresyev's bedside and began slowly and solemnly, like a conjuror, to untie it. The creak of leather could be heard, and the pleasant, pungent, acrid smell of tan pervaded the ward.

When the wrappings were removed a pair of new, yellow, creaking artificial limbs, skilfully constructed and made to measure, were exposed to view. On the artificial limbs were a pair of new, brown army boots; and they fitted the limbs so well that one might have thought that they were living, booted feet.

"All you want is a pair of overshoes, and they'd be nice enough to go to your wedding in," said the craftsman, gazing admiringly at his handiwork over his spectacles. "Vasily Vasilyevich himself ordered them. 'Zuyev,' he said, 'make a pair of feet that will be better than real ones.' Well, here they are! Zuyev has made them. Fit for a king!"

Meresyev's heart shrank at the sight of the artificial feet; it shrank, froze, but that feeling was soon vanquished by his eagerness to try them on, to walk, to walk unaided. He thrust out the stumps of his legs from under the blanket and hurriedly urged the craftsman to put them on him. But the old man, who claimed that long ago, before the Revolution, he had made an artificial limb for a "big duke" who had broken his leg at the races, did not like to be hurried. He was very proud of his work and wanted to prolong the pleasure of delivering the order to his customer.

He wiped the limbs with his sleeve, scraped a small stain from one of them with his finger-nail, breathed on the spot and polished it on his snow-white smock, then stood the limbs on the floor, slowly folded the wrapper and put it into his pocket.

"Come on, Grandpa, let's try them!" said Meresyev impatiently, sitting on the edge of his bed.

He now looked at the bare stumps of his legs with the eyes of a stranger and felt pleased with them. They looked strong and sinewy, and it was not fat that usually accumulates with enforced immobility, but firm muscles that rippled under the dark skin, as if they were the muscles not of stumps, but of the sound limbs of a man who did a lot of fast walking.

"What do you mean 'come on, come on'? Sooner said than done!" grumbled the old man. "Vasily Vasilyevich said to me, 'Zuyev,' he says, 'make the best pair you've ever made in your life. This lieutenant,' he says, 'intends to fly without feet.' Well, I've made 'em! Here they are! With feet like that you'll not only be able to walk, but ride a bike and dance the polka with the ladies.... Good work, I tell you!"

He inserted Alexei's right stump into the soft, woollen socket of the artificial limb, fastened it firmly with the straps and then stood back and clicked his tongue admiringly.

"It's a nice boot! Does it fit? Doesn't pinch anywhere, does it? I should say so! You'll not find a better craftsman than Zuyev in the whole of Moscow!"

With deft hands he put the other limb on, but scarcely had he fastened the straps when Meresyev, with a sudden jerk, sprang from the bed on to the floor. A dull thud followed. Meresyev uttered a cry of pain and dropped full length to the floor by the side of the bed. The old craftsman was so surprised that his spectacles shifted to his forehead. He had not expected his customer to be so frisky. Meresyev lay on the floor stunned and helpless, his booted artificial feet spread wide apart. His eyes expressed perplexity, pain and fear. Had he really been deceiving himself?

Bringing her hands together in amazement, Klavdia Mikhailovna rushed to him. Assisted by the old craftsman, she raised Alexei and sat him on his bed. There he sat limp and dejected, a picture of despair.

"He-eh, young man! You mustn't do that!" expostulated the old craftsman. "Jumps up as if they were real, live feet! But you mustn't be down-hearted, either. You've got to learn to walk, right from the beginning. Forget that you are a soldier for the time being. You're a little toddler, and you've got to learn, step by step, first with crutches, then holding on to the wall, and after that with a stick. You can't do it all at once; you've got to do it gradually. But you go and jump up like that! They're good feet, but not your own. Nobody can make feet as your papa and mama made them for you!"

Alexei's legs ached after this unlucky jump, but for all that he was eager to try the artificial feet at once. They brought him a pair of light, aluminium crutches. He rested the ends on the floor, pressed the pads under his arm-pits and, slowly and cautiously this time, slipped from his bed and rose to his feet. And indeed, he stepped out like an infant just learning to walk, instinctively guessing that it can walk, but fearing to let go of the lifesaving support of the wall. Like a mother or grandmother taking an infant for its first walk with a towel round its chest, Klavdia Mikhailovna carefully supported him on one side and the old craftsman on the other. He stood for a moment, feeling acute pain where the feet were fastened to the legs. Then he hesitatingly put one crutch forward and then the other, rested the weight of his body upon them, brought up one foot and then the other. The sound of creaking leather was heard, followed by two loud taps on the floor.

"Good luck! Good luck!" said the old craftsman under his breath.

Meresyev took a few more cautious steps, but these first steps of his artificial feet cost him so much effort that after reaching the door and returning to his bed he felt as though he had carried a piano up four flights of stairs. He flung himself upon the bed face downward, sweating profusely, too weak to turn over on his back.

"Well, how do you like 'em? You ought to thank God there's a man like Zuyev in the world," chattered the old man boastfully as he carefully unfastened the straps and released Alexei's legs, which were slightly swollen from the unaccustomed pressure. "With them on you'll be able to fly not only in the ordinary way, but right up to the Lord himself. It's good work, I tell you!"

"Thank you! Thank you, Grandpa. It is good work. I can see that," mumbled Alexei.

The craftsman stood fidgeting for a while as if wishing to ask a question and not daring to, or else, perhaps, expecting to be asked a question. At last, heaving a sigh of disappointment, he said, moving slowly towards the door:

"Well, good-bye. I hope you like them."

But before he reached the door Struchkov called out:

"Hey, old man! Take this and have a drink to celebrate the feet fit for a king!" With that he handed him a batch of bills.

"Thanks! Thank you very much! The occasion is certainly worth a drink!" answered the old man, and raising the skirt of his smock as if it were a craftsman's apron, he slipped the money into his hip pocket with an important air. "Thanks. I certainly will have a drink. As for these feet, I tell you, I put my best into 'em. Vasily Vasilyevich said to me: 'Zuyev, this is a special case. Do your best.' But has Zuyev ever done anything but his best? If you see Vasily Vasilyevich, tell him you are pleased with the work."

With that the old man left the ward, bowing and mumbling to himself. Meresyev lay gazing at his new feet standing on the floor at his bedside, and the more he looked at them the more he liked their skilful design, the excellence of their finish and their lightness. "Ride a bike, dance the polka, fly a plane, right up to the Lord! Yes, I will! I'll do all these things!" he reflected.

That day he sent Olya a long and cheerful letter in which he informed her that his job of receiving new aircraft was drawing to a close and that he hoped that in the autumn, or at the latest in the winter, his chiefs would grant his request to leave this dull job in the rear, with which he was absolutely fed up, and send him to the front, to his own wing, where his comrades had not forgotten him and were, in fact, looking forward to his return. This was the first cheerful letter he had written since the disaster happened to him, the first letter to his beloved, in which he told her that he was always thinking of and longing for her and expressed, rather timidly, his cherished dream of meeting her again when the war was over and, if she had not changed her mind, of setting up a home together. He read the letter over again several times and at last, heaving a sigh, he carefully crossed out the last lines.

The letter he wrote to the "meteorological sergeant" simply bubbled with high spirits and merriment, eloquently describing the events of this great day. He made a sketch of the artificial feet such as no emperor ever wore, described how he had taken his first steps, and told her about the garrulous old craftsman and his prophecy that he, Alexei, would be able to ride a bike, dance the polka and fly right to heaven. "And so, expect me in the wing; tell the Commandant to arrange for a place for me at the new base," he wrote, casting a sidelong glance at the floor. The feet protruded from under the bed as though somebody were hiding there. Alexei looked round to see if anybody was watching him and then bent over and lovingly stroked the cold, shining leather.

There was another place where the appearance in ward forty-two of a pair of "artificial feet fit for a king" was the subject of eager discussion; this was the third-year course of the medical department of Moscow University. The whole of the feminine section of that course, and it was by far the largest section at that time, was fully informed about the affairs of ward forty-two. Anyuta was very proud of her correspondent, and alas, Lieutenant Gvozdev's letters, which were not written for public information, were read aloud, in part or whole, except for the more intimate passages, which, incidentally, appeared more and more often as the correspondence continued.

The entire third-year medical course was in love with heroic Grisha Gvozdev, disliked surly Kukushkin, admired Meresyev's indomitable spirit, and regarded as a personal bereavement the death of the Commissar whom, after Gvozdev's rhapsodic descriptions of him, all were able to appreciate and love. Many were unable to restrain their tears when they heard that this big, vivacious man had departed this life.

The interchange of letters between the hospital and the university became more and more frequent. The young people were not content with the ordinary post, which in those days was too slow. In one of his letters, Gvozdev quoted the Commissar as saying that nowadays letters reached their destinations like light from distant stars. A person's life may be extinguished, but his letters would travel slowly on and eventually tell the recipients about the life of a man who had died long ago. Practical and enterprising, Anyuta looked for a more perfect means of communication and found it in the person of an elderly nurse who worked both at the university clinic and at Vasily Vasilyevich's hospital.

From that day onward, the university learned of the happenings in ward forty-two on the second or, at the latest, the third day and was able to respond to them quickly. In connection with the "artificial feet fit for a king", a dispute arose about whether Meresyev would be able to fly or not. It was a youthful and ardent dispute, in which both sides sympathised with Meresyev. Bearing in mind the complexity of handling a fighter plane, the pessimists claimed that he would not be able to fly. The optimists, however, argued that for a man who, to get away from the enemy, had crawled through a dense forest for a fortnight, heaven knows how many kilometres, nothing was impossible. And to back their argument, the optimists quoted examples from history and from fiction.

Anyuta took no part in this dispute. The artificial feet of an airman unknown to her did not interest her very much. In her rare spare moments, she pondered over her feelings towards Gvozdev, which, it seemed to her, were becoming more and more complicated. At first, on hearing of this heroic officer, whose life had been so tragic, she had written to him under the impulse of an unselfish desire to assuage his grief. But as their acquaintance grew in the course of their correspondence, the abstract figure of a hero of the Patriotic War gave way in her mind to a real, living youth, and this youth began to interest her more and more. She noticed that she felt anxious and sad when no letters came from him. This was something new, and it gladdened and frightened her. Was it love? Was it possible to love a man you have never seen, whose voice you have not even heard, whom you know only from his letters? More and more often there were passages in the tankman's letters that she could not read to her fellow-students. After Gvozdev had confessed in one of his letters that he had "fallen in love by correspondence", as he expressed it, Anyuta realised that she too was in love, that hers was not a schoolgirl's love, but real love. She felt that life would lose its meaning for her if she ceased to receive these letters to which she now looked forward with such impatience.

And so they confessed their love for each other without having met, but after this something strange must have happened to Gvozdev. His letters became nervous, uneasy and vague. Later, he plucked up courage to write to Anyuta that it had been a mistake for them to have confessed their love for each other without having met, that Anyuta probably had no idea how terribly his face was mutilated, that he was totally unlike the old photograph he had sent her. He did not want to deceive her, he wrote, and requested her to cease writing about her feelings towards him until she had seen with her own eyes whom it was she loved.

On reading this, Anyuta first felt indignant and then frightened. She took the photograph from her pocket. A thin, youthful face with determined features, a fine, straight nose, a small moustache and a nicely shaped mouth looked at her. "And now? What are you like now, my poor darling?" she whispered, gazing at the photograph. As a medical student, she was aware that burns heal badly and leave deep, indelible scars. For some reason, she recalled that in the anatomical museum she had seen a model of the face of a man who had suffered from lupus: a face scarred by bluish furrows and pimples, with irregular, corroded lips, eyebrows in small clumps, and red eyelids without eyelashes. What if he were like that? Her face paled with horror at the thought; but at once she mentally scolded herself. Well, suppose he is? He fought our enemies in a burning tank, defending her freedom, her right to education, her honour, her life. He was a hero. He had risked his life so many times and was now yearning to return to the front to fight and to risk his life again. But what had she done in the war? She had dug trenches, performed air defence duty and was working in a base hospital. But what was this compared with what he had done? "These doubts alone make me unworthy of him!" she railed at herself, making an effort to drive away the frightful vision of that mutilated face that rose before her eyes.

She wrote him a letter, the longest and tenderest she had written throughout their correspondence. Naturally, Gvozdev never learned about these doubts. On receiving this splendid letter in answer to the anxious one that he had written, he read it over and over again. He even told Struchkov about it, and the latter, after listening to the story with an indulgent air, said:

"Show your pluck, man. You know the saying: 'A pretty face and a heart that's cold; a plain one and a heart of gold.' All the more so today, when men are so scarce."

Naturally, this candour failed to reassure Gvozdev. As the day of his discharge from hospital drew nearer he looked at himself more often in the mirror, sometimes from a distance, with a running, superficial glance, and sometimes, bringing his face almost up against the glass, he would massage his scarred and pitted face for hours.

At his request, Klavdia Mikhailovna bought him some face powder and cream, but he soon saw that no cosmetics would conceal his scars. At night, however, when everybody was asleep, he would steal to the toilet and stay there a long time massaging the scars, powdering them and massaging them again, and then look hopefully into the mirror. From a distance he looked a splendid fellow: a sturdy figure, broad shoulders and narrow waist, set on straight, sinewy legs. But close up! The sight of the red scars on his cheeks and chin and the drawn, ribbed skin drove him to despair. "What will she think when she sees it?" he asked himself. She would be terrified. She would look at him, turn away and walk off with a shrug of her shoulders. Or what would be worse, she would talk to him for an hour or so out of politeness, then say something official and cold and—good-bye! He grew pale with anger, as if that had already happened.

Then he would draw a photograph from the pocket of his gown and critically examine the features of a round-faced girl with soft, thin but fluffy hair combed back over a high forehead, a blunt, upturned, truly Russian nose and tender, childish lips. On the upper lip there was a barely perceptible mole. From this guileless, sweet face a pair of grey, or perhaps blue, eyes, slightly bulging, gazed at him honestly and frankly.

"Tell me, what are you like? Will you be frightened? Will you run away? Will you have heart enough not to see what a monster I am?" he would ask, gazing intently at the photograph.

Meanwhile, with tapping crutches and creaking leather, Senior Lieutenant Meresyev passed him, tirelessly hobbling up and down the corridor—once, twice, ten times, twenty times. He did this every morning and evening, according to a programme he had set himself, increasing the length of the exercise every day.

"He's a fine chap!" commented Gvozdev to himself. "A real sticker. Pluck isn't the word for it. Learnt to walk on crutches in a week! Some take months. Yesterday he refused a stretcher and walked down the stairs to take his treatments and then walked up again. Tears were rolling down his face, but he kept on, and even bawled at the orderly who wanted to help him. And you should have seen his smile when he reached the landing unaided! You'd think he had climbed Mount Elbrus."

Gvozdev turned away from the mirror and watched Meresyev hobbling rapidly on his crutches. "Look at him! Actually running! And what a nice, fine face he has! A small scar across the eyebrow, but it doesn't spoil his looks a bit, rather an improvement, in fact." If only he, Gvozdev, had a face like that. What's feet? You can't see feet. And of course, he'll learn to walk, and to fly! But your face! You can't hide an apparition like this, which looks as if drunken devils had threshed peas on it at night.

Alexei Meresyev was on his twenty-third lap along the corridor during his afternoon exercise. All over his tired body he felt the burning of his swollen thighs and the aching of his shoulders from the pads of his crutches. As he hobbled along he cast a sidelong glance at the tankman standing at the mirror. "Funny chap!" he thought to himself. "What's he worrying over his face for? He will never be a cinema star now, of course. But a tankman. What's to stop him? Your face doesn't matter, as long as you've got a sound head, and arms, and legs. Yes, legs, real legs, not these stumps which hurt and burn as if the artificial feet were made not of leather but of redhot iron."

Tap, tap. Creak, creak. Tap, tap. Creak, creak.

Biting his lips and trying to suppress the tears which, in spite of himself, were forced to his eyes by the acute pain, Senior Lieutenant Meresyev with difficulty completed the twenty-ninth lap along the corridor and finished his exercise for the day.

14

Grigory Gvozdev left the hospital in the middle of June.

A day or two before he left he had a long talk with Alexei. The fact that they were comrades in misfortune and that their personal affairs were equally complicated had drawn them together and, as happens in such cases, they opened their hearts to each other, frankly told each other of their apprehensions about the future and all about what each of them found doubly hard to bear because pride prevented them from sharing their troubles with others. Each showed the other the photograph of his girl.

Alexei had a rather worn and faded photograph of Olga that he himself had taken on that clear, bright day in June when they had raced barefoot across the flower-covered steppe on the other side of the Volga. A slim girl in a pretty print frock, she sat with her legs drawn in and with flowers in her lap. Among the daisies, she herself looked white and pure, like a daisy in the morning dew. While arranging the flowers she thoughtfully inclined her head and her eyes were wide open and enraptured, as if she were seeing the magnificent world for the first time in her life.

After looking at this photograph, the tankman said that a girl like that would never desert a fellow in misfortune; but if she did—well, to hell with her, it only showed that appearances are deceiving, and in that case it would be better if she did leave him, because she was a rotter, and it was no use tying yourself up for life with a rotter, was it?

Alexei liked Anyuta's face and, without noticing it, he expressed to Gvozdev, but in his own way, the very thoughts that Gvozdev had just expressed to him. There was nothing profound in this talk, and it did not in the least help to solve their problems, but both felt the better for it, as if a severe and long-festering boil had burst.

They arranged that when Gvozdev left the hospital, he and Anyuta, who had telephoned and promised to come and meet him, would pass the ward window, after which Alexei would write to Gvozdev, telling him what impression the girl had made upon him. Gvozdev, in his turn, promised to write Alexei and tell him how Anyuta had met him, how she had reacted when she saw his mutilated face, and how they were getting on. Alexei thereupon decided that if things went well with Grisha he would at once write to Olya and tell her all about himself, but ask her not to tell his mother, who was still very sick and scarcely able to leave her bed.

This explains why both were so nervously anticipating the tankman's discharge. They were so worried that neither could sleep, and at night both stole out into the corridor—Gvozdev to give his scars another massage in front of the mirror, and Meresyev, after padding the tips of his crutches to deaden the sounds, to do an extra turn in his walking exercises.

At ten o'clock, Klavdia Mikhailovna came into the ward, with a sly smile informing Gvozdev that somebody had come for him. Gvozdev jumped up from the bed as if he had been blown off it by a blast of wind. Blushing so furiously that the scars on his face stood out more conspicuously than ever, he began hurriedly to collect his things.

"She's a nice girl, and looks so serious," said the nurse with a smile, watching Gvozdev's hurried preparations to leave.

Gvozdev's face beamed with pleasure.

"Do you mean it? Do you like her? She is a nice girl, isn't she?" he asked and, in his excitement, ran out of the ward forgetting to say good-bye.

"Jackass! Just the kind that are caught in the net," growled Major Struchkov.

Something had gone wrong with this wild fellow during the past few days. He became morose, often had fits of anger for no reason at all, and being now able to sit up in bed, would sit all day staring out of the window with his cheeks propped up by his fists, and refuse to answer when spoken to.

The entire ward—the gloomy major, Meresyev, and the two new patients—leaned out of the window to see their former wardmate appear in the street. It was a warm day. Soft, billowy clouds with radiant, golden edges were sailing swiftly across the sky, changing their shape. Just at that moment, a small, grey, puffy raincloud was passing hurriedly over the river, scattering large raindrops that glistened in the sun. The granite walls of the embankment shone as if they were polished; the asphalt road was covered with dark, marblelike patches, and from it arose such a fine moist vapour that one wanted to stick one's head out of the window to catch these pleasant raindrops.

"He's coming!" whispered Meresyev.

The heavy oak doors at the entrance opened slowly and two people emerged: a rather plump young woman, bare-headed, her hair combed back from her forehead, wearing a white blouse and a dark skirt; and a young soldier whom even Alexei did not at once recognise as the tankman. In one hand he carried his suitcase and over his other arm he carried his greatcoat; and he walked with such a springy step that it was a pleasure to watch him. Evidently, he was trying his strength, and was so delighted at being able to move freely that he did not run but seemed to glide down the steps. He took his companion's arm and, sprinkled with heavy, golden raindrops, walked with her along the embankment—towards the window of the ward.

As Alexei watched them his heart was filled with joy: so everything had passed off well! No wonder she has such a frank, sweet, simple face. Such a one would not turn away. No! Girls like that don't turn away from a man in trouble.

They drew near the window, halted and looked up. The young couple stood against the rain-polished parapet of the embankment where the slowly falling rain sketched a background of bright, slanting streaks. And here Alexei noticed that the tankman looked embarrassed and worried, and that Anyuta, who really was as pretty as in the photograph, also looked worried and embarrassed, that her arm lay loosely on the tankman's arm, and that altogether she looked agitated and irresolute, as if she were about to withdraw her arm and run away.

They waved their hands, smiled a strained smile, walked further along the embankment and vanished round the corner. Silently the patients returned to their beds.

"Poor Gvozdev hasn't hit it off," observed the major, but on hearing the tap of Klavdia Mikhailovna's heels in the corridor, he gave a start and abruptly turned to the window.

Alexei felt troubled for the rest of the day. He even missed his evening walking exercise and turned in before everybody else; but the springs of his mattress twanged long after the rest of the patients had fallen asleep.

Next morning, before the nurse was barely in the room, he asked her whether there were any letters for him. There were no letters. He washed and ate his breakfast listlessly, but he took a longer spell of walking exercise than usual; to punish himself for the weakness he had shown the previous evening he did fifteen extra laps to make up for the exercise he had missed. This unexpected achievement caused him to forget his anxiety. He had proved that he could move freely on his crutches without growing too tired. The corridor was fifty metres long. Multiplied by forty-five, the number of times he had walked up and down, that made two thousand two hundred and fifty metres, or two and a quarter kilometres, the distance from the officers' mess to the airfield. He mentally went over that familiar track that led past the ruins of the old village church, past the brick block of the gutted school which gazed mournfully at the road out of the hollow sockets of its paneless windows, through the wood where the fuel trucks covered with fir branches were hidden, past the commander's dugout, and past the little wooden hut where, poring over maps and charts, the "meteorological sergeant" performed her rites. A good stretch! By heaven, quite a good stretch!

Meresyev decided to increase the daily exercises to forty-six laps, twenty-three in the morning and twenty-three in the evening, and to try next morning, when he was fresh after the night's rest, to walk without crutches. This at once diverted his mind from his gloomy thoughts, raised his spirits and put him in a practical frame of mind. In the evening, he commenced his exercise with such enthusiasm that before he was aware of it he had done over thirty laps. Just at this moment he was interrupted by the appearance of the cloak-room attendant with a letter. The letter was for him. The small envelope was addressed: "Senior Lieutenant Meresyev. Strictly confidential." The word "strictly" was underlined, and Alexei did not like the look of that. The letter inside was also marked "strictly confidential" and also underlined.

Leaning against the windowsill, Alexei opened the letter and the further he read the lengthy epistle, which Gvozdev had written at the railway station the night before, the gloomier his face became. Gvozdev wrote that Anyuta had turned out to be exactly as he had pictured her, that she was probably the prettiest girl in Moscow, that she had met him like a brother, and that he liked her more than ever.

"...But the thing we talked about turned out exactly as we said. She is a good girl. She did not say a word to me, and did not even hint at anything. She behaved like a brick. But I am not blind. I could see that my blasted, ugly face frightened her. Everything seemed to be all right, but suddenly I would see her looking at me as if she were ashamed, or frightened, or sorry for me—I can't say which.... She took me to her university. It would have been better if I had not gone. The girl students gathered round and stared at me.... Would you believe it? They knew all of us! Anyuta had told them all about us.... I could see that she was looking at them apologetically as much as to say: 'Forgive me for bringing this fright here.' But the main thing, Alyosha, is that she tried to hide her feelings: she was so nice and kind to me, and kept on talking and talking as if afraid to stop. Then we went to her place. She lives alone. Her parents have gone away with the evacuees. Evidently, they are quite respectable people. She made me some tea and while at the table she kept looking at my reflection in the nickel kettle and sighing. To cut it short, I thought to myself: 'Well, this can't go on.' I put it to her straight: 'I can see that my appearance is not to your liking. You are right. I can understand. I am not offended.' She burst into tears, but I said to her: 'Don't cry. You are a nice girl. Anybody could fall in love with you. Why ruin your life?' Then I said to her: 'Now you see what a beauty I am. Think it over. I will return to my unit and will send you my address. If you don't change your mind, write to me.' And I also said to her: 'Don't make yourself do anything you don't want to. I'm here today and there tomorrow—we're at war.' Of course, she says: 'Oh, no, no!' and goes on crying. Just then the blasted siren began to screech. She went out and I took advantage of the commotion to slip away, and I went straight off to the officers' regiment. They gave me an appointment at once. Everything is all right now. I've got my railway ticket and I'll soon be off. But I must tell you, Alyosha, I am more in love with her than ever, and I don't know how I'm going to live without her."

Reading his friend's letter it seemed to Alexei that he was gazing into his own future. No doubt this was what would happen to him. Olya would not repel him, would not turn away from him, she too would want to make the same noble sacrifice, she would be kind to him, smile through her tears and try to suppress her aversion.

"No, no! I don't want that!" he exclaimed.

He limped back to the ward, sat down at the table to write a letter to Olya—a short, cold, matter-of-fact letter. He dared not tell the truth. Why should he? His mother was ill, and why should he add to her grief? He wrote Olya that he had pondered a great deal over their relationship with each other and had come to the conclusion that it must be hard for her to wait. Nobody knew how much longer the war would last, but time, and youth, were passing. War is such a thing that there may be no sense in waiting. He may be killed and she will be left a widow without even having been a wife: or what would be worse, he may be disabled and she will have to marry a cripple. What was the use of that? Let her not waste her youth, and let her forget him as quickly as possible. She need not answer this letter, he will not be hurt if she did not. He understood her position, although it was hard for him to confess it. But it will be better that way.

The letter seemed to burn his hands. Without going over it he put it in an envelope and quickly hobbled to the blue letter-box that hung in the corridor behind the water heater.

He returned to the ward and sat down at the table again. With whom could he share his grief? Not with his mother. With Gvozdev? He, of course, would understand, but where was he? How could he find him in the infinite maze of roads that led to the front? Write to his unit? But will those lucky men engaged in their everyday war occupations have time to worry about him? The "meteorological sergeant"? Yes, that's the one! He at once began to write, and the words came freely, as freely as the tears that come in the embrace of a friend. Suddenly he stopped in the middle of a sentence, thought for a moment, crumpled the letter and then tore it up.

"There is no agony worse than the agony of authorship," said Struchkov in his customary bantering tone.

He was sitting in his bed holding Gvozdev's letter, which he had picked up from Alexei's bedside cupboard and read.

"What's come over everybody today?... And Gvozdev too! Oh, the jackass! A girl turns her nose up, so he's all in tears. Psychological analysis. You are not angry with me for having read the letter, are you? What secrets can there be among us soldiers?"

Alexei was not angry. He was thinking: "Perhaps I should wait for the postman tomorrow when he comes to clear the box and take the letter back?"

Alexei slept badly that night. First he dreamt that he was on a snow-covered airfield where there was a plane of strange design, a "La-5", with bird's feet instead of landing gear. Yura the mechanic climbed into the cockpit and said Alexei's "flying days are over", and that it was now his turn to fly. Then he dreamt that he was lying on a bed of straw and Grandpa Mikhail, in a white shirt and wet pants, was steaming Alexei's body, laughing and saying: "A steam bath's just the thing before your wedding." And just before morning, he dreamt of Olya. She was sitting on an overturned boat with her strong, tanned legs in the water, light, slim and radiant. She was shading her eyes from the sun with one hand and, laughing, beckoned to him with the other. He swam towards her, but the current was strong and turbulent and carried him away from the bank and from the girl. He worked harder and harder with his arms, his legs, with all the muscles of his body, drew nearer and nearer to her and could already see her hair fluttering in the wind and the drops of water glistening on her tanned legs....

With that he woke, feeling bright and happy. He lay for a long time with eyes shut, trying to fall asleep in the hope of dreaming that pleasant dream again. But that happens only in one's childhood. The image of that frail, tanned girl in his dream seemed to have lit up everything.

He was not to worry, not to mope, but to swim towards Olya, swim against the stream, swim forward at all costs, exert every ounce of strength and reach the girl! But what about that letter? He wanted to go to the letter-box and wait for the postman, but he changed his mind, and with a wave of his hand said to himself: "Let it go. It won't frighten real love away." And believing now that love was real, that it was waiting for him whether happy or sad, sound or sick, whatever condition he would be in—he felt a new accretion of strength.

That morning, he tried to walk without crutches. He cautiously got up from the bed and stood with his feet apart, helplessly trying to keep his balance with his outstretched arms. Holding on to the wall, he took a step. The leather of the artificial feet creaked. His body swayed, but he kept his balance with his arms. He took another step, still holding on to the wall. He had never dreamed that walking was such a difficult job. When he was a boy he had learnt to walk on stilts. He would lean his back against a wall, get up on the stilts, push away from the wall and take one step, then a second and then a third—but his body would sway to one side, he would jump off, leaving the stilts lying in the grass growing in the suburban street. It was not so bad learning to walk on stilts, however, for you could jump off, but you can't jump off artificial feet. And when he tried to take the third step his body swayed, his foot gave way and he fell prone on the floor.

For his exercises he had chosen the hour when the other patients took their various treatments and there was nobody in the ward. He did not call for help. He crawled to the wall and, supporting himself against it, slowly rose to his feet, rubbed his side that he had hurt in his fall, looked at the bruise on his elbow, which was beginning to grow livid, and, clenching his teeth, took another step forward, pushing himself from the wall. It looked as though he had learned the trick. The difference between his artificial feet and ordinary ones was that they lacked elasticity. He was as yet unfamiliar with their properties and had not yet acquired the habit, the reflex, as it were, of changing the position of his feet in the process of walking, of transferring the weight of his body from heel to toe in taking a step, and from toe to heel in taking the next one, and also, of placing his feet not parallel to each other, but at an angle, toes outward, which lent more stability to the body when walking.

A man learns all this in his infancy when he takes his first awkward steps on his short, feeble legs under the care of his mother. These habits are acquired for the rest of one's life and become a natural impulse. When, however, a man is obliged to wear artificial limbs and the natural harmony of his body is disturbed, this impulse acquired in infancy, far from helping, impedes his movements. In learning to acquire new habits, he is obliged to combat the old impulse. Many people who have lost their limbs, if they lack sufficient will-power, never again learn the art of walking that we so easily learn in childhood.

Having set himself a goal, Meresyev was determined to reach it. Realising the mistake he made in his first attempt, he tried again. This time he turned the toe of his artificial foot outward, rested on the heel and then threw the weight of his body on the toe. The leather creaked angrily. The moment the weight was transferred to the toe, Alexei lifted the other foot from the floor and threw it forward. The heel struck the floor. He now stood away from the wall, balancing his body with his outstretched arms, not daring to take the next step. And there he stood, his body swaying, trying to keep his balance and feeling a cold sweat breaking out on the bridge of his nose.

It was in a moment like this that Vasily Vasilyevich discovered him. He stood at the door watching, then stepped towards him and, supporting him by the armpits, exclaimed:

"Good going! Why are you alone, without a nurse or an orderly? Proud, I suppose.... But never mind. As in everything you do, the first step is the most important, and you've got over the most difficult part."

Shortly before this Vasily Vasilyevich had been appointed head of an extremely important medical institution. It was a big job and took up an enormous amount of time. He was obliged to drop his work at the hospital, but the old veteran was still a consultant, and although others now directed its affairs, he came to the hospital every day, and if he had the time, went around the wards and gave advice. But he was a different man after the loss of his son. His former boisterous cheerfulness was gone; he no longer shouted and railed, and those who knew him well regarded this as a sign of approaching age.

"Now, Meresyev, let's learn this together," he proposed. Turning to his retinue, he said: "You go along, this is not a circus, there's nothing to look at. Finish the round without me." And then again to Meresyev: "Now then, boy ... one! Hold on, hold on to me, don't be shy! I'm a general, and you've got to obey me. Now, two! That's right. Now the right foot. Good! Left! That's fine!"

The famous surgeon rubbed his hands cheerfully as if in teaching a man to walk he was performing a God knows how important experiment. But such was his nature, to become enthused with everything he did, and to put all his great, energetic soul into it. He compelled Meresyev to walk the length of the ward, and when Alexei dropped completely exhausted on to a chair, he drew another chair up, sat down beside him and said:

"Well, are we going to fly? I should say so! In this war, my boy, men with an arm torn off lead companies in attacks, mortally wounded men fire machine-guns, men block enemy machine-guns with their bodies.... Only the dead are not fighting." A shadow crossed the old man's face and he added with a sigh: "But even the dead are fighting ... with their glory. Yes.... Now, young man, let's start again."

When Meresyev stopped to rest after his second lap across the ward, the professor pointed to the bed that Gvozdev had occupied and inquired:

"What about the tankman? Has he been discharged?"

Meresyev told him that the tankman had recovered and had rejoined his unit. The only trouble with him was that the burns had terribly mutilated his face, especially the lower part.

"So he has written to you already? I suppose he is heartbroken because the girls don't love him. Advise him to grow a beard and moustache. I mean it, seriously. It will look original, and the girls will take a fancy to him."

A nurse came panting into the ward and told Vasily Vasilyevich that there was a telephone call from the Council of People's Commissars. The professor rose heavily, and from the way he rested his puffy, peeling hands on his knees and bent his back in doing so, one could see how much he had aged during the past few weeks. At the door he turned round to Meresyev and said cheerfully:

"So don't forget to write to ... what's his name ... your friend, I mean ... and tell him that I prescribe a beard for him. It's a tried remedy ... and extremely popular with the ladies!"

That evening, an old attendant at the clinic brought Meresyev a walking-stick, a fine, old ebony stick with a comfortable ivory handle bearing a monogram.

"The professor sent you this," said the attendant. "Vasily Vasilyevich. It's his own. Sent it to you as a present. He said that you were to walk with a stick."

Things were dull in the hospital on that summer evening and so the patients in the wards on the right, the left and even from the floor above, took excursions to ward forty-two to see the professor's present. It was, indeed, a fine walking-stick.

15

The lull before the storm at the front dragged on. The communiqués reported fighting of local importance and skirmishes between scouting parties. There were fewer patients in the hospital now, and so the chief ordered the unoccupied beds in ward forty-two to be removed. Meresyev and Major Struchkov had the ward to themselves; Meresyev's bed was on the right and the major's on the left, near the window facing the embankment.

Skirmishes between scouting parties! Meresyev and Struchkov were experienced soldiers, and they knew that the longer the lull, the longer this strained calm lasted, the fiercer would be the storm that would follow it.

One day there was a reference in the communiqué to sniper Stepan Ivushkin, Hero of the Soviet Union, who had killed twenty-five Germans somewhere on the Southern Front, bringing his score up to two hundred. A letter arrived from Gvozdev. He did not, of course, say where he was, or what he was doing, but wrote that he had returned to the outfit of his former commander, Pavel Alexeyevich Rotmistrov, that he was satisfied with life, that there were lots of cherries where he was and all the boys were overeating themselves with them, and asked Alexei to drop a line to Anyuta upon receipt of this letter. He had written to her too, he said, but did not know whether his letters reached her.

These two communications were enough to tell a military man that the storm would break somewhere in the South. It goes without saying that Alexei wrote to Anyuta, and also sent Gvozdev the professor's advice to grow a beard; but he knew that Gvozdev was in that state of feverish anticipation of battle which causes such anxiety and yet such joy to every soldier, and so would have no time to think about a beard, or even, perhaps, about Anyuta.

Another happy event occurred in ward forty-two. A decree was published conferring on Major Pavel Ivanovich Struchkov the title of Hero of the Soviet Union; but even this joyful news failed to cheer the major up for long. He fell into the dumps again and cursed his shattered kneecaps, which tied him to his bed in a hectic time like this. There was another reason for his dejection which he tried to conceal, but which Alexei discovered in the most unexpected manner. Concentrating his mind entirely on one object—to learn to walk—Meresyev now scarcely noticed what was going on around him. He lived strictly in accordance with a daily schedule he had drawn up for himself: for three hours every day—one in the morning, one at midday and one in the evening—he practised walking in the corridor on his artificial feet. At first the patients in the other wards were annoyed by the figure in the blue gown passing by their open doors with the regularity of a pendulum and by the creaking of the leather limbs that echoed down the corridor; but later they grew so accustomed to this that they could not conceive of certain parts of the day without this figure passing their doors. So much so, indeed, that one day, when Meresyev was down with the flu, messengers were sent from the other wards to inquire what had happened to the footless lieutenant.

In the morning, Alexei did his physical exercises and then, sitting on a chair, he would train his feet to perform the motions necessary to control an aircraft. Sometimes he exercised until his head swam, until he heard a ringing in his ears and bright green circles swam before his eyes and the floor seemed to heave under him. When that happened he would go to the washstand, douse his head with cold water and lie down for a while in order to recover quickly so as not to miss his hour of walking and gymnastics.

That day, after walking until he grew dizzy, he groped his way into the ward, seeing nothing in front of him, and sank on to his bed. Recovering a little, he became conscious of voices in the ward: the calm, slightly ironical voice of Klavdia Mikhailovna, and the excited, pleading voice of Struchkov. Both were so taken up with their conversation that they failed to notice Meresyev coming into the ward.

"Believe me, I am talking seriously! Can't you understand? Are you a woman, or not?"

"Yes, of course I am a woman, but I don't understand, and you can't talk seriously on this subject. Besides, I don't want your seriousness!"

Struchkov lost his temper and shouted in a railing tone:

"I love you, damn it! You are not a woman, you are a block of wood not to see that! D'you understand now?" With that he turned away and drummed his fingers on the window-pane.

Klavdia Mikhailovna walked towards the door with the soft, cautious footsteps of the trained nurse.

"Where are you off to? Aren't you going to answer me?"

"This is neither the time nor the place to talk about that, I am on duty."

"Why don't you talk straight out? Why are you tormenting me? Answer!" There was a note of anguish in the major's voice now.

Klavdia Mikhailovna stopped at the door; her slim, graceful figure stood out clearly against the background of the dark corridor. Meresyev had never suspected that this quiet nurse, no longer young, could be so femininely firm and attractive. She stood in the doorway with her head thrown back and looked at the major as if from a pedestal.

"Very well," she said. "I will answer you. I do not love you, and probably will never be able to love you."

She went away. The major flung himself on his bed and buried his head in the pillow. Meresyev now saw the reason for the major's strange behaviour during the past few days, his irritableness and nervousness when the nurse came into the ward, and his sudden turns from cheerfulness to outbursts of violent anger.

He must have been enduring real torment. Alexei was sorry for him and at the same time pleased. When the major got up from his bed, Alexei could not forgo the pleasure of teasing him.

"Well, can I spit you in the face, Comrade Major?"

Had he foreseen the effect these words would have upon the major, he would not have uttered them even in jest. Struchkov rushed to Alexei's bed and in a voice of despair shouted:

"Spit! Go on, spit! You will be right. I deserve it. But what shall I do now? Tell me! Teach me what to do! You heard us, didn't you?..."

He sat down on the bed, clutching his head in his hands and swaying his body from side to side.

"Perhaps you think I was having a lark? But I wasn't. I was serious. I proposed in earnest to that ninny!"

In the evening, Klavdia Mikhailovna came into the ward on her usual round. As always, she was quiet, kind and patient. She seemed to radiate repose. She smiled at Meresyev and also at the major, but looked at the latter with perplexity, and even fear. Struchkov was sitting at the window biting his nails, and as the sound of Klavdia Mikhailovna's footsteps receded down the corridor he looked after her with an expression of anger mixed with admiration.

"Soviet angel!" he growled. "What fool gave her that name? She's a devil in a nurse's smock!"

The nurse from the office, a scraggy, middle-aged woman, came into the ward and inquired:

"Meresyev, Alexei, is he a walking patient?"

"No, a running one!" barked Struchkov.

"I did not come here for a joke," observed the nurse sternly. "Meresyev, Alexei, senior lieutenant, wanted on the telephone."

"A young lady?" asked Struchkov, livening up and winking at the irate nurse.

"I did not see her marriage certificate," hissed the nurse, sailing majestically out of the ward.

Meresyev leapt up from his bed. Cheerfully tapping his walking-stick, he overtook the nurse and actually did run down the stairs. For about a month he had been expecting a reply from Olya and the thought had flashed through his mind: perhaps it is she? But that could not be. She could not travel from that place near Stalingrad to Moscow at a time like this! Besides, how could she have found him here in the hospital, since he had told her that he was serving in some rear administration, and not in Moscow itself, but in a suburb? But at that moment Meresyev believed in miracles, and not noticing it himself, he ran, ran for the first time on his artificial feet, in a rolling gait, leaning on his stick only now and again, while his boots creaked: creak, creak, creak....

He picked up the receiver and he heard a pleasant, deep, but totally strange voice. He was asked whether he was Senior Lieutenant Alexei Petrovich Meresyev from ward forty-two. In a sharp and angry tone, as if there had been something offensive in that question, Meresyev barked:

"Yes!"

There was a moment's pause, and then the voice, now cold and strained, apologised for having troubled him and, evidently offended by the curt reply, went on to say with obvious effort:

"This is Anna Gribova speaking, a friend of Lieutenant Gvozdev's. You don't know me."

Meresyev grasped the receiver with both his hands and shouted into it, at the top of his voice:

"Are you Anyuta? Anyuta? I know you perfectly well! Grisha told me about...."

"Where is he? What has become of him? He went away so suddenly. I went out of the room when the alert was sounded. I am in a first-aid unit, you know. When I came back he was gone, and he left no note or address.... Alyosha dear ... excuse me for calling you that.... I know you too.... I am very worried about him. I'd like to know where he is, and why he left so suddenly...."

Alexei felt a warm feeling surge through his heart. He was glad for his friend's sake. The funny chap had been mistaken, too sensitive. So genuine girls are not scared by a soldier's disablement. And that meant that he too could count on somebody being worried about him and seeking him in the same way. These thoughts flashed through his mind like lightning as he shouted into the receiver, almost spluttering in his excitement:

"Anyuta! Everything's all right! It was a regrettable misunderstanding. He is quite well and on active service again. Of course! F.P.O. 42531-B. He is growing a beard! Honestly, Anyuta! A fine beard, like ... er ... like ... er, like the partisans wear! It becomes him!"

Anyuta did not approve of the beard. She thought it was superfluous. Still more delighted to hear this, Meresyev answered that since that was the case, Grisha would have the beard off in a jiffy, although everybody thought that the beard greatly improved his looks.

In the end, they both hung their receivers up as fast friends, arranging that Meresyev would telephone her before he left the hospital. On his way back to the ward Alexei remembered that he had run to the telephone. He tried to run again, but nothing came of it. The sharp impact of the artificial feet caused acute pain to shoot through his whole body. But never mind! If he couldn't run today he would tomorrow, and if not tomorrow, then the day after, but hell, he would run! Everything would be all right. He certainly would be able to run and fly, and fight, and being fond of pledges, he pledged himself, after his first air battle, after he had brought down his first German, to write and tell Olya everything, come what may!

PART THREE

1

At the height of the summer of 1942, a young, thickset man in the regulation step-collared coat and trousers of the Air Force, with the insignia of a senior lieutenant on his collar, emerged from the heavy oak doors of the army hospital in Moscow, leaning on a stout, ebony walking-stick. He was accompanied by a woman in a white smock. The kerchief with a red cross, of the kind nurses wore during the First World War, lent her kind, pretty face a solemn expression. They halted on the porch. The airman removed his crumpled, faded forage-cap and awkwardly bent to kiss the nurse's hand. The nurse took his head in both her hands and kissed his forehead. After that, the airman, with a slightly rolling gait, quickly descended the stairs and without looking back strode down the asphalted embankment past the long hospital building.

Patients in blue, yellow and brown pyjamas were standing at the windows waving their hands, walking-sticks or crutches and shouting parting advice to him. He waved his hand in reply, but it was evident that he was eager to get away from this big, grey building as quickly as possible, and he turned his head away from the windows to conceal his agitation. He walked quickly, with a queer, springy step, leaning lightly on his walking-stick. Were it not for the soft creak that accompanied every step, nobody would have thought that this well-built, sturdy-looking, active man had no feet.

On his discharge from hospital, Alexei Meresyev was sent to convalesce to the Air Force sanatorium near Moscow. Major Struchkov was sent to the same place. A car had been sent to take them to the sanatorium, but Meresyev had told the hospital authorities that he had relatives in Moscow and could not leave without visiting them. He left his kit-bag with Struchkov and went on foot, promising to get to the sanatorium in the evening by the electric train.

He had no relatives in Moscow, but he wanted very much to have a look round the capital, eager to try his strength in walking unaided, and to mix in a noisy crowd that was not in the least concerned about him. He had telephoned Anyuta and had asked her whether she could meet him at about twelve o'clock. Where? Well, say the Pushkin Monument.... So now he was striding along the embankment of the majestic, granite-bound river, the ruffled surface of which was glistening in the sun. As he walked, he deeply inhaled the warm summer air that was impregnated with a sweet, familiar fragrance.

How good everything was all round!

All the women he passed looked beautiful to him, and the green trees looked astonishingly bright. The air was so balmy that it turned his head like an intoxicant, and so clear that he lost his sense of perspective, and it seemed to him that he had only to stretch out his hand to touch the battlement walls of the Kremlin that he had never seen before except in pictures, the cupola of Ivan the Great belfry, and the huge, low arch of the bridge hanging heavily across the water. The sweet, intoxicating smell that filled the city reminded him of his boyhood. Where did it come from? Why was his heart throbbing so fast, and why was he thinking of his mother, not the present shrunken old lady, but young, tall, with magnificent hair? He had never been in Moscow with her!

Until now, Meresyev had known the capital only from illustrations in the magazines and newspapers, from books, from what he had heard from those who had visited it, from the slow midnight chimes of the ancient clock that rang out over the sleeping world, and from the medley of sounds that came through the radio receiver during holiday demonstrations. And now, here it was, spread before him, beautifully refracted in the hot summer light.

He walked down the deserted embankment along the Kremlin wall, stopped to rest against the cool granite parapet and gazed at the grey, oily water splashing against the foot of the granite wall, and then slowly ascended the hill leading to Red Square. The lime-trees in the asphalted streets and squares were in bloom, and amidst the simple, sweet-smelling blossoms in their clipped crowns bees were busily humming, completely ignoring the horns of passing automobiles, the clanging and rattling of street-cars and the shimmering, petrol-fume-laden haze that arose from the heated asphalt.

So this is Moscow!

After four months in hospital, Alexei was so amazed by this summer magnificence that he did not, at first, notice that the capital was in war garb and in the state of "readiness No. 1", as they called it in the Air Force, that is to say, ready to rise to meet the enemy at any moment. The wide street near the bridge was blocked by a big, ugly barricade consisting of log squares filled with sand: looking like toy cubes left on the table by a child, square, concrete gun emplacements with four embrasures towered at the corners of the bridge. On the grey surface of Red Square, houses, lawns and avenues were painted in different colours. The shop windows in Gorky Street were boarded up and protected with sandbags, and in the lanes, also looking like playthings abandoned by children, lay rusty "hedgehogs" made from rails. A soldier from the front, particularly one who had not been in Moscow before, would not see anything extraordinary in this. The only things that might have surprised him were the TASS windows, looking down at passers-by from walls, and shop windows, and the queer way in which the fronts of some of the houses were painted, reminding one of the absurd futurist pictures.

Fairly tired by now, Meresyev, with creaking boots, and leaning more heavily on his stick, walked up Gorky Street, looking round for and amazed not to find bomb pits and craters, wrecked buildings, gaping spaces and shattered windows. Having served in one of the most westerly airfields he had been accustomed to hear wave after wave of German bombers flying eastward over his dugout almost every night. Before the sounds of one wave had died out in the distance another would come rolling over, and sometimes the sky would be roaring all night. The airmen knew that the fascists were making for Moscow, and pictured to themselves the inferno that must be raging there.

And now, roaming through war-time Moscow, Meresyev sought the traces of air raids, but failed to find any. The asphalted roads were smooth, the buildings stood in serried ranks. Even the windows, criss-crossed with strips of paper, were, with few exceptions, intact. But the fighting line was near, and this could be seen from the care-worn faces of the inhabitants, half of whom were soldiers in dusty top-boots, tunics sticking to their shoulders from sweat, and with knapsacks on their backs. A long column of dusty lorries with dented mudguards and shattered wind-screens burst out of a lane into the sunlit main street. The soldiers in the battered lorries, their capes flying in the wind, looked around them with curiosity. The column moved on, overtaking trolley-buses, automobiles and trams, a living reminder that the enemy was not far away. Meresyev followed the column with longing eyes, thinking: if he could jump into one of those dusty lorries he would be at the front, at his own airfield, by evening! He pictured to himself the dugout which he had shared with Degtyarenko, the trestle beds made of fir logs, the pungent smell of tar, pine and of petrol in the primitive lamp made from a flattened cartridge, the roar of engines being warmed up in the morning, and the sound of the swaying pine-trees overhead that never ceased day or night. To him that dugout seemed to be a real, quiet, cosy home! If only he could get there soon, to that bog which the airmen cursed because of the dampness, the soggy ground and the ceaseless buzzing of mosquitoes!

With difficulty, he dragged his feet to the Pushkin Monument. On the way, he stopped to rest several times, leaning on his stick with both hands and pretending to examine some trifling articles in shop windows. With a sigh of relief he sat down, or rather dropped, on to a green, sun-warmed seat near the monument and stretched his legs, which ached and burned from the straps of his artificial feet. Tired as he was, the joyous feeling did not leave him. That bright sunny day was wonderful! The sky over the statue on the roof of the building on the corner of the street seemed infinite. A gentle breeze carried the fresh, sweet smell of the lime-trees along the boulevard. The trams clanged merrily, and merry was the laughter of the children who, though pale and thin, were busily burrowing in the warm, dry sand at the foot of the monument. Farther down the boulevard, behind a rope barrier, and guarded by two rosy-cheeked girls in smart military tunics, could be seen the silvery, cigar-shaped body of a barrage balloon, and this implement of war looked to Meresyev not like a night-watchman of the Moscow sky, but like a large, good-natured animal that had escaped from the Zoo and was now dozing in the cool shade of the trees.

Meresyev shut his eyes and turned his smiling face up to the sun.

At first, the children paid no attention to the airman. They reminded him of the sparrows on the windowsill of ward forty-two, and amidst the sound of their twittering he absorbed with his whole body the warmth of the sun and the noise of the street. But one little fellow, running away from his playmates, tripped over Alexei's outstretched feet and went sprawling in the sand.

For an instant, the little fellow's face was contorted by a tearful grimace, then it assumed an expression of perplexity, which gave way to a look of horror. The child cried out in fear and scampered off. The entire flock of children gathered around him and for some time chirped and twittered with alarm, casting sidelong glances at the airman. Then they slowly and furtively drew near him.

Absorbed in his reflections, Alexei noticed nothing. He opened his eyes and saw the children gazing at him in surprise and fear, and only then did he become conscious of what they were saying.

"You're fibbing, Vitamin! He's a real airman. A senior lieutenant," gravely observed a pale, thin lad of about seven.

"I'm not fibbing!" protested Vitamin. "May I drop down dead! Honestly, they're wooden! Not real, but wooden, I tell you!"

Meresyev felt a stab at the heart, and at once the brightness of the day was dimmed for him. He raised his eyes, and at his glance the children backed away from him, still gazing at his feet.

Piqued by his companion's scepticism, Vitamin said to him challengingly:

"If you like, I'll ask him. Think I'm afraid? Want to bet?"

He detached himself from the rest and sidled up to Meresyev, slowly, cautiously, ready to dart away in an instant, like "Submachine-Gunner" on the hospital windowsill. At last, standing strained, hunched like a runner on the mark, he ventured to ask:

"Comrade Senior Lieutenant, what kind of feet have you got, real ones or wooden? Are you an invalid?"

The small boy saw the airman's eyes fill with tears. Had Meresyev jumped up and yelled at him and gone for him with his funny walking-stick with the gold letters on it, he would not have been surprised, but to see an Air Force lieutenant cry! He did not so much realise as feel in his little heart the pain he had caused this soldier with the word "invalid". He silently drew back into the crowd of children, and the crowd vanished as if it had melted away in the hot air that smelt of honey and heated asphalt.

Alexei heard his name called. He jumped up at once. Anyuta stood before him. He recognised her immediately, although she was not as pretty as she looked in the photograph. Her face was pale and tired, and she wore a tunic and top-boots, and an old, faded forage-cap perched on her head. But her greenish, slightly bulging eyes looked at Meresyev with such brightness and simplicity, they radiated such friendship, that this girl, a stranger to him, seemed to be an old acquaintance, as if they had played in the same courtyard together as children.

For a moment, they gazed at each other in silence. At last she said:

"I pictured you altogether different."

"How did you picture me?" asked Meresyev, feeling unable to drive the not very appropriate smile from his face...

"Well, how shall I put it? You know, heroic, tall and strong. Yes, that's it, and a heavy jaw, like this, and, of course, a pipe in your mouth.... Grisha wrote so much about you!"

"Now your Grisha, he is a real hero!" interrupted Alexei, and seeing the girl brighten up at this he continued in the same strain, stressing the word "your". "Your Grisha is a real man! What am I? But your Grisha.... I suppose he told you nothing about himself...."

"D'you know what, Alyosha? I may call you Alyosha, mayn't I? I got used to that name from his letters. You have no other business in Moscow, have you? Then come to my place. I've come off duty and am free for the whole day. Come! I have some vodka at home. Do you like vodka? I'll treat you to some."

In an instant, out of the depth of his memory, there flashed before Alexei's eyes the sly face of Major Struchkov, and he seemed to hear him say gloatingly: "There you are! D'you see the kind she is? Lives alone! Vodka! Aha!" But Struchkov had been so discredited that he would not believe him now for anything. It was a long time before evening, so they strolled along the boulevard, chatting merrily like good old friends. It pleased him to notice that the girl bit her lips to restrain her tears when he told her what misfortune had befallen Gvozdev at the beginning of the war. Her greenish eyes flashed when he described his adventures at the front. How proud she was of him! How furiously she flushed when she questioned him to get more and more details? How indignant she was when she told him that Gvozdev, for no reason whatever, had sent her his pay certificate! And why did he run off so suddenly? Without saying a word, without leaving a note, or an address? Was it a military secret? But is it a military secret, when a man goes away without saying good-bye and doesn't write a word?

"By the way, why did you so strongly stress the fact that he is growing a beard?" asked Anyuta, looking at him inquisitively.

"Oh, just blurted it out. There's nothing in it," answered Meresyev evasively.

"No, no! Tell me! I'll not let you alone until you do. Is that a military secret, too?"

"Of course not! It's simply that our Professor Vasily Vasilyevich, well ... prescribed a beard ... so that the girls ... I mean, so that a certain girl should like him more."

"Ah, so that's it! Now I understand everything!"

Suddenly, the light went out of Anyuta's greenish eyes, she seemed to grow older. The paleness of her face became more marked, and tiny wrinkles, so fine that they seemed to have been traced with a needle, appeared on her forehead and at the corners of her eyes, and altogether, in her old and worn tunic and with the faded forage-cap on her chestnut hair, she looked tired and weary. Only her small, full, bright red mouth with the barely perceptible down and tiny mole on the upper lip showed that she was still young, that she had barely reached twenty.

It happens in Moscow that you walk along a wide street in the shade of magnificent houses and then you turn off that street, take a dozen steps or so, and you find yourself before a small, squat house with tiny windows dim with age. It was in a house like this that Anyuta lived. They climbed a narrow staircase that smelt of cats and kerosene to the upper floor. The girl opened the door with a key. Stepping past a bag of provisions and some tin bowls and billycans that were kept in the cool of the small passage, they entered a dark and deserted kitchen, passed through a short corridor and came to a low door. A little, lean old woman poked her head out of a door opposite.

"Anna Danilovna, there's a letter for you," she said and, gazing inquisitively at the young people until they had entered the room, she vanished.

Anyuta's father was a lecturer at an institute. When the institute was evacuated, Anyuta's parents went with it, and the two rooms, crowded like an antique store with furniture in linen covers, were left to the girl's care. The furniture, the old, heavy hangings over the door and windows, the pictures on the walls and the statuettes and vases on the piano gave off an odour of mustiness and desolation.

"You must excuse the disorder. I am living at the hospital and from there I go straight to the university. I only visit this place now and again," said Anyuta flushing, hastily removing the litter from the table together with the tablecloth.

She left the room, returned and replaced the tablecloth, carefully smoothing the edges.

"Even when I do get a chance to come home I am so tired that I have just strength enough to drag myself to the couch and fall asleep without even undressing. So there's not much time for tidying up!"

A few minutes later, the electric kettle was singing: old, faded china cups were glistening on the table, some thin slices of rye bread were lying on a china bread plate, and at the very bottom of a sugar bowl lay some sugar broken up into tiny pieces. A teapot, hidden under a tea-cosy with woollen tassels, also a last-century product, was filling the room with a fragrant odour which was reminiscent of prewar times, and in the middle of the table stood an unopened bottle with a bluish tint, guarded on either side by a thin goblet.

Meresyev was sitting in a deep, velvet-covered armchair. So much stuffing was peeping out from under the green velvet upholstery that the embroidered woollen rugs that had been carefully fastened to the back and the seat were unable to conceal it. But the armchair was so comfortable, cosily and kindly embracing the sitter, that Alexei at once leaned back in it and luxuriously stretched out his tired, aching legs.

Anyuta sat on a low stool beside him and, looking up into his face like a little girl, began to question him again about Gvozdev. Suddenly, remembering her duty as a hostess, she jumped up scolding herself and pulled Alexei to the table.

"Will you have a glass? Grisha told me that tankmen and airmen too, of course...."

She pushed a glass towards Alexei. The bluish tint of vodka sparkled in the bright sunbeams that slanted into the room. The smell of the alcohol reminded Alexei of the airfield in the distant forest, the officers' mess, and the cheerful hum that accompanied the issue of the "fuel ration" at dinner. Seeing that the other glass remained empty Alexei asked:

"What about you?"

"I don't drink," answered Anyuta simply.

"But suppose we drink to him, to Grisha?"

The girl smiled, silently filled her glass, held it by its slender stem and with a thoughtful look in her eyes clinked with Alexei and said:

"Here's luck to him!"

She raised her glass with a flourish, emptied it at a gulp and at once began to cough and splutter. Her face turned red and she could barely catch her breath.

Not having tasted vodka for a long time, Meresyev felt the liquor go to his head and send a warm glow through his body. He refilled the glasses, but Anyuta shook her head resolutely.

"No, no! I don't drink. You saw what happened."

"But won't you drink good luck to me?" urged Alexei. "If you only knew, Anyuta, how much I need it!"

The girl looked at him very gravely, raised her glass, nodded to him with a smile, gently squeezed his elbow and emptied the glass again, but again she coughed and spluttered.

"What am I doing?" she exclaimed when, at last, she caught her breath. "And after a twenty-four hours' spell of duty! I am doing it only for your sake, Alyosha. You are ... Grisha wrote a lot about you.... I do wish you good luck, I wish it very, very much. And you will have good luck, I am certain. Do you hear what I say? I am certain." And she broke into a merry peal of laughter. "But you are not eating! Take some bread. Don't be shy. I have some more. This is yesterday's. I haven't received today's ration yet." She pushed the china bread plate with the slices cut as thin as paper towards him. "Eat, you silly boy, otherwise you'll get tipsy, and what will I do with you then?"

Alexei pushed the bread plate away, looked straight into Anyuta's eyes and at her small, full, bright red lips and said in a low voice:

"What would you do if I kissed you?"

She gave him a frightened glance, sobering up at once. There was no anger in her eyes, but inquiry and disappointment, as if they were looking at something that a moment ago had sparkled in the distance like a precious stone and now turned out to be but a piece of common glass.

"I would probably chase you out and then write Grisha and tell him that he is a bad judge of people," she answered coldly. Pushing the bread plate towards him again she added insistently: "Eat something, you're drunk!"

Meresyev's face beamed.

"And you would be absolutely right! Thanks for that! I thank you in the name of the entire Soviet Army! And I'll write to Grisha and tell him that he is a very good judge of people!"

They chatted until about three o'clock, when the dusty sunbeams that slanted into the room began to creep up the wall. It was time for Alexei to catch his train. Sadly and reluctantly, he got up from the green velvet armchair, taking some of the stuffing with him on his coat. Anyuta saw him off to the station. They walked arm in arm and, having rested, Alexei stepped out so confidently that Anyuta asked herself: "Was Grisha joking when he wrote that his friend had no feet?" She told Alexei about the base hospital where she and other medical students now worked, sorting the wounded. There was plenty of work, she said, because several trainloads of wounded were coming in every day from the South. And what wonderful men these wounded were, and how bravely they bore their sufferings! Suddenly she interrupted herself and asked:

"Were you serious when you said that Grisha was growing a beard?" She was silent and pensive for a moment and then added: "I understand everything now. I'll tell you honestly, as I told my Dad: at first I could not bear to look at his scars. No, not bear, that's not the right word. I mean—frightened. No! That's not right, either. I don't know how to describe it. Can you understand me? Perhaps it was not nice of me, but what can one do? But to run away from me! The silly boy! Lord, what a silly boy! If you write to him, tell him that I am hurt, hurt very much by his behaviour."

The vast railway station was filled almost entirely with soldiers, some hurrying on definite errands and others sitting silently on the forms ranged round the walls or on their kit-bags, or squatting on the floor, with frowning, care-worn faces, their minds seemingly concentrated upon a single thought. At one time, this line was the main connection with Western Europe; the enemy had now cut the road to the West about eighty kilometres from Moscow. Only troop trains ran on the short remaining stretch, and in a matter of two hours the men travelled from the capital straight to the second echelon of their respective divisions that were holding the defence line here. And every half-hour an electric train unloaded on the platform crowds of workers who lived in the suburbs, and peasant women bringing in milk, fruit, mushrooms and vegetables. For a while, these noisy crowds flooded the railway station, but they soon flowed into the square, leaving the station once again in the sole possession of the military.

In the main hall, stretching right to the ceiling, hung a huge map of the Soviet-German front. A plump girl in military uniform was standing on a step-ladder holding a newspaper with the latest communiqué of the Soviet Information Bureau and marking the fighting line with a string attached to pins.

In the lower part of the map, the string turned at a sharp angle to the right. The Germans were advancing in the South. They had broken through in the Izyum-Barvenkovo region. Their Sixth Army had driven a blunt wedge into the heart of the country and was pointing towards the blue vein of the Don salient. The girl fastened the string on the line of the Don. Quite near to it wound the thick artery of the Volga, with Stalingrad marked with a large circle, and Kamyshin, indicated by a dot, above it. It was evident that the enemy wedge which had struck the Don was driving towards this main artery and was already near it. In grim silence, a large crowd, over which the girl on the step-ladder towered, watched the girl's plump hands changing the position of the pins. A young soldier with a perspiring face, in a new, as yet uncreased greatcoat that hung stiffly from his shoulders, said, mournfully thinking aloud:

"The bastards are pushing hard.... Look how they are pushing!"

A tall, lean railwayman with a grey moustache, and wearing a greasy railwayman's cap, looked down frowningly upon the soldier and growled:

"Pushing, are they? But why are you letting them? Of course, they'll push if you back away from them! Fine fighters you are! Look where they've got to! Almost up to the Volga!" His voice expressed pain and grief, like that of a father rebuking his son for having made a grave and unpardonable blunder.

The soldier looked round guiltily and, hunching his shoulders to adjust his brand-new greatcoat, began to push his way out of the crowd.

"You are right! We've lost a lot of ground," sighed another man, and shaking his head bitterly, he exclaimed: "Ekh!"

Here an old man in a canvas dust-coat, a village schoolteacher or, perhaps, a country doctor, spoke up in defence of the soldier:

"Why blame him? Is it his fault? How many of them have been killed already! Look at the force that's pushing against us! The whole of Europe—and in tanks! How can you hold that up all at once? By rights we ought to go down on our knees and thank that boy that we are still alive and walking freely about Moscow. Look how many countries the fascists have trampled with their tanks within a week! But we have been fighting for over a year and we are still hitting back—and how many we have laid out! The whole world ought to go down on its knees to that boy! And you say 'back away'."

"I know, I know, for God's sake don't give me any propaganda! My mind knows it, but my heart aches fit to burst!" answered the railwayman gloomily. "It's our land the Germans are trampling, it's our homes they are destroying!"

"Is he there?" asked Anyuta, pointing to the southern part of the map.

"Yes. And she's there, too," answered Alexei.

Right on the blue loop of the Volga, above Stalingrad, he saw a dot over which was the inscription "Kamyshin". For him it was something more than a dot on the map. The vision rose before his eyes of a small green town, grassy suburban streets, poplar-trees with rustling, shiny, dusty leaves, the smell of dust, fennel and parsley coming from wattle-fenced vegetable plots, the round, striped melons looking as if they had been scattered among the dried leaves on the dry earth of the melon patches, the wind of the steppe impregnated with the pungent smell of wormwood, the indescribable shining expanse of the river, a graceful, grey-eyed, sun-tanned girl, and his mother, grey-haired and helplessly fussy....

"They're both there," he repeated.

2

The electric train sped through the Moscow suburbs, its wheels rattling out a merry tune and its siren sounding angrily. Meresyev sat near the window, forced right up against the wall by a clean-shaven old man wearing a broad-brimmed Maxim Gorky hat and gold-rimmed pince-nez attached to a black cord. Between his knees he held a hoe, a spade and a pitchfork, carefully wrapped in newspaper and tied with string.

Like everybody else in those grim days, the old man thought of nothing but the war. He vigorously waved his thin hand in front of Meresyev's nose and whispered into his ear in an important manner:

"You mustn't think that I don't understand our plan because I'm a civilian. I understand it perfectly. It's to entice the enemy into the steppes of the Volga, yes, and get him to stretch his lines of communication, to lose contact with his base, as they say nowadays, and then, from there, from the west and the north, cut his communications and smash him. Yes. And it's a very clever plan. We haven't got only Hitler against us. He is whipping the whole of Europe against us. We are fighting single-handed against six countries. Single-handed! We've got to weaken the force of their blow at least with the aid of space. Yes. This is the only reasonable way. After all, our allies are keeping quiet, aren't they? What do you think?"

"I think you are talking piffle. Our land is too precious to use it as a shock absorber," answered Meresyev in an unfriendly tone, suddenly remembering the desolate, gutted village he had crawled through in the winter.

But the old man went on buzzing in Meresyev's ear, breathing the smell of tobacco and barley coffee into his face.

Alexei leaned out of the window and, letting the gusts of warm, dusty wind buffet his face, gazed eagerly at the passing stations with their faded green fences and gaily painted kiosks now boarded up, at the little cottages peeping out of the green woods, at the emerald banks of the now dried-up streams, at the wax-candle trunks of the pine-trees shining like amber in the light of the setting sun, and at the wide expanse looming blue in the twilight beyond the woods.

"...You are a military man, tell me, is it right? For over a year now we've been fighting fascism single-handed. What do you think of that? But where are our allies, and the second front? Now you just picture it to yourself: Robbers attack a man who, suspecting nothing, was labouring in the sweat of his brow. But this man doesn't lose his head. He goes for those robbers and fights them. He is bleeding all over, but he keeps on fighting with whatever weapon he can lay his hands on. One against many; they are armed, and had been lying in wait for him a long time. Yes. And the man's neighbours see this fight. They stand at their doors and sympathise with the man, encourage him and say: 'Good for you, boy! Give it to 'em! Give it to 'em hot!' And instead of going to his assistance they offer him sticks and stones and say: 'Here you are! Hit 'em with this! Hit 'em hard!' But they keep out of the fight themselves. Yes. That's how our allies are behaving!... Passengers, that's all they are...."

Meresyev turned round and looked at the old man with interest. Many other passengers in the crowded car were looking in their direction, and from all sides came exclamations:

"Yes, he is right! We're fighting single-handed! Where's the second front?"

"Never mind! We'll buckle in and beat the enemy ourselves. They'll, no doubt, come along with their second front when it's all over!"

The train made a short stop. Several wounded men in pyjamas, some on crutches and others with walking-sticks, and all carrying paper bags with sunflower seeds or berries, got into the car. They must have come from some sanatorium to the market at this place. The old man in the pince-nez at once jumped up and almost forcibly pushed a red-haired lad on crutches, with a bandaged leg, into his seat.

"Sit here, my boy, sit here!" he cried. "Don't worry about me. I'll be getting off soon."

To prove that he meant it, the old man picked up his gardening tools and made for the door. The milk women squeezed up to make room for the wounded men.

Behind him Alexei heard a feminine voice say in reproach: "He ought to be ashamed of himself, letting a wounded man stand next to him and not offering him a seat! The poor lad is being crushed, but he doesn't care a bit! Sits there, quite sound himself, as if bullets will never touch him. An Air Force officer, too!"

Alexei flushed at this undeserved rebuke. His nostrils quivered with anger ... but suddenly he got up with a beaming face and said:

"Take this seat, buddy."

The wounded man started back in confusion:

"No thanks, Comrade Senior Lieutenant. Don't trouble, I can stand. We haven't far to go. Only two stops."

"Sit down, I tell you!" said Alexei with affected sternness, seeing the humour of the situation.

He made his way to the side of the car, leaned against the wall, supported himself on his walking-stick with both his hands and stood there smiling. Evidently the old woman in the check kerchief who had rebuked Alexei saw that she had been mistaken, for her reproachful voice was heard again:

"Look at them! Hey, you over there, in the hat! Sitting there like a princess. Offer the officer with the stick a seat! Come over here, Comrade Officer, you can take my seat. For God's sake, make way there, and let the officer get through!"

Alexei pretended not to hear. The amusement he had felt passed off. At this moment, the conductress called out the name of the stop at which he was to get off and the train slowly came to a standstill. Pushing his way through the crowd to the door he came up with the old man in the pince-nez. The latter nodded to him as if to an old acquaintance and asked in a whisper:

"Well, what do you think, will they open the second front after all?"

"If they don't, we'll manage ourselves," answered Alexei, stepping on to the wooden platform.

Grinding its wheels and loudly sounding its siren the train vanished round the bend, leaving a thin trail of dust. The platform, with only a few passengers, was soon enveloped in fragrant evening repose. This must have been a pleasant, restful place before the war. The tree tops in the pine wood that pressed closely around the station rustled in soothing rhythm. No doubt, two years ago, on lovely evenings like this, crowds of people—smartly dressed women in light summer frocks, noisy children, and cheerful, tanned men returning from town carrying parcels of provisions and bottles of wine—must have poured from the station along the lanes and paths through the shady wood to the cottages. The few passengers that had alighted from this train carrying hoes, spades, pitchforks and other garden tools quickly left the platform and gravely entered the wood, each absorbed with his own cares. Meresyev alone, with his walking-stick, looking like a holiday-maker, stopped to admire the beauty of the summer evening, deeply inhaled the balmy air and screwed up his eyes as he felt against his face the warm touch of the sunbeams that broke through the pine-trees.

In Moscow, he had been told how to get to the sanatorium and, like a true soldier, he was soon able, by the few landmarks he had been given, to find his way to the place. It was about a ten minutes' walk from the station, on the shore of a small, peaceful lake. Before the Revolution a Russian millionaire decided to build a summer palace here unlike any other palace of its kind. He told his architect that money was no consideration as long as he built something entirely original. And so, pandering to the tastes of his patron, the architect erected on the shore of this lake a huge brick pile with narrow latticed windows, turrets and spires, flying buttresses and intricate passages. This absurd structure was an ugly patch on the typical Russian landscape, on the lake shore, now overgrown with sedge. And it was a beautiful landscape! On the edge of the water, as smooth as glass in calm weather, stood a clump of young aspen-trees with trembling leaves. Here and there the speckled trunks of birch-trees towered up from the undergrowth, and the lake itself was framed in a wide, bluish, serrated ring formed by the ancient wood. All this was reflected upside down in the cool, calm, bluish surface of the water.

Many famous painters had paid long visits to this place, the owner of which was noted all over Russia for his hospitality; and this landscape, in whole and in part, has been reproduced for posterity in numerous canvases as an example of the mighty and modest grandeur of the Russian scene.

This palace now served as a sanatorium of the Soviet Air Force. In peacetime airmen had visited this place with their wives and children. Now, wounded airmen were sent here from hospital to convalesce. Alexei arrived at the place not by the wide, roundabout, birch-lined, asphalted road, but by the track through the wood that led from the station straight to the lake. He approached it from the rear, so to speak, and mingled unnoticed in a large, noisy throng that surrounded two crowded buses standing at the main entrance.

From the conversation, farewell greetings and wishes of good luck Alexei gathered that they were saying goodbye to airmen who were leaving the sanatorium for the front. The departing airmen were merry and excited as if they were going not to a place where death lurked behind every cloud, but to their own, peacetime garrisons. The faces of those who were bidding them goodbye expressed sadness and impatience. Alexei knew that feeling; he himself had been feeling that same irresistible attraction ever since the beginning of the gigantic battle that was raging in the South; and it had intensified as the situation on the front developed and became graver. And when Stalingrad was mentioned in military circles, quietly and cautiously as yet, this feeling grew into an infinite longing and his enforced idleness at the hospital had become unbearable.

Tanned, excited faces looked out of the windows of the smart buses. A short, lame Armenian in striped pyjamas, with a bald patch on his head, one of the generally recognised wits and voluntary comedians that one always finds in every contingent of convalescents, hobbled and fussed around the buses, waving his stick and shouting his parting greetings:

"Fedya! Give my regards to the fascists in the air! Pay them out for not letting you finish your course of moon bath treatment! Fedya! Fedya! Make them feel that it is caddish to prevent Soviet aces from taking their moon baths!"

Fedya, a young man with a tanned face and round head, with a large scar running across his high forehead, leaned out of the window and shouted that the Moon Committee could rest assured that he would do his duty.

There was an outburst of laughter from the crowd, and amidst this laughter the buses started off, moving slowly towards the gates.

"Good hunting! Safe journey!" were the greetings that came from the crowd.

"Fedya! Fedya! Send us your P.O. number as soon as you can! Zinochka will send your heart back by registered post!..."

The buses vanished behind the bend. The dust, turned into gold by the setting sun, settled. The convalescents in gowns or striped pyjamas dispersed and strolled round the park. Meresyev entered the vestibule where airmen's caps with blue bands were hanging on cloak-room hooks, and skittles, balls, croquet mallets and tennis-rackets were lying on the floor in the corners. The lame Armenian led him to the reception-room. A closer inspection showed that he had a serious, clever face and fine, large, mournful eyes. On the way, he jestingly introduced himself as the Chairman of the Moon Committee and asserted that moon baths were the best means of healing every kind of wound, that he insisted on strict order and discipline in the taking of moon bath treatments and that he personally made the arrangements for strolls in the moonlight. He seemed to joke automatically, while his eyes retained their grave expression and peered keenly and inquisitively into the face of his listener.

In the reception-room, Meresyev was received by a girl in a white smock and with hair so red that her head seemed to be in flames.

"Meresyev?" the girl inquired sternly, putting aside the book she was reading. "Meresyev, Alexei Petrovich?" She cast a critical glance at the airman and said: "Don't try to play any tricks on me! I've got you down here as 'Meresyev, senior lieutenant from the Nth hospital, amputated feet!'... but you...."

Only then did Alexei see her round face, white, as all red-haired girls have, and almost hidden by a mass of fiery hair. A bright flush diffused her tender skin. She looked at Alexei in amazement with her bright, round, impudent eyes.

"Still, I am Alexei Meresyev. Here are my papers.... Are you Lyolya?"

"No! Why? I am Zina." She looked suspiciously at Alexei's feet and added: "Have you got such good artificial feet, or what?"

"Yes. So you are the Zinochka that Fedya lost his heart to!"

"So Major Burnazyan has been gossiping already! Oh, how I hate that man! He makes fun of everybody. I taught Fedya to dance. There's nothing particular about that, is there?"

"And now you will teach me to dance, all right? Burnazyan promised to put me down for moon baths."

The girl looked at Alexei in still greater amazement.

"What do you mean, dance? With no feet? Nonsense! I suppose you, too, like to make fun of everybody."

Just then, Major Struchkov came running into the room and flung his arms around Alexei.

"Zinochka!" he said to the girl. "It's arranged, isn't it? The senior lieutenant comes into my room."

Men who have spent a long time in hospital together meet later as brothers. So pleased was Alexei to see the major that one would have thought he had not seen him for years. Struchkov already had his kit-bag in the sanatorium and felt quite at home; he knew everybody, and everybody knew him. In the course of one day, he had managed to make friends with some and to quarrel with others.

The windows of the small room they both occupied faced the park, of which the tall, straight pine-trees, green bilberry bushes and a slender mountain ash from which hung as from a palm a few gracefully patterned leaves and only one, but a very heavy, bunch of berries, came right up to the house. Soon after supper, Alexei went to bed, stretched out between the cool sheets and at once fell asleep.

He dreamed strange, troubled dreams that night. Bluish snow. Moonlight. The forest enveloped him like a furry net. He tried to break out of this net, but the snow held him by the feet. He struggled hard, conscious that some frightful disaster awaited him, but his feet had frozen into the snow and he lacked the strength to tear them away. He groaned, twisted and tossed—and he was no longer in the forest, but in the airfield. Yura, the lanky mechanic, was in the cockpit of a strange, soft and wingless aircraft. He waved his hand, laughed and shot up in the air. Grandpa Mikhail took Alexei into his arms as if he were an infant, and said soothingly: "Never mind! We'll have a nice steam bath. That will be fine, won't it?" But instead of putting him in a warm bath, Grandpa laid him in the cold snow. Alexei tried to get up but the snow held him fast. No, it was not the snow; the hot body of a bear was lying on top of him, snorting, crushing and suffocating him. Busloads of airmen passed by, looking cheerfully out of the windows, but they did not see him. Alexei wanted to call to them for assistance, to run towards them, at least to signal to them with his hand, but he could not. He opened his mouth, but only a hoarse whisper came from it. He was beginning to choke, he felt his heart stop beating, he made one last effort and for some reason the laughing face and impudent, inquisitive eyes of Zinochka flashed before him amidst a mass of flaming hair.

Alexei awoke with a feeling of unaccountable alarm. Silence reigned. The major was asleep, snoring softly. A phantomlike moonbeam crossed the room and struck the floor. Why had those terrible days returned to him? He had almost stopped thinking about them, but when he did they seemed unreal. Together with the cool and fragrant night air, a soft, sleepy, rhythmic sound poured through the wide-open, moonlit window, now rising in an agitated tremor, now subsiding in the distance, and now halting at a high note as if checked by alarm. It was the sound of the wood.

The airman sat up in bed and listened for a long time to the mysterious rustling of the pines. He vigorously shook his head as if driving away an enchantment and again became filled with stubborn, cheerful energy. His stay at the sanatorium was to last twenty-eight days, which would decide whether he would fly, fight, live, or whether he would for ever meet sympathetic glances and be offered a seat in the street-car. Therefore, every minute of these long and yet short twenty-eight days must be devoted to the struggle to become a real man.

Sitting in his bed in the ghostly light of the moon amidst the sounds of the major's snoring, Alexei mentally drew up a plan of exercises. In it he included morning and evening gymnastics, walking, running, special foot training, and what attracted him most, what promised to provide all-round development for his legs, was the idea that had occurred to him when he had talked to Zinochka.

He decided to learn to dance.

3

On a clear, tranquil August afternoon, when everything in nature was sparkling and glittering, when there already were certain as yet imperceptible signs of the sad touch of autumn in the hot air, several airmen were basking in the sun on the sandy bank of a tiny stream that wound and rippled through the bushes.

Languid from the heat, they dozed, and even tireless Burnazyan was silent, heaping the warm sand on his broken leg, that had healed badly. They were hidden from view by the grey leaves of a hazel bush, but they were able to see a path that had been trodden in the green grass on the upper bank of the stream. While engaged with his leg, Burnazyan happened to look up and a strange spectacle met his eyes.

The newcomer who had arrived the day before emerged from the wood wearing only pyjama trousers and boots. He looked around and finding nobody in sight began to run in queer hops, pressing his elbows to his sides. After running about two hundred metres he dropped into a walking pace, breathing heavily and sweating. After recovering his wind he began to run again. His body shone like the flanks of a winded horse. Burnazyan silently drew his comrades' attention to the runner and they began to watch him from behind the bush. The newcomer was panting from these simple exercises, every now and again he winced with pain, groaned, but went on running.

Unable to restrain himself any longer, Burnazyan called out:

"Hey, friend! Are you training to beat the Znamensky brothers?"

The newcomer pulled up with a jerk. Weariness and pain vanished from his face. He looked calmly in the direction of the bush and without a word walked into the wood with a strange rolling gait.

"What is he, a circus performer, or is he dotty?" inquired Burnazyan in perplexity.

Major Struchkov, who had just woken up from his doze, explained:

"He has no feet. He is training on artificial ones. Wants to go back to Fighter Command."

These words acted like a cold shower upon those languid men. They jumped up and all began to talk at once. They were amazed that the man about whom they had noticed nothing peculiar, except that he walked with a strange gait, had no feet. His idea of his flying a fighter plane seemed absurd, incredible, even blasphemous to them. They recalled stories of men being discharged from the Air Force for trifling things, for losing two fingers, for strained nerves, and even for revealing symptoms of flat feet. Always, even in wartime, the standard of physical fitness demanded of an air pilot was higher than in any other arm of the service. And lastly, they were of the opinion that it was utterly impossible for a man with artificial feet to pilot a complicated, sensitive machine like a fighter.

They all agreed that Meresyev's idea was fantastic; nevertheless, it fascinated them.

"Your friend is either a hopeless idiot or a great man, nothing in between," was Burnazyan's conclusion.

The news that there was in the sanatorium a footless man who dreamed of flying a fighter plane flashed through all the wards in an instant. By dinner-time, Alexei was the centre of attention, although he himself did not seem to notice it. And all those who watched him, who saw and heard him laughing heartily with his neighbours at the table, eating with a hearty appetite, paying the traditional compliments to the pretty waitresses, strolling with companions in the park, learning to play croquet and even taking a hand at the volleyball net, failed to notice anything extraordinary about him, except the slow, springy step with which he walked. He was too ordinary, in fact. Everybody soon got used to him and ceased to pay any particular attention.

Late in the afternoon of the day after his arrival, Alexei went to the reception-room to see Zinochka. He had saved a pastry from his dinner and now held it wrapped in a burdock leaf. He gallantly presented the pastry to Zinochka, unceremoniously sat down at the desk and asked the girl when she intended to keep her promise.

"What promise?" asked Zinochka, raising her arched, pencilled eyebrows.

"You promised to teach me to dance, Zinochka."

"But..." the girl tried to protest.

"I am told that you are such a good teacher that cripples learn to dance, while normal men lose not only their feet but also their heads, as was the case with Fedya. When shall we start? Don't let us lose precious time."

Yes, she positively liked this newcomer. He had no feet, yet he wanted her to teach him to dance! And why not? He was a nice man, dark, with an even flush showing through the dark skin of his cheeks, and soft, wavy hair. He walked like ordinary people and he had lively eyes, bantering and yet a little sad. Dancing occupied no small place in Zinochka's life. She loved to dance, and was, indeed, a good dancer.... And Meresyev, well, he really was handsome!

To cut a long story short, she consented. She told Alexei that she had been taught to dance by Bob Gorokhov, who was famous throughout Sokolniki, and that he, in turn, was the best pupil and follower of Paul Sudakovsky, who was famous throughout Moscow and taught dancing at military academies and at the club of the Commissariat for Foreign Affairs; that she had taken over from these celebrities the best traditions of ballroom dancing and would undertake to teach even him to dance, although, of course, she was not quite sure that it was possible to dance without real feet. The terms on which she consented to teach him were severe: he must be obedient and diligent, try not to fall in love with her, since that interferes with the lessons, and chiefly—he must not be jealous when other partners invite her to dance, because if she were to dance only with one partner she would lose her skill, and besides, there was no fun sticking to only one partner.

Meresyev accepted the terms without reservation. Zinochka tossed her fiery head and there and then, skilfully moving her pretty feet, demonstrated the first steps. At one time Meresyev had shown great agility in dancing the *Russkaya* and the old dances the fire-brigade band used to play in the public park in Kamyshin. He had a sense of rhythm and quickly learned the merry art. The difficulty he was faced with now was to learn to manoeuvre not living, flexible, mobile feet, but leather contraptions strapped to his calves. Superhuman effort, an intense exertion of will-power was required to put life and motion into the heavy and unwieldy artificial feet.

But he compelled them to obey him. Every new step he learned—every glissade, parade, serpent and point— the intricate technique of ball-room dancing, theorised by the celebrated Paul Sudakovsky and provided with an imposing and euphonious terminology, filled him with the utmost joy, made him as jolly as a sandboy. Having learnt it, he would raise his teacher off the floor and whirl her round in celebration of his triumph over himself. And nobody, least of all his teacher, could suspect what pain these diverse, intricate steps caused him, the price he paid for learning to dance. Nobody saw that when he wiped the sweat off his smiling face with a careless gesture, he also wiped away unbidden tears.

One day, he limped to his room completely worn out but happy.

"I'm learning to dance!" he triumphantly announced to Major Struchkov, who was standing thoughtfully at the window, outside of which the summer's day was quietly waning, and through which the last rays of the setting sun could be seen glistening like gold among the tree tops.

The major made no response.

"And I'll succeed!" Meresyev added resolutely, throwing off his artificial feet with relief and vigorously scratching his numbed legs with his finger-nails.

Struchkov kept his face to the window; his shoulders heaved and he uttered strange sounds, as if he were sobbing. Silently, Alexei crept under his blanket. Something strange was happening to the major. This man, no longer young, who only recently had amused and outraged the hospital ward with his jesting cynicism and scorn for the fair sex, had fallen in love, head over heels in love like a schoolboy, and, it seemed, hopelessly. Several times a day he would go to the reception-room to telephone Klavdia Mikhailovna in Moscow. With every departing patient he sent her flowers, fruit, chocolate and written messages. He wrote her long letters and was happy and joked when he was handed a familiar envelope.

But she rejected his advances, gave him no encouragement, was not even sorry for him. She wrote that she loved, and mourned, another, and in friendly terms advised the major to give her up, to forget her, not to go to expense on her account, or waste time on her. It was this friendly but matter-of-fact tone, so offensive in love affairs, that upset the major so.

Alexei already lay stretched out under the blanket, remaining diplomatically quiet, when the major darted away from the window to Alexei's bed, shook him by the shoulder and, bending over him, shouted:

"What does she want? What am I, tell me? Chaff in the field? Am I ugly, old, a leper? Anybody else in her place ... but what's the use of talking!"

He flung himself into an armchair, grasped his head with his hands and rocked to and fro so vigorously that the armchair groaned.

"She's a woman, isn't she? She ought to be at least curious about me! The she-devil. I love her. If you only knew. You knew him, that other one.... Tell me, in what way was he better than me? What did he get her with? Was he cleverer? Better-looking? What sort of a hero was he?"

Alexei recalled Commissar Vorobyov, his big, bloated body, the waxen face against the pillow, the woman standing like a statue over him in the eternal posture of feminine grief, and that amazing story about the Red Army men marching through the desert.

"He was a *real* man, Major, a Bolshevik. God grant that we become like him."

4

News that sounded absurd spread through the sanatorium: the footless airman had taken up dancing. As soon as Zinochka finished her duties in the reception-room she would find her pupil waiting for her in the corridor. He would bring her a bunch of wild flowers, or else some chocolate, or an orange he had saved from dinner. Zinochka would gravely take his arm and they would walk to the recreation hall, which was deserted in the summer, and where the diligent pupil had already shifted the card tables and the ping-pong table to the wall. Zinochka would gracefully demonstrate a new figure. With contracted eyebrows, the airman would watch the intricate designs she traced on the floor with her small, pretty feet. Then the girl, with a grave face, would clap her hands and begin to count:

"One, two, three—one, two, three, glissade to the right!... One, two, three—one, two, three, glissade to the left!... Turn! That's right! One, two, three—one, two, three.... Now serpent! Let's do it together."

Perhaps it was the task of teaching a footless man to dance, something that neither Bob Gorokhov nor Paul Sudakovsky had ever done; perhaps she had taken a liking to her dark, raven-haired pupil with the bantering eyes; perhaps for both reasons—but be that as it may, she devoted all her spare time and all her soul to the task.

In the evenings, when the sandy river-bank, the volley-ball field and the skittle alley were deserted and dancing became the favourite recreation of the patients, Alexei would unfailingly participate in the revels. He danced well, did not miss a single dance, and more than once his teacher regretted that she had bound him to those strict terms. Couples whirled round the room to the tune of an accordion. With flushed face and eyes flashing with excitement, Meresyev performed all the glissades, serpents, turns and points and led his light-footed partner with the flaming locks with agility, and seemingly without effort. And none who watched this gallant dancer could even guess what he did when he left the room now and again.

He would walk out of the house with a smile on his flushed face, carelessly fanning himself with his handkerchief; but no sooner did he pass through the door than the smile gave way to a wince of pain. Clinging to the handrail, he staggered, groaning, down the steps of the porch, dropped on to the dewy grass and, pressing his whole body to the moist and still warm ground, wept with the pain caused by the tight straps of his artificial feet.

He unfastened the straps to relieve his legs. When he felt rested, he fastened them again, jumped up and strode back to the house. He reappeared unnoticed in the hall where the sweating accordion-player was tirelessly pumping out the music, approached red-haired Zinochka who was already searching for him in the crowd with her eyes, smiled a broad smile, exposing his white, regular, porcelainlike teeth, and the agile, graceful couple would again glide into the circle. Zinochka would chide him for leaving her, he would retort with a jest, and they would whirl round in no way different from the rest of the dancers.

These hard dancing exercises soon produced results. Alexei felt less and less fettered by the artificial feet; they seemed to become grafted to his legs.

Alexei was pleased. Only one thing caused him anxiety now—the absence of letters from Olya. More than a month had passed since—after Gvozdev's unfortunate experience with his girl—he had sent her that fatal, as he now regarded it, and at all events absolutely absurd letter, but no reply came. Every morning, after his gymnastics and running exercises, which he daily increased by a hundred paces, he would go to the letter-rack in the reception-room to see whether there were any letters for him. There were always more letters in the pigeonhole "M" than in any of the others, but he sorted the batch in vain.

One day, during a dancing lesson, Burnazyan's dark head appeared at the recreation hall window. In his hand he held his walking-stick and a letter. Before he could utter a word Alexei snatched the envelope, which was addressed in a large, round, schoolgirl's hand, and ran off, leaving astonished Burnazyan at the window and his angry teacher in the middle of the room.

"Zinochka, they're all like that nowadays," said Burnazyan in the tone of a gossiping aunt. "They are all deceivers. Don't trust any of them. Fly from them like the devil from holy water. Better take me as your pupil." With that he threw his stick into the hall and, puffing and grunting, climbed through the window at which Zinochka was standing, sad and perplexed.

Meanwhile, Alexei ran to the lake, holding the letter in his hand as if afraid that someone would run after him and rob him of his treasure. Pushing through the rustling reeds, he sat down on a mossy boulder and, completely hidden by the tall grass, scrutinised the precious envelope, holding it with trembling fingers. What did it contain? What sentence was it about to pronounce? The envelope was worn and frayed; it must have roamed about a great deal before it reached its destination. Alexei cautiously tore a strip from the envelope and his eye caught the last line of the letter: "Darling, ever yours. Olya." A feeling of relief overcame him at once. He now calmly smoothed the sheets of exercise-book paper on his knee—for some reason they were smudged with clay and stained with candle grease. Olya was always so neat and tidy, what had happened to her? And then he read tidings that filled him with both pride and alarm. It appeared that Olya had left the mill a month ago and was now living somewhere in the steppe with other girls and women from Kamyshin, digging anti-tank ditches and fortifications around "a certain big city, the name of which is sacred to us all," as she put it. The name, Stalingrad, was not mentioned anywhere in the letter, but from the love, anxiety and hope with which she wrote about this "big city", it was evident that she meant Stalingrad.

She wrote that thousands of volunteers like her were working in the steppe day and night, digging, carting earth, laying concrete and building. It was a cheerful letter, but from some of the expressions it contained it was clear that those women and girls in the steppe were having a hard time. Only after she had related to him the affairs with which she was evidently entirely absorbed did she answer the question he had put to her. In angry terms she wrote that she had been deeply hurt by his last letter, which she had received "here, in the trenches", and had she not known that he had been at the front where one's nerves are put to such a terrific strain, she would never have forgiven him for it.

"Darling," she wrote, "what kind of love is it that cannot make sacrifices? There is no such love, dear. If there is, in my opinion it is not love at all. I haven't washed for a week, I wear trousers, and boots from which the toes are sticking out. My face is so sunburnt that the skin is peeling and underneath it is all rough and bluish. If I were to come to you now, tired, filthy, skinny and ugly, would you turn me away, or even blame me? You silly boy! Whatever happens to you, I want you to know that I am waiting for you, whatever you are like.... I often think of you, and until I got into these 'trenches', where we all sleep like the dead as soon as we get to our bunks, I often used to dream about you. I want you to know that as long as I live somebody will always be waiting for you, always waiting, whatever you are like.... You say that something may happen to you at the front; but if anything happened to me in these 'trenches', if I met with an accident and were crippled, would you turn away from me? Do you remember, when we were at the apprenticeship school, we used to solve algebra problems by substitution? Well, substitute me for yourself and think. If you do that, you will be ashamed of what you wrote...."

Meresyev sat a long time pondering over this letter. The sun, dazzlingly reflected in the dark water, was scorching hot, the reeds rustled, and blue dragon-flies flitted from one clump of sedge to another. Fleet water-boatmen on their long, thin legs darted to and fro on the water among the reeds, leaving a lacelike ruffle on the smooth surface. Tiny waves silently lapped the sandy beach.

"What is this?" thought Alexei. "Presentiment? Gift of divination?" "The heart is a soothsayer," his mother used to say. Or had the hardships of trench life given the girl wisdom, and she intuitively understood what he had not dared to tell her? He read the letter once again. No, nothing of the kind. This was not presentiment. It was simply an answer to what he had written. And what an answer it was!

Alexei sighed, slowly undressed and piled his clothes on the boulder. He always bathed in this secluded little bay known only to himself, off this sandy spit hidden by the wall of rustling reeds. Unstrapping his artificial feet, he slowly slipped from the boulder, and although it was very painful to step on the shingle with his bare stumps, he did not go down on all fours. Wincing with pain, he entered the lake and plunged into the cold, dense water. He swam some distance from the shore, turned over on his back and lay quite still. He gazed at the blue, limitless sky. Small clouds were hurrying across it, colliding with each other. He turned over and saw the shore reflected upside down on the cool, blue, smooth surface of the water, and the yellow and white water-lilies amidst their floating round leaves. Suddenly he saw the reflection of Olya sitting on the boulder, Olya, as he had seen her in his dreams, in a printed frock. Her legs, however, were not drawn in, but down, although they did not reach the water—two ugly stums dangled over the surface. He slapped the water to drive away this vision. No, the substitution method that Olya had proposed did not help him!

5

The situation in the South had become graver than ever. The newspapers had long ceased to report fighting on the Don. One day the communiqué of the Soviet Information Bureau mentioned the names of Cossack villages on the other side of the Don, on the way to the Volga, to Stalingrad. These names meant little to those who were unfamiliar with these parts, but Alexei, who was born and bred there, realised that the Don defence line had been pierced and that the war had swept to the walls of Stalingrad.

Stalingrad! That name had not yet been mentioned in the communiqués, but it was on everybody's lips. In the autumn of 1942 it was pronounced with anxiety and pain; it was uttered not as the name of a city, but of a near and dear one in mortal danger. For Meresyev, this general anxiety was magnified by the fact that Olya was somewhere near there, in the steppe outside the city, and who could tell what trials she would be subjected to?

He now wrote to her every day, but of what value were these letters addressed to some field post office? Would they reach her in the confusion of retreat, in the inferno of the gigantic battles that were raging in the Volga steppe?

The airmen's sanatorium buzzed like a disturbed beehive. The customary recreations—draughts, chess, volleyball, skittles and the inevitable *vingt-et-un* which the patients who were fond of a thrill used to indulge in among the bushes near the lake—were abandoned. Nobody could give his mind to such things. Everybody, even the most inveterate sluggards, were up in the morning an hour before time in order to hear the first, seven o'clock, war report over the radio. When the communiqué mentioned the feats performed by airmen, everybody walked about gloomily, found fault with the nurses and grumbled at the food and the rules, as if the sanatorium staff were to blame for the fact that they were hanging around here in the sunshine, in the tranquil woods near the mirror-like lake and not fighting over there, over the steppe near Stalingrad. At last the convalescents declared that they were fed up with being convalescents and demanded their discharge so that they could return to their units.

Late one afternoon, a commission from the Personnel Department of the Air Force arrived. Several officers wearing the insignia of the Medical Corps alighted from the dust-covered car. From the front seat, leaning heavily on the back rest, stepped a stout officer. This was Army Surgeon First Rank Mirovolsky, well known in the Air Force and loved by the airmen for the fatherly way in which he treated them. At supper it was announced that next morning the commission would select volunteers among the convalescents who desired to shorten their sick leave and be sent to their units immediately.

Next morning, Meresyev rose at dawn and without performing his customary exercises went off to the woods and remained there until breakfast time. At breakfast he ate nothing, was rude to the waitress when she chided him for leaving his food untouched, and when Struchkov remarked that he had no right to be rude to the girl who only wanted to be kind to him, he jumped up and left the dining-room. In the corridor Zina was reading the communiqué of the Soviet Information Bureau that was posted on the wall. Alexei walked past her without a word of greeting. She pretended not to see him and merely shrugged her shoulders pettishly. But when he had passed her, without really having seen her, she felt hurt and, almost in tears, called him. Alexei angrily blurted out over his shoulder:

"Well, what do you want?"

"Comrade Senior Lieutenant, who do you..." answered the girl softly, flushing so furiously that the colour of her cheeks almost matched her hair.

Alexei at once recovered his temper and his whole body suddenly seemed to sag.

"My fate is to be decided today," he said in a low voice. "Shake hands and wish me luck...."

Limping more than usual, he went to his room and locked himself in.

The commission sat in the recreation hall to which had been brought all its paraphernalia—respiration meters, handgrip meters, sight-testing cards, and so forth. The entire population of the sanatorium gathered outside the room, and those who wished to cut short their sick leave, that is, nearly all the convalescents, formed up in a long line. Zinochka, however, came along and handed each one a slip indicating the hour and minute when he would be called and asked them all to disperse. After the first men had been before the commission, the rumour went round that the inspection was slight and that the commission was not very strict. And how could the commission be strict when such a terrific battle was raging on the Volga and greater and greater effort was called for? Alexei sat dangling his feet on the low brick wall in front of the porch, and when anybody came out he inquired nonchalantly, as if not particularly interested:

"Well, how did you get on?"

"I've passed!" the person would answer cheerfully, buttoning his tunic or tightening his belt.

Burnazyan went in before Meresyev. He left his stick outside the door and stepped into the room, trying not to swing his body and not to limp on his short leg. He was kept a long time. At last angry exclamations reached

Alexei's ears from the open window, the door opened and Burnazyan rushed out looking very heated. He shot an angry glance at Alexei and hobbled into the park, looking straight before him and shouting:

"Bureaucrats! Bunny-holers! What do they know about aviation? Do they think it's a ballet?... Short leg!... Damned enemas and syringes, that's all they are!"

Alexei was conscious of a cold feeling in the pit of his stomach, but he walked into the room at a brisk pace, cheerful and smiling. The commission sat at a long table. Towering in the centre like a mountain of flesh sat Army Surgeon First Rank Mirovolsky. At a side table, in front of a pile of case cards, sat Zinochka, small and pretty like a doll in her white, starched smock, with a wisp of red hair peeping coquettishly from under her gauze kerchief. She handed Alexei his case card and softly pressed his hand.

"Now, young man, strip to the waist," said the surgeon, screwing up his eyes.

Meresyev had not indulged in his exercises in vain. The surgeon could not help admiring his fine, well-developed body, every muscle of which could be seen bulging under the dark skin.

"You would do as a model for a statue of David," said a member of the commission, showing off his knowledge.

Meresyev easily passed all the tests. His handgrip was fifty per cent above the standard, and in the respiration test he blew the indicator up to the highest limit. His blood pressure was normal, his nerves in excellent condition. In the end he pulled the steel handle of the strength-testing machine so hard that he broke the spring.

"A pilot?" inquired the surgeon, looking pleased; and making himself more comfortable in his seat he began to write his decision in the upper corner of "Case Card. Senior Lieutenant Meresyev, A. P."

"Yes."

"Fighter?"

"Yes."

"Well, go and fight! They want fellows like you over there, want them badly!... By the by, what were you laid up with?"

Alexei's face fell. He felt that everything was about to collapse. The surgeon scrutinised his case card and a look of amazement spread over his face.

"Amputated feet.... What's this? Nonsense! This must be a mistake, eh? Why don't you answer?"

"No, it's not a mistake," said Alexei softly and very slowly as if he were mounting the scaffold.

The surgeon and the other members of the commission stared suspiciously at this sturdy, finely-built and vivacious young man and could not understand what was the matter.

"Turn your trousers up!" the surgeon commanded in an impatient tone.

Alexei grew pale, glanced helplessly at Zinochka, slowly rolled up the bottoms of his trousers and stood despondent, with his hands at his sides, exposing his leather feet.

"Have you been trying to make fun of us, or what? Look at the time you've wasted! Surely you don't think you are going back into the Air Force with no feet, do you?" said the surgeon at last.

"I don't think, I'm going!" answered Alexei in a low voice, his dark eyes flashing with stubborn defiance.

"With no feet? You're crazy!"

"Yes, I'm going to fly with no feet," answered Alexei, no longer defiantly, but calmly. Out of the pocket of his old-style airman's tunic he drew the neatly folded clipping from the magazine. "Look," he added, showing the clipping to the surgeon. "He flew with one foot. Why shouldn't I be able to fly with no feet?"

The surgeon read the clipping and then looked up at Alexei with surprise and respect.

"Yes, but you must have a hell of a lot of training to do that. This man trained for ten years. You've got to learn to use your artificial feet as if they were real," he said in a milder tone.

At this point Alexei received unexpected reinforcements. Zinochka fluttered from behind her table, put her hands together as if in prayer, and flushing so furiously that beads of sweat stood out on her temples, she twittered:

"Comrade Army Surgeon First Rank, you should see him dance! Better than anybody with two feet!"

"Dance? What the devil!..." exclaimed the surgeon, looking round at the members of the commission in amazement.

Alexei gladly caught up the idea suggested by Zinochka.

"Don't decide now," he said. "Come to our dance tonight and see what I can do."

As Alexei walked towards the door he saw the reflection in the mirror of the members of the commission talking animatedly to each other.

Before dinner, Zinochka found Alexei in a copse in the neglected park. She told him that the commission had continued to discuss him for a long time after he had left the hall, and that the surgeon had said that Meresyev was a remarkable lad and that, who knows, perhaps he really would be able to fly. What couldn't a Russian do? To this a member of the commission had answered that there had been no case like it in the history of aviation, and the surgeon had retorted that lots of things had not occurred in the history of aviation, and that in this war Soviet airmen had contributed to it a great deal that was new.

A farewell dance was arranged to celebrate the return of the volunteers—about two hundred, as it turned out—to active service, and it was a grand affair. A military band was invited from Moscow and the music echoed like thunder through the halls and passages of the palace, causing the latticed windows to tremble. The airmen, sweat pouring down their faces, danced without end, and the merriest, most agile and vivacious among them was Meresyev, dancing with his auburn-haired lady. A matchless couple!

Army Surgeon First Rank Mirovolsky sat at the open window with a glass of cool beer in front of him, unable to tear his eyes away from Meresyev and his fiery-haired partner. He was a surgeon, and an army surgeon at that, and he knew the difference between artificial and real feet.

And now, watching the dark, well set up airman leading his graceful little partner, he could not rid himself of the thought that there must be some trick behind this. At last, after Alexei had danced a *barinya* in the middle of a ring of applauding admirers, wildly clapping his thighs and cheeks as he leaped and capered, he went up to Mirovolsky, perspiring and excited. The surgeon shook hands with him in silent respect. Alexei said nothing, but his eyes looked straight into those of the surgeon, imploring, demanding an answer.

"You understand, of course," the surgeon said at last, "that I have no right to appoint you to a unit, but I will give you a certificate for the Personnel Department. I will certify that with proper training you will be fit to fly. In any case, you can count on my vote."

Mirovolsky left the hall arm in arm with the head of the sanatorium, who was also an army surgeon of considerable experience. Both were filled with amazement and admiration. They sat for a long time before going to bed, smoking and discussing what Soviet men could do when they were really determined to do it. . . .

In the meantime, while the music was still thundering and the shadows of the dancers thrown by the light from the open windows were still flitting across the ground, Alexei Meresyev was locked in the upstairs bath-room with his legs immersed in cold water, biting his lips until they bled. Almost fainting from pain, he bathed the livid calluses and the wide sores caused by the fierce friction of the artificial feet.

An hour later, when Major Struchkov entered the bedroom, Meresyev, washed and refreshed, was sitting in front of the mirror combing his wet, wavy hair.

"Zinochka is looking for you. You ought to take her for a farewell stroll. I'm sorry for the girl."

"Let's go together!" answered Meresyev eagerly. "Do come, Pavel Ivanovich," he pleaded.

The thought of being alone with that pretty girl who had gone to such trouble to teach him to dance made him feel uneasy; after the receipt of Olya's letter he felt awkward in her presence. He kept on urging Struchkov to go with him until, at last, the latter grumblingly picked up his cap.

Zinochka was waiting on the balcony, holding the remnants of a bunch of flowers; the floor at her feet was littered with flower stalks and petals. Hearing Alexei's footsteps she started forward eagerly, but seeing that he was not alone she suddenly seemed to wilt.

"Let's go to say good-bye to the wood," proposed Alexei in a nonchalant tone.

They linked arms and walked in silence down the old avenue of lime-trees. At their feet, on the moonlit ground, coal-black shadows followed them, and here and there the first autumn leaves glistened like scattered coins. They reached the end of the avenue, went through the gates and walked over the grey, wet grass to the lake. The hollow was covered with a blanket of fleecy mist that looked like a white sheepskin. The mist clung to the earth and, reaching their waists, breathed and shone mysteriously in the cold moonlight. The air was damp and impregnated with the sated smell of autumn. It was cool and even chilly one moment and warm and close another, as if this lake of mist had warm and cold currents of its own....

"Looks as though we are giants walking above the clouds, doesn't it?" said Alexei pensively, uneasily feeling the girl's strong little arm tightly pressed against his elbow.

"Not giants, but fools. We'll wet our feet and catch cold for our journey," growled Struchkov, who seemed to be absorbed in his own mournful reflections.

"I have the advantage over you there. I have no feet to wet, and so I can't catch cold," said Alexei laughing.

"Come on, come on! It must be very nice there now!" urged Zinochka, pulling them towards the mist-covered lake.

They almost blundered into the water and stopped short in amazement when it suddenly loomed black through the wisps of mist right at their feet. Near by was a small jetty with a rowboat faintly outlined in the darkness. Zinochka fluttered off into the mist and returned with a pair of oars. They fixed the rowlocks, Alexei took the oars, and Zinochka and the major sat in the stern. The boat glided slowly through the still water, now plunging into the mist and now appearing in open water, the black, polished surface of which was generously silvered with moonlight. No one spoke, all were absorbed in their own thoughts. The night was calm, the water dripped from the oars like drops of quicksilver, and seemed as heavy. The rowlocks clicked softly, a corn-crake creaked somewhere, and from far away the mournful screech of an owl came barely audible across the water.

"You can hardly believe that there's war raging near by," said Zinochka softly. "Will you write to me, comrades? Now you, Alexei Petrovich, you will write to me, won't you? Even if it's only a short note. I'll give some addressed postcards to take with you, shall I? You'll write: 'Alive and well, greetings,' and drop it into a letter-box, all right?..."

"I can't tell you how glad I am to go. Hell! I've had enough of idling. My hands are itching for work!" cried Struchkov.

Again they all fell silent. The tiny waves lapped softly and gently against the sides of the boat, the water gurgled sleepily under its keel and spread out in a glistening angle from its stern. The mist dispersed and a ruffled, bluish moonbeam stretched across the water from the shore, lighting up the patches of water-lily leaves.

"Let's sing," suggested Zinochka, and without waiting for a reply started the song about the ash-tree.

She sang the first couplet sadly, alone, but the next was taken up by Major Struchkov in a fine, deep baritone. He had never sung before, and Alexei had not even suspected that he had such a beautiful, mellow voice. The pensive and passionate strains of this song rolled over the smooth water; the two fresh voices, male and female, supported each other in their longing. Alexei recalled the slender ash-tree with the solitary bunch of berries outside the window of his room, and large-eyed Varya in the underground village. Then everything vanished—the lake, the wonderful moonlight, the boat and the singers—and in the silvery mist he saw the girl from Kamyshin, but not the Olya that had sat among the daisies in the flowery meadow, but a different, unfamiliar girl, weary-looking, with cheeks sunburnt in patches, cracked lips, in a sweat-stained tunic, wielding a spade somewhere in the steppe near Stalingrad.

He dropped the oars and joined to sing the last couplet of the song.

Early next morning a long train of buses passed through the gates of the sanatorium. While they were still at the porch, Major Struchkov, sitting on the footboard of one of the buses, had struck up his favourite song about the ash-tree. The song was taken up by those in the other buses, and the farewell greetings, wishes of good luck, Burnazyan's witticisms and the parting advice that Zinochka was shouting to Alexei through the bus window were all drowned by the simple but significant words of this old song which had long been forgotten, but which had been revived and had become popular during the Great Patriotic War.

And so the buses drove through the gates, carrying with them the deep, harmonious strains of this melody. When the song came to an end the singers fell silent, and nobody uttered a word until the first factories and workers' settlements on the outskirts of the city flashed past the bus windows.

Major Struchkov, still sitting on the footboard of his bus with his tunic unbuttoned, smilingly admired the landscape. He was in a most cheerful mood; this eternally wandering soldier was again on the move, travelling from one place to another, and he felt in his element. He was going to some unit, he did not yet know which, but whichever it was, it was home to him. Meresyev sat silent and anxious. He felt that his greatest difficulties still lay ahead, and who could tell whether he would be able to surmount those new obstacles?

Straight from the bus, not even troubling to arrange for lodgings for the night, he went to see Mirovolsky. Here he met with his first stroke of ill luck. His well-wisher, whom he had won over with such difficulty, was away; he had flown on some urgent official mission and would not be back for some time. The official Alexei spoke to told him to put in an application in the regulation way. Forthwith he sat down by the windowsill, wrote out the application and handed it to the officer in charge, a thin, little man with tired eyes. The latter promised to do all he could and advised Alexei to call again within two days. Alexei pleaded, begged and even threatened, but in vain. The officer, pressing his small bony fists to his chest, answered that such were the regulations and that he had no power to violate them. In all probability, he really had no power to expedite the matter. With a gesture of disgust, Meresyev went away.

And thus commenced his wanderings from one war office department to another. His troubles were increased by the fact that in the hurry with which he had been brought to the hospital he had not been provided with clothing, food and money allowance certificates, and up till now he had not taken the trouble to obtain them. He did not even have a leave certificate. Although the kind and obliging officer in charge of these matters promised to telephone his regimental headquarters and ask them to send the necessary papers at once, Meresyev knew how slowly everything was done and realised that for some time he would have to live without money, without lodgings and without rations in stern war-time Moscow, where every kilogram of bread and every gram of sugar was precious.

He telephoned to Anyuta at the hospital. Judging by her voice she must have been worried or busy with something, but she was very glad that he had arrived and insisted that he should stay at her place during these few days, the more so that she was quartered at the hospital and he would have the place to himself.

The sanatorium had provided each departing patient with a five-day dry ration for the journey, and so, without thinking twice, Alexei went off to the now familiar dilapidated little house that nestled in the depths of the courtyard behind the tall backs of the lofty new buildings. He had a roof over his head and some food to eat, so now he could wait. He mounted the familiar dark, winding staircase that still smelt of cats, kerosene and damp washing, groped for the door and knocked loudly.

The door was opened, but being held by two stout chains, stood ajar. The little old woman poked her thin face through the narrow space, looked at Alexei distrustfully and searchingly and asked him who he was, whom he wanted and what his name was. Only after that did the chain rattle and the door swing wide open.

"Anna Danilovna is not at home, but she telephoned about you. Come in and I'll show you to her room," said the old woman, scanning his face, his tunic, and especially his kit-bag, with her dull, faded eyes. "Perhaps you need some hot water? There's Anichka's kerosene-stove in the kitchen, I'll boil some...."

Alexei entered the familiar room without the least embarrassment. Evidently, the soldier's ability to feel at home anywhere that Major Struchkov possessed to such a marked degree was communicating itself to him. The familiar odours of old wood, dust and moth-balls, of all these things that had served faithfully and well all these decades, even filled him with emotion, as if he had returned to his own home after many years of wandering.

The old woman followed at his heels, keeping up a constant chatter about a queue at a baker's shop where, if you were lucky, you could get white rolls on your ration card instead of rye bread; about an important army officer she had heard in the street-car the other day saying that the Germans were getting it hot at Stalingrad and that Hitler had gone so mad over this that he had to be put in a mad-house and it was his double who was ruling Germany now; about her neighbour Alevtina Arkadyevna, who really had no right to receive a worker's ration card, and who had borrowed a fine enamelled milk can and had not returned it; about Anna Danilovna's parents, who were very nice people now away with the evacuees; and about Anna Danilovna herself—a very nice girl, quiet and well-behaved, not like others who go gallivanting with God knows whom, and she didn't bring men home. In the end she asked:

"Are you her young tankman, Hero of the Soviet Union?"

"No, I'm an airman," answered Meresyev, and he could barely restrain a smile when he saw the surprise, vexation, distrust and anger that was simultaneously expressed on the old woman's mobile face.

She pursed her lips, banged the door angrily, and from the corridor said, no longer in the cordial tone in which she had spoken before:

"Well, if you need any hot water, you can boil some yourself on the blue kerosene-stove."

Anyuta must have been very busy at the base hospital, for on this dull autumn day the apartment looked quite neglected. There was a thick layer of dust on everything, and the flowers on the windowsill and stands were yellow and wilted, as if they had not been watered for a long time. There were mouldy crusts on the table, and the kettle had not been removed. The piano, too, was clothed in a soft, grey coat of dust, and a large bluebottle, seemingly suffocating in the musty air, was buzzing dejectedly and beating itself against a dim, yellowish window-pane.

Meresyev flung open the windows, which overlooked a sloping garden that had been converted into a vegetable plot. A blast of fresh air blew into the room and stirred up the accumulated dust so vigorously that it looked like a fog. Here a happy idea occurred to Alexei ... to tidy up the room and give Anyuta a pleasant surprise if she managed to get away from the hospital in the evening in order to see him. He begged the old woman to lend him a pail, a rag and a swab and zealously set about a job that for ages men had looked upon with scorn. For an hour and a half he rubbed and scrubbed and dusted, thoroughly enjoying the work.

In the evening, he went to the bridge where, on his way to the house, he had seen girls selling large, bright autumn asters. He bought a bunch, placed the flowers in vases on the piano and on the table, made himself comfortable in the green armchair, and conscious of a pleasant tiredness all over his body, he greedily inhaled the odours of the meal the old woman was cooking in the kitchen from the provisions he had brought.

But Anyuta came home so weary that, barely greeting him, she flung herself upon the couch and did not even notice how tidy the room was. Only after she had rested and had taken a drink of water did she look round in surprise. Smiling a weary smile and gratefully pressing Meresyev's elbow, she said:

"No wonder Grisha loves you so much that it makes me a little jealous. Did you do it, Alyosha ... you yourself? You are a nice boy! Have you heard anything from Grisha? He is over there. I received a letter from him the other day, a short one, just a couple of lines. He is in Stalingrad, and what do you think the silly boy is doing?

Growing a beard! At a time like this! It's very dangerous over there, isn't it? Tell me, Alyosha, isn't it? People are saying such terrifying things about Stalingrad!"

"They're fighting there."

Alexei frowned and sighed. He envied all those who were there, on the Volga, where that gigantic battle about which everybody was talking was raging.

They talked the whole evening, thoroughly enjoyed their supper of tinned meat, and as the other room was boarded up, they, like comrades, turned in in the same room, Anyuta on the bed and Alexei on the couch, and at once fell into the deep sleep of youth.

When Alexei awoke and sat up on the couch, sunbeams were already slanting into the room. Anyuta had gone. He found a note pinned to the back of the couch: "Have hurried off to the hospital. There is tea on the table and bread in the cupboard; I have no sugar. Will not be able to get away again before Saturday. A."

All these days Alexei scarcely left the house. Having nothing to do, he mended the old woman's primus-stoves, kerosene-stoves, saucepans and electric switches, and at her request he even mended the coffee grinder of that awful Alevtina Arkadyevna who, incidentally, had not yet returned the enamelled milk can. In this way he got into the good graces of the old woman as well as of her husband, who worked for the Building Trust, was active in the air defence brigade, and was also absent from home for days and nights on end. The old couple arrived at the conclusion that while tankmen were very nice fellows, of course, airmen were in no way inferior to them, and even, when you know them better, proved to be a serious, home-loving lot in spite of their airy profession.

At last, the day came for Alexei to go to the Personnel Department to get the decision. He spent the night before on the couch with his eyes open. In the morning, he got up, shaved, washed, appeared at the office exactly to the minute and was the first to walk up to the desk of the major in the Administration Service who was to decide his fate. He disliked that major the moment he set eyes on him. Without looking up at Alexei, as if he had not seen him come up, he continued to busy himself at the desk, taking out and sorting folders, telephoned to various people, explained to the clerk at great length how to number files, and then went out and did not return for a long time. By this time Alexei thoroughly hated his long face, long nose, clean-shaven cheeks, bright lips and sloping forehead, which imperceptibly merged with a glistening bald head. At last the major came back, sat down, turned over the leaf of his calendar, and only then did he pay attention to Alexei.

"Do you want to see me, Comrade Senior Lieutenant?" he inquired in a pompous, self-confident bass.

Meresyev told him his business. The major requested the clerk to bring Alexei's papers, and while waiting for them sat with his legs outstretched and with concentrated attention picked his teeth with a toothpick, which out of politeness he covered with the palm of his hand. When the papers were brought to him he began to peruse Meresyev's file. Suddenly he waved his hand and pointed to a chair, inviting Alexei to sit down; evidently he had reached the part about the amputated feet. He continued reading, and on finishing the last page looked up and inquired:

"Well, what do you want me to do for you?"

"I want an appointment to a wing in Fighter Command."

The major leaned back heavily in his chair, looked with astonishment at the airman who was still standing in front of him, and with his own hand drew a chair up for him. His bushy eyebrows slipped higher up his smooth and shining forehead as he said:

"But you can't handle a plane!"

"I can and I will! Send me to a training school for a trial," said Meresyev almost shouting, and such indomitable determination was expressed in the tone in which he said it that the officers at the other desks in the room looked up inquiringly, wondering what the dark, handsome lieutenant was asking for so insistently.

The major was convinced that the man in front of him was a fanatic or a lunatic. Casting a sidelong glance at Alexei's angry face and "wild", flashing eyes, he said, trying to speak in the mildest tone he could:

"But look here! How is it possible to pilot a plane without feet? And who do you think will let you do it? It's ridiculous! It has never been done before!"

"Never been done before! Well, it will be done now," answered Meresyev stubbornly. He drew his notebook from his pocket, exracted the magazine clipping, removed the cellophane wrapping from it and laid it on the desk in front of the major.

The officers at the other desks dropped their work and listened intently to the conversation. One of them got up from his desk and approached the major, as if to inquire about some business matter, asked for a light, and glanced at Meresyev's face. The major ran his eye down the clipping. At last he said:

"We can't go by this. It is not an official document. We have our instructions which strictly define the various degrees of fitness for the Air Force. I could not allow you to handle a plane if you had two fingers missing, let alone two feet. Here's your clipping, that's no proof. I admire your pluck, but...."

Mereseyev was boiling with rage and felt like picking up the inkstand from the major's desk and hurling it at his shining bald head. In a choking voice he said:

"What about this?"

With that he put his last card on the table—the certificate signed by Army Surgeon First Rank Mirovolsky. The major picked it up doubtfully. It was drawn up in due and proper order, it bore the seal of the Department of the Medical Corps, and was signed by a surgeon highly respected in the Air Force. The major read the certificate and his tone became more friendly. The man in front of him was not a lunatic. This extraordinary young fellow seriously wanted to fly, in spite of his not having feet. He had even succeeded in convincing a sober-minded army surgeon of considerable authority that he could do so. The major pushed Meresyev's file aside with a sigh and said:

"I cannot do anything for you, much as I would like to. An army surgeon first rank can write anything he pleases, but we have clear and definite instructions which must not be departed from.... If I depart from them, who will answer for it—the Army Surgeon?"

Meresyev looked with burning hate at this well-fed, self-confident, calm and polite office, at the neat collar of his well-fitting tunic, at his hairy hands and big, close-clipped, ugly fingernails. How could he explain to him? Would he understand? Did he know what an air battle was? Perhaps he had never heard a shot fired in his life. Restraining himself with all his might, he asked in a low voice:

"What am I to do, then?"

The major shrugged his shoulders and answered:

"If you insist, I can send you to the commission of the Formations Department. But I warn you beforehand, nothing will come of it."

"To hell with it then, send me to the commission!" gasped Meresyev, collapsing into a chair.

Then commenced his wanderings from office to office. Weary officials, up to their neck in work, listened to what he had to say, expressed surprise and sympathy and helplessly shrugged their shoulders. Indeed, what could they do? They had their instructions, very good instructions, endorsed by the High Command, and there were the time-hallowed traditions of the service—how could they violate them? And in such an obvious case too! They were all sincerely sorry for this irrepressible, disabled man who longed to go back into the fighting line, and none of them had the heart to give him a definite refusal; so they sent him from the Personnel Department to the Formations Department, from desk to desk, and each, out of pity, sent him to a commission.

Meresyev was no longer put out either by refusals or admonitions, or by humiliating sympathy and condescension, against which his proud soul revolted. He learnt to keep himself in hand, acquired the tone of the solicitor, and although some days he met with as many as two or three refusals, he would not give up hope. The magazine clipping and the Army Surgeon's certificate became so worn from being constantly taken from his pocket that they tore at the creases and he was obliged to stick them together with tape.

The hardships of his wanderings were aggravated by the fact that while waiting for an answer he was living without an allowance. The provisions with which he had been supplied by the sanatorium had been consumed. True, the old couple in Anyuta's apartment, with whom he had become fast friends, seeing that he no longer cooked any food for himself, persistently invited him to dinner; but he knew how hard the old people toiled on their tiny vegetable patch beneath the windows, how precious every onion and every carrot was to them, and how, like little sister and brother sharing some sweetmeat, they shared their bread ration every morning; and so he cheerfully told them that to avoid the bother of cooking he now dined at an officers' messroom.

Saturday came, the day on which Anyuta—whom he had telephoned every evening to report on the unsatisfactory state of his affairs—would be relieved from duty. He resolved to take a desperate step. In his kit-bag he still had his father's old silver cigarette case with a niello design of a sleigh drawn by three dashing horses on the corner, and bearing on the inside the inscription: "On your silver wedding. From your friends." Alexei did not smoke, but his mother had slipped this precious family relic into his pocket when he had left home for the front, and he had kept the heavy, clumsy thing all the time, putting it into his pocket "for luck" when going on a flight. He fished the cigarette case out of his kit-bag and took it to the commission shop.

A thin woman, smelling of moth-balls, turned the cigarette case in her hands, pointed to the inscription with a bony finger and declared that articles bearing an inscription were not accepted for sale.

"But I'm not asking much for it. Name your own price."

"No, no, and besides, Comrade Officer, I should think it's too early for you to accept gifts for your silver wedding," the moth-ball woman remarked caustically, glancing up at Alexei with hostile, colourless eyes.

Flushing hotly, the airman snatched the cigarette case up from the counter and made for the exit. Somebody stopped him by his arm, breathing the heavy smell of wine into his ear.

"Quite a nice-looking little thing you've got there. Cheap, did you say?" asked a man with an ugly, unshaved face and a prominent blue nose. He stretched out a sinewy trembling hand towards the cigarette case. "Massive. Out of respect for a hero of the Patriotic War, I'll give you five 'greys' for it."

Alexei did not bargain. He took the five hundred-ruble bills and rushed out of this kingdom of old, stinking junk into the fresh air. At the nearest market he bought some meat, back fat, a loaf of bread, some potatoes and onions, and even did not forget to buy a few sticks of parsley. Thus loaded, he made his way home, as he now called it, chewing a piece of back fat on the way.

"I've decided to take my ration and to do my own cooking again. The stuff they serve in the messroom is awful!" he lied to the old woman, piling his purchases on the kitchen table.

That evening a splendid dinner awaited Anyuta: potato soup cooked with meat and with bits of parsley floating on its amber surface, fried meat with onions, and even cranberry jelly, which the old woman had made with starch obtained from the potato peelings. The girl came home pale and weary. She forced herself to wash and change. Hurriedly eating the first course and then the second, she stretched out on the old, magic armchair, which seemed to embrace one like an old friend in its kind plush arms and whisper sweet dreams in one's ear, and there she dozed off without waiting for the masterfully made jelly, which was cooling in a can under the running tap.

When, after a short nap, she opened her eyes, the grey shadows of dusk already filled the small and now tidy room so crowded with cosy old furniture. At the dining-table, under the old lamp-shade sat Alexei with his head between his hands, pressing it so tightly that it seemed as though he wanted to crush it. She could not see his face, but from the way he sat it was evident that he was in the depth of despair, and pity for this strong and stubborn man welled up from her heart. She got up, softly stepped towards him, took his big head in her hands and stroked it, running her fingers through his stiff hair. He caught her hand, kissed the palm, jumped up, cheerful and smiling, and exclaimed:

"What about the cranberry jelly? You are a nice one! Here I was doing my best, keeping it under the tap to get the proper temperature, and you go and fall asleep! Isn't that enough to throw any cook into the dumps?"

Each ate a plateful of the "superior" jelly that was as sour as vinegar, chatted merrily about everything except, as if by common agreement, two subjects—Gvozdev and Meresyev—and later made arrangements to turn in on their respective couches. Anyuta went into the corridor and waited until she heard Alexei's artificial feet fall to the floor with a tap, then walked in, put the lamp out, undressed and went to bed. The room was dark, they were silent, but from the rustle of the sheets and the twang of the bed springs, she knew that he was awake. At last Anyuta asked:

"Are you asleep, Alyosha?"

"No."

"Thinking?"

"Yes. And you?"

"I'm thinking too."

They fell silent again. In the street a street-car screeched as it turned the corner. For an instant the flash of an electric spark from its trolley lit up the room, and in that instant each saw the face of the other. Both were lying with eyes wide open.

Alexei had not said a word to Anyuta about his fruitless wanderings, but she guessed that his affairs were in a bad way and that, perhaps, his indomitable spirit was being worn down by disappointment. Her feminine intuition told her how much that man must be suffering, but it also told her that, hard as it may be for him at this moment, a word of sympathy would only aggravate his pain and that commiseration would only offend.

He, in turn, was lying on his back, with his head resting on his hands, thinking about the pretty girl in the bed a few paces away from his own, the sweetheart of his friend and a good comrade. He only had to take a few steps across the dark room to reach her; but nothing in the world could induce him to take those few steps, as if the girl, whom he knew little, but who had given him shelter, was his own sister. Major Struchkov would probably jeer at him, probably not believe him, if he told him about this. But who could tell? Perhaps now he would be able to understand him better than anybody else.... What a fine girl Anyuta is! Poor thing, how tired she gets, and yet how enthusiastic she is about her work at the base hospital!

"Alyosha!" Anyuta called softly.

From Meresyev's couch came the sound of regular breathing. The airman was asleep. The girl rose from her bed, stepped softly with her bare feet to his couch, straightened his pillow and tucked his blanket around him as if he were a child.

7

Meresyev was the first to be called in by the commission. The huge, flabby Army Surgeon First Rank, who had at last returned from his mission, again presided. He recognised Alexei at once, and even rose from behind the table to welcome him.

"They won't accept you, eh?" he said in a kindly, sympathetic tone. "Yes, yours is a hard case. You have to get round the law, and that's not an easy thing to do."

The commission did not trouble to examine Alexei. The Army Surgeon wrote across his application in red pencil: "Personnel Department. Deem it possible to send applicant to training school for trial." With this paper Alexei went straight off to the Chief of the Personnel Department. He was not allowed to see the general. Alexei was about to flare up, but the general's adjutant, a dapper young captain with a little black moustache, had such a cheerful, kindly, friendly face that although he never could stand "guardian angels", as he called adjutants, Alexei sat down at his desk and, to his own surprise, told the captain his story in all its details. The story was often interrupted by telephone calls, every now and again the captain got up and disappeared into his chief's office, but every time he came back he sat down opposite Alexei and, peering at him with his naive, childish eyes which expressed both curiosity and admiration, and also distrust, said hurryingly:

"Well, go on, what happened after that?" Or suddenly he would interrupt the story with the exclamations: "Is that true? Are you serious? Well, well!"

When Alexei told him about his wanderings from office to office, the captain, who in spite of his youthful appearance seemed to be well versed in the intricacies of the official machine, exclaimed angrily:

"The devils! They had no reason to chase you about like that! You are a remarkable, a ... I really don't know how to express it ... an exceptional fellow!... But after all, they were right: men without feet don't fly."

"But they do! Look at this." And Meresyev showed him the magazine clipping, the Army Surgeon's opinion, and the paper directing him to the Personnel Department.

"But how will you fly with no feet? You are a funny chap! You know the saying: a footless man will never make a dancer."

Had anybody else said it, Meresyev would certainly have taken offence, and probably would have flared up and said something rude to him; but the captain's face beamed with such good-will that Alexei jumped up and said with boyish impudence:

"Never, you say? Well, look!" And with that he started a wild step-dance in the middle of the waiting-room.

The captain watched him with admiration for a time and then jumped up and without saying a word snatched up Alexei's papers and vanished behind the door of the chief's office.

There he remained for quite a time. Hearing the subdued sounds of conversation coming from the office, Alexei felt his whole body grow tense, and his heart throbbed rapidly and painfully, as if he were driving in a fast machine.

The captain emerged from the office pleased and smiling.

"Well," he said. "Of course, the general won't hear of you going into the flying personnel, but this is what he has written: 'Applicant to be appointed to serve in M.C.B. without reduction of pay or rations.' D'you get that? Without reduction...."

Instead of joy, the captain was amazed to see indignation flare up in Alexei's face.

"M.C.B.! Never!" he shouted. "Don't you understand? I'm not worrying about rations and pay! I'm an airman! I want to fly, to fight!... Why don't people understand that? What can be simpler?..."

The captain was perplexed. This was a queer applicant indeed. Another man in his place would have danced for joy ... but this one! A sheer crank! But the captain was beginning to like this crank more and more. He sincerely felt with him and wanted to help him in his problem. Suddenly, an idea occurred to him. He winked to Meresyev, beckoned to him with his finger and, glancing at the door of his chief's office, whispered:

"The general has done all he can. He has no power to do any more. On my word of honour. They'd think he himself was mad if he appointed you to the flying personnel. I'll tell you what. Go straight to the big chief. He alone can help you."

Alexei's new friend obtained a pass for him and half an hour later he was nervously pacing up and down the carpeted floor of the waiting-room of the big chief's office. Why didn't he think of this before? Of course! This was where he should have come at once without wasting so much time! It was win or lose now.... It was said that the big chief himself had been an ace in his time. He ought to understand! He won't send a fighter airman to the M.C.B.!

A number of staid generals and colonels were sitting in the waiting-room conversing in low voices. Some, obviously nervous, were smoking heavily. The senior lieutenant paced to and fro in his strange, springy step. When all the visitors had gone and Meresyev's turn came, he briskly stepped up to the desk at which a young major with a round, open face was sitting.

"Do you want to see the chief himself, Comrade Senior Lieutenant?" asked the major.

"Yes. I have a very important personal matter to put to him."

"Perhaps you would tell me something about it first? Take a chair, sit down! Do you smoke?" And he offered Meresyev his cigarette case.

Alexei did not smoke, but for some reason he took a cigarette, crushed it between his fingers, put it on the desk and all at once, as he had done when he had been with the captain, blurted out the story of his adventures. The major listened to his story, not so much courteously as amicably, sympathetically and attentively. He read the magazine clipping and the Army Surgeon's opinion. Encouraged by the sympathy the major displayed, Meresyev, forgetting where he was, wanted once again to demonstrate his ability to dance and ... nearly spoilt the whole show, for just at that moment the office door was vigorously pushed open and a tall, lean officer with raven-black hair emerged. Alexei recognised him at once from the photograph he had seen. Buttoning his greatcoat as he walked, he was saying something to a general who followed him. He looked very worried and did not even notice Meresyev.

"I'm going to the Kremlin," he said to the major, glancing at his watch. "Order a plane for Stalingrad at six o'clock. Land at Verkhnaya Pogromnaya." With that he vanished as quickly as he had appeared.

The major at once ordered the plane and remembering that Meresyev was in the room he said apologetically:

"You're out of luck. We are going away. You'll have to come again. Have you any lodgings?"

The dark face of the extraordinary visitor, who only a moment ago had seemed so determined and strong-willed, suddenly expressed such keen disappointment and weariness that the major changed his mind.

"All right," he said. "I know that the chief would have done the same."

With that he wrote a few lines on official notepaper, slipped the paper into an envelope, and addressed it: "Chief of Personnel Department." He gave the envelope to Meresyev and, shaking hands with him, said:

"With all my heart I wish you luck!"

The note stated: "Senior Lieutenant A. Meresyev has seen the Commander. He is to be treated with all attention. Everything possible must be done to help him to return to combat duty."

An hour later the captain with the little moustache conducted Meresyev into the office of his chief. The old general, a stout man with fierce, shaggy eyebrows, read the note and, raising his merry blue eyes to the airman, laughed and said:

"So you've already been there? Quick, I must say! So you are the fellow that went up in the air because I sent you to the M.C.B.! Ha-ha-ha!" he burst into a merry chuckle. "Good lad! I see you are a thoroughbred flyer. Don't want to go into the M.C.B.! Took offence, did you?... What a joke!... But what am I to do with you, young step-dancer, eh? You'll break your neck, and then they'll screw my head off for being an old fool and appointing you! But who can tell what you can do? In this war our boys have surprised the world with even bigger things than that.... Where's your paper?"

With that the general scribbled across the paper with blue pencil in a careless, illegible hand, barely completing the words: "Applicant to be sent to training school." Meresyev snatched the paper with a trembling hand, read the inscription there and then, at the desk, then read it again on the staircase landing, again downstairs where the sentry examined the passes, again in the street-car, and finally on the pavement in the rain. And of all the inhabitants of the globe, he alone knew the meaning and the value of those carelessly scribbled words.

That day Alexei Meresyev sold his watch—a gift from the Divisional Commander—and with the proceeds went to the market and bought all sorts of food and wine, telephoned Anyuta and implored her to get a couple of hours' leave from her base hospital, invited the old couple in Anyuta's apartment, and arranged a feast to celebrate his great victory.

8

The training school near Moscow, situated close to a small airfield, was very busy during those anxious days. The Air Force had a large share of the battle of Stalingrad. The sky over that Volga stronghold, always aglare and overcast with the smoke of conflagrations and explosions, was the arena of incessant air clashes that developed into regular battles. The losses on both sides were heavy. Fighting Stalingrad was calling for airmen, airmen and more airmen.... The training combat flying school, which trained airmen who had been discharged from hospital, and also pilots who had hitherto flown civil aircraft, was consequently working to full capacity. Training planes, looking like dragon-flies, swarmed over the small and crowded airfield like flies over an uncleared kitchen table, and their buzzing could be heard from sunrise to sunset. Whenever you looked at the wheel-rutted field, there was always a machine either taking off or landing.

The Chief of Staff of the school, a short, stout, red-faced, robust lieutenant-colonel with eyes inflamed from lack of sleep, glared angrily at Meresyev as much as to say: "What the devil has brought you here? I've enough to do without you," and snatched the proffered papers out of his hand.

"He'll object to my feet and tell me to clear out," thought Meresyev, glancing furtively at the dark stubble on the chin of the lieutenant-colonel. But just then the latter received two telephone calls at once. He pressed one receiver to his ear with his shoulder, boomed something irritably into the other, and at the same time ran his eye down Meresyev's papers. Evidently, the only thing he read was the general's scribbled order, for at once, still holding the receiver, he wrote under it: "Lieutenant Naumov, Third Training Unit. To be listed." Then, putting down both receivers, he inquired wearily:

"Have you got your uniform issue papers? Ration papers? You haven't? Yes, I know what you are going to say. Hospital. There was no time for it. But how am I going to feed you? Apply for them at once. I'll not put you through without allowance papers."

"Very well. I will do it at once!" said Meresyev with delight, and saluting smartly. "May I go?"

"Yes," answered the lieutenant-colonel with a listless wave of his hand. Suddenly he yelled: "Wait! What's that?" He pointed to the heavy walking-stick with the gold monogram, the gift from Vasily Vasilyevich. When Meresyev left the office, he had forgotten it in the corner in his excitement. "What is that? Throw the thing away! One would think this was a gypsy camp, not a military unit! Or a park: walking-sticks, canes, riding-whips!... You will soon be hanging amulets round your neck and putting black cats in your cockpit. Don't let me see that damned thing again. Fop!"

"Very good, Comrade Lieutenant-Colonel!"

Alexei knew that many difficulties and hardships lay ahead: he had to put in an application for new papers and explain to the irate lieutenant-colonel how he had lost the original ones; owing to the confusion created by the constant stream of men that passed through the school, the food was inadequate, and no sooner had the trainees had their dinner than they began to long for supper; in the crowded school building which temporarily served as quarters for Unit Three, the steam-pipes had burst, it was frightfully cold, and throughout the first night Alexei shivered under his blanket and leather coat—but for all that, amidst all this confusion and discomfort, he felt as, probably, a fish feels when a wave sweeps it back into the sea after it had been lying gasping on a sandy beach. He liked everything here; even the discomforts of bivouac life reminded him that he was near his goal.

The habitual surroundings, the cheerful men he was accustomed to in their leather coats, now peeling and faded, in their dogskin flying boots, their tanned faces and hoarse voices; the habitual atmosphere reeking with the sweetish, pungent smell of aircraft fuel, and echoing with the roar of engines being warmed up and with the steady, soothing drone of flying craft; the grimy faces of the mechanics in greasy overalls ready to drop from weariness; the irate instructors with faces tanned to the colour of bronze; the cherry-cheeked girls in the meteorological station; the bluish, stratified smoke issuing from the stove in the command post; the low humming of the buzzers and the startling ring of telephones; departing flyers taking away spoons and creating a shortage in the messroom; the wall newspapers written by hand in coloured pencils, with the inevitable cartoon about the youthful airmen who dreamed of their girls while in the air; the soft, yellow mud in the airfield rutted by wheels and skids, and the merry conversation spiced with salacious catchwords and aviation terminology—all this was familiar and settled.

Meresyev blossomed out at once. He recovered the cheerfulness and merry recklessness characteristic of the men in Fighter Command which he seemed to have permanently lost. He pulled himself together, briskly returned the salute of inferiors, smartly took the regulation steps on meeting superiors and, on receiving his new uniform, forthwith had it "altered to fit" by an old quartermaster sergeant in the M.C.B., who had been a tailor in civil life, and who, in his spare time, altered the regulation-sized uniforms to "fit the bones" of smart and fastidious lieutenants.

On the very first day, Meresyev went to the airfield to look for Lieutenant Naumov, the instructor of Unit Three, in whose charge he had been placed. Naumov, a short, very vivacious man with a big head and long arms, was running near the "T" sign looking up into the sky where a tiny plane was flying in the "sector". Railing at the pilot who was in the plane, the instructor was yelling:

"Bloody packing-case! Bag of ... silver! Says he was in Fighter Command! He can't fool me!"

Meresyev stepped up to introduce himself and saluted in the regulation manner, but Naumov only waved his hand, pointed to the sky and shouted:

"See that? 'Fighter'. 'Terror of the air'! Flopping about like ... like a daisy in an ice hole...."

Alexei at once took a liking to the instructor. He liked these slightly crazy men who were head over heels in love with their work, and with whom a capable and zealous airman could easily get on. He made a few practical remarks about the way the pilot in the air was flying. The little lieutenant looked him up and down with a critical eye and inquired:

"Coming into my unit? What's your name? What type of craft have you flown? Have you been in action? How long is it since you have been up?"

Alexei was not sure whether the lieutenant heard all his replies, for he again looked up into the sky and, shading his eyes from the sun with one hand, shook his other fist and yelled:

"Bloody wheelbarrow! ... Look at him veering! Like a hippopotamus in a drawing-room!"

He ordered Alexei to turn up first thing next morning and promised to "give him a trial" at once.

"Go and take a rest now," he said. "You need it after your journey. Have you had any grub? In the confusion here, they can forget to feed you, you know.... Clumsy idiot! Wait till I get you down here, I'll show you 'Fighter'!"

Alexei did not turn in to take a rest, the more so that it seemed to be warmer in the airfield, across which the wind was driving dry and prickly sand, than in classroom "9a", the sleeping quarters he had been assigned to. He found a shoemaker in the battalion and gave him his week's tobacco ration to convert an old officer's belt of his into two straps with loops and buckles with which he intended to fasten his artificial feet to the pedals of the plane he was to fly. In view of the urgency and unusual nature of the order, the shoemaker demanded half a litre of vodka in addition to the tobacco, and promised to make a "good job" of it. Meresyev returned to the airfield and watched the flights as though they were not ordinary training flights, but a competition between super-aces until the last plane was taxied to the line and fastened with ropes. He did not so much watch the flights as breathe the atmosphere of the airfield, absorb the activity, the inceasing roar of the engines, the dull thud of rockets and the smell of fuel and lubrication. His whole being rejoiced, and the idea that tomorrow his plane might refuse to obey him, get out of hand and crash, never entered his mind.

He turned up at the airfield next morning when it was still deserted. Away out on the line the engines being warmed up were roaring, the warming stoves were shooting out flames, and the mechanics, who were starting the propellers, leapt away from them as if they were snakes. The familiar morning cries and responses were heard:

"Ready!"

"Contact!"

"Contact!"

Somebody swore at Alexei and asked him what the hell he was doing hanging around the planes so early in the morning. He answered with a jest and kept on repeating like a merry refrain that for some reason had sunk into his mind: "Ready, contact, contact." At last the planes slowly taxied to the starting line, hopping and rolling awkwardly from side to side with trembling wings which the mechanics were supporting. By this time Naumov arrived, smoking the stump of a cigarette, so short that he seemed to be drawing smoke from his nicotine-stained finger-tips.

"So you've turned up!" he said in answer to Alexei's formal salute. "All right. First come, first served. Get into the rear cockpit of number nine over there. I'll be with you in a minute. We'll see what kind of a bird you are."

He took a few last, hurried puffs at his fag while Alexei hastened to the plane. He wanted to fasten his feet to the pedals before the instructor got there. He seemed to be a decent fellow, but who could tell? He might suddenly get a fit in his head, kick up a shindy and refuse to give him a trial. Meresyev clambered along the slippery wing, convulsively clutching at the side of the cockpit. Owing to his excitement and lack of practice he could not for the life of him throw his leg over the side, and the elderly mechanic with a long, melancholy face looked up at him in surprise and thought: "The bastard's drunk!"

At last Alexei managed to get one inflexible leg into the cockpit, got the other in with incredible effort and dropped heavily into the seat. He fastened his artificial feet to the pedals with the aid of his straps. They turned out to have been well made, and the loops fitted firmly and snugly over his feet like those of a good pair of skates in his boyhood.

The instructor poked his head into the cockpit and inquired:

"Say, are you drunk? Let me smell your breath."

Alexei exhaled. Satisfied that the smell of alcohol was absent, the instructor shook his fist threateningly at the mechanic.

"Ready!"

"Contact!"

"Contact!"

The engine snorted several times and then the pistons began to beat rhythmically. Meresyev almost jumped for joy and automatically pulled the gas lever, but he heard the instructor growling into the intercom:

"Don't go rushing like a bull at a gate!"

The instructor opened the throttle himself. The engine roared and whined, and the plane, hopping and skipping, took the run. The instructor automatically pulled the stick, and the tiny plane that looked like a dragon-fly and bore the pet name of "forest ranger" on the north front, "cabbage grower" on the central front and "corn grower" in the south, the plane that everywhere was the butt of the good-natured chaff of the soldiers and respected as an old, creaky but tried and devoted comrade, the plane on which all airmen had learnt to fly, steeply rose to the sky.

In a mirror fixed at an angle, the instructor could see the face of his new trainee. How many faces of men taking their first flight after a long interval had he seen! He had seen the condescending smile of aces; he had seen the brightly burning eyes of enthusiasts who once again found themselves in their element after weary wandering from hospital to hospital; he had seen those who had been severely injured in a crash grow pale, show signs of nervousness and bite their lips when they got into the air, and he had seen the impudent inquisitiveness of novices taking off for the first time. But in all the years he had been acting as instructor his mirror had never reflected an expression as strange as that which he saw on the face of this dark, handsome senior lieutenant who was obviously no novice at flying.

A feverish flush diffused the dark skin of the new trainee. His lips were pale, not from fright, but from an exalted emotion that Naumov could not explain. Who was he? What was happening to him? Why did the mechanic think he was drunk? When the plane took off and was suspended in the air, the instructor had seen the trainee's dark, stubborn, gypsy eyes, unprotected by goggles, fill with tears, and he saw the tears roll down his cheeks and blown away by a current of air as the plane veered.

"A bit off his nut, I think. I'll have to be careful with him. You never can tell..." mused Naumov. But there was something in the expression of the agitated face that he saw reflected in the oblong mirror that fascinated the instructor. To his own surprise he felt a lump rising in his throat and the instruments before him became hazy.

"Take over, now," he said through the intercom, but he merely loosened his grip on the stick and pedals, ready to take over the instant his queer trainee showed any weakness. Through the duplicate gear he felt the plane being handled by the confident and experienced hands of the new trainee, the "airman by the grace of God", as the Chief of Staff of the school, an old air wolf who had been an airman as far back as the Civil War, was fond of saying.

After the first lap Naumov ceased to have any fears about the new trainee. The plane coursed steadily, "according to regulations". The only strange thing was that in steering along the straight, the trainee, every now and again, veered slightly to the right or left, up or down. He appeared to be testing his own skill. Naumov decided to let the new man go up alone the next day and after two or three flights put him into a "UT-2" training plane, a miniature, plywood copy of a fighter plane.

It was cold. The thermometer on the wing registered 12° C below zero. A piercing wind blew into the cockpit, penetrating the instructor's dogskin flying boots and turning his feet into ice. It was time to land.

But every time he commanded: "Go in for landing!" through the intercom, he saw in his mirror a pair of black, burning, imploring eyes. No, they did not implore, they demanded, and he could not find it in his heart to refuse. Instead of ten minutes, they flew for half an hour.

Leaping out of the cockpit, Naumov stamped his feet and flapped his arms; the early frost certainly had a nip in it that morning! The trainee, however, fidgeted with something in the cockpit for a while and then alighted slowly, and reluctantly it seemed. When he got his feet on the ground he squatted near the wing with a happy, really intoxicated smile on his lips, and with his cheeks flushed by the frost and excitement.

"Cold, eh?" the instructor asked. "It got me right through my flying boots, but you are wearing ordinary shoes! Aren't your feet frozen?"

"I have no feet," answered the trainee, continuing to smile at his own thoughts.

"What!" ejaculated Naumov, his jaw dropping with astonishment.

"I have no feet," Meresyev repeated distinctly.

"What do you mean, you have no feet? Do you mean there's something wrong with them?"

"No, I have no feet at all. These are artificial."

For a moment Naumov stood riveted to the ground with amazement. What that queer fellow had said was unbelievable. No feet! But he had just been flying, and flying well! ...

"Let's see," he said, and there was a note of apprehension in his voice.

This inquisitiveness neither annoyed nor offended Alexei. On the contrary, he wanted to put the finishing touch to the surprise of this funny old fellow, and, with a gesture like that of a conjuror performing a trick, he lifted the legs of his trousers.

The trainee stood on feet made of leather and aluminium and looked merrily at the instructor, the mechanic and the line of airmen waiting for their turn to go up.

In a flash Naumov understood the cause of this man's agitation, of the unusual expression in his face, of the tears in his black eyes, and of the eagerness with which he wanted to prolong the thrill of flying. This trainee amazed him. He rushed towards him and, violently shaking hands with him, exclaimed:

"Boy, how could you? You don't know, you simply don't know what sort of a man you are!"

The chief thing was done now. Alexei had won the instructor's heart. They met in the evening and drew up a training programme. They agreed that Alexei's position was a difficult one. If he committed the slightest blunder, he stood in danger of being barred from flying for ever, and although now more than ever he was burning to get into a fighter plane and fly to the place whither the finest warriors in the country were now streaming—the famous city on the Volga—he consented patiently to undergo all-round training. He realised that in his position only an "A-1" certificate would suffice.

9

Meresyev stayed at the training school for over five months. The airfield was covered with snow, the aircraft were put on runners. When up in the "sector" Alexei now saw beneath him not the bright colours of autumn overspreading the land, but only two colours: white and black. The sensational news of the rout of the Germans at Stalingrad, the doom of the German Sixth Army and the capture of Paulus, were now things of the past. An unprecedented and irresistible offensive was developing in the South. General Rotmistrov's tanks had pierced the German front and were playing havoc in the enemy's rear. At a time like this, when such things were going on at the front, and when terrific battles were raging in the sky over the front, Alexei found it harder to "creak" painstakingly in tiny training planes than it had been for him to pace day after day an innumerable number of times up and down the hospital corridor, or to dance mazurkas and foxtrots on his swollen, excruciatingly painful stumps.

But back in the hospital he had pledged himself to return to active service in Fighter Command. He had set himself a goal, and he strove towards it in spite of sorrow, pain, weariness and disappointment. One day a thick envelope arrived at his new address, which Klavdia Mikhailovna had sent on. It contained some letters and one from herself inquiring how he was getting on, what successes he had achieved, and whether his dream had come true.

"Has it?" he asked himself, but without answering he began to sort the letters. There were several: one from his mother, one from Olya, one from Gvozdev, and one other that greatly surprised him. The address was written in the hand of the "meteorological sergeant" and beneath it was the inscription: "From Captain K. Kukushkin". He read that one first.

Kukushkin wrote that he had been shot down: his plane was hit and set on fire, he bailed out and managed to land within his own lines, but in doing so he dislocated his arm and was now at the medical battalion, where he was "dying from ennui among the gallant wielders of enemas", as he put it. He was not worrying, however, for he was confident that he would soon be back in his plane. He added that he was dictating this letter to his, Alexei's, well-known correspondent Vera Gavrilova, who thanks to him, is still called the "meteorological sergeant" in the wing. The letter also said that Vera was a very good comrade and a mainstay to him in his misfortune. At this point Vera wrote on her own behalf, in parentheses, that, of course, Kostya was exaggerating. From this letter Alexei learned that he was still remembered in the wing, that his portrait had been added to those of the heroes of the wing that hung in the messroom, and that the Guards had not lost hope of seeing him among them again. The Guards! Meresyev smiled and shook his head. The minds of Kukushkin and of his voluntary secretary must be taken up very much with something if they forgot to inform him of such an important event as the presentation of the Guards' Colours to the wing!

Then Alexei opened the letter from his mother. It was the chatty epistle that old mothers usually write, full of anxiety and concern for him: how was he faring, was he not cold, was he getting enough food, did he receive warm winter clothes, and should she knit him a pair of mittens? She had already knitted five pairs and had sent them as gifts to the men of the Soviet Army. And in the thumb of each pair she had put a note saying: "I hope they bring you luck." She hoped he had received a pair of those mittens! They were very nice, warm mittens, knitted from wool that she had combed from the down of her rabbits. Yes, she had forgotten to mention that she had a family of rabbits now—a buck, a doe and seven little ones. Only at the end of the letter, after all this affectionate, old motherly chatter, did she write about the most important thing: the Germans had been driven away from Stalingrad, lots and lots of them were killed there, and people even said that one of their big generals was taken prisoner. Well, and when they were driven away, Olya came to Kamyshin on five days' leave. She had stayed at her house, as Olya's house had been wrecked by a bomb. She was now in a sappers' battalion and was a lieutenant. She had been wounded in the shoulder, but she had recovered now and had been awarded a decoration—what kind of decoration, the old lady, of course, did not think of saying. She added that while staying at her house, Olya slept all the time, and when she was not asleep she talked about him; and they told fortunes with cards, and every time the queen of diamonds came out on top of the king of clubs. Alexei surely knew what that meant! So far as she was concerned, she wrote, she could not wish for a better daughter-in-law than that same queen of diamonds.

Alexei smiled at the old lady's artless diplomacy and carefully opened the grey envelope containing the letter from the "queen of diamonds". It was not a long letter. Olya wrote that after digging the "trenches", the best members of her labour battalion were drafted into a sappers' unit of the regular army. She now had the rank of lieutenant-technician. It was her unit that had, under enemy fire, built the fortifications at Mamayev Kurgan that is now so famous, and also the ring of fortifications around the Tractor Works, for which it had been awarded the Order of the Red Banner. Olya wrote that they were having a very hard time, that everything—from canned meat to shovels—had to be brought from the other side of the Volga, which was continuously under machine-gun fire. She also wrote that not a single building had remained intact in the city and the ground was pitted with craters and looked like an enlarged photograph of the moon.

Olya wrote that when she left the hospital she and others were taken through Stalingrad in a car, and she saw piles of bodies of dead Germans that had been collected for burial. Many were still lying along the roads! "How I wished that your friend the tankman, I have forgotten his name, the one whose whole family was killed, could come here and see all this with his own eyes. Upon my word, I think all this ought to be photographed for the movies and shown to people like him. Let them see what vengeance we have taken on the enemy!" At the end she wrote—Alexei read this unintelligible sentence several times—that now, after the battle of Stalingrad, she felt that she was worthy of him, hero of heroes. The letter had been written in a hurry, at a railway station where their train had stopped. She did not know where they were going and so could not tell him what her P. O. number would be. Consequently, until he received the next letter from her, Alexei was unable to write and say that it was she, that little, frail girl who had toiled so zealously in the very thick of the fight, that was the real "hero of heroes". He turned the envelope over again, and in the sender's address read the distinctly written name: Guards Junior Lieutenant-Technician Olga So-and-so.

Every time he had a moment to spare at the airfield Alexei took this letter out and read it again, and for a long time it seemed to warm him in the piercing winter wind in the airfield, and in the freezing class-room "9a", which still served as his home.

At last, Instructor Naumov fixed a day for his test flight. He was to fly a fighter-trainer, and the flight was to be examined not by the instructor, but by the Chief of Staff of the school, that same stout, ruddy-faced, robust lieutenant-colonel who had welcomed him so coldly when he arrived.

Knowing that he was being closely watched from the ground and that his fate was about to be decided, Alexei excelled himself that day. He handled that tiny, light plane so expertly that the lieutenant-colonel could not restrain outbursts of admiration. When Meresyev alighted from the plane and presented himself to the chief, he could tell from the joy and excitement that beamed from every wrinkle on Naumov's face that he had passed the test.

"You have an excellent style! Yes ... you are what I call an airman by the grace of God," growled the lieutenant-colonel. "Listen, would you like to remain here as an instructor? We need men like you."

Meresyev emphatically refused.

"Well, you're a fool! Anybody can fight, but here you'd be teaching men to fly."

Suddenly the lieutenant-colonel's eye caught the walking-stick that Meresyev was leaning on, and his face turned livid.

"You've got that thing again!" he roared. "Give it to me! Do you think you are going on a picnic with a cane? You're not on a boulevard.... Forty-eight hours in the guardroom for disobeying orders!... Aces! Getting themselves mascots! You'll be painting the ace of diamonds on your fuselage next! Forty-eight hours! D'you hear what I say?"

The lieutenant-colonel tore the stick out of Meresyev's hand and glared round, looking for something to break it on.

"Permit me to say, Comrade Lieutenant-Colonel. He has no feet," intervened Instructor Naumov.

The Chief of Staff's face went more livid; his eyes bulged and he breathed heavily.

"What do you mean? Are you trying to make a fool of me? Is it true what the instructor just said?"

Meresyev nodded and glanced furtively at his precious stick, which was in imminent danger of destruction. Indeed, he was now never separated from the gift of Vasily Vasilyevich

The lieutenant-colonel looked suspiciously at the friends and drawled:

"Well ... if that's the case ... then, of course.... Show me your feet! ... Humph!"

Alexei was discharged from the training school with a first-class certificate. That irate lieutenant-colonel, that old "air wolf", was able to appreciate his great accomplishment more than anybody else, and was not stinting in words of admiration. He certified that Meresyev was "a skilful, experienced and strong-willed airman, fit for any branch of the air service".

10

Meresyev spent the rest of the winter and the early part of the spring at an improvement school. It was an old-established army aviation school, which had an excellent airfield, fine living quarters and a magnificent club-house with a theatre where performances were sometimes given by Moscow theatrical companies. This school too was crowded, but the pre-war regulations were religiously adhered to, and the trainees were obliged to be careful even about minor details of dress, because, if boots were not polished, if a button was missing on a coat, or if a map case had been hurriedly put on over the belt, the offender had to do two hours' drill by order of the Commandant.

A large group of airmen, to which Alexei Meresyev belonged, was training to fly a new type of Soviet fighter plane, the "La-5". The training was thorough and included a study of the engines and other parts of the plane. At the lectures, Alexei was amazed to learn the progress Soviet aviation had made in the short period that he had been absent from the army. What had seemed a bold innovation at the beginning of the war was now hopelessly out of date. The swift "Swallows" and light, high flying "Migs" that were regarded as masterpieces at the beginning of the war, were being decommissioned and replaced by newly-designed machines which the Soviet aircraft factories had put into mass production in a fabulously short time: magnificent "Yaks" of the latest models, "La-5's" which had come into fashion, and two-seater "Ils" —flying tanks which almost shaved the ground and rained on the heads of the enemy bombs, bullets and shells, and which, in their panic, the German forces had already named "black death". The new machines, brought into being by the genius of a fighting people, immensely complicated the art of air fighting and called for not only knowledge of the machine the airman was handling, and not only indomitable daring, but also ability quickly to find one's bearings in the air, to divide an air battle into its component parts and, independently, without waiting for orders, to adopt combat decisions and carry them out.

All this was extremely interesting. But fierce and unrelaxing offensive fighting was proceeding at the front, and while sitting in the bright and lofty class-room at a comfortable, black-topped desk listening to the lectures, Alexei Meresyev longed painfully to be at the front, yearned for the atmosphere of the fighting line. He had learned to overcome physical pain, he was able to compel himself to perform what seemed impossible, but he lacked the will-power to overcome the ennui of enforced idleness, and sometimes for weeks he would roam about the school, morose, absent-minded and bad-humoured.

Fortunately for Alexei, Major Struchkov was at the school at the same time as he. They had met like old friends. Struchkov arrived about two weeks after Alexei, but he at once plunged into the life of the school, adapted himself to its extremely strict rules that seemed so out of place in war-time, and made himself at home with everybody. He guessed the reason for Alexei's blue mood at once, and on leaving the bath-room to go to their sleeping quarters at night he would dig Alexei in the ribs good-humouredly and say:

"Don't grieve, old man! There'll be plenty of fighting left for us! Look how far we are yet from Berlin! Miles and miles to go. We'll have our share, don't you worry. We'll have our fill of fighting."

The major had grown thin and aged during the two or three months that they had not seen each other, he looked "broken", as they said in the army.

In midwinter, the group to which Meresyev and Struchkov belonged commenced flying practice. By this time Alexei was thoroughly familiar with the "La-5", the small, short-winged plane, the shape of which reminded one of a flying fish. Often, during recess, he would go to the airfield and watch these machines rise steeply into the air after a short run and see their bluish undersides glistening in the sun as they veered. He would go up to one, examine it, stroke its wing and pat its side as if it were not a machine, but a handsome, well-groomed, thoroughbred horse. At last, the group was lined up at the start. Every man was eager to try his skill, and a restrained altercation commenced among them as to who was to go up first. The first one the instructor called on was Struchkov. The major's eyes shone, he smiled knowingly, and he whistled a tune excitedly as he strapped on his parachute and drew the hood over the cockpit.

The engine roared, the plane shot off down the air field, leaving a trail of powdery snow that glistened in the sunlight like a rainbow, and in another moment it was in the air, its wings glittering in the sun. Struchkov described a narrow curve over the airfield, banked beautifully several times, rolled over, skilfully, handsomely performed the prescribed number of acrobatics, vanished from sight, suddenly shot out from over the roof of the school and, with roaring engine, swept at top speed over the airfield almost knocking the caps off the heads of the trainees who were waiting for their turn, and vanished again. He soon returned, however, and now, staidly descending, he made a skilful landing. He jumped out of the cockpit excited, exultant, wild with delight, like a boy who had successfully played a merry prank.

"It's not a machine, it's a violin, by God that's what it is!" he shouted breathlessly, interrupting the instructor who was scolding him for his recklessness. "You can play Chaikovsky on it, I tell you!" Throwing his powerful arms around Meresyev, he exclaimed: "It's good to be alive, Alyosha!"

It was, indeed, a splendid craft. Everybody agreed on that. Meresyev's turn came. After strapping his feet to the pedals he rose into the air and suddenly felt that this steed was too mettlesome for him, a footless rider, and needed extra careful handling. When the plane rose into the air he had failed to feel that full and magnificent contact with the machine that creates the joy of flying. It was an excellently constructed machine. It answered to every movement, to every tremor of the hand on the steering-gear and at once performed the corresponding movement. In its responsiveness it was really like a well-tuned violin. It was here that Alexei felt in all its acuteness his irretrievable loss, the irresponsiveness of his artificial feet, and he realised that in a machine like this the best artificial feet, with the best of training, cannot serve as a substitute for living, sensitive, flexible ones.

The aircraft easily and resiliently cut through the air and answered to every movement of the steering-gear, but Alexei was afraid of it. He noticed that when he veered his feet delayed, did not achieve that harmonious coordination that an airman acquires like a sort of reflex. That delay might throw the machine into a spin and prove fatal. Alexei felt like a hobbled horse. He was no coward, he was not afraid of being killed, he had gone up without even making sure that his parachute was in order; but he was afraid that the slightest blunder would cause his expulsion from the Fighter Command and tightly close against him the gates of his beloved profession. He was doubly cautious, and quite upset when he brought the machine down; owing to the irresponsiveness of his feet, he "bucked" so badly that the machine hopped clumsily on the snow several times.

Alexei alighted from the cockpit silent and frowning. His comrades, and even the instructor, hiding their embarrassment, praised and congratulated him, but this condescension only offended him. He waved them aside and, with a rolling gait and dragging his feet, he limped across the snow towards the grey school building. To prove a failure now after he had been in a fighter plane! This was the worst disaster that had befallen him since that April morning when his damaged machine struck the tops of the pine-trees. He missed his dinner, nor did he go in to supper. In violation of the school regulations, which strictly prohibited trainees from being in the dormitories in the day-time, he lay with his boots on his bed, with his hands under his head, and nobody who knew of his grief—neither the orderly nor the officers who passed by—rebuked him for this. Struchkov looked in and tried to speak to him, but getting no reply he went away, commiseratingly shaking his head.

Almost immediately after Struchkov left the room, Lieutenant-Colonel Kapustin, the political officer of the school, came in. He was a short, ungainly individual with thick eye-glasses, wearing a badly fitting uniform that hung on him like a sack. The trainees loved to listen to his lectures on international problems, during which this clumsy-looking man made them feel proud that they were participants in this great war. But they did not think much of him as an officer; they regarded him as a civilian who had got into the Air Force by chance and knew nothing about aviation. Paying no attention to Meresyev, Kapustin looked round the room, sniffed the air and suddenly exclaimed angrily:

"Who the hell's been smoking here? There's a smoking-room to smoke in. Comrade Senior Lieutenant, what does this mean?"

"I don't smoke," answered Alexei indifferently, continuing to lie on the bed.

"Why are you lying there? Don't you know the rules? Why don't you get up when your superior enters? Get up."

This was not a command. On the contrary, it was spoken in the polite manner of a civilian, but Meresyev obeyed listlessly and stood to attention next to his bed.

"That's right, Comrade Senior Lieutenant," said Kapustin encouragingly. "And now sit down and let's talk."

"What about?"

"About you. Let's go out. I want to smoke, and it is not permitted here."

They went out into the dimly-lit corridor—the electric bulbs were coloured blue for the black-out—and stood by the window. Kapustin puffed at his pipe, and at each puff his broad, thoughtful face was lit up by the glow.

"I intend to give your instructor a reprimand today," he said.

"What for?"

"For letting you go up into the sector without first obtaining permission from his superiors.... Why are you staring at me like that? As a matter of fact, I deserve a reprimand myself for not having had a talk with you before. I never have the time, always busy. I intended to, but.... Well, let that go! See here, Meresyev, flying is not such an easy thing for you, and that's why I intend to make it hot for your instructor."

Alexei said nothing. He wondered what kind of a man it was puffing his pipe. A bureaucrat who was annoyed because someone had ignored his authority by failing to report an unusual occurrence in the life of the school? A petty official who had discovered a clause in the regulations governing the choice of flying personnel that prohibited men with physical disabilities from going on flights? Or a crank jumping at the opportunity to exhibit his power? What did he want? Why did he blow in when Meresyev was sick at heart enough as it was, and felt like putting his neck in a noose?

He felt like kicking the man out and restrained himself with difficulty. Months of suffering had taught him to avoid drawing hasty conclusions, and there was something in this ungainly Kapustin that fleetingly reminded him of Commissar Vorobyov whom Meresyev called a real man. The light in Kapustin's pipe glowed and died out, and his broad face, fleshy nose and wise, penetrating eyes emerged from the bluish gloom and vanished again. Kapustin went on:

"Listen, Meresyev. I don't want to pay you compliments, but say what you like, you are the only footless man in the world to handle a fighter plane. The only one!" He unscrewed the mouth-piece of his pipe and peered through it at the dim light of a bulb and shook his head in perplexity. "I am not talking about you wishing to go back to the combat unit. It is certainly praiseworthy, but there is nothing particular in it. At a time like this everybody wants to do his very best to achieve victory.... What's happened to this damn pipe?"

He began to clean the mouth-piece again and seemed completely absorbed in the task; but Alexei, alarmed by a vague presentiment, was now on tenterhooks, eager to hear what he was going to say. Continuing to fidget with his pipe, Kapustin went on speaking, without seeming to care what impression his words made:

"It's not merely the personal matter of Senior Lieutenant Alexei Meresyev. The point is that you, a footless man, have acquired a skill that the whole world had hitherto regarded as attainable only by a man of perfect physical fitness, and then only by one out of a hundred. You are not simply Citizen Meresyev, you are a great experimenter.... Ah! I've got it going at last! It must have been stopped up with something.... And so I say, we cannot, we have no right to treat you as an ordinary airman, no right, do you understand? You have started an important experiment, and it is our duty to help you in every way we can. But in what way? That you must tell us. What can we do to help you?"

Kapustin refilled his pipe, lit up again, and again the red glow, appearing and vanishing, snatched his broad face and fleshy nose out of the gloom.

He promised to arrange with the chief of the school to allow Meresyev an extra number of flights, and suggested to Alexei that he should draw up a training programme for himself.

"But look how much fuel that will take!" said Alexei regretfully, amazed at the simple way this little, ungainly man had dissolved all his doubts.

"Fuel is important, of course, especially now. We measure it out by the thimbleful. But there are things more precious than fuel," answered Kapustin, and with that he carefully knocked the warm ashes out of his pipe against his heel.

Next day Meresyev commenced to train alone, and he did this not only with the perseverance he had shown when he was learning to walk, run and dance; he did it like one inspired. He tried to analyse the technique of flying, to study every detail, to divide it into the minutest motions, and to learn each one separately. He now studied, yes, studied, what he had acquired instinctively in his youth; he acquired intellectually what he had in the past attained by practice and habit. Mentally dividing the process of handling a plane into its component parts, he learned the special knack for each of them and transferred all the working sensations of the feet to his shins.

This was very hard and painstaking work, and the results were so small that they were barely perceptible. Nevertheless, every time he went up Alexei felt that the plane was becoming more and more grafted to him, that it was becoming more obedient to him.

"Well, how's it going, maestro?" Kapustin asked when he met him.

In answer Meresyev raised his thumb. He did not exaggerate. He was making progress, slow, perhaps, but sure; and the most important thing was that he ceased to feel in the plane like a weak rider mounted on a fleet and spirited steed. His confidence in his own skill returned to him, and this, as it were, was conveyed to the plane, and the latter, like a living thing, like a horse that feels a good rider on its back, became more obedient, and gradually revealed to Alexei all its flying qualities.

11

Long ago, in his boyhood, Alexei went out to learn to skate on the early smooth, translucent ice that formed in the inlet of the Volga where he had lived. Actually, he had no skates; his mother could not afford to buy him a pair. The blacksmith, whose washing his mother used to do, made him, at her request, a pair of small wooden blocks with thick wire runners and holes at the sides.

With the aid of string and bits of wood, Alexei strapped these blocks to his old and patched felt boots. On these he went to the river, on to the thin, yielding, melodiously creaking ice. All the boys in the neighbourhood of Kamyshin were sliding to and fro with shouts of delight, dashing along like little devils, racing each other, and hopping and dancing on their skates. Their antics looked easy, but as soon as Alexei stepped on to the ice it seemed to slip from under him and he fell painfully on his back. He jumped to his feet at once, fearing to let his playmates see that he had hurt himself. He tried to skate again, and to avoid falling on his back he bent his body forward, but this time he fell on his nose. He jumped to his feet again and stood for a while on his trembling legs, trying to think how it happened, and watching the other lads to see how they skated. He knew now that he must not bend his body too far forward, nor must he bend back. Trying to keep his body upright, he took several steps sideways and fell on his side; and so he fell and got up over and over again until sunset, and, to his mother's vexation, returned home all covered with snow, his legs trembling with weariness.

But next morning he was back on the ice again. He now moved with greater confidence, did not fall so often and, taking a run, could slide several metres; but try as he would he could make no further progress, although he remained on the ice until dusk.

But one day—Alexei had never forgotten that cold, blizzardy day when the wind drove the powdery snow over the polished ice—he made a lucky move and, to his own surprise, he kept on gliding, more and more swiftly and confidently with every round. All the experience that he had imperceptibly acquired when falling and hurting himself and repeating his attempts again and again, all the little knacks and habits he had gained, seemed suddenly to have amalgamated into one, and he now worked his legs and feet, feeling that his whole body, his whole boyish, fun-loving, persevering being, was exulting and filling with pleasurable confidence.

This was what happened to him now. He flew many times with great perseverance, trying to merge himself with his machine again, to feel it through the metal and leather of his artificial feet. At times he thought that he was succeeding, and this cheered him immensely. He tried a stunt, but he at once felt that his movement lacked confidence, the plane seemed to shy and struggle to get out of hand, and feeling the bitterness of waning hope he resumed his dull training routine.

But one thawing day in March, when in that one morning the ground at the airfield suddenly became dark and the porous snow shrank so much that the planes left deep furrows in it, Alexei rose into the air in his fighter plane. A side wind blew his plane off its course and he was obliged to keep on correcting it. In bringing the plane back into its course, he suddenly felt that it was obedient to him, that he could feel it with his whole being. This feeling came like a flash of lightning and at first he would not believe it. He had suffered too much disappointment to believe his luck at once.

He veered sharply and deeply to the right; the machine was obedient and precise. He felt exactly what he had felt as a boy on the dark, crisp ice in the tiny inlet of the Volga. The dull day seemed to brighten at once. His heart throbbed with joy, and he felt a slightly choking sensation in the throat from emotion.

At a certain invisible line the entire result of his persevering efforts in training was put to the test. He had crossed that line, and now he reaped the fruits of those numerous days of hard work easily and without strain. He achieved the main thing that he had long striven for without success: he had become merged with his machine, felt it as the continuation of his own body. Even the insensitive and inflexible artificial feet did not hinder this. Conscious of the waves of joy that were sweeping over him, he veered deeply several times, made the loop, and had barely completed this when he threw the machine into a spin. The ground spun furiously with a whistling sound, and the airfield, the school building and the tower of the meteorological station with its striped, inflated sleeve—all merged in continuous circles. With a sure hand he brought the machine out of the spin and made another tight loop. Only now did the then famous "La-5" reveal to him all its known and hidden qualities. What a machine it was in experienced hands! It responded readily to every movement of the steering-gear, it easily performed the most intricate stunts, and shot up like a rocket, compact, agile and swift.

Meresyev climbed out of the cockpit, staggering as if he were drunk, his mouth stretched in an idiotic smile. He did not see the infuriated instructor, nor hear his irate raving. Let him rave! Guardroom? All right, he was quite ready to do a spell in the guardroom. What difference did it make now? One thing was clear: he was an airman, a good airman. The extra quantity of precious fuel that had been spent on his training had not been wasted. He would repay that expenditure a hundredfold, if only they would let him go to the front.

At his quarters another pleasant surprise awaited him: a letter from Gvozdev was lying on his pillow. Where, how long, and in whose pocket it had wandered before it reached its destination, it was difficult to say, for the envelope was creased, smudged and oil-stained. It was enclosed in a neat envelope addressed in Anyuta's hand.

The tankman informed Alexei that a damnable thing

had happened to him. He was injured in the head by the wing of a German plane! He was now in the corps hospital, although he was expecting to be discharged within a day or two. And this incredible thing had happened in the following way. After the German Sixth Army had been cut off at Stalingrad, the Tank Corps in which Gvozdev served pierced the front of the retreating Germans and went through the breach across the steppe into the enemy's rear. Gvozdev was in command of a tank battalion in that raid.

It was a lovely raid! The steel armada charged into the Germans' rear, fortified villages and railway junctions, bursting in upon them like a bolt from the blue. The tanks charged through the streets, shooting down and crushing the troops that came in their way, and when the remnants of the German garrisons had fled, the tanks and the motorised infantry, whom they carried on their armour, blew up ammunition dumps and bridges, railway switches and turn-tables, thus blocking the trains of the retreating Germans. They refuelled and took in stocks of provisions from captured enemy stores and continued their advance before the Germans could recover, or at least find out in what direction the tanks would move next.

"We sped across the steppe, Alyosha, like Budyonny's cavalry! And did we put the wind up those fascists! You wouldn't believe it, but sometimes, with three tanks and a captured armoured car, we took whole villages and store bases. In war, Alyosha, panic is a great thing. A good panic among the enemy is worth two full-blooded divisions to the attacking force. Only it must be skilfully sustained, like a camp-fire; fuel—unexpected blows—must be constantly added to prevent it from dying out. We pierced the German armour and found that there is nothing underneath it except stinking tripe. We went through them as easy as cutting cheese.

"...And this is how this silly thing happened to me. The chief called us together and told us that a scouting plane had dropped him a message to the effect that at such and such a place there was a big air base: about three hundred planes, fuel and supplies. He pulled at his ginger moustache and said: 'Gvozdev, go out to that airfield tonight. Go quietly, without firing a shot, as if you are Germans, and when you get near enough, charge in among 'em, bang away with all your guns and turn everything upside down before they know where they are; and see to it that not a single bastard gets away.' This task was given to my crowd and another battalion that was put under my command. The rest of the outfit went on towards Rostov.

"Well, we got into that airfield like a fox into a hencoop. You won't believe it, Alyosha, but we got right to the German traffic regulators near the field. Nobody stopped us—it was a foggy morning and they couldn't see anything, they could only hear the sound of the engines and the rattling of the tracks. They thought we were Germans. Then we let loose and went for them. It was fun, I can tell you, Alyosha! The planes were lined up in rows. We fired armour-piercing shells and each shot went through half a dozen at least. But we saw that we couldn't do the job that way, because the crews that had some pluck began to start the engines. So we closed our hatches and started to ram them in the tails. They were transport planes, huge things, we couldn't reach their engines, so we went for their tails, they couldn't fly without tails any more than they could without engines. And that is where I got laid out. I opened the hatch and popped my head out to take a look round, and just then my tank ran into one of the planes. A fragment of the wing hit me in the head. A good thing my helmet softened the blow, else I would have been a goner. Everything's all right now and I'll be leaving the hospital soon and be among my tank boys again before long. The real trouble is that in the hospital they shaved my beard off. After all the trouble I took to grow it—it was a fine, broad beard—they went and shaved it off without the least pity. Well, to hell with the beard! We are moving pretty fast now, but still, I think I'll be able to grow another before the war's over, and hide my ugliness. I must tell you, though, Alyosha, for some reason Anyuta has taken a dislike to my beard and scolds me about it in every letter."

It was a long letter. It was evident that Gvozdev had written it to while away the tedium of hospital life. Incidentally, at the end of the letter he wrote that near

Stalingrad, when he and his men were fighting on foot—they had lost their machines and were waiting for new tanks—he met Stepan Ivanovich in the region of the famous Mamayev Kurgan. The old man had attended a training course and was now a noncom—a sergeant-major in command of a unit of anti-tank rifles. But he had not abandoned his sniper's habits. The only difference, as he told Gvozdev, was that he was now after bigger game—not careless fascists who crept out of their burrows to bask in the sun, but German tanks, strong and cunning beasts. But even in hunting this game the old man displayed his former Siberian huntsman's skill, stonelike patience, fortitude and splendid marksmanship. When they met they shared a bottle of rotten trophy wine that prudent Stepan Ivanovich had carefully put away, and recalled all friends. Stepan Ivanovich asked to be remembered to Meresyev, and invited both of them to visit him at his collective farm when the war was over and go hunting for squirrels, or tealshooting.

This letter comforted Alexei and yet made him sad. All his friends from ward forty-two had long been fighting again. Where were Grisha Gvozdev and old Stepan Ivanovich now? How were they getting on? Into what parts had the wind of war blown them? Were they alive? Where was Olya?

Again he recalled what Commissar Vorobyov had said about soldiers' letters being like the light from extinguished stars that takes a long time to reach us, so that it happens that a star may have been extinguished long ago, but its bright, cheerful light continues to pierce space, bringing us the gentle radiance of a non-existent luminary.

PART FOUR

1

On a hot summer day in 1943, and old truck raced along a road that had been beaten through neglected fields overgrown with reddish weeds by the baggage trains of advancing Soviet Army divisions. Bumping over pitfalls and rattling its ramshackle body, it headed for the front line. On each of its battered and dust-covered sides there could barely be seen a white painted strip bearing the inscription: "Field Postal Service". As the truck raced along, it left behind a huge, fluffy trail of grey dust which dissolved slowly in the close, still air.

The truck was loaded with mail bags and bundles of the latest newspapers, and in it sat two soldiers in airmen's tunics and peaked caps with blue bands, bumping and swaying in unison with the motions of the truck. The younger of the two, who, judging by his brand-new shoulderstraps, was a sergeant-major in the Air Force, was lean, well-built and fair-haired. His face was of such a virginal tenderness that it seemed as though the blood were shining through the fair skin. He looked about nineteen. He tried to behave like a seasoned soldier, spat through his teeth, swore in a hoarse voice, rolled cigarettes as thick as a finger, and tried to appear indifferent to everything. But in spite of all that, it was evident that he was going to the front line for the first time and was nervous. Everything around—a damaged gun by the roadside with its muzzle pointing to the ground; a wrecked Soviet tank with weeds growing right up to its turret; the scattered wreckage of a German tank, evidently the result of a direct hit of a bomb; the shell craters already overgrown with grass; the mine discs removed from the road by sappers and piled by the roadside near the new crossing, and the birch crosses in the German soldiers' cemetery visible in the distance—traces of the battles that had raged here, and to which a war-seasoned soldier would have paid no particular attention, surprised, amazed the lad, seemed to him to be significant, important and extremely interesting.

On the other hand, it could easily be seen that his companion, a senior lieutenant, was indeed a seasoned soldier. At a first glance you would say that he was twenty-three or twenty-four; but looking into his tanned, weather-beaten face with the fine wrinkles round the eyes, mouth and on his forehead, and into his dark, thoughtful, tired eyes, you would add another ten years to his age. The landscape made no impression upon him. He was not surprised by the rusty wreckage of war machines twisted by explosions that was lying about here and there, or by the deserted streets of the gutted village through which the truck passed, or even by the wreckage of a Soviet plane—a small heap of twisted aluminium and, at a little distance, the wrecked engine and the battered tail with a red star and a number, at the sight of which the younger soldier had turned red and shuddered.

Having made a comfortable armchair for himself out of the bundles of newspapers, the officer sat dozing with his chin resting on the handle of a quaint, heavy ebony walking-stick ornamented with a gold monogram. From time to time he opened his eyes with a start, as if driving away his drowsiness, looked round with a happy smile and deeply inhaled the hot, fragrant air. Away off the road, over a heaving sea of reddish weeds, he caught sight of two specks, which, after scrutinising carefully, he guessed to be two planes, leisurely gliding across the sky, one behind the other. His drowsiness left him in an instant, his eyes lit up, his nostrils quivered, and, keeping his eyes fixed on the two barely perceptible specks, he pounded on the roof of the driver's cabin and shouted:

"Cover! Turn off the road!"

He stood up, scanned the terrain with an experienced eye, and showed the driver the clayey hollow of a stream, the banks of which were overgrown with grey coltsfoot and golden clumps of celandine.

The younger soldier smiled indulgently. The planes were circling harmlessly far away, looking as though they were not in the least concerned with the lone truck that was raising an enormous trail of dust over the dreary, deserted fields. But before he could utter a word of protest the driver turned off the road, and the truck, rattling, raced towards the hollow.

As soon as they reached the hollow the senior lieutenant got out and, squatting in the grass, vigilantly watched the road.

"What are you making all this..." the younger soldier began, glancing ironically at the officer, but before he could finish the sentence the latter dropped flat to the ground and yelled:

"Down!"

In that very instant two immense shadows, engines roaring, swept right over their heads with a strange cluttering noise, causing the air to vibrate. Even this did not frighten the younger soldier much: ordinary planes, no doubt ours. He looked round and suddenly he saw by the roadside an overturned, rusty truck belching smoke and bursting into flames.

"Ah! They're firing incendiaries," said the mail-truck driver with a smile, gazing at the shell-battered and already burning side of the truck. "They're out for trucks."

"Hunters," calmly answered the senior lieutenant, making himself more comfortable on the grass. "We'll have to wait, they'll be back soon. They are scouring the road. You had better bring your truck farther back a bit, boy, under that birch-tree over there."

He said this calmly and confidently, as if the German airmen had just communicated their plans to him. Accompanying the mail was an army post-woman, a young girl who had been sitting with the driver. She now lay on the grass, pale, and with a feeble, perplexed smile on her dusty lips, furtively looking up at the calm sky across which billowy summer clouds were rolling. It was for her benefit that the sergeant-major, although feeling very embarrassed, said nonchalantly:

"We'd do better to get moving. Why waste time? A man destined to hang will never drown."

The senior lieutenant, calmly chewing a blade of grass, looked at the youth with a barely perceptible merry twinkle in his stern dark eyes and said:

"Listen, boy! Forget that silly proverb before it's too late. And another thing, Comrade Sergeant-Major. At the front you're supposed to obey your superiors. If the order is: 'Down!' you must lie down."

He found a juicy stick of horse sorrel in the grass, stripped the fibrous skin with his finger-nails and chewed the crisp plant with relish. Again the sound of aircraft engines was heard, and the same two planes flew low over the road, slightly rolling from wing to wing; they passed so close that the dark-yellow paint on their wings, the black and white crosses, and even the ace of spades painted on the fuselage of the nearest of them, could be seen distinctly. The senior lieutenant lazily plucked a few more "ponies", looked at his watch and commanded:

"All clear! Let's go! And step on it! The farther we are from this place, the better."

The driver sounded his horn and the post-woman came running from the hollow. She offered several pink wild strawberries hanging on their stalks to the senior lieutenant.

"They are ripening already.... We didn't notice the summer coming in," he said, smelling the berries and sticking them in the buttonhole of his tunic pocket like a nosegay.

"How do you know they won't come back and that it is safe to go on?" the youth asked the senior lieutenant, who had fallen silent and was again swaying in unison with the truck as it bumped over the pitfalls.

"That's easily explained. They are 'Messers', 'Me-109'. They carry enough fuel for only forty-five minutes' flying. They have spent it and have gone to refuel."

The senior lieutenant gave this explanation in a tone suggesting that he could not understand how people did not know such a simple thing. The youth now began to scan the sky more vigilantly; he wanted to be the first to signal the return of the "Messers". But the air was clear and so impregnated with the smell of the luxuriantly growing grass, dust and heated earth, the grasshoppers chirped so vigorously and merrily, and the larks sang so loudly over the dreary, weed-covered land, that he forgot about the German aircraft and the danger, and in a clear, pleasant voice began to sing the song that was popular at the front in those days, about a young soldier in a dugout longing for his sweetheart.

"Do you know 'The Ash-Tree'?" his companion inquired, interrupting him.

The youth nodded and started the old song. A look of sadness crossed the senior lieutenant's tired, dusty face.

"You are not singing it right, old man," he said. "It's not a comic song. You've got to put your heart into it." And he picked up the melody in a soft, very low, but clear voice.

The driver stopped for a moment and the post-woman got out of the cabin. She stepped on the wheel and with a light spring jumped into the body of the truck where she was caught by strong, friendly arms.

"I heard you singing, so I thought I'd join you...."

And so they sang in trio, to the accompaniment of the rattling of the truck and the zealous chirping of the grasshoppers.

The youth let himself go. He took a big mouth-organ from his kit-bag, and playing on it one moment and waving it like a baton and joining in the singing another, he acted as the conductor. And on this depressing and now abandoned road, like a whip-lash among the dusty, luxuriant, all-conquering weeds, rang out the powerful and mournful strains of a song as old and as new as these fields languishing in the summer heat, as the vigorous chirping of the grasshoppers in the warm, fragrant grass, as the larks' singing in the clear, summer sky, and as that lofty and infinite sky itself.

They were so taken up with their singing that they were nearly jerked out of the truck when the driver suddenly braked. The truck pulled up in the middle of the road. In the roadside ditch lay an overturned three-ton truck, its dusty wheels in the air. The youth turned pale, but his companion climbed over the side and hurried towards the ditch. He walked with a queer, springy, waddling step. A moment later the mail-truck driver was pulling out of the cabin of the overturned truck the blood-stained body of a quartermaster captain. His face was cut and scratched, evidently by broken glass, and was of an ashen hue. The senior lieutenant lifted his eyelid.

"This one's dead," he said, removing his cap. "Anybody else in there?"

"Yes. The driver," answered the mail-truck driver.

"What are you standing there for? Come and help!" the senior lieutenant snapped at the dismayed youth. "Haven't you seen blood before? Get used to it, you'll see quite a lot! Here you are, this is the hunters' prey."

The driver was alive. He moaned softly but his eyes were shut. There were no signs of injury, but evidently, when the truck, hit by a shell, hurtled into the ditch, the driver struck his chest violently against the wheel and was caught in the wreckage of the cabin. The senior lieutenant ordered him to be lifted into the mail truck. The lieutenant had with him, carefully wrapped in a piece of cotton cloth, a smart, brand-new greatcoat. This he spread out for the injured man to lie on, sat down on the floor of the truck and placed the injured man's head upon his knee.

"Drive for all you're worth!" he ordered.

Gently supporting the injured man's head, he smiled at some remote thought of his own.

Dusk had already fallen when the truck raced down the street of a small village, which an experienced eye could at once see was the command post of a small aircraft unit. Several lines of wire ran suspended from dusty branches of bird-cherry and gaunt apple-trees standing in front gardens, from the sweeps of wells and from the poles of fences. In the thatched sheds near the houses, where peasants usually keep their carts and farm implements, battered "Emkas" and jeeps could be seen. Here and there through the dim panes of the small cottage windows, soldiers wearing peaked caps with blue bands were seen and the taping of typewriters could be heard; and from one house, on which the network of wires conjoined, came the even ticking of a telegraph apparatus.

This village, which stood off the main and minor roads, looked as if it had survived in this now desolate and weed-covered place as a relic to show how good it had been to live in these parts before the Hitler invasion. Even the small pond, overgrown with yellowish duckweed, was full of water. It was a cool, glistening patch in the shade of old weeping willows, and forcing a way through the clumps of weeds, preening and splashing themselves, swam a couple of snow-white, red-beaked geese.

The injured man was carried to a cottage with a Red Cross flag. Then the truck drove through the village and stopped at the neat little building of the village school. From the numerous wires that ran into the broken window, and the sentry standing on the porch armed with a submachine-gun, one could guess that this was staff headquarters.

"I want to see the Wing Commander," said the senior lieutenant to the orderly, who was sitting at the open window solving a cross-word puzzle in a magazine.

The youth, who had followed at the heels of the senior lieutenant, noticed that on entering the building the latter had mechanically straightened the front of his tunic, adjusted its folds under his belt with his thumbs and had buttoned his collar. He forthwith did the same. He had taken a great liking to his taciturn companion and now tried to copy him in all things.

"The colonel is busy," answered the orderly.

"Tell him that I have an urgent dispatch from the Personnel Department of Air Force Staff Headquarters."

"You'll have to wait. He is with the air reconnaissance crew. He said he was not to be interrupted. Go out and sit in the garden for a bit."

The orderly again became engrossed in the cross-word puzzle. The new arrivals went into the garden and sat down on an old bench next to a flower-bed, which had been carefully bordered with bricks but was now neglected and overgrown with grass. Before the war, on quiet summer afternoons like this, the old village school-teacher must have rested here after her day's work. Two voices were distinctly heard coming from the open windows. One, hoarse and excited, was reporting:

"Along this road and this one, leading to Bolshoye Gorokhovo and the Krestovozdvizhensky churchyard, there is considerable movement, continuous columns of trucks, all going in one direction—to the front. Here, right near the churchyard, in a hollow, there are trucks, or tanks.... I suppose a big unit is being concentrated."

"What makes you think so?" interrupted a tenor voice.

"We encountered very heavy barrage fire. We barely got away. There was nothing here yesterday, except some smoking field kitchens. I flew right over them and raked them just to give them a shaking-up. But today! Their fire was terrific! ... Obviously, they're making for the front."

"What about square 'Z'?"

"There is some movement there too, but not so much. Here, near the wood, there's a big tank column on the march. About a hundred. Stretched out in echelons for about five kilometres, moving in broad daylight without camouflage. Perhaps it's a sham move.... Here, here, and here, we spotted artillery, right near the front lines. And ammunition dumps. Camouflaged with wood piles. They were not there yesterday.... Big dumps."

"Is that all?"

"That's all, Comrade Colonel. Shall I write out a report?"

"Report? No! No time for a report! Go to Army Headquarters at once! Do you know what this means? Hey, orderly! My car! Send the captain to A. F. Headquarters!"

The colonel had his office in a spacious classroom. The only furniture in this room with bare log walls was a table, on which lay the leather cases of field telephones, a large aviation map-case with a map, and a red pencil. The colonel, a short, energetic, well-knit man, paced the room with his hands behind his back. Absorbed in his thoughts, he passed the airmen who were standing at attention. Suddenly he halted in front of them and looked at them inquiringly.

"Senior Lieutenant Alexei Meresyev reporting," said the dark officer, clicking his heels and saluting.

"Sergeant-Major Alexander Petrov," reported the youth, clicking the heels of his army boots louder, and trying to salute more smartly.

"Wing Commander, Colonel Ivanov," barked the chief in reply. "A dispatch?"

With precise movements Meresyev pulled the dispatch from his map-case and handed it to the colonel. The latter quickly scanned the short message, cast a rapid, searching glance at the new arrivals, and said:

"Good! You've come at the right time. But why have they sent so few?" Suddenly a look of surprise crossed his face as if he had remembered something. "Wait a minute!" he exclaimed. "Are you the Meresyev? The Chief of Staff of A. F. telephoned me about you. He warned me that you...."

"That's not important, Comrade Colonel," interrupted Alexei, not very politely. "Permit me to proceed to my duties."

The colonel looked at the senior lieutenant with curiosity and, nodding, said with an approving smile:

"Right! Orderly! Take these men to the Chief of Staff, and give orders in my name to have them fed and provided with sleeping quarters. Say that they are to be listed in Guards Captain Cheslov's squadron."

Petrov thought that the Wing Commander was a bit too fussy. Meresyev liked him. Men like this—brisk, able to grasp things at once, capable of thinking clearly and of taking resolute decisions—were just after his own heart. The air scout's report that he had heard while sitting in the garden had sunk into his mind. From many signs which a soldier could read: from the congestion of the roads they had hitch-hiked on after leaving Army Headquarters, from the fact that at night the sentries on the road had insisted on strict black-out and threatened to fire at the tyres of those who disobeyed, from the noise and congestion in the birch woods off the main roads caused by the concentration of tanks, trucks and artillery, and from the fact that even on the deserted field road they had been attacked by German "hunters" that day—Meresyev guessed that the lull at the front was coming to an end, that the Germans intended to strike their new blow in this region, that the blow would be struck soon, that the Soviet Army Command was aware of this and had already prepared a worthy reply.

2

The restless senior lieutenant would not let Petrov wait for the third course at dinner, but made him jump with him on a fuel truck that was going to the airfield, which was situated in a meadow outside the village. Here the new men introduced themselves to Guards Captain Cheslov, the Squadron Commander, a frowning, taciturn, but, for all that, an extremely good-natured fellow. Without much ado, he led them to the grass-covered earthwork caponiers in which were standing two brand-new, brightly varnished, blue "La-5's" with numbers "11" and "12" painted on their rudders. These were the machines the new-comers were to fly. They spent the rest of the afternoon in the fragrant birch wood—where even the roar of aircraft engines could not drown the singing of the birds —inspecting the machines, chatting with the new mechanics, and acquainting themselves with the life of the wing.

They were so absorbed in what they were doing that they returned to the village with the last truck when it was already dark, and missed their supper. But this did not worry them. In their knapsacks they had the remains of the dry rations that had been issued to them for the journey. Sleeping quarters was a more serious difficulty. This little oasis in the desolate, weed-grown wilderness was greatly overpopulated with the crews and staff personnel of two aircraft wings. After wandering from one overcrowded house to another and indulging in angry altercations with the inmates who refused to make room for the new-comers, and after philosophical reflections about the regrettable fact that houses were not made of rubber and did not stretch, the quartermaster at last pushed them into the very next house they came to and said:

"Sleep here tonight. I'll make some other arrangements for you in the morning."

There were already nine men in the little hut, and they had all turned in. A smoking kerosene-lamp made from the flattened body of a shell, the kind that were called "Katyushas" in the first years of the war and were renamed "Stalingradki" after Stalingrad, dimly lit up the dark figures of the sleepers. Some slept on beds and bunks and others on hay spread on the floor and covered with capes. In addition to the nine lodgers, the hut was occupied by the owners, an old woman and a grown-up daughter, who, for the want of room, slept on the ledge of the huge Russian stove.

The new-comers halted on the threshold, wondering how they were to step over the sleeping bodies. The old woman shouted at them angrily from the stove:

"There's no room, there's no room! Can't you see we're overcrowded? Where are we going to stick you, on the ceiling?"

Petrov felt so embarrassed that he was ready to retreat, but Meresyev was already picking his way to the table, trying to avoid stepping on the sleepers.

"We only want a corner where we can eat our supper, Grandma. We haven't eaten all day," he said. "Could you get us a plate and a couple of cups? We won't inconvenience you by sleeping here. It's a warm night, and we can sleep in the garden."

From the depths of the stove-ledge, from behind the back of the irate old woman, two small bare feet appeared; a slim figure silently slipped away from the stove and, balancing skilfully between the sleepers, vanished behind the passage door and soon returned, carrying some plates. Two coloured cups were hooked on to her slender fingers. At first Petrov thought it was a child, but when she got to the table and the dim yellow light picked her face out of the gloom, he saw that she was a young woman, and a pretty one too; only her beauty was marred by her brown blouse and sack-cloth skirt, and by the tattered shawl she wore crossed on her chest and tied at the back like an old woman's.

"Marina! Marina! Come here, you slut!" hissed the old woman on the stove.

But the young woman made no sign that she had heard. Deftly, she spread a newspaper on the table and placed the plates, cups and forks upon it, casting sidelong glances at Petrov the while.

"Well, eat your supper. I hope you enjoy it," she said. "Perhaps you want to cut up or heat something? I could do that in a sec. Only the quartermaster said we were not to light a fire outside."

"Marina, come here!" the old woman called.

"Don't pay any attention to her, she's a bit touched. The Germans have scared her to death," said the young woman. "As soon as she sees soldiers at night, she gets worried about me. Don't be angry with her, she's like that only at night. She's all right in the day-time."

In his knapsack Meresyev found some sausage, a tin of meat, even two dry herrings with the salt glistening on their lean sides, and a loaf of army bread. Petrov proved to be less provident; all he had was some meat and rusks. Marina cut all this up with her small deft hands and laid it out appetisingly on the plates. More and more often her eyes, concealed by long lashes, scrutinised Petrov's face, while Petrov cast furtive glances at her. When their eyes met they both flushed, frowned and turned their heads away; and they conversed only through Meresyev, never addressing each other directly. It amused Alexei to watch them, amused and yet saddened him a little: they were both so young. Compared with them he felt old, tired and with a large part of his life behind him.

"Marina, you don't happent to have some cucumbers, eh?" he asked.

"We do," the young woman answered with a roguish smile.

"And perhaps you can find a couple of boiled potatoes?"

"Yes—if you ask for it properly."

She left the room again, skipping over the bodies of the sleepers lightly and noiselessly, like a moth.

"Comrade Senior Lieutenant!" protested Petrov. "How can you be so familiar with a girl you don't know? Asking her for cucumbers and...."

Meresyev broke into a merry laugh.

"Listen, old man, where do you think you are? Are we at the front, or aren't we?... Hey, Grandma! Stop grousing! Come down and eat with us!"

Grunting and mumbling to herself, the old woman got down from the stove, came to the table and at once pounced on the sausage, of which, it appeared, she had been very fond before the war.

The four of them sat down at the table and to the accompaniment of the snores and sleepy mumbling of the other inmates, supped with great relish. Alexei chatted all the time, teased the old woman and made Marina laugh. Finding himself at last in his element of bivouac life, he enjoyed it thoroughly, feeling as if he had come home after long wanderings in foreign lands.

Towards the end of the supper the friends learned that this village had survived because it had been the headquarters of a German unit. When the Soviet Army launched its offensive, the Germans fled so hurriedly that they had no time to destroy the village. The old woman went out of her mind when the fascists raped her eldest daughter in her presence. Later the girl drowned herself in the pond. During the eight months the fascists were in the district, Marina had lived in the empty threshing-barn in the back yard, the entrance to which had been concealed with piles of straw and junk. All this time she never saw the sun. At night her mother brought her food and drink, passing it to her through the smoke hole. The more Alexei chatted with the girl the more often she glanced at Petrov, and her eyes, impudent and yet shy, expressed barely concealed admiration.

Chatting and laughing, they finished their supper. Marina thriftily put the remnants of the food back into Meresyev's knapsack, saying that everything comes in handy for a soldier. After that, she whispered something to her mother and then turned round and said emphatically:

"Listen! Since the quartermaster has put you in here, I want you to stay! Get up on the stove, and mother and I will go into the cellar. You need a rest after your journey. Tomorrow we'll find a place for you."

Again stepping lightly over the sleepers, she went out and came back with a bundle of straw, spread it over the wide stove-ledge and rolled up some clothing for pillows; she did all this briskly, deftly, noiselessly, and with feline grace.

"A nice girl, isn't she, old man?" commented Meresyev, lying down on the straw with pleasure and stretching his limbs until the joints cracked.

"Not bad," answered Petrov with affected indifference.

"Did you see how she kept looking at you!..."

"I did not! She was chatting with you all the time!"

A moment later his regular breathing was heard. But Meresyev did not fall asleep. Lying on the cool, fragrant straw, he saw Marina enter the room and search for something, every now and again casting a furtive glance at the stove. She trimmed the lamp on the table, glanced at the stove again, and picking her way among the sleepers, softly made for the door. For some reason, the sight of this pretty, graceful girl clothed in rags filled Alexei's soul with melancholy repose. The problem of sleeping quarters had been solved. He was to make his first combat flight in the morning. He was paired with Petrov—he, Meresyev, to be leader. How would it work out? He seemed a nice lad. Marina had fallen in love with him at first sight. Well, he'd better get some sleep!

He turned over on his side, rustled the straw for a bit and fell fast asleep.

He woke up feeling that something terrible had happened. He did not realise at once what it was, but with the soldier's instinct he jumped up and clutched his pistol. He could not tell where he was. A cloud of acrid smoke that smelt like garlic enveloped everything; and when the cloud was blown away by the wind he looked up and saw strange, huge stars glittering brightly over his head. It was as light as in broad daylight and he could see the logs of the hut scattered like matches, the displaced roof, jutting beams and some shapeless thing burning a little way off. He heard groans, the undulating roar of aircraft engines and the dreadful whine of dropping bombs.

"Down!" he yelled to Petrov who was kneeling on the stove-ledge that towered above the ruins and looking wildly around him.

They dropped flat on the bricks and pressed their bodies against them. In that instant a large bomb splinter struck the chimney and a shower of red dust and dry clay rained down upon them.

"Don't move! Lie still!" commanded Meresyev, suppressing a desire to jump up and run, no matter where, so long as he could be on the move, the desire that every man feels during a night air raid.

The bombers could not be seen. They were circling in the darkness high above the flares they had dropped. But in the flickering, glaring light the bombs could be distinctly seen plunging into the zone of light like black drops and, visibly increasing in size, hurtle to the ground and shoot red flames into the darkness of the summer night. It seemed as though the earth was splitting up and roaring.

The airmen clung to the stove, which swayed and trembled with every explosion. They pressed their bodies, cheeks and legs to the ledge, trying to flatten themselves, to merge with the bricks. The droning of the engines died away, and at once the roar of the flames of the burning ruins on the opposite side of the street was heard.

"Well, they gave us a refresher," said Meresyev, with affected coolness brushing the straw and clay dust from his clothes.

"But what about the men who were sleeping here?" anxiously asked Petrov, trying to restrain the nervous twitching of his jaw and the hiccup that was forcing itself to his throat. "And Marina?"

They got down from the stove. Meresyev had a torch. He searched under the planks and logs that littered the floor. There was nobody there. Later they learned that the airmen had heard the alert and had managed to run to the slit. Petrov and Meresyev searched all the ruins, but they failed to find Marina or her mother. They called them, but no answer came. What could have become of them? Did they survive the raid?

Patrols were already in the street restoring order. Sappers extinguished the fires, dismantled the ruins and unearthed the dead and injured. Orderlies ran through the streets calling out the names of airmen. The wing was quickly transferred to another base. The flying personnel was mustered in the airfield so as to leave with their machines at dawn. A preliminary count showed that the casualties were not heavy. One airman was injured, and two mechanics and several sentries were killed at their posts. It was believed that many of the villagers had perished, but how many it was difficult to say owing to the darkness and confusion.

Just before dawn, on the way to the airfield, Meresyev and Petrov could not help stopping at the house they had slept in. Out of the chaos of logs and planks two sappers were carrying a stretcher on which lay something covered with a blood-stained sheet.

"Who is that?" asked Petrov, his face pale and his heart heavy with foreboding.

One of the stretcher-bearers, an elderly sapper with whiskers, who reminded Meresyev of Stepan Ivanovich, explained at length:

"An old lady and a girl. We found them in the cellar. They were hit by falling bricks. Killed outright. I don't know whether the young one is a girl or a woman, she's so small. Must have been pretty by the look of her. A brick hit her in the chest. She is pretty—like a little child."

That night the German army launched its last big offensive; and in attacking the lines of the Soviet forces started the Battle of the Kursk Salient which proved fatal for it.

3

The sun had not yet risen; it was the darkest hour of the short summer night, but the engines being warmed up in the airfield were already roaring. On a map spread out on the dewy grass, Captain Cheslov was showing the airmen of his squadron their new airfield and the route to it.

"Keep your eyes open," he was saying. "Don't lose sight of each other. The airfield is right in the forward lines."

The new base was, indeed, in the fighting line marked on the map with blue pencil, on a salient that jutted into the dispositions of the German forces. To get there they flew not back, but forward. The airmen were delighted. In spite of the fact that the enemy had taken the initiative again, the Soviet Army was not preparing to retreat, but to attack.

When the first rays of the sun lit up the sky, and the pink mist was still rolling over the field, the Second Squadron rose into the air in the wake of their commander, and the planes set course for the south, keeping in close formation.

Meresyev and Petrov kept close together in their first joint flight, and short as it was, Petrov was able to appreciate the confident and truly masterly style of his leader; and Meresyev, deliberately veering sharply and suddenly several times on the way, noticed that his follower possessed gumption, a good eye, strong nerves, and what he regarded as most important, a good flying style, though not yet confident.

The new air strip was situated in the rear of an infantry regiment. If the Germans discovered it, they would be able to reach it with their light guns and even with their heavy trench mortars. But they had no time to bother with an airfield that had appeared under their noses. While it was still dark they had opened fire on the fortifications of the Soviet troops with all the artillery they had accumulated here in the course of the spring. A red, quivering glare rose high in the sky over the fortified area. Explosions blotted out everything like a dense forest of black trees that sprang up every instant. Even when the sun rose darkness prevailed. It was difficult to distinguish anything in the droning, roaring, quivering gloom, and the sun was suspended in the sky like a dim, grimy-red pancake.

The reconnaissance flights the Soviet aircraft had made over the German positions a month before had not been in vain. The intentions of the German Command were disclosed; its positions and points of concentration were plotted on the map and studied square by square. The Germans, as was their habit, thought that they would be able to plunge their dagger with all their might into the back of their sleeping and unsuspecting foe; but the foe only pretended to be asleep. He caught the assailant's arm and crushed it in his steel-like, powerful grip. Before the roar of the artillery preparation that raged on a front of several tens of kilometres died down, the Germans, deafened by the thunder of their own batteries and blinded by the gun-powder smoke that enveloped their positions, saw the red balls of the explosions in their own trenches. The marksmanship of the Soviet artillery was perfect, and it aimed not at squares, as the Germans had done, but at definite targets, batteries, concentrations of tanks and infantry already drawn up on the line of attack, at bridges, underground ammunition dumps, blindages and command posts.

The German artillery preparation developed into a terrific artillery duel in which tens of thousands of guns of the most diverse calibres participated on both sides. When the planes of Captain Cheslov's squadron landed in the new airfield, the ground was quaking, and the roar of explosions merged into a continuous, mighty roar, as if an endless train were on a railway bridge, hooting and rattling and clanging, and never crossing it. The entire horizon was blotted out by voluminous, rolling smoke. Over the small wing airfield came wave after wave of bombers, some in goose, some in stork and some in open formation, and the dull thuds of their exploding bombs could be distinguished amidst the steady roar of artillery.

The squadrons were ordered to be in "readiness No. 2". That meant that the airmen were to be in their cockpits so as to take off as soon as the first rocket shot into the air. The planes were wheeled to the edge of a birch wood and camouflaged with tree branches. The cool, raw air of the wood had a mushroomy fragrance, and the mosquitoes, whose buzzing was drowned by the roar of battle, furiously attacked the faces, necks and hands of the airmen.

Meresyev took off his helmet and, lazily waving the mosquitoes away, sat deep in thought, enjoying the pungent morning fragrance of the wood. In the next caponier stood the plane of his follower. Every now and again Petrov got up from the seat of his cockpit and even stood on it to look in the direction in which the battle was raging, or to follow the passing bombers with his eyes. He was eager to go into the air to meet a real foe for the first time in his life, to direct his tracer bullets not at a wind-inflated sleeve hauled by an "R-5", but a real, live, agile enemy plane in which, perhaps, like a snail in its shell, sat the fellow whose bomb had killed that slim, pretty girl whom he now thought of as having seen in a beautiful dream.

Meresyev watched his restless follower and thought to himself: "We are about the same age. He is nineteen and I am twenty-three. What does a difference of three or four years signify for a man?" But by the side of his follower he felt like an experienced, staid and tired old man. Just now Petrov was wriggling about in his cockpit, rubbing his hands, laughing and shouting something at the passing Soviet planes, while he, Alexei, had stretched himself out comfortably in his seat. He was calm. He had no feet, it was immensely more difficult for him to fly than for any other airman in the world, but even that did not stir him. He was firmly convinced of his skill and he trusted his mutilated legs.

The wing remained in "readiness No. 2" until evening. For some reason it was kept in reserve. Evidently they did not want to disclose its position prematurely.

The dugouts assigned to the wing as their sleeping quarters had been built by Germans who had held this place. To make them more comfortable they had covered the plank walls with cardboard and packing-paper. Still hanging on the walls were pin-ups of movie stars with rapacious mouths, and oleograph views of German towns.

The artillery battle raged on. The earth quaked. Dry sand dribbled down the wallpaper, causing creepy, rustling sounds, as if the dugout were teeming with vermin.

Meresyev and Petrov decided to sleep in the open on their capes. The orders were to sleep fully dressed. Meresyev merely loosened the straps of his feet. He lay on his back, gazing at the sky, which seemed to quiver in the red flashes of the explosions. Petrov fell asleep at once, and in his sleep he snored, mumbled, worked his jaws, smacked his lips and curled up like a sleeping child. Meresyev covered him with his greatcoat. Realising that he would not be able to sleep, he got up, shivering with cold, performed several vigorous physical jerks to get warm and sat down on a tree stump.

The artillery tempest blew over. Only now and again a battery, here and there, reopened sporadic fire. Several stray shells swept over and exploded somewhere in the vicinity of the airfield. This so-called harassing fire usually did not disturb anybody. Alexei did not even turn his head at the sound of the explosions; his gaze was directed towards the fighting line. It was distinctly visible in the darkness. Even now, at this late hour of the night, there raged an intense, unrelaxing, heavy battle, which was reflected on the sleeping earth by the red glare of immense conflagrations that had flared up along the whole horizon. Over it flashed the flickering lights of flares— the bluish-phosphorous German ones, and the yellowish ones shot into the sky by the Soviet troops. Here and there a huge tongue of flame leaped up, lifting the curtain of darkness from the earth for an instant, and after it came the heavy sigh of an explosion.

The drone of night bombers was heard and the entire front became ornamented with the multicoloured beads of tracer bullets. The shells of quick-firing anti-aircraft guns shot up like drops of blood. Again the earth trembled, moaned and groaned. The beetles that droned in the tops of the birch-trees were not disturbed by this, however; deep in the wood an owl hooted in a human voice, foreboding evil; in the bushes in the hollow, having recovered from its day-time fear, a nightingale sang, at first hesitatingly, as if trying its voice, or tuning an instrument, and then with full throat, trilling and twittering as if its heart would burst at the sounds of its own music. Its song was taken up by others, and soon the whole front line rang with the melodious trilling that came from all sides. No wonder the nightingales of Kursk are famous throughout the world!

And now they were making the welkin ring with their song. Alexei, who was to go up for a trial next day, not before a commission, but before death itself, was kept awake by this nightingale chorus. And his thoughts were taken up not with the morrow, not with the forthcoming battle, not with the possibility of being killed, but with the distant nightingale that had once sung for them in the suburbs of Kamyshin, with "their" nightingale, with Olya, with his native town.

The eastern sky paled. Gradually the trilling of the nightingales was drowned by the noise of gun-fire. The sun rose slowly over the battlefield, large and red, scarcely able to penetrate the dense smoke of shots and explosions.

4

The Battle of the Kursk Salient continued with unrelaxing fury. The original plan of the Germans to smash our fortifications south and north of Kursk by swift, powerful blows with tanks, and, by a pincers operation, surround the whole of the Kursk group of the Soviet Army and organise a "German Stalingrad" there, was frustrated by the staunchness of the defence. After a few days the German Command realised that they would be unable to break through this defence and that, even if they did succeed in doing so, their losses would be so heavy that they would not have enough forces left for the pincers operation, but it was too late to stop. Hitler had placed too much hope—strategical, tactical and political —upon this operation. The avalanche was let loose. It rushed downhill with increasing momentum, sweeping up and carrying with it everything in its way; those who had let it loose had not the power to stop it. The Germans' advance was measured in kilometres, their losses in divisions and army corps, hundreds of tanks and guns and thousands of vehicles. The advancing armies bled and lost strength; German headquarters were aware of this, but they were no longer in a position to retard developments and were therefore obliged to throw more and more reserves into the inferno of battle.

The Soviet Command parried the German blows with the forces that were holding the defence line here. Watching the growing fury of the Germans they held their reserves deep in the rear until the enemy's drive had lost its impetus. As Meresyev learned later, the function of his wing was to cover an army concentrated for a counter-stroke. That explained why the tanks, and the fighter units that were to act in conjunction with them, were mere spectators in the first stage of the great battle. When all the enemy forces had been brought into action, "readiness No. 2" was rescinded at the airfield. The crews were permitted to sleep in the dugouts and even to undress. Meresyev and Petrov rearranged their quarters. They threw out the pin-ups and foreign views, tore down the German cardboard and packing-paper and decorated the wall with fir and birch twigs; after that the creepy rustle of dribbling sand no longer disturbed the dugout.

One morning, when the bright sunbeams were already streaming through the open entrance of the dugout on to the pine-needles carpeting the floor, and when the friends were still stretching in the bunks which had been built in niches in the walls, hurried footsteps were heard on the path overhead and somebody shouted what was a magic word at the front: "Postman!"

Both simultaneously threw off their blankets, but while Meresyev was tightening his foot straps, Petrov ran up, caught the postman and came back, triumphantly carrying two letters for Alexei, one from his mother and one from Olya. Alexei snatched the letters out of his friend's hand, but in that instant the rapid beating of the gong came from the airfield, calling the crews to their machines.

Meresyev slipped the letters inside his tunic and, forgetting about them at once, hastened after Petrov along the track in the wood leading to the machines. He ran fairly fast, using his stick and waddling only slightly.

When he reached his machine the cover had already been removed from the engine and the mechanic, a pockmarked, laughter-loving lad, was waiting impatiently for him.

An engine roared. Meresyev watched the "6", his Squadron Commander's plane. Captain Cheslov taxied his machine on to an open glade. He raised his arm—that meant "Attention!" The other engines roared. The whirlwind bowed the grass to the ground and caused the green tresses of the weeping birches to flutter in the breeze as if straining to break away.

As he was running to his machine Alexei was overtaken by another airman who managed to shout to him that the tanks were passing to the offensive. That meant that the fighters were to cover the tanks' passage through the shattered enemy lines, to clear and cover the air for the attackers. Cover the air? What did it matter? In an intense battle like this, it could not mean a peaceful flight. Sooner or later he was sure to meet the enemy in the air. Now came the test! Now he would prove that he was not inferior to any airman, that he had achieved his object.

Alexei was nervous, but not because he was afraid of being killed; not even because of the sense of danger that affects even the bravest and coolest of men. Something else was worrying him: Had the armourers tested the machine-guns and cannon? Were the ear-phones in his new helmet, which he had not yet worn in battle, in order? Would Petrov lag behind, or rush in too hastily if they had to fight the enemy? Where was the stick? He wouldn't like to lose Vasily Vasilyevich's gift, and he was even worried that somebody might take the book he had left in the dugout, a novel that he had read the previous day up to the most thrilling part and which he had left on the table in his hurry. He remembered that he had not said good-bye to Petrov, so he waved his hand to him from the cockpit. But Petrov did not see him, he was impatiently watching the Commander's raised arm, his face, framed by his leather helmet, suffused with a patchy flush. The arm dropped. The cockpit hoods were drawn.

A trio of machines snorted at the line and ran off, followed by another, and by a third. As soon as the first three planes were in the air, Meresyev's group hopped off and followed them, leaving the flat earth swaying beneath them. Keeping the first trio in sight, Meresyev lined his up behind it, and behind his came the third.

They reached the forward line. The ground, pitted and torn up by shells, looked from the air like a dusty road after the first drops of a heavy rain. Ploughed-up trenches, blindages looking like pimples, and gun emplacements now nothing but heaps of logs and bricks. Yellow sparks flashed all along the mutilated valley; they came from the conflagration of the gigantic battle raging below. How small, toylike and strange it all looked from above! One could scarcely believe that down below everything was burning, roaring, in convulsion, that death was prowling amidst the smoke and soot on the mutilated earth, reaping an abundant harvest.

They flew across the battle-line, made a half-circle over the enemy's rear and recrossed the battle-line. Nobody fired at them. Those down below were too busy with their own grim earthly affairs to pay attention to the nine tiny aircraft that were spiralling above them. But where were the tanks? Aha! There they were! Meresyev saw them creep out of the wood, one behind the other, looking from the air like grey, awkward beetles. Soon quite a large number had emerged, but more and more came creeping out of the greenery and moved along the roads and hollows. The first of them raced up the hill and reached the shell-ploughed ground. Red sparks appeared from their trunks. A child, even a nervous woman, would not have been frightened by this tremendous tank attack, by this impetuous rush of hundreds of machines against the remnants of the German lines, if they had viewed it from the air together with Meresyev. At this moment, amidst the crackling and buzzing in the ear-phones in his helmet, he heard the hoarse and even now listless voice of Captain Cheslov:

"Attention! I am Leopard three! I am Leopard three, 'Stukas', 'Stukas' to starboard!"

Ahead of him Alexei saw a short horizontal line. It was the Commander's plane. The plane rocked. That meant: "Do as I do!"

Meresyev repeated the order for his own flight. He looked round: his follower was suspended by his side, keeping almost parallel with him. Good lad!

"Hold tight, old man!" he shouted to him.

"I am," came the answer amidst the chaotic crackling and buzzing.

Again he heard the call:

"I am Leopard three, Leopard three!" And then the order: "Follow me!"

The enemy was near. Just below them, in the tandem formation that the Germans favoured, was a unit of "Ju-87's", single-engine dive-bombers. These notorious dive-bombers, which had won piratical fame in battles over Poland, France, Holland, Denmark, Belgium and Yugoslavia, the new German weapon, about which the press of the whole world related such horrors at the beginning of the war, soon became a back number in the expanses of the Soviet Union. In numerous air fights our Soviet airmen discovered their weak points, and our Soviet aces began to regard the Junkers as an inferior sort of game, like wood grouse or hares, that did not require real hunter's skill.

Captain Cheslov did not lead his squadron straight against the enemy but made a detour. Meresyev thought that the cautious captain intended to "put the sun behind him" and then, masked by its dazzling rays, creep unseen close up to the enemy and attack him. Alexei smiled to himself and thought: "He's doing those junkers too much honour by performing this complicated manoeuvre. Still, it will do no harm to be careful." He looked round again. Petrov was behind him. He could see him distinctly against a white cloud.

The German unit was now on their starboard. They sailed in beautiful formation, in perfect unison, as if tied together by invisible threads. Their wings were dazzling bright from the sunrays that poured down upon them.

Alexei heard the last snatches of the Commander's order:

"...Leopard three. Attack!"

He saw Cheslov and his follower swoop like hawks upon the enemy's flank. A string of tracer bullets lashed at the nearest Junkers; the latter dropped, and Cheslov, his follower, and the third man in his flight plunged through the breach in the German line. The Germans at once closed up and the Junkers continued on their way in perfect formation.

Alexei gave his call signal and wanted to shout: "Attack!" but he was so excited that all he could say was "A-a-a!" He was already swooping down, seeing nothing except the smooth-sailing German line. He chose as his target the plane that had taken the place of the one Cheslov had shot down. He heard a ringing in his ears, his heart throbbed so violently that he almost choked. He caught the target in his sight and, keeping his two thumbs on his trigger-buttons, swept towards it. Wisps of grey, fluffy string shot past him. Aha! They're shooting! Missed! Again. Nearer this time. No damage! What about Petrov? Not hurt, either. He's on port side. Dodged 'em. Good lad! The grey side of the German plane grew longer in his sight. His thumbs felt the cool aluminium buttons. Just a little closer....

That was the moment when Alexei felt that he had become completely merged with his machine. He felt the throbbing of the engine as if it were beating in his breast, with all his being he felt the sensation of the wings and the rudder, and it seemed to him that even the clumsy, artificial feet had acquired sensitiveness and did not prevent him from uniting with his machine in its swift movements. The graceful, streamlined body of the fascist machine slipped out of his sight, but he caught it again and pressed his trigger. He did not hear the shots, he did not even see the string of tracer bullets, but he knew that he had scored and rushed on, convinced that his victim would drop and he would not collide with him. Glancing away from his sight he was surprised to see another plane hurtle down. Had he hit two? No. That was Petrov's doing. He was on his starboard. Not bad for a greenhorn! His young friend's luck pleased him more than his own.

The second flight slipped through the breach in the German formation. And then the fun began. The second wave of German machines, evidently piloted by less experienced airmen, broke formation. The planes of

Cheslov's group dashed in among the scattered Junkers, chased them away and forced them hastily to unload their bombs over their own lines. This was exactly what Captain Cheslov had calculated on in undertaking his manoeuvre—to compel the enemy to bomb his own lines! Getting the sun behind him had not been his chief aim.

The first line of Germans closed up again, however, and the Junkers continued on their way towards the spot where the tanks had broken through. The third flight's attack was unsuccessful. The Germans did not lose a single machine, and one of the fighter planes vanished, shot down by a German gunner. They were drawing near to the place where the tanks were to develop their attack, there was no time to increase altitude. Cheslov decided to risk an attack from underneath. Alexei mentally approved of this. He himself was eager to take advantage of the "La-5's" splendid qualities in vertical manoeuvring to "dig" the enemy in the belly. The first flight was already shooting upward, spouting tracer bullets like a fountain. Two Germans dropped out of line at once. One of them must have been cut in two, for it suddenly split, and its tail just barely missed Meresyev's engine.

"Follow!" shouted Meresyev, and casting a sidelong glance at the silhouette of Petrov's machine, he pulled his stick.

The ground turned upside down. Alexei fell back in his seat as if he had been struck a heavy blow. He felt the taste of blood in his mouth and on his lips, a red haze appeared before his eyes. His machine shot up almost vertically. As he lay back in his seat the spotted belly of a Junkers, the funny, streamlined spats of its thick wheels, and even the clods of earth from the airfield sticking to them, flashed into his sight.

He pressed his trigger-buttons. Where he hit the enemy plane—in the fuel tank, engine, or bomb rack—he did not know, but the plane vanished instantly in the brown smoke of an explosion.

The blast threw Meresyev's machine to the side and it shot past the clump of fire. He levelled his machine and scanned the sky. His follower was on his starboard side suspended in the infinite blue above a sea of white clouds that looked like soap-suds. The sky was deserted; only on the horizon small dots could be seen against the background of distant clouds—they were the Junkers scattering in different directions. Alexei looked at his watch and was amazed. It had seemed to him that the fight had lasted at least half an hour and that his fuel must be running low; but the watch showed that it had lasted only three and a half minutes.

"Alive?" he asked, glancing at his follower who had "crawled over" and was now flying parallel with him.

Amidst the jumble of sounds in his ear-phones he heard a distant, exultant voice:

"Alive.... Down.... Look down...."

Down below, in a battered, mutilated, hilly valley, fuel tanks were burning in several places, and clouds of dense smoke were rising in columns in the still air. But Alexei did not look at these burning remains of enemy planes. His eyes were glued upon the green-grey beetles that were scurrying widely across the fields. They had crept up to the enemy's positions along two hollows and those in front were already crossing the trenches. Spouting red sparks from their trunks, they crawled through the enemy's lines and crept on farther and farther, although shots still flashed in their rear and the smoke from the German guns was visible.

Meresyev realised what these hundreds of beetles in the depths of the enemy's shattered positions meant.

He was witnessing what the Soviet people, and the people of all freedom-loving countries, read about in the newspapers next day with joy and exultation. On one of the sectors of the Kursk Salient, the army, after a terrific artillery preparation which lasted for two hours, pierced the enemy's defences, entered the breach and cleared the road for the Soviet forces that had passed to the offensive.

Of the nine machines in Captain Cheslov's squadron two failed to return to their base. Nine Junkers were shot down. Nine to two was certainly a good score when counting machines. But the loss of two comrades marred the joy of victory. On alighting from their machines the airmen did not exult or shout and gesticulate in ardent discussion of the battle, and live over again the dangers they had passed through, as they usually did after a successful engagement. Gloomily they stepped up to the Chief of Staff, reported results in dry, curt phrases and went off without looking at each other.

Alexei was a new man in the wing. He did not know the two men who had perished. But he was affected by the prevailing mood. The biggest and most important event in his life, the thing he had striven for with all the power of his body and mind and which was to determine his future course of life—his return to the ranks of the sound and fit—had occurred. How many times had he dreamed of this—in his hospital bed, and later, when learning to walk and to dance, and when recovering his skill as an aviator by hard training! And now, when the long-hoped-for day had arrived, after he had downed two German planes and he was again an equal in the family of fighter-pilots, he, like the rest, stepped up to the Chief of Staff, reported his score, explained the circumstances and praised his follower, and then sat down in the shade of a birch-tree and thought of those who had not returned that day.

Petrov was the only one who ran around the airfield, bareheaded, his fair hair fluttering in the breeze, and clutching those he encountered by the sleeve, related to them:

"...right next to me he was, within arm's reach almost.... Well, listen.... I saw the senior lieutenant aiming at the leader. I got the one next to him in my sight. Bang!"

He ran up to Meresyev, dropped down at his feet on the soft, grassy moss and stretched out; but unable to stay in this restful position he jumped up and exclaimed:

"You did some wonderful stunts today! Grand! Took my breath away!... Do you know how I downed that fellow? Just listen.... I followed you and saw him right next to me, as close as you are to me now...."

"Wait a minute, old man," interrupted Alexei, patting his pockets. "Those letters! What did I do with those letters?"

He remembered the letters he had received that day and had not had time to read. He felt a cold sweat break over him when he failed to find them in his pockets. He slipped his hand inside his tunic, felt the rustling envelopes and breathed a sigh of relief. He took Olya's letter and, paying no heed to the story his enthusiastic young friend was telling, cautiously tore a strip from the envelope.

Just then a rocket spluttered. A red, fiery serpent shot into the sky, arched over the airfield and died out, leaving a grey, slowly dissolving trail. The airmen sprang to their feet. Alexei slipped the letter inside his tunic without having been able to read a word of it. In opening the envelope he had felt something hard in addition to the writing-paper. Flying at the head of his flight along the now familiar course he felt the envelope now and again, wondering what was in it.

The day on which the tank army breached the enemy's positions marked the beginning of a very busy period for the Guards Fighter Aircraft Wing in which Alexei now served. Squadron after squadron flew to the area of the breach. Before one had time to land after battle another was in the air, and the fuel trucks were already rushing towards the machines just returned. The petrol flowed into the empty tanks in generous streams. A quivering haze hovered over the heated engines like that over a field after a warm, summer rain. The airmen did not leave their cockpits even to take their dinner; it was brought to them in aluminium billycans. But nobody was in the mood to eat, the food stuck in their throats.

When Captain Cheslov's squadron landed again and the machines, after they had been taxied to the wood, were being refuelled, Meresyev sat smiling in his cockpit, conscious of a pleasant, aching tiredness, impatiently looking up into the sky and hurrying the fillers. He yearned to be in the scrap again, to put himself to the test once more. He frequently slipped his hand inside his tunic and felt the rustling envelopes, but in this situation he was not in the mood to read.

It was not before the evening, when dusk was beginning to fall, that the crews were dismissed. Meresyev walked to his quarters not by the short cut through the wood, as he usually did, but by the longer road through the weed-covered field. He wanted to collect his thoughts, to rest after the din and clatter, after all the swiftly changing impressions of that seemingly endless day.

It was a clear evening, fragrant, and so quiet that the rumble of the now distant gun-fire sounded not like the noise of battle, but like the thunder of a passing storm. The road ran through what had formerly been a rye-field. The dreary weeds which in the ordinary human world timidly send up slender stalks in the corners of a yard, or on a heap of stones on the edge of a field, in those places that the master's eye rarely reaches, stood here like a solid wall, huge, arrogant and strong, overpowering the land that had been made fruitful by the sweat of many generations of toilers. Only here and there could a few thin ears of wild rye, like feeble blades of grass, be seen struggling against this mass. The weeds devoured all the substances of the soil, absorbed all the rays of the sun, deprived the rye of light and sustenance, and so these few ears had withered before they had bloomed and never filled with grain.

Meresyev reflected: that is how the fascists wanted to take root in our fields, to devour the substances of our soil, to rob us of our riches, to rise up terrible and arrogant, to shut out the sun and drive our great, labour-loving, mighty people from their fields and gardens, deprive them of everything, overwhelm and crush them as these weeds had crushed these feeble ears which had now lost even outward resemblance to a strong and beatiful cereal. Overcome by a wave of boyish energy, he swung his ebony stick and hacked at the reddish, feathery weeds, and was filled with elation when whole batches of the arrogant heads were cut down. The sweat poured down his face, but he kept on hacking at the weeds that had choked the rye, rejoicing in the sensation of struggle and action that filled his tired body.

Quite unexpectedly a jeep snorted behind him and with squeaking brakes pulled up on the road. Without looking round, Meresyev guessed that the Wing Commander had overtaken him and had seen him in this boyish occupation. He flushed up to his ears and, pretending he had not heard the approach of the car, began to dig the earth with his stick. But he heard the colonel say:

Cutting 'em down? It's a useful occupation. I've been looking for you all over the place. Everybody's asking for our hero. And here he is warring with weeds."

The colonel jumped out of the car. He liked to drive and in his spare time potter about with his car just as he liked to lead his wing in difficult exercises and in the evening potter about with the oily engines with the mechanics. He usually wore blue overalls, and only his lean, masterful features and his smart, new peaked cap distinguished him from that grimy crew.

Meresyev, still embarrassed, dug the earth with his stick. The colonel placed his hands on his shoulders and said:

"Let's have a look at you! Humph, the devil take it! Nothing particular! I can confess it now. When you came to us I did not believe, in spite of all that was being said about you at Army Headquarters. I did not believe that you could go through a fight. And yet you have! And how!... That's our Mother Russia! Congratulations! I congratulate you and admire you. Going to 'Molestown'? Get in, I'll give you a lift."

The jeep raced along the field road at top speed, swerving like mad at the bends.

"Tell me, perhaps you are in need of something, having difficulties of some kind? Don't hesitate to ask for assistance, you have deserved it," said the colonel, skilfully driving the car through a trackless copse and between the "molehills", as the airmen had dubbed their quarters.

"I don't need anything, Comrade Colonel. I am no different from anybody else. It would be better if people forgot that I have no feet," answered Meresyev.

"Yes, you are right. Which is yours? This one?"

The colonel pulled up sharply at the entrance of the dugout and Meresyev had barely alighted when the car was already chugging through the wood, winding between the birches and oaks.

Alexei did not go into the dugout. He lay down on the woolly, mushroom-scented moss under a brich-tree and carefully drew Olya's letter from the envelope. A photograph slipped out and fell on to the grass. Alexei quickly picked it up, and his heart beat rapidly and painfully.

A familiar and yet almost unrecognisable face gazed at him from the photograph. It was Olya in military uniform: tunic, sword-belt, Order of the Red Star, and even the Guards' badge—and it all suited her so well! She looked like a lean, good-looking boy in an officer's uniform. Only this boy had a tired face, and his large, round, lustrous eyes had an unyouthful, penetrating look.

Alexei gazed at those eyes long and hard. His heart was filled with that unaccountable sweet sadness that one feels on hearing in the evening the distant strains of a favourite song. In his pocket he found the old photograph of Olya, taken in a print frock in the meadow among the white, starry daisies. Strange to say, the girl in the tunic with the tired eyes that he had never seen, was dearer to him than the one he had known. On the back of the new photograph was the inscription: "Always remember."

The letter was brief, but cheerful. The girl was now in command of a platoon of sappers, only this platoon was not engaged in war but in peaceful work; it was helping to rebuild Stalingrad. She wrote little about herself, but went into raptures about the great city, about its reviving ruins, about the women, girls and youths who had come here from all parts of the country to rebuild the city, living in cellars, gun emplacements, blindages and bunkers left after the fighting, and in railway cars, plywood shacks and dugouts. People were saying, she wrote, that everybody who worked well would receive an apartment in the rebuilt city. If that were true, then Alexei could be sure of having a place after the war.

The twilight was short, as it usually is in the summer. Alexei read the last lines of the letter by the light of his torch. When he had read it he threw a beam of light on the photograph. The soldier gazed at him with stern, honest eyes. "Darling, you are having a hard time.... The war has not spared you, but it has not broken you! Are you waiting? Wait. I will come. You love me. Love me for ever, dear." And suddenly Alexei felt ashamed that for eighteen months he had kept from her, a Stalingrad fighter, the misfortune that had befallen him. He felt an urge to go down into his dugout at once and frankly write her about everything—let her decide, and the sooner the better. It would be easier for both of them when everything was settled.

After his achievement that day he could speak to her as an equal. He was not only flying, but fighting. Had he not pledged himself to tell her everything either when his hopes had definitely collapsed or when he had become the equal of others in battle? He had now achieved his object. The two planes that he had shot down fell into the scrub and burned there in sight of all. The officer of the day had recorded this in the wing log, and the report had gone to Divisional and Army Headquarters, and to Moscow.

All this was true. He had fulfilled his pledge and he could now write. But when you come to think of it, was a "Stuka" a worthy foe for a fighter plane? A really good hunter would not claim in proof of his skill that he had shot, say, a hare, would he?

The humid night grew darker in the wood. Now that the thunder of battle had receded southward and the glare of the now distant conflagrations was barely visible through the network of tree branches, all the night sounds of the fragrant, luxuriant summer wood could be distinctly heard—the frenzied rasping of the grasshoppers in the glades, the guttural croaking of hundreds of frogs in the bog near by, the shrill cry of a corn-crake, and high above all this, the singing of the nightingales that reigned in the damp semi-darkness.

Alexei was still sitting under the birch-tree on the soft but now dewy moss while patches of moonlight interspersed with black shadows crept along the grass at his feet. Again he drew the photograph from his pocket, placed it on his knee, and gazing at it in the light of the moon, he became lost in thought. One after another, small, dark silhouettes of night bombers sped southward overhead in the clear, dark-blue sky. Their engines droned in a low, bass key, but even this voice of war now sounded in the moonlit wood that rang with the singing of the nightingales like the peaceful buzzing of cockchafers. Alexei sighed, put the photograph back into his tunic pocket and, springing to his feet, shook himself to throw off the enchantment of that night. Rustling the dry twigs on the ground, he quickly descended into the dugout where, stretched like a giant on his narrow soldier's couch, Petrov was sound asleep and snoring lustily.

5

The crews were roused before dawn. Army Headquarters had received information that on the day before a large German aircraft unit had arrived in the area where the Soviet tanks had broken through. Ground observations and intelligence reports justified the assumption that the German Command appreciated the danger created by the break-through of the Soviet tanks at the very base of the Kursk Salient and had called up the Richthofen Air Division, which was manned by the finest aces in Germany. This division had been last routed near Stalingrad, but had been re-formed somewhere deep in the German rear. The wing was warned that the enemy was strong in numbers, equipped with the latest type of machines—Fokke-Wolf-190's—and was highly experienced in battle. It was ordered to be on the alert and to provide reliable air cover for the second echelon of the mobile forces that had begun that night to follow the tanks through the breach.

Richthofen! That name was well known to experienced airmen as that of the division that enjoyed the special patronage of Hermann Goering. The Germans sent it whenever their forces were being hard pressed. The flyers of this division, some of whom had conducted their piratical operations over Republican Spain, were fierce and skilful fighters, and were reputed to be a dangerous foe.

"The men are saying that some sort of 'Richtovens' have been sent against us. Gee! I hope we meet 'em soon! We'll show 'em 'Richtovens'!" declaimed Petrov in the messroom, hurriedly swallowing his food and glancing at the open window where Raya, the waitress, was picking flowers from a large bunch and placing them in shell bodies that had been polished with chalk until they shone.

It goes without saying that this defiance was hurled at the "Richtovens" not for the benefit of Alexei who was finishing his coffee, but of the girl who was busy with the flowers and was now and again casting sidelong glances at handsome, ruddy Petrov. Meresyev watched them with an indulgent smile, but he disliked jokes and frivolous talk where serious business was concerned.

"Richthofen, not Richtovens," he said. "And 'Richthofen' means: keep your eyes peeled if you don't want to burn among the weeds today. It means: keep your ears wide open and don't lose contact. The Richthofens, my boy, are wild beasts that can get their teeth into you before you know where you are!"

At dawn, the first squadron went up under the command of the colonel himself. While it was in the air a second group of twelve fighter planes got ready for flight. It was to be commanded by Guards Major Fedotov, Hero of the Soviet Union, the most experienced airman in the wing, bar the commander. The machines were ready, the men were in their cockpits, the engines were in low gear, sending gusts of air across the space at the edge of the wood like the wind that sweeps the ground and shakes the trees before a storm, when the first, big, heavy drops of rain are already splashing on the thirsty earth.

From his cockpit, Alexei watched the machines of the first group descending steeply as if they were slipping out of the sky. Involuntarily, in spite of himself, he counted them and his heart leapt with anxiety when an interval occurred in the landing of two of the machines. But the last one landed. All had returned. Alexei breathed a sigh of relief.

Scarcely had the last machine taxied away when Major Fedotov's "No. 1" tore off the ground, followed by the other fighter planes in pairs. They lined up beyond the wood. Rocking his plane, Fedotov lay on his course. They flew low, cautiously keeping in the zone of the breach made the day before. Now Alexei saw the ground speed under his plane not from a great height, not in distant perspective which lends everything a toylike appearance, but close to him. What the day before had appeared to him from above like a game, now presented itself as a vast, boundless battle-field. Fields, meadows and copses, ploughed up by shells and bombs and scarred by trenches, raced madly under his wings. Dead bodies were scattered in the fields; abandoned guns, singly and in whole batteries; wrecked tanks; long heaps of twisted iron and shattered wood where artillery had pounded the columns; a large wood, completely razed to the ground, looking from above as if it had been trampled down by a vast herd— all raced past like the scenes in a cinema film, and it seemed as though this film were endless.

All this testified to the stubborn and sanguinary nature of the fighting that had raged here, to the heavy losses sustained and to the magnitude of the victory achieved.

The tanks had left innumerable double, criss-cross tracks all over the wide expanse, leading on and on deep into the enemy's positions, right to the horizon, as if a vast herd of strange animals had stampeded across the fields southward, trampling down everything in their way. Endless columns of motorised artillery, fuel tanks, huge mobile, tractor-drawn repair shops, and covered lorries followed in the trail of the tanks, leaving grey tails of dust that were visible in the distance. From the air it seemed that these columns were moving at a snail's pace; and when the fighter planes rose to a greater height all this looked like an army of ants crawling along a forest track in the spring.

Diving into these tails of dust that rose high in the still air as if diving into clouds, the fighter planes flew over the columns to the leading jeeps, in which, evidently, the commanders of the tank force were riding. The sky over the columns was clear of the enemy, and in the distance, on the hazy horizon, irregular puffs of the smoke of battle were already to be seen. The group turned back, spiralling in the sky like a toy kite. At that moment Alexei saw right on the horizon, first one, and then a whole swarm of dark specks floating low over the ground. Germans! They too flew hugging the ground, obviously aiming at the tails of dust that were visible in the reddish, weed-covered fields. Alexei instinctively glanced round. His follower was behind him, keeping as close to him as he dared.

He strained his ears and heard a distant voice:

"I am Sea-Gull two, Fedotov; I am Sea-Gull two, Fedotov. Attention! Follow me!"

Discipline in the air, where the airman's nerves are strained to the utmost, is such that he sometimes carries out his commander's intentions even before the latter has finished his command. Before the next command was heard amidst the whining and buzzing, the entire group veered in pairs, but in close formation, to intercept the Germans. Sight, hearing and mind were concentrated to the limit. Alexei saw nothing but the enemy planes that were growing rapidly before his eyes; in his ears there was nothing but the crackling and buzzing of the ear-phones in which he was to hear the next command. But instead of that command he very distinctly heard an excited voice cry in German:

"*Achtung! Achtung! La-fünf! Achtung!*"

It must have been the German ground observer warning his planes of danger.

As was its custom, the famous German aircraft division had carefully covered the battle-field with a network of markers and ground observers who, furnished with radio transmitters, had been parachuted the previous night in the anticipated area of air battles.

Then, less distinctly, came another voice, hoarse and angry, shouting in German:

"*Donnerwetter! Links! La-fünf! Links! La-fünf!*"

In addition to vexation, there was a note of alarm in that voice.

"Richthofen, you are not afraid of our 'Lavochkins', are you?" muttered Meresyev grimly, watching the approaching enemy formation and feeling a thrill of elation shoot through his tense body.

The enemy could be seen distinctly now. They were attacking planes, Fokke-Wolf-190's, powerful, swift machines which had just been put into commission.

They outnumbered Fedotov's group two to one. They flew in that strict formation that distinguished the units of the Richthofen Division, in pairs, in step-ladder fashion, in such a way that each pair protected the rear of the pair in front. Taking advantage of his higher altitude, Fedotov attacked the enemy. Alexei had already chosen his target and, while not losing sight of the rest, headed for it, trying to keep it in his sight. But somebody forestalled Fedotov. A group of "Yaks" swept in from the other side and swiftly attacked the Germans from above. The blow was so successful that it at once broke up the enemy formation. Confusion reigned in the air. Both sides broke up into fighting twos and fours. The fighter planes strove to intercept the enemy with

6

The noise of the air battle that was fought over the roads along which the rear administrations of the attacking armies were streaming was heard not only by the men in the cockpits of the planes engaged in battle. It was also heard through a powerful radio set at the airfield by Colonel Ivanov, the Commander of the Guards Fighter Wing. An experienced flyer himself, he could tell by the sounds that came to him over the ether that the fight was a hot one, that the enemy was strong and stubborn and was refusing to surrender the sky. The news that Fedotov was fighting an unequal battle quickly spread through the airfield. All those who could came out of the wood into the glade and looked anxiously to the south from where the planes were expected to return.

Surgeons in their white smocks came hurrying out of the messroom, chewing as they ran. Ambulance cars with big red crosses painted on their roofs emerged from the bushes and stood with their engines humming, ready for action.

The first pair came flying over the tree tops and, without circling over the airfield, landed and taxied down the spacious field. It consisted of "No. 1", piloted by Hero of the Soviet Union Fedotov, and "No. 2", piloted by his follower. Right on their heels came the second pair. The air over the wood echoed with the roar of the engines of the returning machines.

"Seven, eight, nine, ten," counted the watchers, scanning the sky with growing anxiety.

The machines that landed left the field, taxied to their caponiers, and fell silent. Two machines were still missing.

An expectant hush fell upon the waiting crowd. Minutes passed with tormenting slowness.

"Meresyev and Petrov," said somebody quietly.

Suddenly a joyous female voice rang over the field: "There's one!"

The roar of an aircraft engine was heard. Over the tops of the birch-trees, almost grazing them, came "No. 12". The plane was damaged, a piece of its tail was missing, the tip of its left wing had been cut off and the piece was hanging by some wire. The plane, on landing, hopped in a queer way; it jumped high, came down and jumped again, and in this way hopped to the very end of the airfield and came to a dead stop with its tail raised up. The ambulances with the surgeons on the footboards, several jeeps, and the whole of the waiting crowd rushed towards the machine. Nobody rose out of the cockpit.

They drew back the hood. Huddled in the seat in a pool of blood lay Petrov. His head was sunk helplessly on his breast. Strands of wet fair hair covered his face. The surgeons and nurses unfastened the straps, removed his parachute bag that was gashed by a shell splinter, carefully raised the motionless body and laid it on the ground. The airman was wounded in the leg and arm. Dark patches spread quickly over his blue overalls.

Petrov was given first aid and placed on a stretcher. As he was being lifted into the ambulance he opened his eyes. He whispered something, but so faintly that he could not be heard. The colonel bent over him.

"Where's Meresyev?" the wounded man inquired.

"Hasn't landed yet."

The stretcher was lifted again, but the wounded man vigorously rolled his head and even tried to get out.

"Wait!" he said. "Don't take me away. I don't want to go. I'll wait for Meresyev. He saved my life!"

The airman protested so vigorously, threatening to tear off his bandages, that the colonel waved his hand and turning his head away said through clenched teeth:

"All right. Leave him alone. He won't die. Meresyev has only enough fuel left for not more than one minute."

The colonel glued his eyes to his stop-watch and saw the red second hand tick round its circle. Everybody else was gazing at the grey wood, over the top of which the last plane was expected to appear. Ears were strained to the utmost, but except for the distant rumble of gun-fire and the muffled tapping of a woodpecker near by, nothing was heard.

How long a minute drags sometimes!

7

Meresyev turned to face the enemy.

The "Lavochkin-5" and the "Fokke-Wolf-190" were fast planes. They approached each other at lightning speed. Alexei Meresyev and the unknown German ace of the famous Richthofen Division charged each other head on. A head-on attack lasts an instant, even less than what it takes an experienced smoker to light a cigarette. But that instant creates such a nervous strain, puts all the airman's nerves to such a test as a fighter on the ground is not subjected to even in the course of a whole day's battle.

Picture yourself in one of the two fast fighters charging at each other at full combat speed. The enemy plane grows in size before your very eyes. Suddenly it confronts you in all its details: wings, the glistening circle of the revolving propeller, the black dots that are its guns. In another instant the planes will collide and split into so many fragments that it will be impossible to sort the remains of the pilot from the remains of the machine. Not only the pilot's will-power, but also all his moral fibre, is put to the test in that instant. The weak-nerved will not stand the strain. A man not prepared to die for the sake of victory will instinctively pull the stick and leap over the deadly hurricane sweeping towards him; and in the next instant his machine will be hurtling to the ground with a ripped underside or a hacked-off wing. Nothing can save him. Experienced airmen know this perfectly well, and only the bravest dare to make a head-on attack.

The planes tore through the air.

Alexei was aware that the man coming against him was not a greenhorn from the Goering enrolment, hastily trained to fill the gaps that had been formed in the German Air Force by the heavy casualties on the Eastern Front. He was an ace of the Richthofen Division, in a machine that no doubt had depicted on its sides the silhouettes of planes recording many a victory in the air. He would not falter, he would not swerve, he would not avoid battle.

"Look out, 'Richthofen'!" muttered Alexei through his teeth. Biting his lips until they bled and contracting his firm muscles, he glued his eyes to his sight and exercised all his will-power to prevent them from shutting in the face of the enemy machine that was charging straight at him.

He strained his senses to such a degree that through the haze of his whirling propeller he thought he could see the transparent screen of the enemy's cockpit, and through that, two human eyes intently staring at him; and those eyes burned with frenzied hate. It was a vision called up by nervous tension, but Alexei was convinced that he saw them. "This is the end," he thought, contracting all his muscles still tighter. "This is the end." He looked ahead and saw the rapidly growing plane rushing towards him like a whirlwind. No, that German would not swerve either. This was the end.

He prepared for instant death. Suddenly, when it seemed to him that he was within arm's length of the German machine, the German pilot lost his nerve and his plane leapt upward; the blue, sunlit underside of the German machine flashed like lightning in front of him. In that instant Alexei pressed all his triggers, stitched the German with three fiery threads and looped; and as the ground swung over his head he saw the plane fluttering helplessly against its background.

"Olya!" he yelled in frenzied triumph, and forgetting everything he spiralled down in narrow circles, accompanying the German machine on its last journey, right down to the red, weed-covered ground, until it struck the earth and sent up a column of black smoke.

Only then did his nervous tension and tightened muscles relax, leaving him with a sense of intense weariness. He glanced at the fuel gauge. The pointer was trembling almost at zero.

There was fuel left for three, at best four minutes' flying. It would take at least ten minutes to get back to the airfield, plus some time for increasing altitude. He had been a fool to descend with that damaged "Fokke"! "Like a foolish kid!" he said, scolding himself.

As is always the case with brave, cool men in moments of danger, his mind was clear and worked with the precision of clock-work. The first thing to do was to gain altitude, not by spiralling, but by an oblique ascent in the direction of the airfield. Good!

He laid his machine to the required course, and seeing the ground drop beneath him and a haze come over the horizon, he continued his calculations in a calmer mood. It was no use counting on the fuel. Even if the gauge was slightly at fault he would not have enough. Land before he got to the airfield? But where? He mentally went over the whole of the short route. Woods, scrubby bog and the bumpy fields in the zone of permanent defences, all ploughed up in criss-cross fashion, pitted with craters and bristling with barbed wire.

"No! I'll only kill myself if I land!"

Bail out? That could be done. Right now. Open the hood, veer, push the stick—and that's all. But what about the machine, this wonderful, swift and agile bird? Its fighting qualities had saved his life three times that day. Abandon it, smash it, convert it into a heap of twisted metal? It was not that he would be to blame for this. He was not afraid of that. In fact, he had a right to bail out in a situation like this. At that moment the machine seemed to him to be a strong, generous and devoted living thing, and to abandon it would be downright treachery. And then—to return without his machine after the very first combat flights, to wait in the reserve until he got another, to be idle in a hectic time like this when our great victory was starting at the front, to hang around doing nothing at a time like this!

"No fear!" said Alexei aloud, as if somebody had proposed this to him.

Fly until the engine stops. And then? Then we'll see.

And he flew on, first at three and then at four thousand metres, scanning the ground in the hope of finding a small glade. The wood behind which the airfield was situated was already looming on the horizon; it was about fifteen kilometres away. The pointer of the fuel gauge was no longer trembling, it was lying firmly on the limit button. But the engine was still working! What was feeding it? Higher, still higher.... Good!

Suddenly, the steady drone, which the airman's ear does not notice any more than a healthy man notices the beating of his heart, changed to another key. Alexei caught the change at once. The wood was distinctly visible; it was about seven kilometres away, and it was three or four kilometres wide. Not much. But there was this sinister change in the regular beat of the engine. An airman feels this with his whole being, as if it were not the engine, but he himself gasping for breath. Suddenly there comes the ominous "chuck, chuck, chuck", that shoots through his body with frightful pain.

"No! It's all right. It's working steadily again. It's working! Hurrah! And here is the wood!" He could see the tops of the birch-trees like a green sea heaving in the sunlight. It was impossible to land anywhere now except at the airfield. There was only one thing to do now: forward, forward!

Chuck, chuck, chuck!

The engine droned again. For long? He was over the wood. He could see the sandy path running smooth and straight through it like the parting on the Wing Commander's head. The airfield was now three kilometres away: it was behind that serrated border, which Alexei thought he could already see.

Chuck, chuck, chuck! And suddenly silence reigned, so deep that he could hear the tackle humming in the wind. The end! A cold shiver ran down Meresyev's back. Bail out? No! Go a little further. He turned the machine into a sloping descent and glided down, trying to keep as level as possible and at the same time avoid dropping into a spin.

How terrible was this absolute silence in the air! It was so intense that he could hear the crackling of the cooling engine, and the throbbing of his temples and noise in his ears from the rapid descent. The ground was rising fast to meet him, as if a huge magnet were drawing it towards the plane!

He could see the edge of the wood and the emerald-green patch of the airfield beyond it. Too late? The propeller stuck at a half-turn. It was terrible to see it motionless in the air! The wood was quite close. Was this the end? Would she never know what had happened to him, what superhuman efforts he had made during the past eighteen months, that after all he had achieved his goal, had become a real, yes, a real man, only to crash in this absurd way as soon as he had achieved it?

Bail out? Too late! The wood was rushing past beneath him and in his hurricane flight the tree tops merged in continuous green strips. He had seen something like this before. When? Why, of course! During that spring, at the time of his frightful crash. Then the green strips had raced beneath him in the same way. He made the last effort and pulled the stick....

8

Petrov heard a ringing in his ears from loss of blood. Everything—the airfield, the familiar faces and the golden afternoon clouds—suddenly began to sway, turn upside down slowly and fade away. He moved his injured leg and the acute pain it caused brought him round.

"Hasn't he come?" he asked.

"Not yet. Don't talk," came the answer.

Could it be that Meresyev, who that day had unaccountably appeared like a winged god in front of that German at the very moment when Petrov had thought that his end had come, was now nothing but a shapeless heap of burnt flesh lying somewhere on that shell-scalped and mutilated ground? And would Sergeant-Major Petrov never again see the black, slightly wild and kindly bantering eyes of his leader? Never?

The Wing Commander pulled his sleeve down. He no longer needed his watch. Stroking his smooth hair with both his hands he said in a dull voice:

"That's all!"

"Is there no hope?" somebody asked.

"No. Fuel's run out. Perhaps he has landed somewhere or bailed out.... Take this stretcher away!"

The colonel turned away and began to whistle some melody, all out of tune. Petrov again felt a lump rising in his throat, so hot and large that he almost choked. A strange coughing sound was heard. The people still standing silently in the middle of the airfield looked round and at once turned their heads away. The wounded airman in the stretcher was sobbing.

"Take him away! What the hell!..." shouted the colonel in a choking voice, and he strode off, turning his face away from the crowd and screwing up his eyes as if to protect them from a sharp wind.

The people began to disperse, but in that instant a plane glided over the edge of the wood as noiselessly as a shadow, its wheels just grazing the tops of the trees. Like an apparition it glided over the people's heads, over the ground, and as if drawn to it touched the grass with all three wheels. A dull thud, the crunching of gravel and the swish of grass were heard, which was unusual, for airmen never hear it owing to the noise their engines make when they land. All this was so sudden that nobody realised what had happened, although it was the most ordinary thing: a plane landed, and it was "No. 11", the very one they had all been waiting for so anxiously.

"It's him!" somebody shouted in an hysterical, unnatural voice, and at once all awoke out of their stupor.

The plane finished its run and came to a standstill at the very edge of the airfield, in front of the wall of young, curly, white-barked birch-trees that were lit up in the orange-coloured rays of the setting sun.

Again nobody rose from the cockpit. People rushed to the machine as fast as they could, panting, and filled with foreboding. The colonel ran ahead of them all, jumped on to the wing, drew back the hood and looked into the cockpit. Meresyev was sitting there, bare-headed, his face as white as a summer cloud, and with a smile on his bloodless, greenish lips. Two streams of blood trickled down his chin from his bitten lip.

"Alive? Are you hurt?"

Meresyev smiled weakly and looking at the colonel with dead tired eyes answered:

"I'm all right. I was just scared.... For about six kilometres I hadn't a drop left."

The airmen crowded round the plane, noisily congratulating Alexei and shaking his hand.

"Go easy chaps, you'll break that wing off! You mustn't do that! Let me get out!" Alexei chided them with a smile.

At that moment, from below the crowd of heads that were hovering over him, he heard a familiar voice, but so faint that it seemed to come from very far:

"Alyosha, Alyosha!"

Meresyev recovered his strength in an instant. He jumped up and, drawing himself up heavily with his arms, threw his awkward feet over the side of the cockpit, nearly kicking someone on the wing, and leapt to the ground.

Petrov's face seemed to have merged with the pillow he was lying on. Two large tears lay in the deep, dark hollows of his eyes.

"Old man, you're alive! You ... you old devil!" cried Alexei dropping down on his knees beside the stretcher. He took the helpless head of his comrade in his hands and looked into his suffering and yet joyfully sparkling eyes.

"You're alive!"

"Thank you, Alyosha, you saved me. You are ... Alyosha, you are...."

"Damn you all! Take the wounded man away! Standing there gaping like a lot of fools!" came the thundering voice of the colonel.

The colonel was standing near by, short, virile, swaying on his sturdy legs, his close-fitting, shining boots showing from under the trousers of his blue overalls.

"Senior Lieutenant Meresyev, report on your flight. Any planes shot down?" he demanded in an official tone.

"Yes, Comrade Colonel. Two 'Fokke-Wolfs'."

"Under what circumstances?"

"One in a vertical attack. He was hanging on Petrov's tail. The other in a head-on attack, about three kilometres north of the area of the general engagement."

"I know. The groundsman has only just reported.... Thanks."

"Serving..." Alexei began, wishing to give the regulation response, but the colonel, who was usually so strict in matters of form, interrupted him and said in an informal tone:

"Very good! Tomorrow, you will take command of.... The Commander of Squadron Three has not returned to the base."

They walked to the command post together. As flying was finished for the day, the entire crowd followed them. They were already nearing the green mound of the command post when the officer on duty came running towards them. He pulled up sharply in front of the colonel, bareheaded, looking very pleased and excited, and opened his mouth to say something, but the colonel interrupted him in a dry, stern voice:

"Why are you uncovered? What do you think you are, a schoolboy during recess?"

"Comrade Colonel, permit me to report," blurted out the excited lieutenant, standing to attention and barely able to catch his breath.

"Well?"

"Our neighbour, the Commander of the 'Yaks', wants you on the telephone."

"Our heighbour! What does he want?..."

The colonel briskly made for the dugout.

"It's about you..." the officer on duty began to tell Alexei, but from down below came the colonel's voice:

"Send Meresyev to me!"

When Meresyev stood stiffly at attention before him, his hands at his sides, the colonel put his palm over the telephone receiver and growled at him angrily:

"Why did you misinform me? Our neighbour wanted to know who flew our 'No. 11'. I answered: 'Meresyev, Senior Lieutenant.' Then he asked: 'How many did you put down to his score today?' I answered: 'Two.' He says: 'Add one more to his credit. He knocked a "Fokke-Wolf" off my tail today. I myself saw it go down.' Well! Why are you silent?" The colonel frowned at Alexei and it was hard to say whether he was joking or in earnest. "Is it true? Here you are, speak to him yourself.... Hello! Are you there? Senior Lieutenant Meresyev on the phone. I'm handing him the receiver."

An unknown, hoarse bass voice came over the wire:

"Thanks, Senior Lieutenant. You made a splendid showing. I appreciate it. You saved me. Yes. I followed it right to the ground and saw it crash.... Do you drink? Come over to my C.P., I owe you a litre. Well, thanks again. We'll shake when we meet. Carry on."

Meresyev put the receiver down. He was so tired after what he had gone through that he could hardly stand. His one thought was to get to "Molestown" as quickly as possible, to get on his dugout, throw off his artificial feet and stretch out on the bunk. Stepping about awkwardly at the telephone for a moment, he slowly made for the door.

"Where are you off to?" said the colonel, intercepting him. He took Meresyev's hand and squeezed it with his own small, wiry hand so hard that it hurt. "Well, what can I say to you? Good lad! I am proud to have men like you under me.... Well, what else? Thanks.... Yes, and that pal of yours, Petrov I mean. He's a good lad, too. And the others.... I tell you, we can't lose the war with men like you!"

And again he firmly squeezed Meresyev's hand.

It was night before Meresyev found himself in his dugout, but he could not fall asleep. He turned his pillow over, counted up to a thousand and then counted backwards, recalled all his acquaintances whose names began with "A", then with "B", and so on, and then started unblinkingly at the dim light of the kerosene-lamp—but all these welltried methods of inducing sleep proved ineffective. No sooner did he shut his eyes than familiar pictures rose before him, now vividly, and now barely distinguishable in the gloom: Grandpa Mikhail's troubled eyes looking at him from under his silvery locks; Andrei Degtyarenko blinking his "cow's eyelashes"; Vasily Vasilyevich shaking his grey-streaked mane and scolding somebody; the old sniper, his soldier's face wrinkled up in a smile; he saw the waxen face of Commissar Vorobyov against the white background of his pillow, gazing at him with his clever, penetrating, bantering, understanding eyes; Zinochka's red hair flashed before him, fluttering in the breeze; little, vivacious Instructor Naumov smiled and winked at him with sympathy and understanding. Many splendid, friendly faces looked and smiled at him out of the darkness, rousing recollections and filling his already overflowing heart with warmth. But from among these friendly faces, and at once blotting them out, arose the face of Olya, the lean face and large, tired eyes of a boy in an officer's uniform. He saw her as clearly and distinctly as if she were really before him—and in a way he had never seen her in real life. So vivid was the vision that it startled him.

What was the use of trying to sleep! Conscious of an influx of joyous energy, he sat up, trimmed the "Stalingradka", tore a page out of an exercise book, sharpened the point of his pencil and began to write.

"My darling," he wrote in an illegible hand, barely able to keep up with the thoughts that rushed through his mind. "Today I shot down three Germans. But that's not the main point. Some of my comrades are now doing this nearly every day. I would not boast to you about this. My darling, my beloved. Today I want, I have a right, to tell you about what happened to me eighteen months ago, and which—forgive me, please forgive me—I have kept from you. But today, I have at last decided. . . ."

Alexei became lost in thought. Mice squeaked behind the planks with which the dugout was lined, and the dribbling of dry sand was heard. Together with the fresh and humid scent of birch and flowering grass that was wafted through the open doorway, came the slightly muffled but unrestrained trilling of nightingales. Somewhere in the distance, beyond the gully, probably outside the officers' mess, male and female voices were singing the mournful song about the ash-tree. Softened by the distance, the tune acquired a particularly tender charm at night and filled the heart with sweet sadness, the sadness of expectation, the sadness of hope.

And the remote and muffled rumble of gun-fire, now almost inaudible at the airfield, which was already deep in the rear of our advancing forces, drowned neither the melody, nor the trilling of the nightingales, nor the soft, dreamy rustling of the wood.

1946

POSTSCRIPT

One day, when the battle of Orel was drawing to its triumphant end and the forward regiments that were advancing from the north were reporting that from the Krasnogorsk hills they were able to see the burning city, Headquarters of the Bryansk Front received a report to the effect that during the preceding nine days the men of the Guards Fighter Aircraft Wing that was operating in that area had shot down forty-seven enemy planes. Their own losses amounted to five machines and only three men, as two of the men brought down had bailed out and had reached their base on foot. Such a victory was unusual even in those days of the Soviet Army's swift advance. I got a seat in a liaison plane, that was flying to the airfield of that wing, with the intention of getting a story for an article for *Pravda* on the achievements of these Guards airmen.

The airfield of this wing was situated in a common pasture which had been roughly cleared of clumps and molehills. The planes were hidden like a brood of grouse chickens on the edge of a young birch wood. In short, it was a field air strip of the type that was common in the hectic days of the war.

We landed late in the afternoon, when the wing was finishing a hard, busy day. The Germans were being exceptionally active in the air in the area of Orel, and on that day each fighter plane had made as many as six combat flights. At sundown, the last planes were returning from their seventh flight. The colonel, a short tightly-belted, brisk man with a tanned face, hair carefully parted, and wearing new, blue overalls, frankly confessed that he was unable to give me a connected story that day, that he had been at the airfield since six in the morning, that he had been up three times himself and was so tired that he could hardly stand. Nor were the other officers in the mood to grant newspaper interviews that evening. I realised that I would have to wait until next day; in any case it was too late to return. The sun was already touching the tops of the birch-trees and gilding them with molten gold.

The last of the machines landed and with engines still running they taxied straight to the wood. The mechanics swung them round. The pale, weary airmen slowly alighted from their cockpits only when the machines had been safely housed in their green, turf-covered caponiers.

The very last plane to arrive was that of the Commander of Squadron Three. The transparent hood of the cockpit was drawn back. First, a big ebony walking-stick with a gold monogram came flying out and dropped on the grass. Then, a tanned, broad-faced, black-haired man drew himself up on powerful arms, nimbly swung his body over the side, lowered himself to the wing and stepped heavily to the ground. Somebody told me that he was the best airman in the wing. Not to waste the evening, I decided to talk to him. I distinctly remember him looking at me with his merry, vivacious, dark eyes, in which unquenched, boyish impudence was strangely combined with the weary wisdom of a man who had gone through a great deal, and saying to me with a smile:

"Man alive! I am dog-tired. It's all I can do to drag my feet, and my head is going round. Have you eaten? No! Then come to the messroom with me, we'll have supper together. They give us two hundred grams of vodka for supper for every plane we shoot down. I'm entitled to six hundred grams tonight. That's enough for two. Will you come? We can chat while we are eating, since you are so impatient to get a story."

I consented. I liked this candid, cheerful officer. We went by the path the airmen had trodden through the wood. My new acquaintance walked briskly and now and again he bent down to pluck a bilberry or a cluster of pink whortleberries, which he there and then flipped into his mouth. He must have been very tired, because he walked with a heavy step, but he did not lean on his strange walking-stick. It hung on his arm, and only at rare intervals did he take it in his hand to swipe at an agaric mushroom or a willow-herb. When, in crossing a ravine, we climbed up the slippery, clayey slope, the airman found the going difficult and pulled himself up by clutching at the bushes, but he did not lean on his stick.

In the messroom, his tiredness vanished at once. He chose a table near the window from which we could see the cold, red glare of the sunset, which airmen regard as a forecast of windy weather the next day, eagerly gulped down a large mugful of water, and chaffed the good-looking, curly-haired waitress about a friend she had in hospital, because of whom, the airman said, she made life a misery for all the others. He ate with relish and gnawed the bone of his mutton chop with his strong teeth. He exchanged banter with his comrades at the next table, asked me to tell him what was new in Moscow, about the latest books and plays, and regretted that he had never been to a Moscow theatre. When we had finished the third course—bilberry jelly, which the airmen here called "thundercloud"—he asked me:

"Have you fixed up lodgings for tonight?" I said, "No."
"Then come and stay in my dugout," he said. He frowned for a moment and added in a low voice: "My room-mate did not return today... so there's a spare bunk. I'll dig up some fresh bed linen. Come on, then."

Evidently, he was one of those who were fond of chatting with a new arrival. I consented. We descended into the ravine, on both slopes of which, amidst thick growths of wild raspberry, lungwort and willow-herb and the raw smell of decaying leaves and mushrooms, the dugouts were built.

When the wick of the smoky homemade kerosene-lamp known as "Stalingradka" was well alight and lit up the interior of the dugout, the latter proved to be rather spacious and cosy, and looked as if it had been long inhabited. In recesses dug in the clayey walls were two neat bunks covered with mattresses made of ground sheets filled with fresh, fragrant hay. Some young birch-trees, their leaves still fresh, were stuck in the corners "for the aroma", as the flyer explained. Neat, straight shelves had been cut in the walls amidst over the bunks, and on the shelves, which were covered with newspaper, lay stacks of books, shaving tackle and a cake of soap and a tooth-brush. Over the head of one of the bunks could be dimly seen two photographs in pretty, homemade frames of plexiglass, of the kind that were made in great number by wing handy men from the wreckage of enemy planes to while away the tedium of inaction in periods of lull. On the table stood a billycan filled with fragrant wild raspberries covered with a burdock leaf. The raspberries, the young birch-trees, the hay and the fir twigs with which the floor was carpeted, gave off such a sweet pungent smell, the dugout was so cool, and the chirping of the grasshoppers in the ravine was so soothing that we were overcome by a pleasant languor, and we decided to put off until morning both our talk and the raspberries.

The airman went outside. I heard him noisily cleaning his teeth and dousing himself with cold water, making the wood echo with his grunting and snorting. He came in refreshed and cheerful, with drops of water on his hair and eyebrows, turned down the wick in the lamp and began to undress. Something heavy clattered on the floor. I looked down and could not believe my eyes. His feet were lying on the floor! A footless flyer! And a pilot of a fighter plane! A pilot who had made seven combat flights that day and had shot down three enemy planes! It was unbelievable.

But the fact was that his feet, artificial feet, of course, with nicely fitting army shoes, were lying on the floor! The upper parts were under the bunk and it looked as though a man were hiding there with his feet protruding. Evidently my face expressed the amazement I felt, for my host looked at me and asked with a pleased, sly smile:

"Didn't you notice it before?"

"I would never dream...."

"I'm glad to hear that! Thanks! But I am surprised that nobody told you. There are as many busy-bodies in this wing as there are aces. Funny they let a new man come in, and a *Pravda* correspondent at that, and didn't rush to tell him about the freak they have here."

"But it is an extraordinary thing, you'll admit. To fly a fighter plane with no feet! That wants doing. Nothing like it is known in the history of aviation."

The airman whistled merrily and said:

"History of aviation! It did not know lots of things, but has now learned of them from our flyers in this war.

But what is there to be glad about? You can believe me, I would much rather fly with real feet than with these. But it can't be helped. It turned out that way." The airman sighed and added: "To be exact, the history of aviation does know such cases."

He fumbled in his map case and fished out a magazine clipping, torn and tattered and stuck together on a sheet of cellophane. It told about an airman who had lost a foot and yet had piloted a plane.

"But he had one foot. And besides, he did not fly a fighter plane, but an ancient 'Farman'," I said.

"But I am a Soviet airman," came the reply. "Only don't think I am boasting. Those are not my words. They were spoken to me by a very good, a *real* man" (he laid special stress on the word "real"). "He is dead now."

An expression of sweet, tender sorrow crossed the airman's broad, energetic face, his eyes shone with a kind, clear light, his face looked at least ten years younger, almost youthful, and to my surprise I realised that the man, whom only a moment ago I had taken to be middle-aged, was scarcely twenty-three.

"I hate to have people ask me what, and when, and how it happened.... But just now it all comes back to me.... You are a stranger to me. We'll say good-bye tomorrow and may never meet again.... If you like, I'll tell you the story about my feet."

He sat up in his bunk, drew his blanket up to his chin and began his story. He seemed to be thinking aloud and to have entirely forgotten about me; but he told the story well and vividly. It was evident that he had a keen mind, a good memory and a big heart. Realising at once that I was about to hear something important and unprecedented, and what I might not hear again, I snatched up from the table a school exercise book which bore the inscription on the cover "Log of the Combat Flights of Squadron Three", and began to take down what he said.

The night glided imperceptibly over the woods. The lamp on the table spluttered and hissed, and many an incautious moth that had scorched its wings in its flame lay around it. At first the strains of an accordion were wafted to our ears by the breeze. Then the wailing of the accordion ceased, and only the night sounds of the woods, the sharp cry of a bittern, the distant screech of an owl, the croaking of frogs in the bog near by, and the chirping of grasshoppers accompanied the rhythmic sounds of the low, pensive voice.

The amazing story this man told was so thrilling that I tried to get it down as fully as I possibly could. I filled the exercise book, found another on the shelf and filled that, and failed to notice that the sky, visible in the narrow doorway of the dugout, had paled. Alexei Meresyev had brought his story up to the day when, after shooting down three planes of the Richthofen Division, he felt that he had become again a fully fit airman equal to the rest.

"While we've been chatting the night's slipped by, and I have to go up first thing in the morning," he remarked, interrupting his story. "I must have wearied you. Let's get some sleep."

"But what about Olya? What was her answer?" I asked, and then checked myself and said: "I'm sorry! Perhaps that's an awkward question. Don't answer it if it is...."

"Why?" he said, laughing. "We were cranks, both of us. It turned out that she knew all about it. My chum, Andrei Degtyarenko, wrote her at once—first about my crash, and then that my feet had been amputated. But she, seeing that I was keeping this from her, decided that it was hard for me to tell her about it and pretended not to know anything. We were deceiving each other, heaven knows why! Would you like to have a look at her?"

He turned the wick up and carried the lamp to the photographs in the neat plexiglass frames hanging on the wall over the head of his bunk. One, an amateur photograph, almost completely faded and worn, barely showed the features of a smiling, carefree girl, sitting among the flowers in a meadow. The other showed the same girl in the uniform of a junior lieutenant-technician, with a stern, thin, clever face and a concentrated expression in her eyes. She was so small that in her uniform she looked a pretty boy, but this boy had tired and unboyish, penetrating eyes.

"Do you like her?"

"Very," I answered in all sincerity.

"So do I," he answered with a genial smile.

"And Struchkov, where is he now?"

"I don't know. The last letter I had from him was in the winter, from somewhere near Velikiye Luki."

"And that tankman, what's his name?"

"You mean Grisha Gvozdev? He's a major now. He took part in the famous battle at Prokhorovka, and later in the tank break-through in the Kursk Salient. We were in action in the same area, but we did not meet. He is in command of a tank regiment. He hasn't written for some time now, I don't know why. But never mind. We'll find each other if we live through the war. But, then, why shouldn't we.... Well, now! Let's get some sleep! The night's gone!"

He blew out the light and the dugout was immersed in semi-darkness; in the dim, grey light of the frowning dawn we could hear the droning of mosquitoes, which perhaps, were the only inconvenience in this splendid habitation in the woods.

"I would very much like to write about you in the *Pravda*," I said.

"That's up to you to decide," answered the airman with no particular enthusiasm. And then, very sleepily, he added: "But perhaps you'd better not. Goebbels will get hold of the story and trumpet all over the world that the Russians are compelling footless men to fight, and that sort of thing.... You know what those fascists are."

A moment later he was snoring lustily. But I could not sleep. The simplicity and grandeur of this confession had thrilled me. It might have been a beautiful fable were not the hero of the story sleeping right opposite me and his artificial feet lying on the ground glistening with moisture and distinctly visible in the grey light of dawn.

I did not meet Alexei Maresyev for a long time after that, but wherever the tide of war carried me I had with me the two school exercise books in which near Orel I had recorded the remarkable odyssey of this airman. How many times during the war, during the lull and after, when travelling through the countries of liberated Europe, did I start writing my story about him, but put it aside because all that I succeeded in writing seemed but a pale shadow of his real life!

I was present at a sitting of the International Military Tribunal in Nuremberg. It was on the day when Hermann Goering's cross-examination was drawing to a close. Shaken by the weight of documentary evidence and forced to the wall by the interrogation of the Soviet Prosecutor, "German Nazi No. 2" reluctantly, through clenched teeth, told the court how the huge and hitherto invincible army of fascism had collapsed and melted away under the blows of the Soviet Army in battles fought in the vast expanses of my country. Justifying himself, Goering raised his dull eyes to heaven and said: "Such was the will of Providence."

"Do you admit that, in treacherously attacking the Soviet Union, as a result of which Germany was routed, you committed a most heinous crime?" Roman Rudenko, the Soviet Prosecutor, asked Goering.

"It was not a crime, it was a fatal blunder," answered Goering in a low voice, frowning and lowering his eyes. "All I can admit is that we acted recklessly, because, as became evident during the course of the war, we were ignorant of many things, and many things we could not even have suspected. The chief thing we did not know, nor understand, was the character of the Soviet Russians. They have been and remain a riddle. The best intelligence service in the world cannot discover the Soviets' real war potential. I don't mean the number of guns, aircraft and tanks. That we knew approximately. Nor have I in mind the capacity and capability of their industry. I have in mind their people. The Russians have always been a riddle to a foreigner. Napoleon, too, failed to understand them. We merely repeated Napoleon's mistake."

This forced "confession" about the "riddle of the Russians", about our country's "unknown war potential", filled us with pride. We could well believe that the Soviet people, their ability, talent, courage and self-sacrifice, which so astonished the world during the war, had been and remained a fatal riddle to all these Goerings. How, indeed, could the inventors of the wretched "theory" about the Germans being the *Herrenvolk* understand the soul and strength of a people reared in a socialist country? And I suddenly remembered Alexei Maresyev. His half-forgotten image vividly rose before me there in the grim, oak-panelled hall. And right there, in Nuremberg, the cradle of fascism, I felt an urge to tell the story about one of the millions of common Soviet people who had smashed Keitel's armies and Goering's air fleet, who had sent Roeder's ships to the bottom, and with powerful blows had shattered Hitler's predatory state.

I had with me in Nuremberg the yellow-covered school exercise books, one of which bore the inscription in Maresyev's hand: "Log of the Combat Flights of Squadron Three." On returning to my lodgings from the sitting of the Tribunal I went over the old notes and began to write again, and tried truthfully to relate all I knew about Alexei Maresyev from what he had told me.

Much of what he told me I had not managed to get down, and much had slipped my memory during those four years. In his modesty, Alexei Maresyev had left out a great deal about himself and I was obliged mentally to fill these gaps. The portraits of his friends that he had drawn so vividly and cordially that night had faded from my memory and I was obliged to restore them. Unable to adhere strictly to the facts here I slightly changed the name of the hero and gave new names of his companions and helpers on his arduous and heroic road. I hope they will excuse me for this if they recognise their portraits in this story.

I have given this book the title: *A Story About a Real Man* because Alexei Maresyev is a real Soviet man, the likes of whom Hermann Goering never understood until the day of his shameful death, and to this day are not understood by all those who are prone to forget the lessons of history, by those who even now are secretly wishing to take the path of Napoleon and Hitler.

That is how *A Story About a Real Man* came to be written. After the manuscript had been prepared for the press I wanted the principal hero of the book to read it before it was published, but I had lost all trace of him in the hurly-burly of the war; neither the airmen with whom we were both acquainted nor the official quarters where I made inquiries could help me find Alexei Petrovich Maresyev.

The story was already appearing in a magazine and was being read over the radio when, one morning, my telephone rang. I lifted the receiver and heard a rather husky, manly, and vaguely familiar voice:

"I would like to meet you."

"Who is it speaking?"

"Guards Major Alexei Maresyev."

A few hours later Alexei Maresyev walked into my room with his bearlike, slightly rolling gait, brisk, cheerful and efficient-looking as ever. The four years of war had wrought scarcely any change in him.

"I was sitting at home reading. The radio was switched on, but I was absorbed in the book and paid no attention to the broadcast. Suddenly my mother exclaimed: 'Listen, son! They are talking about you!' I pricked up my ears. So they were. Telling about my adventures. That was a surprise—who could have written it? I did not remember telling about it to anybody. And then I recalled our meeting near Orel, in that dugout, and how I had kept you awake all night with the story of my experiences.... But how can that be?—I thought to myself. It was so long ago, nearly five years. But there it was. The reader finished the chapter and mentioned the author's name. So I decided to hunt you up."

He blurted all this out almost in one breath, smiling his broad, somewhat shy, Maresyev smile that I had seen before.

As always happens when two soldiers meet after they had not seen each other for a long time, we fought our battles over again, talked about officers with whom we were both acquainted and had a kind word for those who did not live to see our victory. As before, Alexei was reluctant to talk about himself, but still, I learned that he had fought many a successful battle after our meeting. With his Guards wing he went through the campaings of 1943-45. Near Orel, after I left him, he shot down three enemy planes, and later, during the battles in the Baltic seaboard, he added two more to his score. In short, he made the enemy pay heavily for the loss of his feet. The government conferred upon him the title of Hero of the Soviet Union.

Alexei also spoke about his private affairs, and in this respect too I am glad to add a happy ending to my story. After the war he married the girl he loved and they now have a son, Victor. Maresyev's mother came from Kamyshin and is now living with them, rejoicing in the happiness of her children and nursing little Victor.

Today, the name of the principal hero of my story is often mentioned in the newspapers. The Soviet officer who set such a striking example of courage and fortitude in the struggle against the enemy who had encroached upon our sacred Soviet soil is now an ardent champion of world peace. The working people of Budapest and Prague, Paris and London, Berlin and Warsaw have seen him more than once at conferences and rallies. The amazing life of this Soviet soldier is known far beyond the borders of his own country; and the noble demand for peace sounds exceptionally convincing when coming from the lips of one who so courageously bore the severest trials of war.

A son of his mighty and freedom-loving people, Alexei Maresyev is fighting for peace with the same ardour, determination and confidence in victory as he fought and vanquished the enemy during the war.

Thus, life itself is writing the sequel to this story about Alexei Maresyev—a Real, Soviet Man.

Moscow, November 28, 1950

You may also enjoy ...

Wandering Between Two Worlds: Essays on Faith and Art
Anita Mathias
Benediction Books, 2007
152 pages
ISBN: 0955373700

Available from www.amazon.com, www.amazon.co.uk
www.wanderingbetweentwoworlds.com

In these wide-ranging lyrical essays, Anita Mathias writes, in lush, lovely prose, of her naughty Catholic childhood in Jamshedpur, India; her large, eccentric family in Mangalore, a sea-coast town converted by the Portuguese in the sixteenth century; her rebellion and atheism as a teenager in her Himalayan boarding school, run by German missionary nuns, St. Mary's Convent, Nainital; and her abrupt religious conversion after which she entered Mother Teresa's convent in Calcutta as a novice. Later rich, elegant essays explore the dualities of her life as a writer, mother, and Christian in the United States-- Domesticity and Art, Writing and Prayer, and the experience of being "an alien and stranger" as an immigrant in America, sensing the need for roots.

About the Author

Anita Mathias was born in India, has a B.A. and M.A. in English from Somerville College, Oxford University and an M.A. in Creative Writing from the Ohio State University. Her essays have been published in The Washington Post, The London Magazine, The Virginia Quarterly Review, Commonweal, Notre Dame Magazine, America, The Christian Century, Religion Online, The Southwest Review, Contemporary Literary Criticism, New Letters, The Journal, and two of HarperSanFrancisco's The Best Spiritual Writing anthologies. Her non-fiction has won fellowships from The National Endowment for the Arts; The Minnesota State Arts Board; The Jerome Foundation, The Vermont Studio Center; The Virginia Centre for the Creative Arts, and the First Prize for the Best General Interest Article from the Catholic Press Association of the United States and Canada. Anita has taught Creative Writing at the College of William and Mary, and now lives and writes in Oxford, England.
Website: www.anitamathias.com/
Blog: wanderingbetweentwoworlds.blogspot.com/

CPSIA information can be obtained
at www.ICGtesting.com
Printed in the USA
BVHW03033518O119
537843BV00032B/57/P